THE FIRST APPRENTICE

THE STREYAN SAGA

A. P. JOYNSON

ACKNOWLEDGMENTS

I'll begin once more by thanking my editors and my mentor, without whom, my writing would be intolerable.

To Mum and Dad, thank you for raising me on stories of magic, and wizards and witches and gods and monsters. Letting me slip into an imagined world, when I showed barely a whisper of interest in the physical. Who needs football when you've got fantasy?

To Jake, thank you for believing in my writing, more often than not, more than I do. It is thanks to you that my dreams didn't wither on the vine.

But most of all, for this book in particular, I must thank my brother Henry. The world that this book takes place in, is as much his as it is mine.

I still remember summer days we spent playing make believe together, when sticks became magical staffs and our back garden could contain whole worlds. You were my scene partner and my co-writer and my very best friend.

I love you all.

south BlueTooth Range
Forest of Cerunos
Burning Mantle
STREYA
Dragon Back Ridge
Golden Cradle
Great Marsh
Evergreen Forest
Titanic Lands
North Steampeak Range
Black Crater

First published in 2025 by Ace Publishing.

ISBN: 978-1-9193932-0-9

Cover design by Miblart.

1

A Day in the Life of Aster Shepard

They'd got her chin right, but not her hair; it was too bouncy, too full. When they'd carved Cora Olympia into marble-white with seams of black, they'd flattered her. Of course they had. We all flattered her, at least we did at first. How could you not? Your first meeting with a god is bound to be a little clumsy. Cora Olympia is my mentor, and of course, she's not really a god. That's what she tells us anyway, but for all intents and purposes. What else do you call a person who has been around for a millennium, and who built a city and a civilisation on their back?

That is the kind of person you carve into marble. White marble, with seams of black. My favourite had always been the statue in Infinite Park, the one with the hair that was a bit too full. Another, smaller statue had been added behind it almost fifty years ago to commemorate one of Cora's lost apprentices: Sky Everbright, gone too soon. At the same time, a little plaque had been added beneath Cora's statue to commemorate all the infinites that had come before her. The plaque read, *Her coming set the sky alight.* Evidently, the people of Streya were feeling in a very commemorative mood at the time. The oldest of them had been thirty-three. As far as history went back at least, as far back as the plaque beneath the statue remembered.

And then there was Cora Olympia herself; infinite for over a thousand years. Founder of Streya, the City of Stars, the greatest city to have ever... lived? Lived wasn't quite the right word, since cities aren't born, and they don't die. But it may cease to exist one day. Shone would be a better word.

Because as the City of Stars, Streya does just that: it shines. All of Streya was designed around light, and built beneath it. The tall buildings of Streya's skyline were generously adorned with thousands of mirrors, all focused and arranged to bounce magical light off of one another throughout the city. At night, it was as though a perpetual web of starlight floated just above our heads, hence the name. Unfortunately, by day, resulting glare was quite overbearing. It was typical of light walkers to have created a city so resplendent in the dark, but headache inducing during the day.

Truthfully, it had hurt my eyes from the moment I'd arrived, ten years prior. I'd been a student of the University of Streya, the greatest centre for magical learning in the world. I was chosen to become an apprentice, one of three, and eventually, I became a professor. Today, I was to become the Master.

I'd not slept. I'd left Percy, my husband, in our bed

after tossing and turning for hours. He'd be gone by now. He had an early start; he'd told me as much. Some important mission in the blue tooth range. He'd tell me more about it tonight, use it to distract me from my day. And what a day I was about to begin; my first day as Master of Streya. Only the second Master of Streya in its history. Perhaps, one hundred years hence, there would be a plaque beneath a statue with my name carved into it. The second of many to come, but for now, I was the second of only two. The first, Cora: master for a millennium. The second, me: master for now.

I stood. I'd been in the garden for hours, and now it was finally time for me to leave. You could walk from the garden to the university fairly quickly. It was situated in the old town, which had been built around the university's lofty towers. But the streets of Streya can be frantic, with self-propelled carts, carrying anything from bushels of apples to people, zooming by in every direction. Miraculously, they never crashed into each other, but even if it wasn't dangerous, the streets of Streya were at the very least a little scary to navigate on foot. So, I preferred a different mode of travel. One last time, out of nervous habit, I performed my little sequence of rituals. I checked my pocket for my rabbit's foot, brushed my finger across the frame of my glasses, fiddled with the sapphire ring upon my finger, and felt the outline of my coal studded cane beneath my cloak. Watching my breath fog the crisp air, I readjusted my wide rimmed black sunhat, taking just a moment to admire the frosted garden grass, and looked within myself. To my light. A great roaring green flame at the very centre of my being. Some people would call it a soul, I don't know if that's quite right, I just know it's my light. Drawing it out to my eyes, I passed it through my glasses, shifting its hue from green to bronze, until it formed a soft glow all around me. Beginning with my wavy, dark brunette hair, little by little, I felt myself getting lighter. Strands of hair began to stand on end above my head, and my arms, hanging loosely at my sides, began to drift upwards, as if weightless. Finally, I felt my whole body leave the ground, like a marionette doll lifted by its strings. Rising, higher and higher, past the thousands of beams of reflected light, I glided above the buildings, light as a feather, with wind whistling through my hair. I took a deep breath, inflating my chest. Tingles ran along my skin, as my face broke into a broad smile. It doesn't matter how often you do it, flying never gets old. All around me, crafts, unaccompanied chests, and even other light walkers like me whizzed by, all bathed in a soft bronze glow.

The city laid out before me as a tapestry of roofs, with towers that housed the many beacons jutting out at odd angles. Behind me was the sprawling metropolis of new town. Up ahead, at the centre of the city, the University of Streya stood boldly. A great, soaring, looming behemoth, the university was like an enormous oak tree towering high above the forest canopy, with roots that spread the length and breadth of the forest floor. I set my sights on the school, bracing my hat against my head with one hand, and set off. Hurtling through the sky, with my hair whipping at my face, the wind left streaking tears down my cheeks. Percy says I fly too fast, but there's no other feeling like it; watching the world blur around you as you become one with the air.

I only slowed down once I was dangerously close to crashing into the school boundaries. I barely remember my flights, just the elated feeling of freedom they gave me. For just a moment, my spirits took a little anxious dip as I remembered the day that lay before me.

* * *

The door to my office was a large, dark oak slab covered in twisted vines, which spelled the words *Professor A Shepard's Office* across the front. The door groaned open, and to my annoyance, two of the seats opposite my desk were already occupied. My usual class, on the magic of dragon riders and the relations between riders and light walkers, took place in a classroom. A classroom much bigger than my office, with more seats, and critically, a larger gap between my desk and the students. Unfortunately, tradition dictates that meetings between a master and their apprentices should be a more intimate affair, so on such occasions we all had the pleasure of being crammed into my office.

The office itself, although small, was homely. A large, sturdy bookshelf, stood proudly against the full length of the wall opposite my desk. The cosy room boasted a fireplace on the far-left wall, with two windows spaced evenly along the wall directly opposite. I'd been very excited about the installation of the long, green velvet couch that sat snugly beneath the windows, but never seemed to sit on it.

"You're late, sir," said Astrid, in an imperious tone that was already all too familiar. I'd begun to worry that this was her default speaking voice. I was not late, of course; she was just impressively early.

This was technically only our second meeting, and so far, she'd made a fairly poor first impression. Astrid had terrifically pale skin, betraying a childhood spent almost exclusively in the library. Her poker straight blonde hair was slicked back away from her face and fastened in a painfully high ponytail, which seemed to further widen her large, white eyes. Whatever the case may be, her magnificently white irises were unmistakable and unmissable. Ever coordinated, she wore a white blazer and white skirt to match them. She must have lived in fear of dripping teapots.

To her left sat Orion, mutely rolling his eyes. He was equally pale, but with jet black hair, and dressed in black from head to toe. It was as though he was worried any colour might rob him of his magical talents; talents made evident by his inky black irises. When making eye contact with Orion, you were immediately drawn in; it was almost impossible not to stare. His dark irises blended almost seamlessly into his pupils, making his eyes appear as deep holes in his face. I'd never met a void-eyed individual before, and despite my best efforts to steel myself, I still found myself a little unsettled.

Sitting side by side, they made for an odd pair, almost like two pieces from a chessboard had come to life and run away together.

"Actually, Astrid, I think you're early," I said, trying to keep my tone level.

"I bet Professor Olympia was never late when she was tutoring her apprentices," Astrid continued.

"No, you're quite right, Astrid. She wasn't." I offered a placating smile, perhaps naively, hoping to disarm my young interrogator. It didn't work.

"Of course, you'd know, sir, since yours was the last generation to be mentored by Olympia herself, wasn't it?" asked Astrid, although she already knew the answer.

"Right again, Astrid. You've done your research," I replied, opening a book that was resting on my desk. I pretended to scan the pages in the vain hope that redirecting my attention might slow her down.

"I always research my teachers. She handpicked you, alongside Professor Copper, and Head Mistress Vega."

It didn't.

"Yep," I said, reminding myself not to grit my teeth. Astrid was clearly building up to something.

"And is it true that Professor Olympia handpicked you to take over her duties as master, too?" she asked.

Obviously, I thought to myself, as I focused my eyes on a dark, twisted knot of wood on my desk.

"She did indeed," I replied.

"Why does she keep picking you?" Astrid finally loosed the shot she'd been lining up for the past several, increasingly excruciating moments. She asked the same question people in my life had been asking me for over a decade. So true was her aim that she elicited a sound from Orion. An almost imperceptible puff of air escaped from his nose; his version of hysterics.

"You'd have to ask her that," was my well-practiced response. Astrid had managed to make me so tense that when my office door swung open a moment later, I almost ripped the book I wasn't really reading in half.

"Sorry I'm late!" bellowed Sirius, leaning down so as to avoid hitting his head on the doorframe.

"Why are you so big?" Astrid asked rather pointedly.

"I've been working out, you impressed, Teach?" Sirius asked. He was grinning at me cockily, and his grey eyes flashed with mischief. At a guess, he looked to be currently about 7 feet tall, with a bulging chest, and enormous arms that threatened to burst through the sleeves of his shirt at any moment. He had a warm olive complexion, and his sun-bleached hair was long enough to cover his eyes when it fell forward. Sirius was the only one of my apprentices that regularly enjoyed sunlight. He was also sporting a faint grey glow, as if surrounded by a halo of morning mist.

"Working out doesn't make you a foot taller overnight," Astrid rightly pointed out.

"I'm impressed by your use of transforming light, if that's what you mean. Perhaps now you can give us an example of the effects in reverse," I suggested, watching with mild amusement as Astrid and Orion glared at their slightly more relaxed classmate.

"For you, sir, anything," said Sirius. As he shot me an entirely in-appropriate wink, the greyish glow abated and he began to shrink, with his arms and chest deflating to their more usual size. Even when he was finished, he remained the tallest and most athletic person in the room at roughly six foot, but his chest and arms no longer threatened to burst the seams of his shirt.

"Wonderful, well, that brings us nicely to our first proper lesson. We are going to be talking about hues today," I said.

Our first meeting had just been an introduction. An introduction that had gone over like a lead balloon when they were introduced to me instead of Cora, or rather, Professor Olympia, as they'd been expecting.

"We already know all about hues," said Astrid. Orion rolled his eyes for a second time in agreement.

"Wonderful. Well then, you can tell me all about them. Orion, how many hues are there in total?" I asked, keeping one eye on Astrid. I could see she was already simmering to have not being called on to answer the first question of the class, even if it was beneath her.

"There are thirteen," said Orion, in his low, raspy, most likely under-used voice.

"And into how many categories are these hues broken up?" Astrid's hand shot into the air. "Sirius?" I asked, ignoring her hand.

"Three. There are the most commonplace hues, also known as the wild hues. For instance, red, gold or green, like your lovely self, sir." He offered another wink.

"And the other two categories?" I asked, leaving the wink unacknowledged.

"There are the rarer, functional hues, like bronze, or silver or grey, like my lovely self. And of course, the rarest of all, the pure hues: white, void and opal. Like my steamed colleagues to the left," he said, gesturing to Astrid and Orion. This elicited a barely stifled snort of laughter from me.

"I think you mean 'esteemed,'" Astrid corrected him, although I suspect he knew exactly what he was doing.

"Well done, Sirius, correct. And what do we mean by a

hue?" Again, Astrid's hand shot into the air. This time, I chose to indulge her. "Astrid?"

"A hue is something all light walkers, that is to say, people like us, are born with. Magic is simply us pushing out light into the world. The hue will determine the nature of the magic we perform. Only one in one thousand light walkers is born with a pure hue, like me and Orion. And only one in two of those is born with the potential to become a beacon. Which makes Orion and I one in two thousand." Astrid scarcely stopped to draw breath during her word vomit, and when she was finished, she positively bloomed with pride.

"Yes, quite right, Astrid. Although, I'm not sure I asked for all of that maths. Now, what is a beacon?"

"You know what a beacon is, sir." She glowered

"Humour me."

Astrid huffed forcefully. "A beacon is a light walker, powerful enough to use a lens."

"Like this?" I asked, withdrawing my coal-studded cane from within my robe. For the first time, all three pairs of eighteen-year-old eyes were suddenly staring, transfixed.

"Is that a lens, sir?" asked Astrid.

"It is indeed. Can anyone tell me what a lens is?" I enquired.

Astrid's hand shot up once again. "A lens is something that beacons can push light through to change its hue, thereby changing the nature of the magic they might perform with it," she blurted out, not even waiting for me to call on her this time.

"Like this," I said, looking inside myself, and drawing

out my flickering green light. I pushed it into my hand through the coal studded cane, which began to shimmer faintly red. Once glowing, I pointed it at yesterday's teacup, which was still sat on my desk. The air between the staff and the teacup began to ripple ever so gently, and before long, a thin wisp of steam rose from my day-old tea.

"A red lens," Astrid breathed.

"Now, have any of you ever used a lens?" As expected, my question was met with shaking heads. Lenses were rare, powerful, and strictly controlled. In fact, they were inaccessible to students until their third year. Or second, in the case of an apprentice.

"Well then, I suppose today's the day. But we'll not be practicing in my lovely office. Let's go somewhere a bit less flammable," I said, leading my newly enraptured apprentices towards the door. Once outside, we headed to one of the university's many practice ranges. The closest was an open-air arena situated on the roof of the north library.

"Who'd like to go first?" I asked. For the first time, three hands shot up at once.

Each of them in turn, did exactly what novices always do when first introduced to a lens. At first, they were too gentle, barely producing enough energy to warm a pair of socks. Then on the next attempt, they were altogether too strong, releasing massive bursts of scarlet flame. I was relieved that I had brought them to the roof! Plus, it was a bit nippy, so after a while I was glad of the flames.

"Professor Shepard, at our next meeting, do you think we might move onto something more advanced, like one of the functional hues?" Astrid asked, hopefully. Her disappointment with having me as a tutor over Cora seemed to have been quelled, even if only temporarily.

"What did you have in mind?" I responded.

"Well, not right away, of course, but my ambition is to master an opal lens," she said, confidently.

Orion snorted derisively. "You know there's no record of anyone ever having done that, right?" he sniped, suddenly more talkative than I'd ever known him be.

"Of course, I know that. That's why I want to do it. I want to be the first!" Astrid puffed out her chest defiantly, as the palest pink flushed her cheeks. Orion didn't respond, he just smirked provokingly.

"Well, it's a noble ambition, if a rather lofty one," I said, "but for now, I think we'll stick with red until you've all got to grips with channelling your light."

"Why red particularly, Professor Shepard?" Astrid asked.

"Because it's the simplest hue to master. It'll give you all a chance to get used to lenses without any added complications," I said. *And also, because I have mastered it myself, and happen to have a red lens to hand,* I thought but kept to myself. I wasn't about to admit that to my apprentices, not now I finally seemed to be winning them over.

"I thought you might have started us on green, Professor, given it's your native hue. And, with it being one of the most common hues, I expect it can't be that complicated," Astrid continued. I don't think she was intending to sound as condescending as she did.

"You'd be surprised, Astrid," I replied. "Rarity

doesn't always equate to complexity. The wild hues are not always the most simple. Although they are quite common, green, and indeed gold, can be quite complex hues to master. That said, if any of you do find yourselves drawn towards green-hued magic as we continue our studies, I'd of course be happy to help in any way I can. But now, I think that should be all for today," I concluded, as we arrived back at the dark oak door to my office.

Astrid and Orion hastily scooped up their things and scuttled off, walking so quickly they were virtually jogging. Presumably they were racing off to the library to research everything there ever was to know about using red lenses. Sirius lingered a little while longer.

"Is there something you needed?" I asked him, planting myself at my desk, letting the smell of the wood fill me.

"Errm, not really, Professor. just, thanks for picking me. I mean, I know my hue isn't as rare as Astrid's and Orion's. So, I just wanted to thank you for selecting me to be one of your first apprentices. My parents were thrilled." Sirius's vulnerability caught me a little off guard. I had been wondering how long he intended to maintain the class clown persona. I'd expected it would drop eventually, but not quite this quickly.

"My pleasure. Remember, Sirius, I was picked from my generation by Professor Olympia herself, and my hue is quite a bit more common than yours. I wouldn't set too much store in the rarity of your hue. Talent, hard work, and creativity account for just as much as having dazzling white eyes." I offered a smile, and Sirius's eyes darted to the floor, just for a second. When he looked back up, his mischievous signature grin had returned.

"Thanks, Teach, I owe you one. Let me know if you need anything heavy shifting, I'm your man," he said, offering me a final wink as he stepped out the door. His body was already visibly swelling, as a dull grey glow issued from his eyes.

The truth was, Cora had also been the one to pick this crop of apprentices. It was the last thing she did before she dropped the job of master onto me. But since he seemed so happy to have been picked by me, I saw no reason to burst his bubble.

* * *

Later that day, I taught my usual classes on rider magic and the relations between the Court of the Sovereign Family and the Magocracy of the City of Streya. Following my teaching duties, I found myself back in my office. I was ineffectually moving papers around and floundering over lesson plans, when Nick Copper, also known as Professor Copper, bounded in.

"How was your first proper class with the new apprentices, then?" he boomed, in his deep baritone voice. He extended a hand for me to shake, and then yanked me out of my chair into a big hug when I accepted it. Nick was a giant of a man, and had been a fellow apprentice alongside Vega, now Headmistress Vega, and me. His skin was a deep warm brown, and his nature was jovial and friendly. Nowadays, he tended to swan around in long silky robes; today's was purple. But in his heyday, before his desk job had caught up with him, he had been infamous for his risqué outfits. Like me, he was now a teacher in the school, although he spent most of his time working on his own research. He was the foremost expert in his specialist field, the study of the stars and their light, save for Cora of course.

"It was good. I think I'm winning them round at least. They were a bit disappointed with me when they first met me, I think."

"What's to be disappointed about? You're young, you're bright, you've got more to do with the riders and more dragon knowledge than the rest of us combined. Dragons must be a bit exciting!" Nick chuckled, slapping me encouragingly, and slightly too hard, on the back.

"I'm not Cora though, am I? They want Cora, or rather, the great Professor Olympia, as they call her. And I can't even blame them really. Cora has been mentoring generations of kids for hundreds of years; she's pulled more talent out of this place than anyone else ever will. When you get the letter saying you've been selected from this generation's crop of students to be an apprentice, you expect to be mentored by her, not her skinny, speccy student nobody's ever heard of. If we're being honest, I don't even know why I got the job."

Nobody did, truth be told. Although, Nick was far too polite to say it, and I suspect, pleased he hadn't been lumbered with the task himself.

"Cora knows why, she'll have her reasons," Nick reminded me, as Percy had so many times. They were likely correct. That being said, it wouldn't hurt to hear those reasons from her.

"I suppose so," I grumbled.

"Walk with me, Rider," said Nick, a mischievous grin playing at his lips, as he took my hand in his and led me out of my office. He loved that nickname, which had stuck ever since the early days of mine and Percy's romance.

"Through here," he said, waving a faintly glowing silvery hand. For a second, the air trembled. Then all at once, space seemed to fold and warp around some imperceptible point, and a void opened before us. Nick's hue was silver, granting him control of space, and he used it liberally to avoid long walks and staircases.

The portal led to Nick's office, which was housed at the top of the very highest tower of the university. Ceilinged by a crystal-clear glass dome, it allowed perfect vision of the sky, which shifted from blue to more dusky purple shades as night drew in. The very first stars were just barely twinkling into being in the half night. It was a large office, bigger than mine, and it used to be quite lavish. But when Nick moved in, he made some changes, mostly in favour of comfort over aesthetics.

"Any progress?" I asked, taking a seat in one of Nick's many squashy reclining chairs as I gazed up into the sky above.

"They're definitely disappearing," Nick grumbled, slumping down into another chair beside me.

"Do we know why?" I asked.

"Nope, but it seems to me like something, somewhere, is sucking them away." Nick had been studying the stars since our days as apprentices, and he was the first of us to realise they'd been dimming. Now, they were vanishing wholesale.

"It does rather put my three slightly snarky eighteen-year-olds into perspective," I said, with a sigh.

"That's not even the worst of it," said Nick, waving another silvery portal into being. Through the portal, one could see a star. Not a tiny twinkling fleck of light in the distance, but a great roiling boil of flaming majesty, lighting the universe.

"What's the worst of it?" I asked, not able to take my eyes away from the epic wildness of the thing.

"It's definitely related to the dim sickness," he said grimly. With a lazy flick of his wrist, a ribbon of solar heat whipped free of the star and lashed towards the portal, which snapped shut just moments before impact.

"How can you tell?" I asked.

"The timelines match, looking at ancient light and historical logs, and with Cora's help winding things back so I could get a better look at the sky. I can confirm, the stars started dimming about sixty years ago. Two years later, there were more cases of dim children at birth in one year than we'd seen in the last fifty combined. The dimmer the stars got, the dimmer the babies. I mean, we've always known light walkers are more powerful at night. We didn't know why, but it's always been something we've understood to be true. Mothers have always told their kids before bed that our light is bolstered by the light of the stars. It's a connection we don't understand, sure, but we know that we're connected. Heck, this whole darn city is like a shrine to the night sky!" Nick waved his arms grandiosely towards the city below his tower.

"So as long as stars keep dimming, more and more

people will be born without light," I said, now understanding Nick's grim tone.

"Certainly seems like it," Nick confirmed.

"Any ideas about how to help?" I asked.

"Not yet, but me and Cora are working on it, and she's talking to the golden court about it too."

"Good luck to her with that." I huffed, remembering my last, less than friendly interactions with the court.

"She's probably going to rope you into that whole mess, by the way," said Nick, his signature rumbling chuckle returning.

"Ugghhh," I groaned, rolling over in my chair and burying my face in the squashy cushions.

"I'll tell her you can't wait for the new challenge, shall I?" Nick said, his chuckle growing to a full belly laugh.

"Why not, it's not as if I can say no to the woman." I huffed again, climbing rather awkwardly out of the chair.

"None of us can," Nick agreed.

"Well, for now, I'm going home before she finds me."

"Want a lift?" asked Nick, waving another silvery portal into being.

"I'd rather fly. If you could just give me a doorway."

"Of course," said Nick. He clicked his fingers, and suddenly I was falling, with the wind whistling in my hair and my stomach lurching as Nick's booming laugh filled the sky. I snatched for my hat, pinning it to my head with one hand.

"I hate it when you do that!" I yelled into the already closing portal, which had been momentarily below my feet, but was now rapidly becoming a vanishing speck above my head. Clouds and night sky zoomed past me at eye watering speeds, as I focused inwards. I drew out my light and pushed it through my glasses, bathing myself in the bronze glow, until all at once, I wasn't falling, I was floating.

High above the City of Streya, I dipped below the cloud level and let the view wash over me. By day, a bustling city of carts and mirrors and sun visor glare. By night, the city was an endless maze of beaming lights. The world was blanketed in a web of every hue; green and gold and silver and red and navy, cascading out across the land-scape. Glistening like a spider's web, wet by the morning dew. Streya at night, the most beautiful and complex star map ever seen. A ripple ran through me, and goosebumps pimpled my skin, only partly because it was very cold up there.

I took one last look before the shivering set in, and I set off for home, gliding down to be closer to city level. I darted between the high spiralling beacon's towers and the bustling sky traffic of self-propelled carts and taxis. Losing myself in the wind, I felt my cloak whip around me as all of my troubles melted into the background. I was enrobed in peace, until a shaft of light breaking through the blanket of beams caught my eye. I stopped dead, turning on the spot towards the maze of streets where old and new Streya met, and my heart sank. The symbol of the free folk was being projected into the night sky. I kicked off against the air, rocketing towards the distress signal.

Deep within the twisting streets of Streya, hidden in the centre of the old town, was a sanctuary of sorts, run by the benevolent free folks. Inhabited mostly by fairies, the occasional kindly hag, and on one occasion, a unicorn, the centre offered shelter and relief to those born dim. Wrongly, some light walkers feared that the plight of the dim was infectious, and so the sick were often shunned. Luckily, the free folks's magic is quite different from our own, more like a form of inherited alchemy, and as such they share none of those fears. Vega had always taken an active interest in the place, and I tried to help out where I could. Largely out of guilt.

"What's wrong?" I asked, coming to a running stop. I'd made a fairly rapid landing next to a fairy I knew by the name Ailsa. She was about two feet tall, but floated at head height, bedecked in wispy orange bolts of taffeta that contrasted her green hair and eyes quite nicely.

"Riders taking offence at the Golden Courts donations, I guess." She spoke as she worked. Pulling open a rickety wooden door built into the alley, she beckoned towards a figure I only now noticed. The figure was crouched a few feet away, hidden in the shadows. I watched as a small girl straightened up, stepping out of the dark. From her height, I'd guess she was five or six years old, but couldn't be certain as the sickness tended to stunt growth. Her skin was pale, almost grey and papery. Her white-blonde hair was thin and wispy. She trembled with each step and glanced up into my face as she passed. My stomach dropped like lead as our eyes met; hers were dull and tired, but unmistakably faintly golden.

I shuddered, as the image of a woman, tall and strong,

with mousey hair and bright golden eyes, cradling a too-small babe in her arms, flashed through my mind, bringing a torrent of guilt with it. By the time I'd pulled myself together, Ailsa had drawn a glistening veil of blackened dust out of a pouch at her waist and cast it over the now closed door. It shimmered for a moment before a cloak of shadow consumed it.

"I'll see if I can talk to them," I said. I staggered half dazed from the doorway, already wishing I hadn't come. Instinctively, I rubbed my rabbit's foot for luck, checked for my sapphire ring on my right hand and slipped my coal-studded cane into my left sleeve. Taking one last deep breath, I stepped out of the side street into the ancient and rather ramshackle square, which formed the centre of the dim sickness relief operation. My eyes fell immediately on a sight that flipped my stomach and broke me out in a cold sweat.

Two armoured riders were standing in front of their respective dragons. On the right was a hulking swamp dragon. Hunched on all fours, it was as tall as a bungalow and would fill a good-sized dining room, though were it to stretch itself to full height, I suspect it would have reached three stories. A murky green liquid leaked from its jaw, burning a crater at its feet. Its mouth hung slightly open by necessity, as needle-like teeth jutted out at all kinds of vicious angles; common problem among swamp dragons. My one solace was its immaculate emerald green scales. They were spotless, meaning the creature was likely young and had probably never seen real battle. On the left sat a fire dragon, with smoke issuing from its nostrils. Fire drag-ons, although usually half the size of their larger, slower cousins from the swamp, are swifter, more athletic and twice as aggressive. Like its companion, its scales were immaculate, though in this one's case they were a deep ruby red. Its teeth were less haphazardly aligned too.

"Is something the matter?" I heard myself calling to them from across the square. Immediately, I thought to myself that I should probably have formed a plan first. Unfortunately, the planning part of my brain kept screaming, *Run away.*

"Are you in charge here?" asked the man standing before the red dragon. It was hard to tell much about him, hidden as he was beneath his armour, but his voice was young. Barely an adult at all, I suspected.

"I'm afraid not, but I'm sure I can help." I wasn't sure at all, in fact, I was deeply unsure.

"We're here for the eggs," grunted his larger friend, in a much deeper voice.

"Do you mean eggshells?" I said, cursing the teacher in me that saw the need to correct people at every turn.

"You know what we mean, we want them back," snarled the fire dragon's rider, his voice cracking in the process. All the while, fairies were flitting about above our heads, casting glistening nets over doorways and ushering people to shelter.

"I'm afraid those shells were donated by the Sovereign family. I don't imagine they'd be best pleased to hear they'd been stolen. Much less by dragon riders such as yourselves," I said, hoping the weight of the name might scare them off.

Traditionally, dragon eggshells had been ground into a meal to feed baby dragons. It was believed to make them more powerful. More recently, it had been discovered that this same meal could relieve some of the suffering of dim-born light walkers. In fact, I was the first to think it. I'd had the brainwave in my second year at Streya.

"And who's going to tell them who we are?" asked the swamp dragon's rider, gesturing to the helmets covering their faces.

"Well, I could certainly help narrow it down for them. One fire dragon rider, late teens to early twenties, at a push I'd guess five foot nine, slight of build, in what looks to be basic first rank squire's uniform of the third battalion of the royal court. Accompanied by a stockier companion with a swamp dragon, mid-twenties, six feet with a… more generous build. Wearing the second rank squire's uniform of the same battalion if I'm not mistaken." I prayed that I'd remembered my military regalia correctly.

"And how the fuck does a poxy little star scum like you know all that?" snarled the swamp rider, confirming that I had.

"I'm somewhat of an expert on the subject, actually."

"Well then, I guess we can't leave you around to tell about it. Get him!" commanded the swamp dragon rider.

The fire dragon rider hesitated, just for a moment, but it was enough for me to start pushing light into my coal-studded cane. On his signal, the fire dragon craned its neck over his shoulder, gave a bone-rattling roar and released a plume of red-hot fire towards me. I thrust the cane out of my sleeve, focusing on the billowing jet of flames, and kicked off the ground, taking to the air at the same moment. Wrapping red light around the dragon's breath, I twisted it through the air towards the swamp dragon rider.

It would be folly to try to overpower a dragon, but if you were lucky or smart enough to match your hue to their elemental nature, manipulating their magic was a possibility.

The lumbering green beast used its wing to shield its rider, leaving a blackened stain along the leathery membrane. The creature gave a guttural howl, which threatened to shatter windows in every direction.

"Get him!" commanded the swamp dragon rider again, as he mounted the great beast. The swamp dragon began to clumsily flap its wings, struggling to heave its great mass into the air from a standing position. Meanwhile, the fire dragon rider was releasing arrows from a flaming bow in my general direction. Either his aim wasn't great, or the wingbeats of the swamp dragon were throwing him off. In any case, his poor accuracy gave me time to level my right hand at him. I pushed my light into my sapphire ring, and released a powerful jet of water. The blast was met with another bout of red-hot flame from his dragon. There was a hissing sound, and the square filled with an explosion of steam. Hidden inside the cloud, a temporary calm fell over the area.

A moment later, the swamp dragon erupted out of the blanket of white. It climbed into the air, but I was rising faster.

"Can't keep up?" I called out, baiting the hot-tempered rider.

"Blast him!" The dragon let out a hoarse roar, propelling a stream of green towards me as I'd hoped it would. Drawing again on my inner light, I focused and released a globe of bronze energy from my spectacles, enveloping the green jet as it cascaded upwards. As the caustic slime was wrapped in light, its climb through the air slowed until it came to a stop. Then all at once, with a thrust of my arm, it tumbled back towards its sender. Seconds later, there was a hissing sound, accompanied by pained groaning and screaming.

I sighed, watching the dragon tumbled backwards through the sky towards the dissipating steam. Wiping sweat from my brow, I felt my limbs begin to grow a little heavy. Using so much light was already catching up with me. I closed my eyes, just for a second, and took in a long, deep breath to cease my panting. I'd barely realised how tight my chest was, when I felt heat prickle the back of my neck. Instinct kicked in, and I let myself drop out of the sky.

As I fell, I saw a wall of flame fill the sky where my body had been just moments before. The red dragon and its rider glided overhead with agility the swamp dragon, nor I, for that matter, could ever hope to match. Forcing yet more light through my spectacles, I caught myself at roof level and took to the streets, taking shelter in a narrow alleyway. Occasionally, the shadow of the fire dragon's wing would cast over my hiding spot, but it flew so fast there was little chance of me being spotted.

"Come out, come out wherever you are!" The swamp dragon rider's voice echoed through the streets of lower Streya with the unmistakable snarl of someone who'd just been bathed in caustic acid. A pink fairy flitted into my alleyway with a panicked look on her tiny face.

"He's got—" Her strangled whisper was severed by his booming voice, as it filled the streets again.

"Or the fairy gets it!"

"Ailsa," she hissed.

Well shit.

"I'm coming out," I called, raising my hands as I inched cautiously back towards the square. In the centre was the swamp dragon rider, with his dragon behind him. He had a knife to Ailsa's throat, which had done nothing to stop her struggling. She was currently squirming in his arms and in-effectually gnawing on his leather-clothed thumb.

Tendrils of chemical smoke rose from his armour and dragon's scales, as the dragon licked its wounds rather sheepishly… for a dragon.

"Stop fucking wriggling you runt, and no sudden moves from you!" He snarled, tightening his grip. The dragon, craning its long neck, passed its rider to level its hungry amber eyes at me.

"Maybe we can come to some kind of agreement," I called across the square, careful to keep my distance. I hoped my heavy breathing and sweating would go unnoticed.

"Yeah, we can come to some agreement, you give us the eggs, and we'll let the sparkly little rat go."

"Well, perhaps—"

"And you die," he added, as his dragon snarled, peeling back its lips to reveal yet more needle-like teeth. I took a step back. Panic filled me up, as I found myself unable to break eye contact with the massive, cruel, hungry looking thing. My heart was thundering in my chest, and my body felt stiff. I wanted to run. I took another step back, but froze as the wind buffeted the back of my neck, followed by the heart wrenching sound of something landing just behind me.

"You're not going anywhere," came the younger rider's voice, as I felt something cold and hard and pointy level itself against the back of my neck.

Shit, shit, shit.

"So, where are the eggs?"

I gulped, cleared my throat and prepared to speak. Then I froze. All at once, the world was awash with an opal glow. The heaving chest of the swamp dragon was still, and Ailsa also ceased to move, seemingly having been trapped mid wiggle. Dispersing steam suddenly appeared as if drawn in place with a pencil, and the chemical smoke spewing from the rider's burns was now a solid column reaching into the air. The world was absolutely, perfectly quiet, as if nothing was moving and nothing was breathing anywhere. Just pure, deafening silence. Suddenly, the hush was penetrated by the unmistakable sound of footsteps, behind me.

I turned on the spot, looking past the frozen fire dragon rider, with his sword inches from my face. Up close, he looked to be no older than 18: a new recruit.

I'd turned just in time to see a silvery portal shut behind two familiar figures. One with flowing silvery grey hair, held back from her face by a tiara detailed with tiny cogs and hourglasses. Like me, she wore a fitted black robe, which swept down to the floor. Unlike mine, hers had long, wide, intricately detailed sleeves, woven with opal threads. Her hands were brazenly exposed, each finger had a different coloured metallic line running over the back of it, like a strange kind of piercing. On the back of her left hand rested a black stone and, on the right, a white one. She stood tall, her face bore no wrinkles, austere in its beauty, but somehow ageless. Her eyes radiated power, like glowing opals. Behind her was an older looking woman. She wore a long, billowing, blue and white robe, and her long, grey hair was plaited down to the floor. She leant against a black wooden cane, which seemed somehow to be twisted into a rod of stone.

"Cora." I breathed a sigh of relief, side stepping the rider and his dragon, and embracing my old teacher.

"And what am I? Invisible?" said Magda, her old voice creaking as she spoke.

"Oh, give the kid a break, he's just had a skirmish with two riders, you can't expect him to be pleased to see a third," said Cora, releasing me to deliver a playful nudge to Magda's shoulder.

"I'm nothing like these fools," said Magda. She smacked her cane against the fire dragon rider's helmeted head, eliciting a loud clanging sound.

"I'm relieved to see you both!" I said, finally finding my voice.

"So, what do the fools want then?" asked Magda, fixing the closest of the riders with her steely, blue-eyed glare.

"They came for the eggshells the golden court had donated. More recently they'd added killing me to the to do list," I joked, leaning lazily against the fire dragon, which was pleasantly warm to the touch.

"Well, that would be annoying, I'd have to find someone else to teach the new crop of apprentices. How's that going, by the way?" Cora asked.

"Rocky at first, but I think I'm winning them over, although they'd still rather have you."

"They don't know how lucky they are to have you teaching them," said Cora, giving me a gentle shoulder squeeze.

"We should stand back, she's about to release them," said Magda. She took my hand in her old, leathery, and surprisingly firm grip as she began dragging me backwards.

"What are you going to do to them?" I asked.

"Teach them, of course," said Cora, rather chipperly.

"Give them some regrets," said Magda, in a rather grave tone.

The next moment, Cora clicked her fingers, and the shimmering opal light evaporated into the air. Suddenly, the world was moving again. Ailsa was wriggling, smoke was coiling, and the fire dragon rider was panicking.

"Where'd he go?!" he squealed, his voice cracking again.

"Who the fuck are you?" barked the swamp dragon rider from across the square. The fire dragon rider and his dragon wheeled round on the spot, and the rider quickly began to back away.

"W-we've gotta get out of here," he squeaked, almost falling over himself in his haste to back away. His dragon snarled as he cowered behind it, smoke issuing from its nostrils.

"Why, who is she?" asked the swamp dragon rider, nervously adjusting his grip on Ailsa, who was wriggling with renewed vigour.

"She's the fucking infinite," said the fire dragon rider,

still backing away with his sword outstretched ineffectually in Cora's direction.

"I prefer Cora, or Professor Olympia," Cora corrected him, as she began advancing calmly on their position.

"She's still just a star scum! We've got dragons, I'm not scared," said the swamp dragon rider. His tone suggested he was convincing himself as much as his friend.

"You should be," said Cora. She casually flicked her right hand in the direction of the fire dragon, releasing a bolt of white energy which shot through the air and crashed into the beast with such force that a shock wave issued in all directions. The force of it blasted my hair back and left it standing on end. The resulting explosion of pure white power sent the dragon hurtling towards one of the buildings the fairies had been sheltering with their nets. However, before it could make a devastating impact, a silver portal winked into being in its path, and the dragon vanished.

"Where'd Nova go?" yelped the fire dragon rider.

"You can have her back," responded Cora, wrenching another portal open just above the lumbering beast with a lazy flick of the wrist. The fire dragon jettisoned out of it having lost none of its momentum, and crashed with a sickening crunch into its larger brethren. A cloud of dust billowed from the resulting wreckage, followed by a series of groans and yelps.

"Scared yet?" asked Cora, making a point to check her nails as the two riders staggered out of the dust cloud.

"We should leave," the fire dragon rider whimpered.

"We've still got our hostage. Any more of your tricks and she's dead, bitch," snarled the bedraggled rider.

"Do you?" asked Cora, as Ailsa was engulfed in grey light. A moment later, the rider's knife went clattering to the floor. His grip on Ailsa buckled, as in the blink of an eye, she transformed into a rhino turtle as tall as a shire horse and twice as wide. Her four, powerful grey legs and horned face extended out of a huge, mottled brown shell. She delivered a swift kick with her hind legs to her would be assassin, sending him flying into the mangled mound formed by his injured dragon.

"Fuck you!" were the last words he managed to groan, before passing out in the heap of entangled limbs.

"Mercy!" cried the fire dragon rider, flinging himself to his knees at Cora's feet.

"Well, that's embarrassing," I muttered, as Cora raised her hand and with another flash of grey Ailsa, was herself again.

"That was bloody brilliant!" Ailsa chirped.

"Glad you liked it," said Cora with a smile, before returning her attention to the snivelling assailant at her feet.

"You had your sword at my student's neck. Were you intending to show him mercy?"

"I'm s-sorry it was Rod, he talked me into it, I'm so sorry, this wasn't the plan, we just wanted to scare people, t-to get the shells. N-not supposed to kill anyone," he whimpered, with snot streaming down his face into his mouth in a way that made me feel uncomfortable.

"His friend was definitely the bigger bastard of the

two," I said, feeling a wave of pity wash over me as I approached the wreckage.

"Well then, I suggest you stop hanging out with Rod, he's a bad influence. Fetch him out of that pile for me, would you?" instructed Cora, in an eerily familiar, teacherly tone.

"Y-yes, m-mam, I mean, Your Infinite... ness." The rider fumbled his words, in an odd attempt at deference. We watched, bemused, as he struggled to heave his larger friend out of the groaning, steaming wreckage of dragons, and presented him at Cora's feet.

"Good lad, and I already told you, I prefer Cora," she said, waving a hand over Rod's body, releasing a flash of green.

Moments later, vines were surging out of the ground, ripping their way through the cobbled streets to coil around Rod, again and again until he was wrapped from head to toe in stiff, tough plant matter.

"I'm going to keep hold of him for now. He'll have to answer for all this mess he's made," she said, gesturing broadly towards the scorched square. The fire rider nodded obediently.

"What's your clan's name, son?" asked Magda, poking her cane into his face as she hobbled up behind me.

"The Hearth Scales," he said, feebly.

"I'll be having words with your elders," she snarled, giving him a swift jab to the chest.

"Yes, ma'am," he whimpered, rather piteously.

"Well, go stand by those two sorry souls," instructed Cora, gesturing to the rather bedraggled dragons. They called to mind an image of two dogs who'd hurt their snouts in a tussle with a rose bush, only they were as big as a cottage and covered in scales.

"What now?" he asked, obediently.

"Bye bye," said Cora, offering a wave, as a portal opened up beneath their feet. Before he had a chance to say anything else, the boy and the two dragons tumbled into it, before it closed behind them.

"Where d'ya send them?" I asked.

"Third battalion of the royal court's commanding officer's barracks. He'll have a job explaining how he got there," she said, offering me a mischievous look.

"Thanks for turning up when you did," I said with a smile.

"You can thank Magda for that one, she foresaw your need of a helping hand."

"Thank you, Magda." She offered me a wink of her sky-blue eyes. It was a rare gift, but riders of mountain dragons, like Magda, had been known to receive visions. She was one of only two people I'd ever known to use the ability with any level of reliability, though.

"Well, she'd have been in such a strop if you'd got maimed, didn't leave me with much of a choice, did it?"

"It's true, I would have been. Now, how are you getting home, still flying about are you?" asked Cora.

"That was the plan, but I'm a bit worn out now," I said, yawning for theatrical effect.

"Say no more," she said, as a silver portal materialised. Looking through it, I could see my rocking chair, sitting by the fire in the centre of my home. I stepped through it without another word.

* * *

"Was that one of Cora's portals?" came Percy's voice from just behind me. I took a deep breath and let the heavenly aromas of goat stew and baking sourdough fill me up.

"Good eye," I said, turning to face him as the portal snapped out of existence.

There he was, in his ridiculous white apron with red love hearts dotted across it, and *Kiss the Chef* in bubble writing. His hair fell across his face in loose, shiny black curls, partly covering his icy blue eyes. He shared my pale complexion and slim physique. Unlike me, though, he was broad shouldered, tall, at least six foot two, and had an ease about him I'd always envied. His chiselled features and appraising eyes could fool people into believing he was a harsh and aloof figure. Nothing could be further from the truth.

"Hard to miss, once you know what you're looking for," he said, looking up at me from the stew he was stirring diligently. Concern shot across his smiling face when his eyes met mine, sending my stomach fluttering.

"Something wrong?" I asked.

"Your eyes look a little dull, what happened?" he enquired, abandoning his stew. He crossed the length of the room in three long strides, and pulled me into his arms. Most people would never notice a barely perceptible dulling in a light walker's eyes, a tell-tale sign of overexertion. Percy never missed it though. Not when it came to me anyway.

"I ended up in a bit of a scuffle," I said, hugging him

back. I breathed him in, squeezing him as close to me as possible before I let him go.

"Not with one of your students?" he asked, looking half shocked, half curious as he took me by the hand and led me back to his pot so he could continue stirring.

"No, actually I think I might be winning them over."

"I knew you would, but then, who did you end up scuffling with? It's not like you to scuffle with anyone," he said, sprinkling something unpronounceable but no doubt delicious into the pot.

"A couple of riders and their dragons attacked the free folk outpost where the dim sick are being treated," I said, speaking as quickly as possible in the vain hope he'd glaze over it.

"Two dragons and their riders? That sounds like more than a scuffle, how many of you were involved?" he asked, dropping his spoon into the stew.

"Oh, you know… it was mostly me and the fairies and a couple of others," I said, diverting my eyes to focus on the sinking spoon.

"You went on your own, didn't you?" he asked, seeing through me like a freshly cleaned window.

"Well, in fairness, I didn't know it would be two riders and their dragons when I set off," I said, offering a rather feeble smile.

"And when you saw that it was two riders and their dragons, you called for help, right?" he asked, cupping my chin in his hand, gently lifting it until our eyes met. He wasn't angry, his eyes were searching, looking for something. He was frightened. I'd have preferred it if he were angry.

"Not exactly…," I said, fidgeting awkwardly as the recklessness of my earlier escapades dawned on me.

"You fought two riders and their dragons on your own and you didn't even call for help? Are you mad? They could have killed you! I should have been there," he said, bracing my arms, and then hugging me again, squeezing me tight. His voice was a palpable mix of surprise and fear and frustration and exasperation and any number of other guilt-inducing emotions.

"But I wasn't, and I'm fine, everything's fine. And you weren't to know," I said, patting his back reassuringly as he gradually squeezed all the air out of my lungs. I felt like an accordion.

"You're absolutely barking mad."

"You're choking me!" I wheezed.

"Oh right, sorry," he said, letting me go again.

"It's okay, I'm sorry for frightening you," I said, leaning against him as he set about trying to fish his spoon out of the pot clumsily.

"So, who were they anyway? Why were they attacking?"

"Oh, they were after the most recent batch of eggshells the court donated, and I don't think they were anybody really, just young and stupid. One fire dragon and one swamp, the swamp guy was a bit of prick."

"Sounds like they both were, what ended up happening to them?"

"Well, lucky for me, Cora turned up, and she sent one of them back to his barracks with his tail between his legs. She took the other one captive."

"He'll be a bargaining chip then, next time you end up

going with her to meet the courts," said Percy, taking the stew off the fire.

"Ugh, you don't think so, do you?" I groaned.

"Oh definitely, it's doubly awkward for the court, cause not only did their people attack and try to steal back the court's gift, but one of Cora's diplomats ended up being caught in the crossfire. I bet she's secretly over the moon about the whole thing," he said, pouring the stew into two bowls.

"You're probably right," I said, fetching his loaf out of the oven.

"I'll go with you when it comes up, I'd like to meet one of the men that attacked my husband," said Percy, a hint of steel peeking into his tone.

"How was your day anyway," I asked, changing the subject.

"Oh, I've got something to show you actually," he said, leaving the loaf to cool. He led me out of the kitchen area, past our comfy rocking chairs, which I so longed to melt into, and towards the bedroom. Which I also wouldn't have minded melting into.

"I do like a surprise," I said, as we stopped outside our bedroom door.

"So, I was up and out early because a hag had foreseen an abandoned clutch of dragon eggs. Somehow, she managed to get word to one of the leaders of the free folk. They told the golden court, and because the clutch was supposed to be in the Tomb Stone Mountains, the courts wanted a grave dragon rider. As we know, that's not a very long list, and my name was near the top of it."

"So, you went to find an abandoned clutch of dragon

eggs? Weird to think someone would have abandoned one at all." Even the spent eggshells of dragons are valuable. Unhatched eggs are to diamonds what diamonds are to coal, in terms of value.

"Yes, well, that is being looked into. I'm sure they'll figure it out, not really my problem, my problem was getting the eggs."

"And did you?" I asked.

"Sort of, they weren't what we thought they were, they were petrified."

"Really?" I asked, as my eyes peeled wide. A petrified dragon egg was considered one of the most valuable items in all of Streya. They were capable of powering huge permanent spells, or could even be broken up to create lenses in matching hues.

"Yep, and best of all, they let me keep one," said Percy, a large grin spreading across his face. Presumably in response to my mouth dropping open with such force that I'm sure I heard my jaw click. He leant over my shoulder, and pushed open our bedroom door, before turning me on the spot, to manoeuvre me in my shocked state into the bedroom. There, laying on the bed was a perfect, ever-green egg, about the size of a newborn baby.

"A forest dragon egg," I breathed dropping to my knees. I reached out and hesitated, my fingers an inch from the shell. Half of me wanted to pick it up, hold it, feel it, gaze at it, but part of me was too scared to touch it in case I spoiled it somehow.

"What are you going to do with it?" I asked, turning back to Percy, he was kneeling just behind me now.

"What are you going to do with it? It's yours after all,"

he said, smiling even wider. My heart leapt and excitement fluttered through me.

"What, don't be daft, it can't be mine, it's too precious, don't be, are you mad? That's... you're being, what? Sorry." I floundered, struggling to get my words out in any logical order.

"Do you like it? I knew you would."

"You're being silly, don't mess with me, how could it be mine?" I asked, a little lump forming in my throat as the reality of the situation inched its way into my mind.

"How could it not be? As soon as I saw that colour, I thought of you, and your beautiful eyes. And then, when they said I could keep one as payment, the decision was already made," he said, before pressing our lips together and kissing me tenderly, with his afternoon shadow tickling my face. His strong hand clasping the back of my head as he began to gently massage my scalp. Comforting shivers ran down my spine as I finally melted into him

"Is it safe to have it here?" I asked, breaking the kiss to look up into his deep, hungry eyes.

"I'll keep you safe," he said, his voice low and husky. My cheeks flushed hot, and I crashed my lips into his. Whilst he lifted me effortlessly off the ground, and kicked the door closed behind us.

2

"Eat something," said Percy, thrusting a bowl of porridge into my hands. He bustled around the cottage, hopping from the kitchen to the bedroom, wielding coffee cups and yanking socks on with all the grace and elegance of a hippopotamus ballerina. I loved that man.

"Why are you rushing?" I asked, turning back to the little shrine of fruit plants, mushrooms and flowers I'd allowed to grow around my forest egg. I picked a couple of raspberries to drop into my porridge.

"Because Cora, as in your mentor, as in The Infinite, sent a message into my head personally this morning, and I wasn't awake enough to pay attention. I cannot be late for the meeting on top of sleeping through the message."

"For the hundredth time, she will not mind if you're a bit late."

"That is easy for her favourite pupil to say," he said, fiddling frantically with the clasp of a necklace.

"Let me, and for the record I am not her favourite. Vega is headmistress, and Nick is going to be the one to cure this whole dim sickness, what have I done?" I said, as I fixed the silver chain with its onyx pendant around his neck.

"You took over her apprentices. She didn't let any of the others take over for her, did she?" said Percy, planting a kiss on my cheek.

"No, but—"

"I've gotta dash, see you tonight." He cut me off, still floundering for an argument as he hurried out of the door. It slammed behind him, the gust kicking up a small letter that had been left on the doormat.

"Love you!" I called after him, stooping to pick it up. It was sealed with golden wax formed into a shape vaguely reminiscent of a crooked staff. I felt a lump in my throat as I ran my finger up the seal, lifting it without breaking the wax.

Dear Aster & Percy

Hello, my handsome boys! It has been too long since we saw you last. Anna has had the baby. Turns out it was babies: triplets! Can you believe it? You're an uncle again, three times over. You must come and see them soon, they're darling.

Remember, you're welcome anytime you like, be it for an hour or a day or a week. We'd love to meet your new apprentices. Our Aster, The Master of Streya, my goodness me, I got goosebumps just writing that down. I'm sure you're very busy of course, but even so it would be nice. I know darling little Ava would love to spend some time with her uncle.

Perhaps you and Percy could visit for the week of Frost Stars Eve. We haven't had you for the holidays in years. Anyway, I know you're busy, darling. So, I won't keep you.

Love and kisses and all my best wishes,
    Your mum.

Once I'd read it, I folded the letter up and put it back in the envelope. On tiptoes, I placed it onto the pile on the top shelf of the winter clothes closet. Then I blinked my eyes several times until they stopped stinging, and pushed the thought of darling little Ava out of my head. I knew I should write back, but all my note would say was that I was happy to hear about Anna's kids, but that I didn't have the time to visit just at the moment. The thought of Mum opening my letter full of excitement, only to be disappointed was a bit too painful to bear this early in the morning.

Darling little Ava pushed her way back in as I turned back to my porridge. She was my older sister's only child, the first of the next generation of Shepards. I'd met her only twice. She had been born dim, and was so small, and fragile. Holding her felt like cradling a paper doll, as if one wrong move might crush her. And then there were her eyes. The innocent, wide eyes of a baby, dim but faintly golden. The thought of her made me ache. I swallowed hard around the lump in my throat, and as I pushed the image out of my mind, the little girl in the alley of the dim sick centre followed in its wake.

I didn't write a letter. I didn't eat my porridge either. I just cherry picked the raspberries and tried to ignore the guilt.

* * *

"How many lenses have you mastered, Professor Shephard?" asked Astrid, who seemed to think the start of each of our sessions was personal question time.

"Four," I said, not lifting my head from my desk.

"I heard that Professor Olympia has mastered all twelve hues, along with her native light of course," said Astrid, who'd apparently reverted back to resenting my being her mentor.

"Isn't she like, one thousand years old though? I bet most people would have mastered every hue if they'd been around that long," said Sirius.

"Yes, but the point is, she *has* been around that long, so she is *that* knowledgeable," Astrid snapped back.

"It's not like she's going to teach you to be one thousand years old," Sirius retorted.

"Let's not snipe at each other two minutes into the meeting, it will make the rest of our time together intolerable," I said, finally giving up on my plan to bury my head in the proverbial sand. Their response was to shoot glares at each other from either side of Orion, who sat between them.

"Can anyone tell me what the most controlled hue of lens is? I assume you've been reading up since our last meeting," I asked in my best teacher voice, deciding not to acknowledge their childish antagonism.

"Violet hued lenses," said Orion, ignoring Astrid's hand shooting up into the air.

"And why is that?"

"Because violet magic allows us to affect the minds of those around us, which presents a whole host of security and agency-based risks," said a familiar voice from my doorway, which briefly preceded three stifled gasps.

"Professor Olympia," Astrid and Orion whispered at a barely audible volume.

"Quite right, Professor," I said, not bothering to hide my amusement at my apprentice's awe-struck faces.

"Sorry, can I borrow you, Professor Shepard?" she asked, still with only her head poking through the doorway.

"You've got to promise to bring him back," said Sirius. He seemed to have gathered his senses more quickly than Orion and Astrid, who simply nodded their heads dumbly.

"Cross my heart," she said, drawing a cross in the air. As she did so, the gems and bars that adorned the back of her hand glistened in the light.

"One moment," I said, following her out of my office.

"Put this on," said Cora. She immediately started struggling to pin a golden broach with emerald detailing to my robe. It signified my status as a diplomat to the golden court.

"What are you doing here?" I asked, directing my question to Vega, who was standing behind Cora, or more accurately, towering over her. Vega was unusually tall, and always had been for as long as I'd known her. She stood a head higher than most of the faculty. Her blazing white eyes and platinum blonde hair added impact to her already rather impressive form. She'd chosen an immaculate white robe with golden inlay as her uniform when she became headmistress, which made her stand out even further. The white and gold academic giantess was overall quite an intimidating presence. Even to me, someone who'd been present for many of her early blunders. Like the first time she'd tried to use a navy hued lens and almost drowned our apprentice class.

"I'm here to take over your class for the afternoon, apparently," said Vega, making no effort to veil her annoyance.

"Don't be spikey, Vega," said Cora, still struggling with my pin.

"Why do I need a stand in?" I asked, affixing the pin myself.

"You're coming with me to a meeting with the golden court, so I asked Vega to stand in for you," said Cora. The smile on her face told me she found the situation hilarious.

"This is highly irregular. Might I remind you that I am the headmistress of this school? I'm far too busy to be running the apprentice class," said Vega.

"Yes, well, the dim sickness centre being attacked by some errant dragon riders is also somewhat irregular."

"Yes, but—"

"And might I add, you'd told me that was a pet project of yours, and yet who did I find defending it? Our learned colleague, Professor Shephard."

"Thank you, Shephard, but—"

"So, seeing as he stood in for you there, wouldn't it be prudent for you to return the favour here?" asked Cora, with a placid smile cemented to her face.

"I suppose," said Vega, sagging in the face of an all too familiar flattening by Cora.

"Well then, that's settled. You should probably introduce your class to your stand in, I'll wait here."

"Class, Headmistress Vega will be taking your lesson today, as I've been called away on Golden Court business. Be good, and when I get back, I expect to find a report of the three hues you'd each like to start studying. And please, for now, no pure hues. Trust me, you'll thank me later," I said, barely popping my head back through the door, before letting Vega into the office.

"Percy is waiting with Magda on the roof," said Cora, opening a silvery portal with a flick of her wrist and stepping through it. I followed, and my hair was immediately caught in the breeze as the expansive view of Streya stretched out before us. We were standing on the roof of the second highest tower in the school building, which housed, among other things, Cora's office.

"This was what the morning call was about," Percy shouted over the wind as he waved at me.

He, Magda and their dragons were quite a striking sight. Percy in his black chainmail and pauldrons, with black stone detailing. Besides him, Styx, his grave dragon, with dazzling ice-blue eyes, and sleek, black scaled body with deep blue membranous wings.

Grave dragons are the smallest and fastest of all dragons; similar in height and length to a shire horse, but with a wingspan twice that length. They're also one of the rarest breeds of dragon. Styx and Percy were both dwarfed by Eurus, Magda's dragon, a huge, blue serpentine creature. She was a mountain dragon, an even rarer breed. In fact, there was some concern that they might be at risk of going extinct. Unlike other dragon's, mountain dragons had no wings at all, conjuring powerful currents of air to haul their enormous frames through the sky. As to the reason for this, scholars were unsure; some speculate that mere wings had been found insufficient to hold aloft such enormous creatures. That said, historical records of the now extinct meteor dragons depicted those creatures as being born aloft by wings, and they were even larger than their mountain brethren.

Magda had already mounted the beast. Her grey hair whipped around her, and she was bedecked in her jewelled blue and grey robes, which signified her position as a court sage.

"Hey, Styx," I said, hurrying over. I braced my hat against the breeze, which Eurus was whipping into somewhat of a storm already. Styx turned his body, blocking the lion's share of the gale as I approached, and he rubbed his large, scaley black head against my chest. Fixing me with his piercing eyes, his scales were cold to the touch, a little like stone.

"He likes you better than me, I swear." Percy chuckled

as he mounted Styx. Styx immediately reared up, bucking him off again.

"What's the problem?" I asked, feigning ignorance. I was barely able to stop myself grinning.

"He says it's rude of me to get on before you," Percy said with a roll of his eyes, before lifting me, with impressive ease onto Styx's back and remounting himself.

"He really does like me better." I chuckled, as Percy's arms wrapped around my waist and took hold of Styx's reigns. We took to the sky, gently gliding above Eurus's altitude to stay clear of the wind tunnel she was creating.

"He wants to know if the princess is too cold," Percy said, planting a peck on my cheek as he spoke into my ear.

"Still calling me that then?" I chuckled.

"He's such an old man," said Percy, eliciting a warning grumble from Styx, which rumbled through my whole body.

"Well, he needn't worry, I've got this," I said, producing my coal studded cane. I began to warm my admittedly quite chilly hands on it. Percy didn't really feel the cold; riders of grave dragons almost never did.

"I love it up here," I shouted against the wind, as we flew over the great canyons of the titanic lands, which lay at the footstep of Streya. The titanic lands existed on two levels. First, the arid, dusty, reddish brown surface, where giant folks like cyclops roamed. The second existed within the valleys of the great black scars that littered the landscape. From above, you'd be forgiven for thinking that the scars were so deep that you might find yourself falling to the centre of the world, were you to slip through. The truth, which for many years had gone unknown, was that within these great caverns were verdant forests, fed by the waterfalls that were sprinkled along its cavernous mouth. Within them, in the humid microclimates, existed a world we knew scarcely anything about.

"You should have been born a rider, you'd love it," Percy said.

Look up and to your left, Cora's voice echoed through my mind like someone shouting into a cave. It was quite an unnerving experience if you weren't used to it. My eyes were drawn to a large, shadowy cloud high above the rest.

"What's that?" I asked, pointing it out to Percy.

"It couldn't be…," Percy gasped. There was a momentary shift in the air pressure, my skin prickled and lightning sparked, crackling around the giant cloud formation. A huge black silhouette of some impossibly large creature flashed through the sky.

"A Leviathan," we both whispered in unison.

"How can they be that big?" I asked in wonder. The silhouette burned into my mind, almost like a whale against the clouds, only it must have been a mile from tip to tail.

"There is a skeleton of one in the Tombstone mountains. From end to end, it's almost a mile long, and the ribs stretch hundreds of feet into the air," said Percy, steering Styx a little away from the clouds.

"The bone woods you mean?" I asked, remembering a book about mountain ranges my father had brought me as a child when I showed an interest in dragons.

"Yep. You know, I saw a herd of them once."

"Did you see the Shephard?" I asked, craning my head back as the clouds fell behind us.

"Nope, but there were seven of them, I counted the silhouettes, so there must have been a Shepard amongst them somewhere."

* * *

The rest of our flight was significantly less eventful and not at all awe-inspiring, until we crested the top of the dragon's back ridge. This formation of mountains bordered the titanic lands and the draconic territories. The most varied and expansive land on the continent, it contained within it great forests, each as big as Streya itself, bordered by toxic swamp lands. Pocked with mountainous and even volcanic ranges, to the very north stood the frigid Tombstone Mountains, and to the south, steam peaks. The lands of the dragon riders are so vast and wild that no other civilisation could ever hope to survive there in any sense. Only the speed of dragon flight connected these lands. Each territory, each forest or swamp or mountain range, was home to a clan, each with its own ruling elders.

We were flying right to centre. As I looked past Styx's deep blue wings and through the clouds, the Golden Cradle sent a shiver up my spine. Though a relatively small canyon, its walls were riddled with seams of pure gold. It is the only place where golden dragons have ever been known to reside. The seat of power for all the draconic lands, ruled over by the Sovereign family: an ancient dynasty. It was a place that radiated power, and that few outsiders ever got to see.

As Styx and Eurus descended below the cloud line towards the Golden Cradle, we were met by a retinue of the 1st battalion of the royal court; the home guard effectively. At a quick count, they numbered four fire dragons, three swamp dragons and a forest dragon to our left, and four fire dragons and four swamp dragons to our right. Without thinking, I found myself clutching Percy's wrists and pulling his arms tighter around my waist, trying to make myself small. It's an intimidating thing, to be flanked by sixteen dragons flying in formation.

"Don't panic, they're just doing their jobs," Percy whispered into my ear. He let his arms hug around me, whilst Styx snapped his jaws at the nearest lumbering swamp dragon on our right.

"We're here on official court business, with diplomats under the wing of Magda of the Blue Tooth Range, and Percy of the Burning Mantle. Leave us!" commanded Magda, her voice omnidirectional, whipping around us carried by the wind. The guard retinue hesitated for a moment before dispersing. I breathed a sigh of relief, and realised I'd been holding my breath.

"I love it when she does that," I said.

"I wish I could do it." Percy chuckled.

Eurus descended into the Golden Cradle first, and we followed once she'd landed, not wanting to get caught in her wind tunnel in such a confined cavern. The Golden Cradle was for the most part a series of craggy brown rocks speckled with gold and with little vegetation, but towards the centre lay The Clutch. A great castle carved out of the same brown rock, topped with a golden dome, and with four more great spires at each of the four corners. The castle was flanked all around by a crystal moat of blue water, fed by the roaring waterfall that crashed into the canyon behind it. A bridge of stone, about as wide as Eurus's great serpentine body, formed the path into the structure.

Once we'd dismounted, Eurus took again to the sky, leaving our hair and robes billowing in her wake.

"Where is she going?" I asked, approaching Magda and Cora.

"She's trying to lay, so she's spending most of her time at home amongst the blue teeth, what with the whole going extinct issue." Magda rolled her neck, eliciting a series of cracks.

"How are you getting back then?" I asked, watching Eurus's goliath form disappear into the clouds.

"Cora taxis me around, don't you, dear?"

"Sure do," said Cora, offering Magda a wink as she straightened out her wind-swept hair.

"Don't you miss her?" I asked.

"Not particularly, she's a moody old bag, and at my age, flying plays absolute havoc with the bones. It suits us both that she's had to dedicate so much time to the laying," said Magda, pressing her hands into her lower back and pushing her hips forward, eliciting another quite concerning crack.

"We'd have left her to it, but you know how they are about diplomats," said Cora, referring to the golden court's insistence that all diplomats from Streya have an accompanying member of the court, to be held accountable if they do something wrong. We were expected to arrive on said court member's dragon; they were very big on ceremony.

"Do you mind if I enter first?" I asked Cora, as we strode down the stone bridge.

"Why?" The mischievous grin on her face suggested she knew exactly why.

"Because you're a tough act to follow," I said, rolling my eyes.

"Well, since you asked so nicely, of course."

Once inside, we were ushered into what they call the announcement chamber. It was a gaudily decorated room, adorned with golden tapestries and couches that looked like they were designed to be admired but not sat on. In the centre of the room was a large, golden arched doorway, but instead of a door, there was a curtain of golden beads. The entire room felt as though it was conceived as a run up to this doorway. Which in a way, it was. Through the golden archway was the golden throne room, and as such, the sight of it made me sweat. A lot.

"Ready?" asked Percy, giving my hand a quick squeeze. His implacable smile transported me away from this place for a moment to our cottage, where the most intimidating thing was the stove.

"Ready," I replied. I let him lead me just one step forward, through the golden beading and into the throne room, where I did my best not to gasp. But gasp I did, and it echoed embarrassingly loudly off the high walls and bounced around the white marble columns riddled with rivers of gold, until it arrived at the throne.

Sitting there, patiently waiting, was Lance Sovereign of The Cradle, who struck an appropriately intimidating figure. His skin was a deep golden brown, and his black hair was twisted into fine dreads, laced with gold. Standing, he was just over seven feet tall; unusual even among the statuesque Sovereign family. But at present, he sat reclined on his throne, his chin rested against his gauntleted hand. He wore a loosely tied white tunic with golden lacing, which did nothing to hide his well-developed chest. Even at rest, his biceps bulged intimidatingly. Although nothing held a candle to his piercing golden eyes. I remember thinking upon our first meeting that this could be what it felt like to stand in the presence of a god.

Lance, despite his stature, was two years my junior, aged twenty-six. He had only ascended the throne recently, after his mother, its former occupant, had passed birthing her fourth child, and Lance's youngest sister, Gilda. To his right, rested Sol. Curled in behind her glistening golden wings, she was the most impossible being in all of creation: a golden dragon. Little bigger in stature than a fire dragon, but said to contain all the power of the sun itself. She seemed, for now at least, to be asleep. My skin prickled in her presence, and something primal and instinctual in the back of my mind wanted more than anything for me to run away.

Mercifully, a trumpeter sounded to our left, announcing our presence and snapping me out of my trance in doing so.

"Presenting, Aster Shepard, Emerald Eyed, Professor of Dragon Studies at the Magical University of Streya, Master of the Apprentices of Streya, under the wing of Grave Rider, Percival of the Burning Mantle, first of his clan to mount a grave dragon, out rider of the golden court."

The court was pretty big on titles. We bowed and made our way down the golden carpet that stretched from the doorway to the throne. All the while, I wished

Percy would walk quicker. Once we reached the stairs, we stepped aside to the left, away from Sol, thank goodness; and the curtain was drawn back once more as Magda and Cora stepped out. Again, the trumpet sounded.

"Presenting, Cora Olympia, Opal Eyed, The Infinite, The Eternal One, The Wandering Woman, Champion of the City of Streya, Saviour of the Blue Tooth Clan, Hero of the Battle for the Wide Marshes, Victor of The Clutch Uprising, Aide to the Sovereign Dynasty, Sun Hearted, Prismatic Master, Council to the Forest of Cerunos, Professor of Antiquities at the Magical University of Streya, under the wing of Mountain Rider Magda of the Blue Tooth Range, Sage of the golden court."

The announcer looked as though he might collapse from the effort of doing that all in one breath. I couldn't help wondering how many times he'd practiced it. I'd never managed to get all her titles right without becoming tongue tied. Let alone get them all out in one go. I could barely get to The Clutch uprising bit.

Once they'd finally finished announcing her, Cora and Magda strode down the golden carpet in lockstep. Notably, Lance actually sat up in his chair and paid attention.

As they reached the steps to Lance's throne, he rose and descended. Cora and Magda bowed as he approached, his golden bordered boots clacking on the steps.

"No courtiers?" Cora asked, shaking Lance's rather massive hand as he reached her.

"They're performing their duties to the throne; courtiers get too comfortable around the palace if you let them," said Lance.

"Perhaps they'd be able to offer wise council," suggested Magda.

"If I need council, I'll request in," snapped Lance. His tone was not dissimilar to a fourteen-year-old snapping at his mother when asked to clean his room.

"Of course, Your Majesty," said Magda, offering another, almost imperceptible bow.

"Enough small talk, I've got things to attend to. What was so pressing that our meeting had to be moved forward, Olympia?" asked Lance, as he ascended the steps once again. Taking his throne, he left us standing beneath him at the bottom of the stairs. His mother had been a much more delicate diplomat than Lance was turning out to be.

"We'll get to that in a moment, if it pleases. First, since we're here, should we discuss the incident at the dim sick centre in Streya?" said Cora.

Lance's face shifted just for a moment. Whether it was a twinge of annoyance or embarrassment was hard to make out.

"If we must," he conceded, flexing his gauntleted hand in and out of a fist.

"Well, first thing's first. If I may, I've got a prisoner to return to you," Cora continued, raising a glowing silvery hand.

Lance nodded his approval, and with a flick of her wrist, Cora opened a portal a few feet into the air at the foot of the golden throne. There was a loud, echoing clatter of armour as the swamp dragon rider was unceremoniously dumped in front of the steps, still bound in thick, twisted roots and vines. Then a moment later, a groan. Lance observed the prisoner with the disgust of a child looking at a snail they'd just stepped on.

"What would you like done to him?" her asked, as guards emerged from the corners of the room and began dragging the prisoner away.

"Whatever you feel is best, I wouldn't presume to tell you how to run your kingdom," said Cora.

"That's that then," said Lance, apparently bored with proceedings.

"Not quite."

I felt my body clench involuntarily, as nerves flushed palpably through the room. The unmistakable clinking of armour betrayed the guards at the edges of the room, also seizing with shock. I couldn't imagine when they'd last seen their king contradicted. Regardless, Cora barrelled on. She either didn't notice or didn't care; I suspect the latter.

"You see, if it weren't for my colleague, Professor Shepard, two of your people could have caused significant damage to Streya, its citizens and some members of the free folk offering relief to the sick. It seems prudent that the golden court might see fit to offer some kind of amends." As Cora spoke, a little steel entered her voice, and for the first time, Lance levelled his blazing golden eyes in my direction.

"I suppose outrider Percival was there to defend you when you saw fit to intervene?" he asked, although it didn't sound like a question.

"Regrettably not, Your Majesty, I was elsewhere," said Percy, bowing low as he spoke. He was demonstrating some impressive lower back flexion in an effort to avoid Lance's withering gaze.

"So, you fought off two riders and their mounts single handed?" he asked sceptically, his eyes narrowing to suspicious slits. I gulped, finding my mouth was suddenly extremely dry.

"I did, until Professor Olympia arrived," I said, averting my eyes to inspect the hem of Magda's dress.

"He's being modest. By the time I got there, it was mostly a case of tidying up." Cora lied as naturally as she drew breath.

"Perhaps I underestimated you, Professor Shepard." Lance had never much liked my appointment to the diplomatic seat of Streya. He respected might, as many dragon riders did. The fact that I'm a leading expert on draconic history, politics and magic doesn't hold a great deal of weight. Marrying Percy also doesn't seem to have helped matters.

"You're too kind, Your Majesty," I said, offering a smile. At that moment, I felt my armpits break out in a heavy sweat.

"Quite, so what amends did you have in mind?" asked Lance, mercifully fixing his gaze back on Cora.

"Well, I have given it some thought. First, I'd like to offer thanks; the eggshells you kindly donated have been a source of great relief to the sick. Therefore, our first request would be for you to send another shipment. Secondly, whilst Professor Shepard is exceptionally capable, many other light walkers in Streya would not have fared so well in his shoes. I would suggest that a guard posting of your own men would be much appreciated."

Lance paused, with furrowed brows. His chest muscles

flexed seemingly involuntarily as he considered Cora's suggestions.

"Who would oversee the guard? Not you, Professor Shepard, I presume?" said Lance, cracking a half smile. This was probably as close as he dared venture to a joke.

"I could do that, Your Majesty, if it pleased you?" said Percy, taking a step forward literally and figuratively. I had to resist the instinct to take cover and hide behind him.

"That would be possible. I shall provide four members of the First Battalion, Fire Dragon Riders. They should suffice. Now, why did this meeting need to happen today?" asked Lance, leaning forward slightly in his throne as he fixed his eyes with renewed intensity upon Cora.

"Very well," said Cora, taking a deep breath, which made me even more nervous than I was already.

"I shall be stepping down from my position as chief diplomat between Streya and the golden court, and relinquishing all my official duties, rights and responsibilities to Professor Shepard."

There was a beat before I felt my mouth open and close soundlessly, as the words reverberated around my brain.

Relinquishing all my official duties, rights, and responsibilities to Professor Shepard.

Relinquishing all my official duties, rights, and responsibilities to Professor Shepard.

Relinquishing all my official duties, rights, and responsibilities to Professor Shepard.

I was delivered from my trance when I was dragged back a step or two. It was Percy, I could tell by the way his hands settled on my waist. Lance was stalking down his steps, barely containing the fury on his face. Even Magda had retreated, leaving only Cora standing before him.

"You have held your position in this court for centuries," said Lance through gritted teeth as he reached the bottom of the steps. I half expected him to begin circling her like a wolf. The two of them stood facing each other before the golden throne. Every hair on my body was on end; it was like watching a standoff between two lions. Only much, much worse.

"All good things must come to an end." Cora spoke so casually. My stomach flipped, and for a second, I thought I might be sick in the throne room.

"And you have chosen to end them in the wake of my mother's death," he barked, almost breaking into a yell.

"The timing is unfortunate, I agree, however, Profess—"

"You would leave us? When we are at our most…" He stopped himself, his hands balling into fists. He couldn't let himself finish that sentence. Even unsaid, the ghost of that forbidden word lingered in the air. *Vulnerable.*

"I leave you with Professor Shepard, he can—"

"He cannot replace you," said Lance, shooting me a look filled with the disappointment of ten Astrids.

"There's nothing I do for you as a diplomat that he cannot."

At this, Lance audibly snorted. Percy stepped forward, placing himself between me and Lance, which would have been heart melting, if I wasn't worried Lance might declare it an act of treason. Lance didn't speak for a moment. He took several paces away from Cora, before turning back to her, appraising her.

"Why are you doing this?" he all but growled. His question was met with a rumbling from Sol, as she poked her head out from behind a golden wing. Her sleepy serpentine eyes surveyed the room. I almost wet myself when they fell on me.

"I'm afraid that finding a solution to the dim sickness epidemic is taking up so much of my time and focus, I would be doing the court a disservice not to give up my position," said Cora, in the placating tone of a mother talking to an unruly child.

Lance fell silent, and we all stood stock still, as resolve set across the king's imperious features.

"I forbid it." He spoke the words, and suddenly it was as though all the air had been sucked out of the room, making everything and everyone rigid. I stepped into Percy's shadow, giving up any pretence. I was hiding. Any diplomat worth their salt would be hiding by now.

"You've no authority to forbid it." Cora's words echoed in my mind for weeks after I heard them bounding off the marble walls. Lance stiffened, their eyes locked on one another, and the atmosphere grew thick with power. It radiated out of them both, diffusing into the air and threatened to give me a nosebleed.

"Do you mean to defy me?" demanded Lance, as bolts of golden energy peeled off his body, scorching the ground. Cora's smile didn't falter, but opalescent light was emanating from her eyes and growing stronger with each passing second, until at last she stepped forward.

"If I must." The words hung in the air, the opalite glow now bathing Cora in her entirety. The outline of her body began to flicker and shift, as if she were only half there, or there were two or three of her, oscillating in the space of one. Fractal light shattered and reformed around her, as if she were some sort of gravity well. For an impossibly long second, no one said anything. A silence fell over the throne room, only broken by the low, bone-shaking rumble emanating from Sol, which prompted Lance to turn his megaton gaze onto me.

"You are the chief diplomat from Streya to the golden court. Do well." He barked his order, turned on the spot and stalked back up the stairs to his throne, golden energy still arcing off him. I found that I couldn't move, I was hardly able to even breathe as I stood paralysed in disbelief.

"Time to go," said Cora, who had already ceased glowing. She offered a low bow to Lance, and then turned on her heel and set off, marching out of the throne room followed by Magda a few paces behind.

My mind and body seemed to have parted company. I couldn't move under my own steam, but nevertheless my legs were moving. Percy placed one hand at small of my back, held my hand in his other, and was doing his best to drag me out of the throne room.

"What the hell was she thinking?" I barked.

"Exactly what she said, I expect," said Percy, whilst stirring a strew that smelt delicious.

"Will you stop being rational and overreact with me?" I said, pacing so severely I was at risk of wearing a hole in the rug.

"I know it wasn't the ideal way for it to all happen, but—"

"Wasn't ideal? I thought Lance was going to eat us!" I snapped, eliciting a snort from Percy.

"Sol would have been the one eating us all," he said, jovially.

"So extremely not the point," I said, jabbing my finger at him. The image of golden lightning peeling off Lance flickered in my memory, like a half-remembered nightmare.

"Like I said, I know it wasn't ideal, but in the end, isn't this what you wanted? You've been studying dragon rider politics since forever, this had to be the eventual conclusion of all of that," said Percy, applying implacable and irrefutable logic.

"Fine, yes, eventually, but she's dumping it on me now. Why would she dump in on me now? The dim sick has been going on forever, why now?" I moaned, not really looking for explanations so much as needing a good whinge.

Percy was about to be logical at me again, when a silver portal opened up in our living room in front of the fire, and I almost paced my way into it.

"Hey, can I come in?" came Nick's voice from inside the portal.

"This does not constitute an adequate attempt at knocking at the door," I said into the portal.

"I'm taking that as a yes," said Nick, as his large frame emerged into our living room.

"Hey, Nick, I'm making stew, want some?" asked Percy.

"I'd never say no to your stew," said Nick, winking at him.

"If you've quite finished flirting with my husband, I'm in the middle of a crisis here!" I huffed, slumping in my rocking chair and pushing light into the wood, forcing a bed of moss to form on the armrest, from which bloomed a little pink flower.

"You're having a crisis too?" asked Nick, as he perched himself against the breakfast bar that divided the kitchen and living room.

"Oh, good. Tell me about your crisis, I could use the distraction," I said.

"Well, you know how the stars are diminishing, fading away?"

"I do."

"They are?" asked Percy.

"Indeed," said Nick.

"Very bad," I added.

"Well, one of them came back," said Nick.

"Came back, what does 'came back' mean? Expand."

"One of them that was almost gone, down to the embers, barely a flicker. Suddenly, it's back, big, massive rollicking ball of fire in space, being a star, shining."

"Isn't that a good thing?" asked Percy.

"Yes, very good," said Nick.

"I am failing to see the crisis," I said, plucking the pink flower and tucking it behind my ear.

"Another one vanished," he said bluntly.

"Like, they swapped?" Percy and I asked in unison.

"Nope. One of the faded ones had rejuvenated, and

another one, a healthy one, poof, gone," said Nick, miming a puffing motion.

"Like, instantly?"

"Well, I don't know if it was instant, I wasn't watching. All I know is, four hours ago, one was dying and the other was fine. Ten minutes ago, the dying one was in the prime of life, and the other was gone."

"Weird," we both said in unison again.

"Very weird. What's your crisis? Distract me," said Nick.

"Cora resigned from literally every single duty she has to the golden throne, in front of Lance Sovereign, and gave it all to me. They very nearly fought in the throne room over it. He was so pissed off, I thought he might eat me."

"Oh, he doesn't even like you, does he?" said Nick.

"No, he does not," I agreed.

"He's just a snob. The only reason he doesn't like you is because you don't have some rare hue, it's exactly the same reason he demoted Lord Commander Illia to captain. Doesn't matter that she was the best military leader in all the draconic lands. She rides a swamp dragon, and that's common, so Lance doesn't like her," huffed Percy.

"He must like you then, with your rare grave dragon," said Nick, dipping a spoon into the stew to taste it.

"Nope," said Percy.

"What's his problem with you then?" asked Nick.

"Percy is from the Burning Mantle. His mum didn't ride a grave dragon, and his grandad didn't ride a grave dragon."

"I'm new money," said Percy, with a snort.

"He is a snob," said Nick, as Percy decanted his delicious stew into three bowls.

* * *

"Okay, call me crazy, but I think it's unpetrifying," I said, as I examined my forest dragon egg. It was losing its almost crystalline emerald lustre, taking on a darker, more matt tone.

"Amazing," said Percy. He kissed me on the cheek before shoving a whole round of toast into his face in one go.

"Is that possible," I asked, running my finger along the cool exterior of the egg.

"Dunno." Percy shrugged, chucking a mug of tea down his gullet as he pulled on his boots.

"If it is, should we give it back?" I asked. I regretted the words as I spoke them.

"No, if being with you is unpetrifying it, if that is a thing, then it should stay with you. What if you give it back and it stops unpetrifying? Then we've lost a potential forest dragon. You keep it, it's yours."

"But what if it goes all the way?"

"We'll cross that impossible bridge when we come to it," said Percy, hopping towards the door as he yanked his other boot on.

"Right, impossible," I said, eyeing the definitely more muted egg.

"Oh, Aster, looks like your mum's written," said Percy, no longer hopping and chucking and shoving, but holding out a letter, with a golden wax seal on it. His face had softened.

"Oh, right." I let my eyes drop. I never did reply to that last letter about the triplets.

"You know, I could fly us over. Just for an afternoon, like a little drop in," said Percy, placing a hand on my shoulder. I swallowed the lump in my throat and shook my head.

"I can already hear the disappointment in her voice when we tell her we're not staying the night." I mumbled the words, too ashamed to say them any louder.

"We could stay longer if that's what you want," he said, in his gentlest voice.

"I'm too busy," I said, wringing my hands guiltily.

"Okay, well, if you change your mind, just say the word," said Percy, leaning down to plant a kiss on my cheek before heading for the door.

I watched him go and then my eyes fell on the letter. I didn't open it, just shoved it on the pile with all the rest and tried to think about literally anything else.

"So, whilst lesser dragon eggshells have been ground down into a meal to be consumed by baby dragons, golden dragon eggshells tend to be kept as treasures."

"But what about the relics of Cerunos, Professor Shepard?" asked Lumin Fletcher, who'd shouted his question before he'd even had time to raise his hand.

"Ah well, they're a special case. Cerunos, the centaur

king of the greenwoods, later known as the forest of Cerunos, rescued a golden dragon egg that was taken during The Clutch Uprising. The loss of a golden dragon egg would have been crippling to the Sovereign family. So, once the egg hatched, they had the shell melted down and made into a bow and bracers. Forever after, it was known as *The Golden Shot and Arms of Cerunos*. Unlike other dragon eggshells, golden eggs have a more metallic nature and don't grind down well."

"Have any other golden dragon eggs been given as gifts?" Lumin asked.

"None on record. You see, Cerunos' were a reward for returning the egg. There were only two other occasions when a golden dragon egg was taken or went missing. Once, during The Clutch Uprising, which involved Professor Olympia. She turned down every reward that might have been offered. And as for the first time on record, a golden dragon went missing. This was long before the founding of the University of Streya. You have already heard the stories of the Sable Sorcerer, a powerful void-hued beacon who led a group of light walkers in the theft of a golden dragon egg. The egg was never recovered, and what they did with it remains a mystery. All we do know is that eventually, the perpetrators were rounded up and—"

"Professor Shepard, you have to come now!" said Orion, looking more agitated than I had ever seen him as he burst into my junior class on draconic history.

"Ah, class, this is one of my apprentices, Orion. Say hello to Orion," I said, half on autopilot, as I wondered what could be so urgent.

"Astrid and Sirius are fighting," he continued, ignoring

the somewhat eerie chorus of twelve-year-olds greeting him.

"Say goodbye to Orion," I said, sweeping out of the room as he started off sprinting down the corridor.

"Why are they fighting?" I shouted down the corridor after him. I was struggling to run in my skirt- cloak-gown thing, and was regretting the decision to wear it immensely.

"You know how Astrid is," Orion shouted, still ahead of me tearing down the corridor. He was right. I did. "And how Sirius gets." That was also true. I did know how Sirius got.

"Gotcha," I said, rounding the turn into the second-floor courtyard, only to find Astrid, surrounded by motes of white light, facing down a twenty-foot-tall, grey glowing cyclops. *Shit.*

"Stand back," I bellowed. My best impression of a bellow, anyway. Kicking off into the air, bathing myself in bronze light, I peppered the floor in front of Sirius the cyclops with bolts of fire issuing from the tip of my coal studded cane, causing him to dance clumsily backwards.

"Orion, neutralise Astrid's light wells before she puts someone's eye out," I commanded. I began to coax twisting vines out of the cracks in the cobbles of the court-yard, and used them to ensnare Astrid's wrists. As they dragged her hands down to the ground, she snarled in an unexpectedly animalistic fashion. At once, the white motes of light, enveloped in black, rapidly began fading out of existence.

"You're taking his side!" Astrid wailed, as the vines

snaked up her forearms towards her shoulders, pulling her to her knees.

"I am not!" I barked, turning my attention to Sirius the cyclops as he prepared to lob a large clump of dirt in Astrid's general direction. I pushed power through my spectacles, bathing him and his weapon in bronze light. The clump left his grip and floated ineffectually into the air, before drifting out of the courtyard. Meanwhile, Sirius the cyclops, was trying to breaststroke his way back towards solid ground.

"Orion, be a dear and turn Sirius back to his normal self," I said, landing with a sigh. I wiped the sweat from my brow as a round of applause erupted from the awe-struck teenaged onlookers. After a moment, inky black darkness coated the cyclops's form, and he began to shrink. He grew smaller and smaller until the black faded away, and Sirius fell to the floor, having returned to himself.

"Now, what on earth was all this about? You two are old enough that you should be able to settle any differences without—"

"Professor Shepard, I need to see you at once," came Vega's imperious voice. Students at the courtyard entrance were parting to let the giant of a woman through.

"I've got this situation well in hand, Headmistress Vega, there's no need to—"

"At once!" She barked over me, and I resisted the urge to roll my eyes as she turned on the spot and began stalking off. Jangling as she went, Vega had each lens she had mastered set into a bracelet. She said it was for the sake of convenience; I thought it was to show off. She was up to nine now, and they jangled when she walked, like a cat with a bell on its collar.

"You two, no attacking each other until I get back. In fact, no attacking each other at all." I gave Astrid and Sirius a stern look, dispelled the vines restraining Astrid, and jogged to catch up with Vega and her ridiculously long strides.

"Okay, Vega, I know it's bad for them to be fighting in the open, but it's not like we didn't have our dramatic moments back in our days as apprentices," I began.

"Shhh."

"Did you just shush me? I was being polite when I said 'we'. We both know you were not above throwing a tantrum in that Courtyard, Vega, and frankly they are my apprentices, not yours, and I don't appreciate you trying to—"

"I don't give a shit about your apprentice's fight in the courtyard, Aster, just shut up and walk faster," she said, increasing her pace as I jogged behind her bewildered.

"What's going on?" I hissed, now whispering, because suddenly I felt like should be whispering.

"Shhh!" Vega hissed back at me again, pushing open the large double doors to her office. Vega's office was in the centre of the school. It was a domed circular room, with pictures of all the past headteachers lining the walls. Each head has the right to furnish the office in their own fashion, and Vega's style was predictably stark. She'd replaced all the windows with one-way glass so that she could see out, but others couldn't see in. Her desk was large, made of black ebony wood, and the chairs were utilitarian in design. Nick was standing by her desk when we entered, anxiously reading over what looked like a letter. We allowed the doors to swing shut behind us.

"Did you get your note?" Vega asked, waving four glowing white beams of energy into being, and barring her office door shut with them.

"What note? And is that necessary?" I asked.

"Aster, she's gone," said Nick, looking up from his note. His eyes were glazed over and lustreless.

"Who's gone?" I asked, shifting on my feet as my chest began to feel tight.

"Cora! She left us these, I'm betting she'll have left you one too, back at the cottage," said Vega, thrusting a similar note to the one Nick had been reading into my hand.

"What are you talking about? Cora wouldn't leave, she's Cora, she's always been around... always," I said, trying to speak it into reality, as my hands grew clammy.

"Read it," she said, jabbing at the note.

Dear Vega

I'm sorry to say that I've decided I have to leave. It's the only way I can see to face the problems ravaging our people. I wish I wasn't leaving so much to you, but equally I know there is no one better suited to the task of leading the light walker people; in many ways you've already taken on that mantle. I know you will want to find me, but trust me when I say any effort spent on that endeavour will be wasted. I hope everything I've been able to teach you in our time together will help see you through what lies ahead.

To that end I leave you with one last piece of advice. There will be a panic in the power vacuum created by my absence. Use the university to fill it, do not let the university close, it must become the anchor for all light walkers. Without it, our people will be vulnerable. Finally, Vega, I must ask you one favour. You must outlaw the use of opalescent lenses. You'll find that I have disposed of the university's entire store of them, do not replenish it.

With all the best wishes in the world, your friend and teacher,

Cora Olympia.

The note slipped from my hand, and I watched as it drifted to the floor, settling so gently it didn't make sense. The message it contained was so heavy, it had crushed my voice down into my chest. It should have left a crater where it landed. I looked up at Vega and Nick, and tried to blink away the tears that were threatening to well in my eyes.

"Why?" I asked aloud, remembering Cora's words to Lance. How just days ago, she'd abandoned that post. Now I knew why.

"I don't know. It's true though, every single opalescent lens is gone, poof, vanished," said Vega. She ran an anxious hand over her tight, platinum blonde bun, knocking a few hairs loose.

"What did your note say?" I asked, looking from Nick's stunned face to his trembling hands.

"She told me not to worry about the dim sickness anymore. She'd found a solution and that's why she had to go, and she told me to cease all research into the anomaly and never to tell anyone about it, to let the knowledge of it die with me."

"What's the anomaly?" I asked.

"It's something I found whilst I was stargazing a few weeks back. It affected Cora like nothing I've ever seen," he said, casting open a silvery portal in front of me.

Immediately my skin prickled, and it was hard to breathe, like something was sitting on my chest. The hairs along my body stood at attention. Whatever it was, it was crushing me down, making me smaller. Through the portal, I stared at it, floating in the darkness, warping the space around it, like it was pulling everything inward. A rolling orb of black energy, surrounded by boiling, exploding twists of flaming star fire, vanishing into the void darkness, and then exploding out of it, like bubbling magma. Occasionally peeking through the storm of pure power was a tiny flash of gold, right at the centre. Sweat poured from my body as I gazed at the thing, and all at once my stomach lurched, and I collapsed to my knees. Overwhelmed by the power of it, I evacuated my breakfast with some force, onto Vega's floor, as the portal winked out of existence.

"Sorry, but what the fuck was that?" I asked, staggering to my feet as Nick opened another portal just above my hand. A glass of water fell out of it, which I just barely caught.

"The anomaly," said Nick gravely, as Vega released a

bolt of searing white energy, vaporising my deposit on her floor.

"Sorry about that," I said, cringing to myself as I chugged my water.

"Oh, don't be, I almost did the same when he showed me," said Vega.

"So, we have to see if there is a note for me too, I suppose," I said, shaking off the oppressive feeling of the anomaly.

"After you," said Nick, waving another portal into being, through which I could see my all too inviting living room.

I was sat in my rocking chair in front of the fire, cradling my egg, which I could have sworn was starting to feel warmer. Cora hadn't left me a note. It made sense really, she'd already left me my job in the golden courtroom. But still, I'd have liked a goodbye. I'd put a brave face on it for Nick and Vega, but once they'd left, I may have shed a self-pitying tear or two.

Percy arrived, looking rugged and windswept and not at all like he'd been given world shattering news and then thrown up in the middle of his workday.

"You're home early," he said, throwing off his long black coat, glazed by the rain that was raging outside, and rattling the windowpanes.

"I had a stomach complaint," I said numbly, running my tongue over my teeth as I ignored the waves of anxious nausea.

"Are you okay?" he asked, kneeling in front of me. He pushed his soaking black hair out of his eyes to see better into my own.

"Not really." I knew I was being vague, but I didn't know where to start, how to say it. To speak the most ludicrous, impossible sentence. Part of me still didn't believe it, couldn't believe it. Refused to believe it. Percy looked concerned. He ran his thumb under my eye, wiping away a tear. I hadn't realised I was crying.

"Do you want to talk about it?" he asked, in his most gentle voice.

I shook my head, unable to speak around the lump in my throat. He placed a hand on my shoulder, and the floodgates opened with a sob as I threw myself into his shoulder and began to cry. His strong arms held me as I whimpered.

"It's okay, I'm here, I love you, it's okay," he whispered soothingly to me. Over and over until the words began to sink in. Eventually, I sat back in my chair, letting him go, and accidentally sent my egg tumbling off my lap. Luckily, Percy caught it before it landed.

"Ooops, careful," he said, gently handing it back to me.

"Sorry." I sniffed, taking it from him. I ran my fingers along its smooth surface.

"Don't be. Hey, this might cheer you up, I've got something for you."

"Not another egg?" I joked, attempting a smile.

"No, it's this, I found it in my bag. I must have swept it up in all my stuff when I was heading out the door." As he spoke, he produced a small white envelope from his back pocket, and my heart almost stopped. My mouth fell open as my eyes peeled back. Without thinking, my hand shot out and took the envelope, turning it over. It was addressed to me.

To Aster Shepard

More tears tumbled down my cheeks as I held the thing in my fist. My knuckles were turning white from the strength of my grip. I couldn't let it go, but I wouldn't open it. If I opened it and it was from her, that meant she was gone, for real.

"Aster, baby, you're scaring me. Please, what's wrong?" Percy's big blue eyes blinked up at me and shot guilt into my nauseating emotional cocktail.

"She's gone." The words tumbled out of me like the first fall of snow before an avalanche.

"What, who?"

"I can't open it, you do it," I said, offering Percy my trembling fist, and dropping the crumpled paper into his hands. Percy took it, looking puzzled. He slipped his finger under the seal and opened the envelope. His eyes peeled wide as he scanned the contents.

"Out loud," I murmured.

"Right, sorry."

Dearest Aster

I wish I could say this all to your face, but I know if I did, you'd try to stop me, and I never could say no to you. One of my few weaknesses. I've found the solution to the dim sickness epidemic, and I'm afraid I'm going to have to go away to put an end to it all. My regret is that of all my students, you will be the one I have to leave unfinished, but the rational part of me knows you're ready. You don't need me anymore, Aster Shepard, you are brilliant.

But please, permit a teacher one last assignment, the very last thing you'll ever do for me. Hold on tight to your apprentices, when I'm gone, they're going to need you. I'm afraid to say I've let myself get a bit too important. My departure is going to cause some unrest, and when chaos reigns, people will go to horrible lengths to assert some control. So, hold fast to those apprentices Aster, they're the future, and they need you.

P.S its very bad form for a teacher to say they have favourite, but now you are one, you'll know that we of course do. You were mine xxx

With all my love, wishing you all the luck in the world, your friend,
   Cora.

"She's gone. She's really gone." I could hear the words; it sounded like my voice speaking, but I wasn't. At least, I didn't think I was. I was staring at Percy, as his eyes frantically scanned the note, over and over. He didn't believe it either. Of course he didn't, because it was impossible. Cora couldn't leave, she's Cora. But she had.

* * *

That night, I fell asleep in Percy's arms, and woke up to his screaming.

"Aster, help!" Percy rarely sounded scared, and when he did, it tore away at me, ripping me from my sleep.

My eyes burst open. The room was in darkness, but not pitch black. There was a dim green glow against the walls, and the bed was moving. Still just waking, I became aware of loud groaning, creaking sounds, echoing just beneath Percy's cry. It was somewhat akin to the sound of trees falling to a woodsman's axe. Cracking, splintering wood.

"What's going on?" I called into the darkness, blinking my eyes, and struggling to sit up on the shifting platform of the bed.

"The beds trying to eat me!" said Percy. I turned to him, following his voice. My eyes were adjusting now, I could see him, or his silhouette at least, struggling against vines that were restraining him at his wrists and ankles. Vines, which appeared to have sprouted from the bed frame. I reached out a hand towards him and realised it was me that was glowing green, my hand sheathed in light, casting shadows across the room.

"It's me, I'm doing it," I said, looking first at my glowing hand, then my glowing arm and down at my glowing body, bewildered.

"Well, bloody stop it," said Percy, struggling against

the groaning wood of the bed. His muscles were rippling, and his veins bulging as he fought to tear himself free.

"Right, sorry," I said. Taking a deep breath, I closed my eyes and looked inward, finding my flickering green light, only now it was a great blinding star. I focused drawing it inward, condensing it. It felt almost like I was learning to control a new lens, not to push out too much power at once. I let out a shaky breath and imagined throwing a black sheet over it, hiding it, though it was no less bright or powerful, but contained. When I opened my eyes, the bed had stopped moving, and the vines had gone dormant. Percy gave a final guttural grunt, as the muscles of his lean body bulged. All at once, his bindings snapped as he ripped himself free.

"Well, that was fucking weird," said Percy, shaking the broken vines off his bruised wrists and ankles.

"I'm sorry… I don't understand what happened. My light, it's like its bigger, brighter or something." I was almost whispering. The image of the great roaring emerald power within me was burned into my mind's eye.

"Is that possible?" asked Percy, putting an arm around my shoulder and pulling me towards him. I rested my head against his chest. His heart was thundering, he was panting, and his skin was wet with sweat. I could smell him, it was intoxicating.

"I don't know." I breathed, my voice was shaky and I could feel the power inside me, raging, aching to be released. I rested a hand against Percy's heaving chest, grounding myself.

"What was that?" asked Percy, as a white light flashed through the room. It was as if a lightning bolt had struck just behind the curtain. I jumped up and clung to Percy. He held me, placing his hand on the back of my head, massaging my scalp, as a shiver ran through me. I held onto Percy tighter as another flash bathed the room, and then another and another in quick succession, until it seemed like the room was permanently lit.

Percy kissed my forehead and moved to the window. His arms were outstretched behind him, keeping me back, shielding me. I admired the muscular ridges of his back, and my cheeks burned. He pulled back the curtain, and both of us gasped as the room was bathed in bright light. From the position of the moon, you could see it was still night, but the sky was lit up, dotted with hundreds of lights.

"The stars," said Percy, watching as with every second, more sources bloomed in the sky. My heart was racing, I was glowing again. I could feel it, power coursing through me, I could barely contain it and didn't want to.

"Come to bed," I commanded, focusing the energy into my hand, and forcing it towards the little shrine where my egg lay, lest it bring the bed to life again.

"But what about the stars?" asked Percy, turning back to face me as a bloom of flowers erupted around the egg.

"After," my voice trembled, as I crawled to the edge of the bed, snaking my arms around Percy's back. One hand twisted into his gorgeous, thick, dark hair, whilst the other dug into his shoulder. He groaned and resisted for a second before collapsing into me, and our lips crashed together. The heat of his skin was fire against my own. His hands, calloused and strong, took hold of my hips as he pulled me into him. His strength took my breath away, pressing me against his muscular frame, I was powerless to resist him. Life poured out of me as I lit the room green, with vines and flowers erupting from every beam and board as Percy took me.

* * *

Percy and I lay awake, entwined with each other, as the light of thousands of stars poured through the drawn curtains and lit up the room as though it were midday. He held me to his side, as my head rested on his chest. I listened to his heartbeat, playing absentmindedly with the dark, curly black hairs reaching up to his clavicle.

"I think we need a gardener." He laughed, his warm, rolling chuckle reverberated through me. Our bedroom, formerly a place of warm brown woods and comfortable throws and blankets, now resembled the jungles of the titanic lands. Every inch teaming with life, flowers and leaves and vines and moss everywhere the eye might fall.

"Yes, I made a bit of a mess, didn't I, I'm sorry about that."

"Don't you ever apologise for that," he said in a low voice, cupping my jaw. He pressed our lips together, and I knew from the burning sensation that my cheeks had gone pink. We were on the precipice of a deepening kiss, when a distant roaring sound reached my ear, and our windows shook in their frames. Percy was at the window in a flash.

"Aster, you need to see this." He was already reaching for his clothes as he beckoned me to the window.

"Well, that doesn't sound good," I said, sliding out of

bed. I was still half asleep in a heady daze. Taking the duvet with me, I approached the window.

"Shit," I muttered, dropping the duvet to my feet. I pressed my face to the glass and stared at the pillar of red and gold flame jutting out of the streets of the old town, a little way off from our cottage.

Percy's hands were wrapped tightly around my waist. The wind was blowing my hair back, and water streamed from my eyes as Styx whipped through the starlit night.

"Faster!" I bellowed over the roaring wind, as a great tree erupted out of a building roof a few streets ahead. Percy's hands took a tighter hold of Styx's back ridges once he had clamped me in place with his arms, and Styx twisted violently through the air. My body lifted off him for a second, I would have been thrown like a rag doll, but Percy held me fast to the dragon's back. Styx's wings folded in tight, and we shot towards the epicentre of the magical explosions like a great black arrow cutting through the sky. I only realised where we were headed when Styx's wings stretched out, creating a windbreak, on the outskirts of the dim sickness centre.

I dismounted before we touched down, coating myself in bronze as I descended into the winding streets. All around me, the normally pallid victims of the sickness appeared to be glowing.

"Help!" A scream from my left stopped me dead. My eyes were drawn to a brunette woman in her early twenties. She was glowing green. I had just caught sight of her before she was enveloped by a creeping web of thorns, cutting and piercing her skin as they coiled around her.

"I'm here, don't panic." I staggered, as the momentum of my landing carried me forward. I released the green light I'd been fighting to contain since the stars exploded overhead. All at once, the thorns bloomed into delicate white flowers of weeping jasmine, dripping their salve into her cuts.

"Thank you, sir," she whimpered, pulling herself free of the vines that were now gently growing-.

"What's happening here?" I asked, taking the chance to wring more salve out of the dripping flower heads into the worst of her cuts.

"Ever since the stars lit up, it's been different around here. I've never felt this way before, it's like we're getting better, it was at first at least, it's hard to explain. I feel like I've been empty my whole life, and tonight I started filling up, but it just kept coming and coming, and I didn't know what to do with it all. People have been losing control all over the centre. I didn't know I could do this, I couldn't do this, never before, not until this morning, I just wanted to make a rose." Her eyes were streaming as she looked in horror at the large, twisted mass she'd created.

"You mean... you were born dim?" I asked, finding myself drawn into her glowing emerald eyes. She looked anything but dim.

"I was... I've never... shone before now." As she spoke, she held her faintly glowing hands up to her face, studying them in disbelief.

"Amazing," I muttered, watching as patches of grass

burst through the cobbles at her feet. My mind was drawn home, to Ava, until the sound of shattering glass one street over brought me back into the chaos. I rounded the corner onto the main square, and my mouth dropped open. Fires were erupting at street corners, and panicking children, glowing red, ran around in disarray. Silvery portals winked in and out of existence in the sky above. Fairies were doing their best to catch falling unfortunates in golden nets, while others were holding down a man who was glowing bronze, and who would otherwise have floated off untethered into the sky.

"Aster! Thank the stars you're here!" I heard Vega's commanding voice bellow from the rooftops, as she floated above the square. Her hands were moving so fast they were almost a blur, shooting out beams of white light. Jets of glowing navy-blue water, and silvery portals opening and closing were all around her, as her eyes scanned the scene for disasters to abate.

"Vega, we need—"

"Look out!" she called, pointing behind me, but her warning wasn't fast enough. Out of the corner of my eye I caught a flash of sky-blue light, and then a great force slammed into my back. The impact sent me hurtling through the air. Helpless, I braced myself as a brick wall zoomed up to meet me, only for a silvery portal to spring into being before me. I was jettisoned high into the sky above the square, where I caught myself in bronze light.

"Thanks," I said, with a quick nod to Vega as I surveyed the scene. I caught sight of Percy slicing through a wall of flames with his weapon, Obol. In its sheath, it would look like any other long sword with a cross-guard hilt, but its blade was ice blue, translucent and constantly poured out waves of mist.

"Any ideas?" she asked, as I watched dozens of explosions of different colours lighting the street. Nothing I could do could quell this, there wasn't a plant in the world. I looked up into the sky in desperation, as if I could beg the stars to stop. And then, I saw it. The darkness in between them, the night, hidden behind the light.

"We need my apprentices, open a portal to the senior commons now."

"Are you mad? This is a disaster, not to mention it's chaos back at the school!" Vega barked.

"Orion is void hued, and Astrid is white hued, get it?" I asked. I watched the realisation dawn on Vega's face, before she flicked her wrist and a silver portal sprung open.

"Astrid, Orion, Sirius, get out here now, and Sirius, give them wings!" I yelled, sticking my head through the portal into the senior common.

It filled with faintly glowing teenagers, their faces rapt in concentration, fighting to contain all this new light. Small gardens, and windstorms were popping up all around, as some lost the battle. It took a moment before my presence began to draw the bemused blinking attention of the common. I'd gathered a few dozen pairs of eyes, before a large blast of grey light dazzled them. I managed to pull myself back from the portal just in time for three blurred figures to shoot out. Astrid, in a silken pink dressing robe, Orion, in a predictably black bed suit which I couldn't imagine was comfortable, and Sirius, wearing only his boxers, a vest and slippers. All three of them were enhanced by a set of broad, brown feathered wings.

"What's going on, sir? Headmistress Vega, why are we here?" asked Astrid, who predictably seemed more excited to see Vega than myself.

"Lots of people losing control all at once, Astrid, I assume you've used your power to enhance another before?" I asked, trying to ignore the sound of screams issuing from street level.

"All the time, in my father's clinic before I came to Streya." Astrid nodded, just barely managing to keep her eyes on me as chaos reigned around us.

"Perfect. Orion, Astrid is going to funnel as much power into you as she can, and you're going to let it—"

"Watch out, sir!"

I groaned, as Sirius's muscular frame slammed into my waist, tackling me through the air and out of the path of a tree trunk that exploded out of the chimney just below where I was floating. I gasped, trying to catch my breath as he squeezed the air out of me.

"Are you okay, sir?" he asked, still holding fast to me. His big grey eyes were focused on me, looking surprisingly concerned.

"Fine, thank you for saving me." I wheezed, offering a smile that was halfway to a grimace as I tapped him on the shoulder. He didn't seem to get the hint. "You can let me go now."

"Oh right, sorry." He let go of me, a concerning shade of pink blooming on his cheeks.

"Good reflexes, young man," said Vega, who'd drifted her way over to us.

"Thanks, ma'am, I am somewhat of an athlete," said Sirius, recovering enough of his class clown bravado to shoot her a wink as he flexed a bicep. In spite of myself, I failed to stifle a titter at the image of the great Vega being flexed at by a hormonal teen.

"Right, good reflexes aside, do you two understand the plan?" I asked, calling back to Orion and Astrid, who seemed to be struggling more with their wings than their grey-hued colleague.

"I think I'll need to be in the centre to cover everyone, sir," said Orion, looking nervously at the particularly volatile centre of the square.

"Let us worry about that. Sirius, have you got one more set of wings in you?"

"For you, sir, I've got all the wings in the world." Sirius flirted particularly weirdly.

"Well, will you give my husband a pair, he hates bronze light," I explained, before calling down to Percy. "Percy, we need you up here!"

His eyes locked onto me instantly amidst the chaos, as a pair of black feathered wings burst from his back. He kicked off the ground without hesitation, darting deftly around another blast of sky-blue wind to reach us.

"What's the plan?" he asked.

"We're clearing a path to the centre for Astrid and Orion, and remember Vega and Sirius, once Orion does his thing we'll be grounded. So be ready to land."

"I'll stay with them till they reach the centre," said Vega, who'd already positioned herself behind Astrid and Orion. Her perfect white eyes scanned the square for upcoming disasters.

"Ready, you two?" I asked. Orion and Astrid shared a nervous glance at one another.

"Ready, sir!" they said in unison.

"Right, everyone, get them to the centre!" I gave the word, and Astrid and Orion folded their wings into a dive. Percy was the fastest of us; within seconds, he was cleaving his way through a large pillar of free-floating masonry blocking the path. Sirius grew to thrice his original size, and used his impressive stature to move intervening citizens clear of the path. He was almost clipped by a high-pressure jet of water shooting from the mouth of a navy-glowing child, but was shielded by one of Vega's walls of white light. I hung back, landing on a roof above the square, and let the green storm inside me flow out. Coaxing roots and vines out of the cracked cobble, I extended my consciousness out into the square, dragging free folk and light walkers alike out of the path of my apprentices'. It felt like I was becoming something more akin to a giant spider, making the square my web. A cold sweat formed on my brow as I forced out more light, quickly wrapping vines round an older gentleman who'd spontaneously exploded into the form of a giant three-headed dog.

As Astrid, Vega and Orion touched down in the now ruined fountain at the centre of the square, darkness immediately began to spread from Orion. Astrid and Vega both planted a hand on his shoulders, and all at once, the small zone of shadow engulfed the square, surging outwards like the centre of a mushroom cloud. The darkness passed over me, and suddenly my light went out. I sighed, as a sense of weightlessness came over me. Then, I stumbled suddenly, realising the world was spinning. My footing on the slate roof slipped, and my vision lurched around me before everything turned quiet and black.

* * *

"Aster, are you okay? Aster, careful, don't move, can you open your eyes?" The world was black, there was cold tile work against my skin, and my head felt as though it was full of rocks.

"Percy?" I croaked, my eyes fluttering open as a pale face started to come into focus.

"Oh, thank the stars, you're okay." Warm muscular arms wrapped around me, as Percy pulled me up into his chest, where I could feel his heart thundering.

"What happened?"

"You passed out, fell off the roof. You're lucky Styx is so obsessed with you, he caught you just in time," said Percy.

"Thanks, Styx," I said, realising the cool tiles I was lying on were in fact Styx's onyx scales. He gave a low, rolling grumble, which I took to mean I was welcome.

"Is he okay?" Vega's voice was unusually soft.

"I'm fine, Percy, help me up."

Percy steadied me as I slipped off Styx back and looked around. Vega was a few feet back, flanked by three surprisingly worried looking apprentices, all of them standing amongst the rubble and stray vines of the now quieted square.

"Your plan worked, sir," said Astrid, with an unfamiliar look on her face. If I didn't know better, I might have mistaken it for admiration.

"That felt amazing!" Orion was smiling more broadly than I'd have thought possible for him before this moment.

"You were amazing, Teach, orchestrating all of us." Sirius eyes were fixed on me in that worrying way of his.

"Let's just agree that we're all amazing," I said, with a chuckle. Taking Percy's hand, I subtly tried to ground myself as the world lurched beneath my feet again.

"So, what do we do now?" Sirius asked, his eyes alight with excitement.

"Bedtime. Remember, you still have class with me in the morning," I said, eyeing each of my apprentices in turn.

"Quite right," said Vega, with a smirk, as she conjured another grey portal into being, which Orion and Astrid dutifully trotted through.

"But, sir, couldn't we—"

"You heard your master, through you go." Vega cut Sirius off mid protest.

"Fine…," he grumbled, trudging after the other two.

"You know there is absolutely no way they're sleeping tonight after all that, right?" Percy asked, leaning down as he whispered into my ear.

"No, but I think I will," I said, allowing myself to sag exhaustedly into him the moment the portal winked shut.

3

A whole new world

"Well, today is going to be an interesting day at the office," I said, as I looked out of the window over the city of Streya. Normally, I'd be groggy for days after exhausting my light to the extent I did last night, but this morning I felt fully recovered. I couldn't help but wonder how well my students, who hadn't spent themselves completely, would be coping with the boost.

"I'm coming with you," said Percy, buttoning up his shirt.

"Why?"

"Because we live in a city of people connected to stars, and the stars just went bonkers. You saw what happened last night, it's dangerous out there." Percy's protective instincts always made my stomach flutter, but today everything felt heightened. It was all I could do not to throw myself into his arms like a hormone-fuelled teenager.

"Don't you have more important work to be getting on with?" I asked, trying not to swoon.

"What could be more important than looking after you?" He took me in his arms as he spoke, bracing his hands on my shoulders as our eyes locked.

"Well, when you put it like that," I spoke breathlessly, gazing up into his loving eyes, whilst my fingers slipped into his shirt and started to work the buttons loose.

"Do we have time?" he asked, with one hand already cupping the back of my neck, sending shivers down my spine as he drew me in, leaving barely an inch between us.

"Astrid tells me off for being late even when I'm early," I said, pressing my lips to his. His stubble grazed my chin as he scooped me up, whirling me through the air before throwing me onto the bed.

"You're late, sir," said Astrid imperiously the moment I stepped into my office. Sweat had beaded on her brow, and she seemed to be faintly glowing.

I was still trying to flatten my wind-swept hair. During the flight to The Clutch, I'd lost my hat, probably because of Eurus. To Astrid's right sat Orion, who'd pushed his chair away from the desk and was sitting gloomily in the corner. It was hard to make out whether that corner of my office was simply poorly lit, or if he was doing that himself. In the opposite corner of the room was Sirius, clearly bathed in a faint grey glow. His body was swelling and shrinking like a set of inflating lungs, and his eyes were shut; either he was concentrating or sleeping.

"You're quite right, Astrid, I am, I do apologise. Tardiness aside, I hope you three don't mind if Percy, my husband, you met him last night, sits in on this lesson," I said, doing my best not to glow with pride as I ushered him in after me.

Percy struck a much more impressive figure than I. In his black leather coat, knee high black leather boots, grey trousers and white shirt, his broad shoulders, dreamy eyes and physique were quite distracting.

"Why is your husband here?" Astrid asked. She was apparently the only one of my apprentices currently capable of acknowledging what I'd said, and quite rudely too. I'd expected a slightly warmer reception after last night's heroics, but clearly controlling their heightened power was taking a toll on my students' manners.

"After the rather explosive night we just had, we thought it was best he come along to help out," I said, pulling up a stool behind my desk for Percy to perch on.

"I'm the human shield," he said cheerily.

"How long do you think this will go on for?" asked Astrid. For a second, she seemed to glow brighter, before taking a low, slow breath and clenching her eyes shut tight. Forcing her light to dim slowly and steadily over a few seconds.

"Who's to say? In the meantime, I think some seat rearranging is in order. Orion, you bring your chair over to be next to Astrid, and swap seats with her. Sirius, pull your chair up on the right of Orion."

"Why?" he grumbled, confirming he was awake.

"Just trust me, you'll learn something," I said, crossing to offer him a hand, which he took. His grip was tight and clammy. Up close, I could see he was taking short, shallow breaths, and that rising from his chair took some considerable effort.

"Percy, could you move Sirius's chair for him?" I asked.

"I can do it," Sirius protested, but made no effort to stop Percy as he placed the chair next to Orion.

"Okay, now Orion, if you're making any efforts to hold back your light, stop. Let it out a little," I said, guiding Sirius to his seat. Orion nodded. Little by little, a deep gloom spilled out of him and inched its way through the room, quickly enveloping Astrid and Sirius in soft blackness. They both gave audible sighs of relief as their respective glows subsided.

"Well, this isn't a permanent solution, I'm not going round holding their hands for the rest of my life," said Orion, curtly.

"I think we're all hoping it's not a permanent problem, but in the meantime, you're giving them a moment's relief."

"Think of it this way, now they both owe you a favour," said Percy from over my shoulder. To my surprise, this actually elicited a smile from Orion.

"What's today's lesson then, Teach?" asked Sirius, in his more characteristic, light-hearted way.

"Well, I was going to review the lenses you've chosen as your main focuses, but perhaps we'll go over exercises in control too."

"What hue was the first lens you mastered?" asked Astrid, as all three of them began pulling out notebooks.

"Red, as is the case with ninety-nine percent of pupils.

I had my sights set on bronze, I'd always wanted to fly, but Professor Olympia insisted on red."

Most students lucky enough to be granted the opportunity to study lenses usually ended up focusing on silver or bronze as one of their first, due to the practicalities of easy transportation magic.

"He flies too fast," Percy said with a chuckle.

"Can't you keep up with him?" asked Sirius, eliciting a snort from Astrid.

"What's funny?" Sirius bristled.

"You don't even know who Professor Shepard's husband is, do you?" she asked, patronisingly.

"What's who he is got to do with flying?" asked Sirius.

"She's probably referring to the fact that I'm a grave dragon rider," said Percy, interjecting before fisticuffs broke out in my office. A flicker of recognition shadowed Orion's face.

"Sir, you married a rider?" asked Sirius.

"How do you not know this? He's practically famous for it," said Astrid.

"I think famous is overstating things a little bit, but yes, it was considered quite a landmark moment. Now, enough about me, can we please focus on the assignment at hand? Orion, you start, what hues did you choose?" I asked, aiming for a change of subject.

"Silver, violet and red," said Orion.

"Why those?" Silver came as no surprise, but violet was interesting.

"Silver for ease of travel, red because I believe it is the simplest hue to master, and thus will form a solid foundation, and violet because I want to be involved in the communications web."

Violet hued light walkers, having power over the mind, can communicate over vast distances by speaking directly into the mind of another. In a world where not everyone can have a silver lens, let alone master one, violet magic allows us to stay connected to light walker settlements outside of Streya.

"Why?" asked Astrid.

"To get out of Streya. To go to one of the furthest colonies and be their link back," Orion said, a glimmer of a smile peeking through his pervasive moodiness.

For most light walkers, getting to Streya was the ultimate goal, however, Orion grew up in the Streyan foster system. I suspected this contributed to his less idealised view of the city. It was one of the few pieces of information Cora had imparted to me about him when she handed over the apprentice class.

"Thank you, Orion, for your honesty. I'll look into finding some lenses for you to begin practice with, and I think I know someone in the web for you to speak to. What about you, Astrid?"

"Silver, for the same reasons as Orion, yellow, because it's what most of my family are born with, and I know you said no pure hues, but I really want to master the opal hue."

"It's because you want to be immortal, isn't it?" said Sirius, leaning forward to talk across Orion.

"What? Opal light walkers aren't immortal, what are you talking about?" said Astrid.

"Yes, they are, Professor Olympia has been around for over a millennium," argued Sirius.

"No, that's because she's the infinite," said Astrid, leaning forward. Their eyes locked, both of them starting to glow threateningly, like candles in a dark room.

"You're both half right," I interjected, before we had a repeat of the other day in the courtyard. My ceiling was far too low for a cyclops.

"How can we both be right?" asked Astrid, still bristling.

"If you'd listen, he'll tell us," Sirius sniped back.

"I am liste—"

"In theory, an opalescent light walker can make themselves immortal by manipulating their own bodies relation to time," I said, cutting Astrid off before their squabbling could continue.

"See!" said Sirius.

"However, to do so would be extremely taxing. Maintaining such an enchantment long term would be strenuous and impractical. Co… that is, Professor Olympia, by virtue of being the infinite, doesn't have to worry about such limitations," I said, fixing my eye on a particularly good book I'd read on the bookshelf opposite. I tried to ignore the stabbing feeling of loss that the mention of Cora brought up.

"And that's why she'll be around forever. Although not teaching forever, apparently," said Astrid, driving the knife deeper.

"You know she chose Professor Shepard to replace her, right? He's probably her favourite pupil. We're lucky to have him," said Sirius, rising unnecessarily to my defence.

"Will you two stop fighting for five minutes?" I barked, trying to forget the final words of Cora's letter.

"Fine," said Astrid, kicking herself and her chair back and away from the table with a huff.

"Errm… Professor Shepard, are you okay?" Sirius asked, his tone suddenly alarmingly gentle.

"What?" I asked, confused.

"You're glowing," Percy said, placing a soothing hand on my shoulder.

"Oh…" I sat for a moment, dazed, as a red rose bloomed out of the middle of my office desk.

"Your magic's very pretty, sir," said Sirius after a short while.

"You should have seen our bedroom this morning."

"Percy!" I barked, spinning round on the spot, eyes wide, as a snigger broke out from my apprentices behind me. Percy looked just as shocked at himself as I was. He cringed, and mouthed his apologies.

"Sirius, tell me the hues you picked, quickly," I commanded, not turning back to face them. I could tell from the burning sensation in my cheeks that they were turning red.

"Errm, well, sir, I picked—"

"Aster, come now," commanded Vega, as my office door swung open with a bang.

"I'm in the middle of a—"

"Sovereign Lance just landed in the gardens. He's in my office." Vega cut me off and brought me out in a cold sweat of dread all at once. I turned slowly to the awe-struck faces of my apprentices, and struggled to make my thoughts line up in a rational order.

"Don't kill each other whilst I'm gone," was the best I could manage, before leaving my office. Percy took my hand and squeezed it as we went.

"What does he want?" I hissed, breaking into a jog to keep up with Vega's long strides.

"Mostly, he seems to want to shout about things," said Vega, curtly.

"Sounds about right," said Percy.

* * *

Lance arrived dressed in the formal wear of a member of the Sovereign family: black robes, with golden dragons stitched into intricate patterns, which wound their way along his chest, back and arms. A single large golden ring indicating his position, and most intimidatingly, two golden scabbards which contained his famed swords, forged from golden dragon shells. Ray, the larger of the two, a bastard sword formerly wielded by his mother, and Lustre, a gladius which looked like a dagger dangling from his giant frame, forged to celebrate his birth. I bowed to him as I entered.

"Your Majesty, to what do we owe the pleasure?" I asked, trying to ignore the beginnings of a tension headache that the thick static of his power was bringing on.

"Why have you not made a report to the courts about the star bloom incident?" he asked, clearly already at the end of his not particularly long fuse.

"I apologise, Your Majesty, as yet we know nothing,

and therefore have nothing to report." I kept my eyes low, careful not to meet his gaze.

"How can you not know? They are stars, and you are light walkers. Are you not connected to the stars?"

"We are, but not in the way you seem to think," said Vega, in a way that made my palms sweat.

"Do you presume to know my mind?" Lance asked, levelling his withering gaze at Vega. She met it unflinchingly, as Cora had. As I could not seem to.

"I'm merely listening to what you're saying and responding." If she was at all intimidated by him, she wasn't giving anything away.

"Has something happened concerning the, ermm, star bloom to cause concern?" I asked. Admittedly, it was a rather good name for the phenomenon.

"A leviathan fell over the Titanic canyon last night. It sent giants of all stripes scattering into draconic lands, causing chaos, and frightening civilians." He seemed to soften slightly as he spoke.

"And you feel the two incidents are related?" I asked, wondering if there was any recorded speculation regarding the relationship between Leviathans and the stars.

"When was the last time you remember a Leviathan falling from the sky?" he snapped, hardening again.

"It's something we can certainly look into," I said, offering another, desperately reverential bow.

"See that you do, and whilst I'm here, I wish to speak to Olympia. To let her know that the red dragon guard we discussed will arrive within the week, along with the eggshells."

"I can pass on words of Your Majesties generosity, if it pleases you," I replied.

"It does not, I wish to speak to her personally." As he spoke, Lance looked around as if expecting to see her emerge from a bookshelf at the mention of her name.

"She's away," said Vega, not looking up from the papers she was poring over at her desk.

"See that the message is passed—"

A thunderous cracking sound cut Lance off. The last thing I saw was his hand shoot to his waist, drawing Lustre, before I was enveloped in Percy's black cloak and pushed down to my knees. A shiver ran down my back as cold air washed over me. Percy must have summoned a shield of ice to shelter us. My world was black, but the sound of creaking, groaning and explosions reverberated, followed by a subdued clattering. A second later, Percy's large, calloused hand took mine and helped me to my feet, pulling back the cloak. Above us, a large hole had appeared in what had been Vega's domed ceiling. Shattered masonry lay about the ground, and the air hummed with Lance's power. A small wisp of steam emanated from the point of Lustre.

"Explain yourself!" commanded Lance, pointing Lustre through the hole in the ceiling towards a giant figure.

"Ummm, sorry, Teach," came a familiar, but unusually low voice.

"Sirius, is that you?" I asked, squinting into the sunlight now pouring into the office."

"Yeah, I kind of... lost control." Sirius's bass-filled voice echoed through the building.

"You know our assailant, Shepard?" asked Lance, his dagger still outstretched in Sirius's direction.

"He's an apprentice," I said, bathing myself in bronze light as I drifted up to Sirius's eyeline, which was currently about twenty feet in the air.

"I'm sorry," he said, looking more upset than I'd expected.

"Don't worry, it's not your fault. Are you hurt?" I asked, drifting around to check his head for wounds.

"No, I just felt this rush of power and then lost control. I was only trying to be a foot or so bigger, you know, just… pump up a bit." He gave a sheepish grin and pointed to a bicep that was now the width of a one-hundred-year-old oak tree.

"Well, you certainly managed that, could you shrink back down for me?" I asked as gently as I could, before landing myself.

"Why do your apprentices have such poor control?" asked Lance accusingly, as I set foot on the floor.

"It's not Professor Shepard's fault, it's the stars, they're charging us all up," said Sirius, valiantly climbing through the rubble to my defence.

"Is there something you needed, Sirius?" I jumped in before Lance could bite his head off, figuratively or literally.

"I just wanted to give you this, since I didn't get a chance to tell you about my lens preferences," said Sirius, rather shyly handing me a crumpled sheet of paper. I unfolded it, scanning the contents. I walked the delicate line between making him feel like I was interested and not enraging the famously short-fused Lance by indulging him. My eyes fell on a small collection of ancient draconic symbols in the corner of the note, which read, *the queens cave.*

"Did you write this?" I asked, shoving the note back into his hand and jabbing at the draconic symbols.

"No, sir," he said, taking the note back, and inspecting the symbols himself. He looked just as confused as me until realisation dawned. "It must have been that old lady."

"What old lady?"

"Oh, she bumped into me in the corridor. I dropped my stuff and she helped me, she could have done it before she gave it back," he explained.

"What did she look like?" I asked, momentarily forgetting that the king of the most powerful nation on the planet was standing just behind me in a strop.

"Hard to say. She was bent forward, with a hood up, she wore faded blue and white robes. I'll find her for you if you like?" he said.

"No, that's quite alright, I have a feeling I know where she will have gone."

"Shepard, I expect a report to the court by week's end," said Lance from behind me, almost making me jump out of my skin.

"Yes, Your Majesty," I said, turning towards him. I caught myself awkwardly in between a bow and a salute, as he strode past me out of the office.

"I suppose nobody is going to help fix this mess then," Vega huffed, kicking some of the smaller chunks of masonry out of her doorway.

"Sorry, Vega, I've got somewhere to be," I said,

already speed walking to where I suspected Magda would be waiting for me.

"Where are we going?" Percy hissed, following me.

"Magda is here," I whispered back, turning a corner rather sharply.

"What, since when?" asked Percy, bewildered.

"Dunno, but she left a symbol for me on my own student's note pad, and if anyone knows what is going on with Cora, it's going to be her, isn't it?"

"True."

I took Percy's hand as we reached the staircase leading to her office, and breathed light through my bronze lens, careful not to push too much of my newfound power. Ever so gently, our bodies began to lift off the ground.

"Ughh, I hate bronze flight," said Percy, clutching his stomach rather dramatically.

"It's better than walking the three hundred steps," I said, as we began to drift rapidly and effortlessly up the spiralling staircase, which led to Cora's office.

Many doorways lined the stairs of the tower, the second tallest in the school, but Cora's was right at the top. Hers was the second to last door, the very highest one bringing you out onto the roof. As usual, Cora's door was unlocked. We gently pushed it open and stepped inside. Normally, candles would be lit and a fire blazing, bathing the room in a warm amber light, and flickering against the bookshelves, which lined all but one wall of Cora's vast office. The final wall was made entirely of glass, and looked out over the quads and the rest of the university. Today, though, there were no candles and no fire. Just the white light of the sun, and unusually, the stars, which gave the room an altogether cooler, less welcoming aura. It felt like an ancient library that you didn't really have permission to be in.

"You made it, I see," came a voice from the armchair, facing the unlit fire.

"Why all the cloak and dagger, Magda? You could have just come to my office," I said, letting the bronze light fade, to Percy's relief.

"Lance doesn't want members of the court coming to Streya without his express permission. He thinks your lot are up to something, what with the stars and everything."

"But we're not," I protested.

"I know that, but he rarely listens to our advice. Especially mine after the stunt Cora pulled in our last meeting." Magda wrung her hands, whilst I perched on another armchair and Percy sat on the floor between us.

"So, what was so urgent that you had to come despite Lance's wishes?" asked Percy curiously, leaning back on his elbows.

"You, that is, the university, need to announce that Cora is gone, and soon," said Magda, gravely.

"Why? That'll cause panic. And why has she gone anyway? Do you know where she is? When is she coming back?" A flood of questions poured out of me.

"Before long, a new infinite is going to emerge. You need to say something before that happens, or Lance, and probably the free folk, will think you've been hiding the truth from them."

I blinked, opening and closing my mouth as the words *new infinite* rolled around my mind on repeat. She'd ignored my questions, but those words answered them all the same. As I sat there, with a lump forming in my throat, my hands started to glow. I could feel it, my chair beginning to root itself to Cora's immaculate hard wood flooring.

"New infinite?" asked Percy. Magda nodded, but offered no explanation.

"It hasn't happened for over a thousand years," I said slowly, as the gravity of what Magda was saying dragged me inside myself. I was vaguely aware of the realisation dawning on Percy's face, too.

"Because the old one has to—"

"Be gone." I interrupted him before he could finish that horrible sentence.

"Exactly," said Magda, heaving herself out of the chair and hobbling towards the window.

"Is that why the stars are doing whatever is it they're doing?" I asked.

"What do you mean?" asked Percy, bewildered.

"It's just something I read, I never thought about what it meant. To be honest, I'd never really understood what it could mean." The statue in Infinite Park flashed through my mind.

"So, a baby is going to be born with infinite light in the new few days?" asked Percy.

"Not necessarily," said Magda.

"The infinite can be passed to any light walker. If I remember rightly, Cora said she was twelve when it passed to her," I explained.

"So, it could be you?" Percy asked, sending a chill down my back as every awful implication of that thought rocked me.

"Ugh, don't. I won't sleep for the dread of it."

"Why does the infinite even happen?" asked Percy, at which Magda and I both shrugged.

"Nobody really knows," I said. There were numerous theories. The goriest was that a collection of hundreds of light walkers had banded together to perform a ritual sacrifice, to create a being powerful enough to lead us. The theory said the nomadic power of the infinite was their collective light. I didn't believe anyone really knew or put much store by any of the theories, but that one certainly had an arresting quality.

"Regardless, it's going to be passed along soon, and if it happens before the world knows about Cora, then it won't look good for the people who kept it secret," said Magda, heading for the exit.

"Wait, where are you going?" I asked, realising that I had no idea how she'd got here. She'd never be able to hide Eurus from Lance.

"To the roof, to get picked up."

"By whom?"

"You remember the lad that attacked the dim sick centre with that awful swamp rider? I've been keeping an eye on him. Wayne, his name is, he's a nice enough boy when he's not being influenced by brutes. I had him take me; he's being assigned to that little guard Lance is putting under Percy's command. As a kind of penance, I think."

"So, I'll be commanding the man that held a sword to my husband's neck?" said Percy, his jaw clenching.

"Oh, I wouldn't fixate on it too much, he really did seem the nicer of the two," I said, offering a conciliatory smile.

"Just give him a chance, get the measure of him," said Magda. As she placed her hand on the door, a wry smile flickered across her face. It was just a momentary flicker before she gently let it open and started hobbling up the stairs. Percy and I stepped out to wave her off, and as the door that led to the roof shut behind her, the hairs on my neck stood on end. The unmistakable feeling of being watched. Percy felt it too and reacted faster than me, wheeling round on the spot and thrusting his arm out to shunt me behind him.

"Oh, it's you," he said, as I stumbled up the stairs, ending up behind him. I turned, and there was Sirius looking winded, sweaty, and very nervous, standing on the last stair before Cora's door.

"How long have you been there?" The words spilled out of me so fast it was a wonder they didn't crash into each other.

"Long enough to know Astrid is going to be devastated." My stomach plummeted.

"I, errm, you can't..." I struggled to find the right words.

"I won't... say anything, if that's what you're worried about," he whispered.

"Thank you, you won't have to keep it a secret for long," I said, stepping past Percy to offer Sirius my hand. He took it, and to my surprise, pulled me into a hug.

"I trust you, Professor Shepard," he whispered into my ear, before letting me go.

"Oh, erm... thank you, Sirius." I was a bit dumbstruck.

"Why did you follow us up?" asked Percy, watching the scene with some amusement.

"Oh right, it's just, Professor Shepard forgot my notes on what lenses I would like to study." He shoved the crumpled paper into my hand for a second time, offering an awkward half smile.

"You walked up all these stairs for that?" asked Percy.

"Yep, and now I'm gonna walk back down them," said Sirius, offering a somewhat awkward wave before setting off down the stairs. I watched him go before letting my eyes drop to his note. To my surprise, he wanted to study red, golden and green hues.

"He's only picked hues I've mastered," I said to Percy, once I guessed Sirius would be out of earshot.

"I am not surprised." Percy chuckled.

"Aren't you?"

"Oh Aster, you can't be this oblivious," said Percy, poking me teasingly.

"What?" I whined.

"He's got a crush on you," Percy's laugh echoed down the stairway. I simply rolled my eyes, but quietly admitted to myself that that would explain a lot of Sirius's odd behaviour.

* * *

That evening, I revisited Vega's office. It was still open to the elements, but the rubble had been cleared away.

"Twice in one day? What have I done to deserve this?" Vega asked, dryly.

"We need to announce that Cora is gone. Today," I said, keeping my voice low.

"Hasn't there been enough chaos for one day?" Vega huffed.

"Before too long, a new infinite is going to emerge, and then everyone will know. We need to announce it before that happens, or it'll look like we were keeping secrets." Vega's brows furrowed for a moment, then her face deflated slightly.

"A new infinite, how do you know?" she asked, her voice softened.

"Magda was here today, she told me," I explained, halfway tempted to place a consoling shoulder on her arm.

"I see." Vega braced herself against her desk and took one deep breath, by which time she'd hardened again. "Fine, I'll make the announcement, but this is going to be a nightmare," she said, angrily summoning another portal, and vanishing through it before I could say another word.

"I'll miss her too," I said to the empty office, before going to meet Percy, who was waiting for me with Styx outside the school gates.

* * *

It was on the flight home that they appeared. Four sets of wings on the horizon, Percy and Styx spotted them before me. We shifted imperceptibly in the air and soared into an updraft, carrying us to a higher vantage point.

"They must be your men," I called over the roaring wind, reminding him of Lance's promise. Four riders to defend the dim sick centre, we could have done with them arriving yesterday.

"I don't really want men," Percy whispered into my ear as they approached, the hairs on my neck standing at rigid attention. Styx slowed his flight, and the four fire dragon riders pulled up alongside him. I knew only one of them by name, courtesy of his last uninvited visit to the centre and Magda.

"You must be Wayne," I called over the roaring wind to the rider on our immediate right. He nodded, shame faced; likely hoping I wouldn't recognise him. Percy diverted our course, leading us to Olympia's Park, another of the large green spaces dotted throughout Streya.

As they landed, the other fire dragon riders stepped back, leaving Wayne by default at the front of the crowd.

"I wanted to apologise for errm—"

"Holding a sword to my neck?" I enjoyed watching him squirm.

"Exactly, I mean… Roderick, he got me all wound up, out of my right mind."

"Do you know who I am?" asked Percy, striding forward, towering over the relatively diminutive Wayne.

"You're Percival of the Burning Mantel, first of your name to ride a grave dragon, Outrider to the Golden Court and Commanding Officer of the newly appointed Draconic Guard of Streya," said Wayne, standing to attention and saluting. The three riders behind him saluted just a split second after.

"And do you know my husband?" The words hung in the air, as Wayne's eyes peeled wide enough that they threatened to pop out like grapes.

"I have a job for you, Wayne," I said, when Wayne failed to reply to Percy's question. He nodded so vigorously he was at risk of giving himself whiplash. "But I'll need some bits from home."

"Say no more," said Percy gently lifting me onto Styx before we set off to the cottage.

"Will you be okay?" asked Percy, as I slipped off of Styx outside our door. Wayne and his dragon landed just a few moments later.

"I think so, come in, Wayne," I said, holding the door to the cottage open for him. His eyes shot to Percy, as if asking for permission, only shuffling in after receiving an affirmative nod.

"I'm gonna show the others where the dragon aerie and dim sick centre are, be back soon." Percy lent down, giving me a peck on the cheek before taking to the air, followed by the other three riders who had remained in the sky, circling overhead. I watched them go, then followed Wayne inside. He was standing nervously at the entrance. It was as if he thought he'd trigger some alarm if he walked into the cottage proper.

"Tea, Wayne?" I asked.

"No, thank you, sir." Wayne wouldn't, or couldn't meet my eyes as he spoke.

"You don't need to call me sir," I said, as I walked past him and sank into my chair.

"Yes, s… I mean… what should I call you?" he asked, looking anxious.

"Never mind, call me sir if you must, just come and sit down, you're making me nervous." He ended up sort of half sitting, half hovering over a breakfast bar stool. Meanwhile, I'd fished out my nice parchment and sliced off a small letter's worth. My handwriting had never been a source of much anxiety for me. That was until I had to write a letter to Lance Sovereign himself.

"Take this, Wayne, and deliver it directly to the golden court," I said, handing him the letter, which I'd folded and sealed with the official wax print of the Streyan Diplomat to the Golden Court. For so long, it had been Cora's print. Today, it sealed the letter informing of her departure.

* * *

Vega announced Cora's disappearance the next morning, using Streya's network of violet lenses to speak to most of the city at once. By mid-afternoon, she had to close the university to outsiders due to the surge of nervous citizens flooding in, looking for answers. I think some of them might have genuinely hoped to find Cora hiding behind a bookcase. Personally, I was happy to be well out of the way, and to know that the message of Cora's disappearance was in the hands of hapless Wayne, and not myself.

* * *

"What do you think happens next?" asked Percy, as we lent over our small balcony looking out across the glowing city of Streya. Whilst the cottage only had one floor, it had been built on a steep incline, creating a balcony at the back of the building. The night sky was lit as bright as day, blazing with hundreds of blooming stars.

"Next?" I asked, wondering how many houses were flooding or exploding in flames as we spoke.

"When the next infinite pops up," said Percy, letting a perfect icicle form on his fingertip before dropping it off the balcony to shatter on the cobbles.

"Well, probably Vega takes charge of tutoring them personally, and they end up some prodigious talent that makes us all embarrassed to call ourselves beacons," I said, only half joking.

"Maybe you should be the one to…" Percy's sentence trailed off as the brightest star in the sky winked out, vanishing into an infinitely small speck of light in the sky. At once, I felt the roaring green flame inside me shrink, as another blooming star all but vanished, and then another and another. They were like flames diminishing to embers in a burnt-out fire. I slumped against Percy, as all my strength and drive seemed to vanish at once.

"Are you okay?" Percy asked, helping me inside.

"It's like the wind was knocked out of me," I explained, gripping his wrist tightly as he lowered me slowly onto our bed. Percy sat himself up against the headboard, pulling me in to rest against him as I lay between his legs. For a man who could pull ice out of thin air, he was always comfortingly warm.

"Take deep breaths," he whispered, stroking my hair back, as I tried not to panic about my heart, as it fluttered disconcertingly in my chest.

"C-can't catch my b-breath," I said, struggling to speak as my breathing ran ragged.

"Don't panic, it'll pass," said Percy, pulling me tighter

to him, gently kissing me behind the ear, sending a distracting ripple of goosebumps surging down my body.

"Do y-you think this is h-happening to everyone?" I took one of his large, calloused hands in mine as I spoke and tried to squeeze it, but found I couldn't muster much strength in my trembling fingers.

"I'm not worried about anyone else right now, don't talk, just breathe, just breathe, just breathe," Percy whispered softly into my ear, gently lulling me into a sort of trance. My breathing and heart gradually calmed, and I was almost asleep when a cracking sound snapped my eyes open.

"What was that?" I asked, my eyes darting around the room for the source.

"No way!" Percy breathed, pointing a finger towards the corner of the room where my egg sat, surrounded by the shrine of plants I'd grown for it.

"That's not possible," I whispered, as another crack appeared along the side of the shell, followed by another, and then another. My mouth fell open, as a small green head with twisting grey slate horns poked out of the top of the shell. Unlike their swamp-dwelling cousins, forest dragon scales aren't emerald green, but a much darker, matt shade, similar to the leaves of a birch tree. Often, their scales resembled the shape of leaves. This one's resembled the heart-shaped leaves of a black mulberry bush. Dwarfed only by mountain dragons and the extinct meteor dragon, forest dragons are some of the largest in the world; similar in scale to swamp dragons, although much less brutish and muscular in build. Forest dragons' limbs are finer and more elegant, and with swanlike necks

, they can grow to be roughly three stories tall and twice as long from their head to the tip of their tail. For now, this one was only just the size of a small house cat.

"That's not possible," I said again, gripping Percy's hand as my heart thundered in my ears. I could feel his tense body leaning forward, watching the little creature as its great, globelike eyes blinked open for the first time. Its snake-like pupils were growing and shrinking as they adjusted to the world, and then all at once its eyes locked with mine. A charge of power ran through me as a voice pierced my mind.

"Hello, Aster." The voice was soft and rumbling, almost like the purr of a cat.

"You're speaking to me?" I asked aloud, crawling to the edge of the bed, drawing up close to the tiny horned head of the creature.

"No way," said Percy from behind me, his voice in utter disbelief.

"Of course, for I am your dragon, and you, my rider."

"I can't be, I'm a light walker, I can't be a rider."

"And yet you are, Aster Shepard, rider of Tera, the forest dragon." As its voice rolled through my head, the little creature's shell cracked completely and fell away, and its wide, brown membranous wings emerged.

"You're Tera?" I asked. The creature nodded, as its delicately thin clawed front legs kicked free of the remains of its shell. It bounded forward, leapt into the air and glided on its outstretched wings, landing before me on the bed.

"Hello, Tera," I said, reaching out a trembling hand,

and gently running my finger to the pointed end of her twisted horns.

"Aster, is she really… speaking to you?" asked Percy, climbing off the bed to survey the creature from above. Percy knew what this meant as well as I did. If she was, it meant I was her rider. Everyone knew that a dragon only ever spoke to its rider. Percy also knew that this was impossible, because a light walker could not be a rider.

"She is," I breathed, my voice catching in my throat.

"Who is this?" the voice issued into my mind again, as Tera returned Percy's gaze.

"My husband, Percy. He rides a grave dragon named Styx," I explained, looking up at Percy with a smile.

"He's much larger than you, a strong paramour is a wise choice." I chuckled, as Tera's words issued into my mind, with a sageness you wouldn't expect from something a minute old.

"What's funny?" asked Percy, dropping to his knees to be eye level with Tera.

"She approves of my choice of husband," I said, and watched a grin burst across Percy's face.

4

A New Infinity

"So, who can tell me what happened in the very first year U.F.?" I asked, looking out at the eager faces of my youngling class on the third day of the somewhat ridiculous Cora Olympia commemoration week. It was Vega's idea, something to help move people towards the idea that she was not coming back. I wouldn't normally be teaching history, but the head of antiquities was the one we were commemorating, so everyone was pitching in. One hand shot up the fastest, little Stella, a yellow-hued girl of seven or eight, I couldn't remember.

"The University of Streya was founded, by Cora Olympia."

"Correct, Stella. At the time it was just one tower, at the centre of what was just a small town. Not unlike the many towers you'll see sprawled throughout the city today. The rest of the university was built around it over the next eight hundred years. But it all started with one tower, and how many pupils?"

"Three sir, three apprentices," said Timmy, a little sky-blue hued boy. He was just coming into his powers, which gave him the appearance of someone perpetually windswept; a rather odd effect to have on a blonde, curly-haired six year old.

"Correct, a tradition that's carried on for generations, with some of the most promising students from each senior class being handpicked to become apprentices by—"

Knock Knock

"Come in," I said to the door.

"Hello class," said Vega. She was greeted by twenty-five echoed 'hellos' and scraping chairs, as the pupils hurried to stand for the headmistress.

"To what do we owe the pleasure?" I asked, gesturing for the class to sit back down.

"I'm just introducing the new head of antiquities, Professor Ithaca, a violet-hued beacon."

As Vega spoke, an older woman hobbled in after her, wearing long black robes that dragged along the floor. She was so stooped she almost had a hunchback, over which was draped an intricately woven, beaded shawl, which snagged my eye for some reason. Her thin, grey hair was tied into a large messy bun on the back of her head. Were she to let it down, it would probably reach her waist.

"Hello, class," croaked Professor Ithaca.

"Hello, Professor Ithaca," the class echoed back to her.

"That'll be all then, carry on," said Vega, waving, and jangling her five bracelets as she went.

"Right, now where were we?" I asked, addressing the class at large.

"You were talking about Cora Olympia's apprentices. My daddy said you were one, sir," Timmy said, struggling to flatten down his fringe, which had caught in his own breeze.

"That's correct, I was."

I remembered Timmy's dad. Streyan by birth, he'd been a contemporary of Nick and Vega's throughout their time at school. I spent my formative years studying in my home village, so didn't know him until I was invited to join their class at seventeen. He was a particularly ambitious bronze-hued light walker named Roma. He ended up being a big wheel in the transport networks of Streya.

"He says it was a mystery why you were ever picked," said Timmy, cheerily.

I smiled, and did my best to believe that Timmy didn't understand the implications of what he'd just said.

* * *

"How's commemorating Cora going?" asked Percy from the kitchen, where he stood stirring an amazing smelling vegetable curry. I was in my rocking chair in front of the fire, stroking Tera, who was curled up in my lap, as she nibbled at the strawberry plant I'd grown out of the floorboards for her.

"Ugh, it's a weird combination of a sad and somewhat pointless feeling. We're teaching them things they already know, every kid in Streya. Heck, every light walker grows up hearing the stories of Cora Olympia. Anyway, I think I might be off the hook now, we've got a new antiquities professor, Ithaca."

"Is she any good?"

"Search me, I've never heard of her, but by the looks of her she's probably old enough to remember most of what she'll be teaching," I said, with a chuckle and then felt immediately guilty.

"And still no sign of the infinite emerging?"

"Nope, and I was hoping to use the news of the infinite emerging to sweep Tera's arrival under the rug."

"Why must I be swept under a rug?" Tera's voice rolled lazily into my head.

"Because something like us has never happened before, I'm scared that some people might not like it, and might try to take you from me."

Percy dropped his spoon and covered the length of the cottage in seconds to wrap his arms around me. "Nobody is going to separate you, and if they try, I won't let them," he said, as a placed a kiss on my cheek.

"Percy is a charming paramour," purred Tera. Her big green eyes were locked onto him, taking in every inch of him. I chuckled, I'd caught myself doing the same thing more than a few times, I understood the appeal.

"What's she's saying," asked Percy, as he smiled back at Tera and gave her a wink.

"Just admiring you, I think," I said. I stifled a laugh as one of Tera's large globes clumsily flickered closed, then snapped open again at Percy.

"I believe Percy will not allow our separation; you have nothing to fear in the reporting of my hatching," said Tera, watching intently as Percy returned to his curry.

"I think really, I'm scared of what Lance will do when I tell him." I ran my fingers along the twisted ripples of Tera's horns, as she curled up into a spiral and began to purr louder. She was growing fast, already becoming slightly awkward to balance on my lap.

"Well, I might have an idea for you on that front," Percy said, whilst sprinkling something into the curry.

"What's that then?"

"I got an invitation today to the golden hunt." He rooted through his pockets and produced a rolled parchment, tied with ribbon and sporting a broken wax seal.

"Have you ever been on one of those before?" I asked.

"Nope, I think it's because I have men under me now." My shoulders vibrated as I tried to contain a snigger at what he'd just said.

"What? Oh…" Percy's cheeks flushed bright red, as the realisation dawned on him too.

"That is not what I meant, Aster, you're twisting my words!" he protested.

"I never said a thing." I giggled.

"Well, you should get your mind out of the gutter," said Percy, unable to suppress his own grin.

"So, as you were saying, now that you've got men underneath you…" I bit my lip, suppressing another fit of giggles.

"Now that I'm a commander, I get invited to the hunt, a hunt which Lance leads," said Percy, rising above my immaturity admirably.

"Oh… hang on, how long is this?" I asked, as I started to realise the point he'd been trying to make.

"Three days in the titan lands, at least."

"Which means someone else will sit in the throne in his absence," I said softly.

"Yep, chances are it'll be Igraine," said Percy.

"Oh perfect, when's this happening?"

"Not tomorrow, the day after. I have to leave ridiculously early in the morning," said Percy, pouring the curry into two separate bowls and bringing them over.

"How will I get there?" I asked. Styx couldn't fly me if Percy was out in the titanic lands hunting.

"I'll assign you one of the dim sick guards, you can have Wayne. You know, he's been surprisingly reliable," said Percy, handing me a bowl as he lowered himself into his rocking chair.

"I expect it's the guilt," I said softly.

"Whatever it is, he's the most competent guy in the guard. He'll get you there."

"Well, Tera, you're going to meet a princess," I said, to the sleeping dragon on my lap.

* * *

Riding a fire dragon is not like riding Styx. Nova was about twice the size, a fair bit slower, and pleasantly warm to the touch, like freshly baked bread. Which was a welcome relief when we burst through the cool, damp clouds and into the open air above the Golden Cradle. Wayne sat behind me, one arm on Nova's spined back, the other clamped tightly around my waist. Clutched in my hands, I held tightly onto Tera, who was watching the sky with rapt attention, having never flown outside our cottage before.

"You know, I can fly, Wayne, you don't have to worry about me falling off," I shouted into the wind.

"Outrider Percy said I was to get you to The Clutch and back safely, sir, that doesn't include you flying yourself there," Wayne shouted back into the wind. He'd somehow become simultaneously more respectful and more assertive since working for Percy. Nevertheless, when the retinue of sixteen riders from the 1st battalion ascended towards our position, he froze up. Nova came to a complete halt, hovering in mid-air.

"Are you okay?" I asked, in a lower register now that the rush of wind wasn't stealing my voice.

"I've never been here before." Wayne was doing a poor impression of an assertive military escort now, his voice cracking as he spoke.

"Don't worry, they're just doing their job. You need to announce why we're here, who I am and who you are, that's all."

"I shall one day become like that." Tera's voice was awestruck inside my mind. I could feel her eyes on the lone forest dragon, the sixteenth member of the guard retinue. Although similar in wingspan to the seven swamp dragons that accompanied it, its body was much finer. With each beat of their wings, they heaved themselves further into the air, falling a little before the next. The forest dragon was much more elegant; its long body almost undulated through the air with its wings outstretched, gliding for the lion's share of the flight. With each flap, it would fold them in, becoming a streak of green ascending rapidly into the air, before unfurling them again to glide.

"State your business," commanded the forest rider.

When I was last here, Magda had seen him off so quickly I'd not had a chance to take a look at his armour. On each pauldron there was a brooch which attached his cloak. The one on the left depicted a gold and emerald inlay of a forest tree on a summer's day, with twisting currents of enamel weaving through the tree branches. This was the crest of the Riders of Whispering Woods. The fact that he was allowed to wear it on his armour signified he must have been an elder of their clan, although as he was helmeted, it was hard to make out his age. On the right pauldron, was a brooch containing three dragon talons to signify he was a knight; the third highest rank of the draconic military. The same rank Percy would hold, were he not an outrider.

"Wayne, you're up," I hissed, realising Wayne hadn't made a peep yet, and even the swamp dragons had managed to catch up with us now.

"Errm, Wayne, I mean, second rank squire Wayne, guardsman of the City of Streya delivering—"

"Escorting!" I hissed.

"Errm, right, sorry, escorting the Chief Diplomat from the City of Streya to the Golden Court, Aster Shepard "

"Why are you not arriving under the wing of outrider Percival?" called the forest rider.

"He is attending the golden hunt, and I have news that couldn't wait," I called back, just as my fringe blew into my face. I ended up poking myself in the eye as I swept it out of the way.

"Very well, your escort may land and wait for you outside The Clutch. I shall accompany you inside."

Without waiting for another word from me, the forest

rider's dragon folded its wings and completed a sort of backwards roll into a dive towards the bridge that covered the crystal blue moat surrounding The Clutch.

"Follow him!" I hissed to Wayne, as we continued to hover inertly above the Golden Cradle.

"Right, yes, sir."

A moment later, water streamed from my eyes as Nova tucked in her wings and went into a dive. By the time we reached the bridge, we'd overtaken the others; for all their elegance, forest dragons are considerably slower than their more athletic, fiery brethren.

"Wait here, squire," commanded the knight, as his dragon gently drifted into land. The brown membranes of its wings billowed gently in the breeze as it touched down. The rest of his retinue of guards were now gone, presumably having returned to their station. He dismounted, and nodded for me to follow him, which I was about to, when I felt a leather glove on my wrist.

"Wait, sir. It's my job to escort you, will you be okay without me?" asked Wayne, with a surprising and somewhat touching level of concern in his voice.

"I'll guard him with my life," said the forest knight, who'd turned to watch the scene. There was not a hint of irony or dramatics in his voice whatsoever. Wayne nodded his ascent, and relinquished his grasp on my wrist.

"He is stealing glances at me." Tera's voice hissed into my head.

"He's a forest rider and you're a forest dragon, he's just curious why you're with me," I responded, speaking directly into her mind, which I'd not yet got used to doing.

"Would it be inappropriate of me to ask your name?" I said, as he led me into the announcement chamber.

"Bors, Elder of the Whispering Woods, and Knight of the first battalion," Bors said, as he removed his gold and emerald helmet, grasping it by the decorative wing details that extended from the visor. He shook out a mop of thick, shoulder-length, white-grey hair, as he placed the helmet onto one of the couches. His olive skin was weathered by the sun, with a small scar running across his chin and dimpled in the centre, creating a cross effect. His eyes were a deep forest green, almost black.

"I think I know the name Bors, have we met?" I asked, watching his eyes drift to Tera.

"Is she something to do with your urgent news?" asked Bors, ignoring my question. His eyes were locked onto Tera.

"I want to bite his face."

Failing to stifle a burst of laughter at Tera's silent outburst, I feigned a weak cough.

"She is part of it," I said, thumping my chest and pretending to clear my throat.

"Are you quite alright?" asked Bors.

"Yep, I think I swallowed a fly on the flight. Shall we go in?"

"Follow me," said Bors with a nod, before turning to the golden beaded curtain leading to the throne room. I stepped through the curtain, cradling Tera in my arms.

In place of Lance was his heir apparent, Crown Princess Igraine Sovereign, Lance's sister. To her right sat the youngest of all the living golden dragons, Eos. The sister of Sol, she was not fully grown yet, and roughly the same size as Styx. For now, she was curled up behind her twinkling golden wings.

Igraine wore a diaphonous gown of white silk and gold lamé. It flowed from her shoulders down to her toes, and trailed several inches behind her when she rose from her throne upon our entrance. She was not as tall as Lance, but would still dwarf me by several inches. Although only twenty-one, she was a thickset woman, with powerful arms, adorned from wrist almost to elbow with golden bangles. Her skin was darker than ebony, with only the slightest hint of bronze warmth. Her hair, twisted into thick ropes of black, had been pinned and bound with gold ribbons into the shape of a crown. Most striking of all though, and most different from her brother, was her smile, which was broad, and warm and white.

The throne room was quite transformed in her presence. The guards almost melted into the pillars, as a band played beautiful music on string instruments from just behind the throne to her left. Couches had been brought in, and courtiers of all stripes were sitting, eating, laughing, and conversing. I guessed they must have been the husbands and wives of those who'd been invited on Lance's hunt. It reminded me of the first time I'd visited the court, under the rule of Lance's mother, Elaine Sovereign.

As Igraine stood, a silence fell over the room, filled by the peel of a trumpet, which sounded to announce us.

"Presenting Aster Shepard, Emerald Eyed, Professor of Dragon Studies at the Magical University of Streya,

Master of the Apprentices of Streya, under the wing of Grave Rider Percival of Burning Mantle, first of his clan to mount a grave dragon, Outrider of the Golden Court, today accompanied by Bors, Elder of the Whispering Wood, Knight of the First Battalion of the Draconic Military."

"Aster, it's been too long," said Igraine, striding towards me. Her gowns billowed behind her as she covered two thirds of the throne room in the time it took me to cover one. I dipped into a bow, but was quickly scooped up into her arms before I could straighten up again.

"Igraine, always a pleasure," I said, as my head flopped over her shoulder. Tera scurried onto my back to avoid being crushed under Igraine's chest.

"Now, what brings Streya's chief diplomat to my brother's court at such short notice?" asked Igraine, setting me down. She was all friendship and warmth, but her eyes were still sharp, and found Tera's head poking over my shoulder immediately.

"Well, something quite unusual has happened concerning—"

"And who is this beautiful hatchling? Did you rescue her by chance?" asked Igraine, cutting me off. She led me over to a couch, which was hurriedly vacated as we approached.

"This is Tera, and no, not quite rescued, you see—"

"You said something quite unusual had happened, but I quite rudely cut you off. Please continue," said Igraine, ironically cutting me off again. She patted a place on the couch next to her for me to sit on.

"Well, you see—"

"Tera, lovely name by the way, sorry, I did it again, continue." Igraine spoke directly to Tera and then back to me.

"This lady is full of power." Tera's voice shuddered into my mind.

"Well, I'm not sure if you were aware, but a few weeks back Percy was dispatched to collect a clutch of eggs foreseen by a hag. They were in the Tombstone Mountains. They turned out to be petrified." I spoke quickly, hoping she'd let me get to the end of a sentence or two.

"I think I remember something about a large clutch of petrified eggs, why what's that got to do with anything?"

"Well, Percy was allowed to keep an egg, a forest egg specifically, which he gave to me." I paused to see if she wanted to cut in, but she seemed suddenly rapt with attention and nodded for me to continue. "During the star bloom, my light, like most light walkers, started errm… overflowing, for want of a better term. And as you may or may not know, my natural hue is green, and somewhat matches the resonance of forest dragon magic."

"Go on…" She now hung on my every word.

"Well, as a way of coping, I'd been funnelling my magic into the petrified forest egg. I don't know for sure if that is why it happened, but it's my best guess."

"Why, what happened?" Her eyes were wide, darting from me to Tera, golden lightning flashing through her pupils.

"The egg… unpetrified."

"You hatched a petrified egg? That's… well, I'd have said it's impossible, but it's unheard of for sure."

"And that's not all," I said, taking a deep breath, before the bit that I'd been dreading.

"You're being quite dramatic about this." Tera craned her neck to look into my eyes as she hissed into my mind.

"This is quite dramatic!" I hissed back. Igraine gasped, and I realised I'd said that out loud.

"You've bonded with her, that is impossible, how is that possible? That is not possible, is that possible? Did you bond with her, say something?" The hubbub of the room fell silent, as Igraine's voice echoed off the marble walls.

"I suppose it would be more accurate to say she bonded with me," I said in a lowered tone, acutely aware of the numerous eyes on me around the court.

"But you're a light walker."

"I said the same thing, but eventually I kind of just accepted it. Accepted her, I suppose I should say."

"Everyone, go back to your music and your conversations," said Igraine, shooting a look around the room.

"Thank you," I said with a sigh of relief, as the string music took up again.

"Have you manifested your bonded treasure yet?" she asked, leaning in close and speaking in a low voice.

"No, I wasn't sure that if that would even happen. Nothing like this has ever happened before, so… I'm just taking each day as it comes."

"Well, it's early days yet. Regardless, I'd say this calls for a party. We have been blessed with not one, but two miracles: a petrified egg of a rare breed of dragon hatched, and a light walker bonded with her."

"A party? So, you're not going to take her away then?" I asked, relieved.

"Let them try!" Tera snarled into my mind. I didn't fight the smile.

"What good would that do? She's not going to bond with someone else for as long as you live. Tell you what, Lance will have a field day when he hears about this."

"Do you think he'll be pleased?" I asked, hopefully.

"Oh, lords no! He's never pleased with anything these days, but he will be shocked. Don't worry, I can see you're worried. I'll tell my brother. Keep an eye on the post, you'll receive a guest of honour invite soon."

"Oh, Igraine, you're a wonder," I said with a smile, as a weight lifted off my chest.

"I know, Aster. Now, unless there is anything else, you have apprentices to see to, and I have one hundred nosey courtiers to fill in on your good news. You'd best get out before I do, or they'll badger you all night."

With that, Igraine shot me a quick wink and then stood. She turned her back to me and strode across the room back to her throne, as a small throng of whispering guests followed her, their eyes flicking occasionally back to me.

"Another worthy ally."

"I take it that means you like her." I was more careful this time to make sure the message reached Tera's mind, not the throne room in general.

"Time to go, Professor Shepard," said Bors. He'd been standing diligently on guard a little way off, and had approached once Igraine took her leave of me.

"I take it that dragon has somehow bonded with you

then?" asked Bors, as we strode through The Clutch's hallowed halls back to Wayne.

"Miraculously," I said, with a smile.

"Well, Aster Shepard, that makes two denizens of the draconic lands that you've charmed. You must have a way about you," said Bors, and at once I remembered who he was.

"You were around when Percy was choosing his station, weren't you? Why didn't you say?" I asked, watching Bors's face for any sign of emotion, but his helmet was back on now, which made emotion tricky.

"What was there to say? Percival chose you and Streya over his duties here. You won."

"He's still an outrider. He performs foreign tasks for the court all the time, he's on a hunt with Lance Sovereign right now." I bristled defensively. The implication that Percy had somehow abandoned his people when he married me was not one I was unfamiliar with.

"He's not here though, is he?" said Bors, stopping in his tracks at the bridge.

"And what of it? Lance Sovereign himself was an outrider before he ascended to the throne. Was he shirking his duties too? Or do you only hold being an outrider against people who marry light walkers?" I snapped, overtaking him as I stormed down the bridge.

"Yes, well, he didn't—"

"I'm not actually interested in whatever you're struggling to conceive, Bors. Good day," I said, turning back to face him once more. Bors, who I'd sensed was a man of few words, seemed to have run out entirely. Tera summarily snapped her jaws at him, and we strode off over the bridge to Wayne.

"Everything go okay, sir?" asked Wayne.

"Take me home, Wayne," I said, more curtly than I'd have liked. I bathed myself in bronze light, and flew the last thirty feet of the bridge, landing on Nova's back.

"Yes, sir!" said Wayne, offering a salute to me. If I didn't know better, I'd have thought he fired off a glare at Bors before we ascended into the sky.

"So, it went well then?" asked Percy, as we lay together in bed. With my head on his chest, I listened to his heart rate steadily slowing, and let my eyes grow heavy as he traced patterns on my back with his finger.

"I'd say so, and your hunt did too?"

"Well, we caught things, so I suppose so. But I didn't enjoy it, really. There's not much sport in hunting animals when you're riding a grave dragon, let alone a golden dragon. I don't think I'll go again if I can avoid it. I did see a leviathan in the clouds though, so that was cool," Percy said, planting a kiss on my forehead.

"I bumped into that old captain, the one that wanted you as a lieutenant. Remember him, Bors?" I said, speaking through a yawn.

"Oh yes, did he have anything to say?"

"I think he's still a bit sore that you didn't take his offer."

"Maybe I'll run into him at Tera's party, mend some fences."

* * *

"Good morning, apprentices," I said, pushing the door to my office open. Astrid, Orion and Sirius were all sitting at my desk in what seemed to be harmony, unusually.

"Morning, Teach," said Sirius, firing off an incongruous wink.

"You seem to be in a good mood, Professor," said Astrid, brightly. I smiled politely and waited, anticipating a subtle jab at the fact I wasn't Cora. But it didn't come, and for a second, I forgot entirely what I was supposed to be doing.

"Yes, errm… what, sorry? Oh yes, very good morning, well, of course, because I have a gift for you three." Their eyes lit up as I produced a small chest from within my desk, and laid it out of the table.

"Lenses, sir?" asked Astrid.

"That would be telling. All three of you, close your eyes and hold out your hands," I said, remembering the first time Vega, Nick and I had been given a lens; Cora had hidden them under our chairs. We'd tried to act cool of course, but I remember a rush of excitement akin to waking on my fifth birthday knowing there were presents downstairs. I could see the same twinkle in my apprentices' eyes before they dutifully closed them and held out their hands. I opened the chest and removed the three lenses, each of them red. Which I expected may cause an issue for Astrid, but we'd cross that bridge when we came to it.

Into Sirius's hands, I placed an ebony armband

peppered with dazzling scarlet flecks made from shards of a petrified fire dragon egg. For Orion, a wand, similar to my cane, made of black volcanic glass, set with small rubies, which looked like embers twinkling in a scorched branch. Finally, for Astrid, a bracelet that resembled a string of black pearls, each of them a perfectly polished piece of lava stone, ejected from the burning mantle.

"Open them," I said softly, and watched their faces light up as they realised what they were holding.

"You hooked us up, Teach," said Sirius, slipping the armband up to his bicep, where it held snuggly in place.

"I'm pleased you like it. Now, Astrid, I do apologise, you asked for an opal lens, which I'm afraid we can't give you. The control of opal lenses is very strict at the moment. Anyway, I thought it would be good for you each to start with a red lens of your own, as it is the simplest to get the hang of." I braced myself for the rebuttal.

"Whatever you think is best, Professor," said Astrid, as she slipped the beads onto her wrist, admiring them gleefully.

"Right, well, up to the roof for practice then, I suppose," I said, trying to contain my joy as I watched my apprentices, seemingly won over at last, trot out of my office.

"Just gently push a little light into the lenses," I said, directing them to aim for the three cauldrons of water, opposite.

One by one, they glowed black and white and grey, and then red. A moment's pause interceded, as the air between the apprentices' outstretched hands and their cauldrons trembled from the heat, then steam began to issue from the cauldrons into the sky.

"Professor, I think something's wrong, I've got too much," said Sirius. His bicep was bulging, as red light exploded out of the band around his arm.

"Just breathe," I said, uselessly, as steam and bubbles exploded out of the cauldron. A moment later, a jet of flame came billowing out of Sirius outstretched hand, melting a hole clean through his cauldron. The plume was getting bigger and yellower and hotter and whiter, as boiling, roiling fire erupted across the sky above the university.

"Lose the lens!" I shouted over the roar of the flame, shielding myself with my coal studded cane as the heat prickled my skin. The jet of fire was spreading wider, and blossoming into a huge sheet of flames engulfing the sky. It didn't make sense; overdoing it was one thing, but this was too much power. Sirius would be exhausted in a moment if he kept this up.

Sirius flailed, flicking the armband from his bicep. It clattered along the floor as the flames vanished, evaporating into the air, but the source was still there. Light was still beaming out of him, so much of it that he could have lit up the night, it was painful to look at. Fractal shards of grey light broke into the atmosphere, distorting the world, before settling on Sirius. I'd only ever seen light like this from one other person, and as Sirius's glow intensified, it dawned on me what was happening.

"Jump for the courtyard!" I bellowed, pushing bronze light over his already growing body. Without hesitation, Sirius ran and leapt off the roof. His body drifted into open space as my light covered him, but then his form swelled again. He was as big as a Hecatonchires now, five times the size of a cyclops, and as he swelled, it was like a punch to the gut. I sank, groaning to my knees, as I struggled to maintain my grip on him.

"I-is he over the courtyard?" I asked, gasping for air as I struggled to keep him afloat. Each time he grew, the wind was knocked out of me again.

"He's over the courtyard, Professor," said Astrid, her voice urgent and panicked.

"Is it clear of people?" I groaned, trembling, as sweat poured out of me. My whole body was tensed, as I held fast to Sirius's growing mass.

"All clear!" Orion declared from the edge of the roof.

I'm afraid to admit that I let out a whimper, as I loosened my grip on Sirius and allowed it to fade. There was a thunderous, booming thud as he touched the ground, and I let myself collapse onto the cool floor, panting and sweating, with my eyes fluttering shut from exhaustion.

"Sir, there are dragons coming," said Astrid a moment later.

"Fuck me," I groaned. I rolled onto my back to see the silhouettes of five dragons emerging against the clouds.

"Are you okay?" Orion asked, kneeling next to me in such a way that made me feel very undignified all of a sudden.

"Astrid, give me a boost!" I was struggling to keep my eyes open, as I watched the grey glowing Sirius steadily expand into the sky.

"Yes, sir," said Astrid, placing a hand on my shoulder as she pushed white light into me.

My skin was suddenly on fire, crackling and full of life. My chest raced ten to the dozen as I struggled to catch my gasping, ragged breath. The fatigue was still there, but now I felt alive, electric, frantic. I pushed light through my bronze lens, and felt my body lift weightlessly from the ground. Rubbing my tired eyes, I ascended, focusing on the smallest of the dragons approaching fast from the head of the formation.

"Make them back off," I called, forcing myself to wake up and fly towards Percy and Styx.

"What is going on?" called Percy, shielding his eyes against the bright grey light emanating from Sirius. Styx was hovering, and buffeting me back slightly with the force of each wing beat. His ice-blue globes were focused on Sirius's ever-growing form.

"It's Sirius, he's lost control, I need to help him before someone gets hurt!"

"How is he powerful enough to even do this?"

"I think you can guess. Just keep your men back, the last thing we need is to startle him," I said. I turned to fly up towards Sirius, as the fire riders pulled up alongside Styx. Each dragon snapped its jaws defensively.

"Be careful," Percy called, obviously recognising the exhaustion in my eyes, as I let myself drift up through the sky towards Sirius's enormous head. I was roughly the size of one of his eyes when I met him.

"Sirius, whatever you're doing, stop!" I called over the roaring wind, covering my own eyes as his were so dazzling.

"I don't know how!" Sirius's voice was low and

bellowing, and rocked my body as it thundered through the air.

"Just focus on your light!" I called, willing myself up again as he grew past my eyeline once more, struggling against the high winds, forcing me backwards as I ascended.

"Here, Professor," said Sirius, gently reaching out a giant hand, each finger longer than I was from head to toe. He plucked me from the air and perched me on his shoulder.

"Now what?" he boomed, as I leant exhaustedly against his neck.

"Imagine throwing a black sheet over it," I yelled, pouring with sweat from the last few moments' exertions.

"It's not working, Professor, what's happening? I don't understand, I'm not this powerful," said Sirius, as his body pulsed with light and grew again.

"Well then use it, rather than trying to stifle it, just use your power to shrink yourself. Grey light has the power to change shape, that can mean smaller too!" I bellowed up to his ear, trying not to shiver as the wind whipped around us, chilling the sweat that had settled over my skin.

"Okay, I'll try, but I still don't understand what's happening, did the stars bloom again?"

"Just focus on shrinking," I said, letting my trembling legs give way, as I slumped down to a seated position on his shoulder.

"I think it's working, are you okay, sir?" asked Sirius. I looked down over his shoulder and saw that the floor looked to be zooming up to meet us, which could only mean that, mercifully, he was in fact shrinking.

"Just a bit worn out. I'd best get down before I'm too big for you," I said, exhaustedly.

"Don't worry about that, sir," said Sirius, as his shrinking hand plucked me off his shoulder. Before long, he had to hold me with two hands, and when he was down to about thirty feet tall, he reached down and placed me on the floor.

"Now, just hold this transformation," I said, as Sirius reached a more normal height. Both of us were now standing in a crater left by one of his formerly huge foot-prints. He was still glowing, and his eyes shone as brightly as lit torches, which made him difficult to look at.

"Aster, are you alright?" I heard Percy's voice and hurried footfall approaching from behind. The moment I felt his hand touch my shoulder, a warm shiver ran through me, and I leant against him tiredly.

"Your eyes are very dim, love, are you okay?"

"Just tired." I yawned.

"What happened to him?" Sirius's voice sounded concerned. He probably looked concerned too, but I'd given myself permission to close my eyes now, and couldn't be bothered to check.

"He wore himself out, making sure you didn't crush anyone." Astrid's voice signified her and Orion's arrival. She sounded out of breath; they must have taken the stairs.

"Thankyou… for helping me, sir. Do you know what's happening to me?" asked Sirius, as he placed what felt like a hand on my shoulder. I opened my eyes so as not to be rude, quickly shutting them again as his were still dazzlingly bright.

"It's my job, Sirius, and it was also my pleasure. And

yes, to answer your question, I think I do know what's happening to you," I said, smiling into his blinding light with my eyes closed.

"Isn't it obvious?" Astrid cut in.

"What is?" asked Sirius.

"You're the new infinite," came Vega's imperious voice from behind me. Her proclamation was followed by a burst of whispers from a crowd of people I hadn't realised were there.

"No way, I can't be, that's… it should be someone who's smarter, Professor, they're wrong, right?" He sounded panicked again.

"Just breathe and focus on not growing again for now," I said softly. Sensing the need for it, I reached up and pulled him into a hug. I didn't have the energy to deal with him growing again. As I opened my eyes, safe from his glowing beams, I could see the courtyard starting to fill up, with students and teachers alike spilling in from every direction. They were jostling each other aside for a look at Sirius, as whispers thundered through the crowd like rain on a tin roof.

"Aster, Sirius, a word in my office," said Vega. A flash of silver burst from her bracelet, as a silvery portal sprang into being, which she strode through, followed nervously by Sirius.

"I'm not leaving you," whispered Percy, as a supporting hand reached around my side and helped me through the portal.

"Aster, sit down before you fall down," said Vega, shoving a chair underneath me as the portal snapped shut behind us.

"Oh, thanks," I said with a yawn, as I let my trembling legs drop me into my seat.

"Now, could you stop glowing?" asked Vega, shielding her eyes as she looked at Sirius.

"I'm working on it, it's not very straightforward."

"Try imagining throwing a black sheet over your light," said Vega, wisely.

"I already tried that one," I said, yawning again. A smile tugged at the corner of my mouth, as she shot me a glare.

"Very well, keep glowing, but keep trying to stop, because this is ridiculous," Vega said, giving up and turning away from Sirius.

"How are you feeling?" I asked, whilst Percy and Vega pulled up more chairs so we could all sit.

"Honestly? Like I could run a marathon and not break a sweat," said Sirius, turning his blinding light back onto me as he spoke, before turning away again when I was forced to squint.

"Sorry, forgot," he said, sheepishly.

"So… what happens now?" Percy asked, looking to me as he took my hand in his.

"Well, as Sirius has emerged as the infinite, it seems prudent that he should receive one-to-one tuition. You already have apprentices, and your position as a golden court diplomat and your other classes take up enough of your time, Aster. Therefore, I propose that I should take Sirius on as my pupil."

Sirius, who, unlike the rest of us, hadn't taken a seat, shifted awkwardly. He seemed to be filled with nervous energy, or perhaps infinite energy.

"But—"

"No. Sirius will remain my apprentice." I didn't mean to cut Sirius off, but Cora's letter was flashing through my mind, and I was too tired to be polite anymore.

"Aster, are you sure you're equipped to deal with this? Look at what happened today," said Vega, doing an impression of concern, but the steel in her voice was giving her away.

"You mean when I single-handedly diffused the problem without anyone getting hurt?" I bristled.

"I mean, when you nearly knocked yourself out in the process," Vega retorted, dropping the act.

"Regardless, Sirius and I know each other, we've built a rapport, it'd be counterproductive to move him now. Sirius needs stability, not disruptions," I argued, trying to ignore the little voice in my head reminding me how nice it would feel to just curl up and go to sleep.

"A little disruption now to ensure the best for—"

"Professor Shepard is the best for me, sorry to interrupt you, Headmistress… Ma'am? But shouldn't what I want count for something in all this?" asked Sirius, fidgeting with his fingers as he spoke. With all his class clown bravado stripped away, he was quite an anxious soul.

"Of course, but you must consider the council of those who know better." Vega spoke through gritted teeth, struggling to maintain her manners.

"Surely, then, we should take the advice of Cora Olympia. She must have known best of all," said Percy, making my heart jump into my chest.

"She isn't here to have a say in the matter, or the matter would not be a subject at all!" Vega snapped.

"But she said in her no—"

"Nothing, she said nothing." I couldn't think of a clever lie as I cut Percy off, avoiding Vega's eyes as they began to narrow suspiciously.

"She said in her what, Percy?" Vega asked, leaning towards him as she spoke.

"N-nothing," said Percy in a tone that sounded more like a question than a statement. He looked nervously from Vega to me.

"She left you a note, didn't she? I cannot believe you didn't tell me!" All pretence dropped, as Vega all but shouted in my face.

"Oh, please, Vega. I didn't know she did at first, it got swept up in Percy's stuff, so we only found it later." Technically, it was only a couple of hours later, but she didn't need to know that.

"Professor Olympia left notes?" asked Sirius.

"Yes, to her old apprentices. Which we all shared with each other, except Aster apparently," said Vega, shooting me a dirty look.

"Did they mention me?" Sirius asked, hopefully.

"No!" Vega snapped. Sirius's face fell.

"Actually, mine did," I said. As Sirius's face lifted again, so did mine.

"What did it say then, or is that still a secret?" Vega huffed.

"That she was sorry to leave us, but it had to be done. And that my last instruction from her was to hold fast to my apprentices, guide them and keep them. That is what Percy was referring to."

"Sorry for spilling the beans," said Percy, sheepishly.

"Don't be, it is what it is," I said, patting him reassuringly on the hand.

"She really said that?" asked Vega, some of the steam she'd built up dissipating.

"Yep, that was my only task. So I'm afraid I can't give Sirius up, nor Orion, nor Astrid."

"Do you think she knew this would happen?" Sirius asked.

"I suspect she had her theories," I said, with a wink.

"She usually did," said Vega, sagging slightly in her chair. I could see it in her face, as a distant look overtook her eyes. It was the look of someone missing Cora, it was easy to spot, because I was too.

"Hey, you stopped glowing!" said Percy, cheerily.

"Oh yeah, I didn't realise," said Sirius. His eyes, whilst still a sparkling grey, were no longer two dazzling torch lights.

"Well, that's something at least," said Vega with a chuckle. It was a creaky, under-used laugh, but it was charming all the same.

"I'm going to cook you something delicious, you just curl up by the fire," said Percy as we staggered through another of Vega's portals, and I dropped myself into my rocking chair.

"Your light is very dim today, Aster." Tera's voice issued into my mind as she leapt off a high shelf. She unfurled her brown membranous wings, allowing herself to glide towards me.

"Big day," I said out loud, too lazy to concentrate on trying to be telepathic with her now.

"You should sleep more and work less," said Tera, as she curled up in my lap. As I ran a hand over her pointed horns, a shiver ran down my back. My skin prickled and my hair stood on end, as a charge surged through me. My light, which had been dim and barely flickering, burst into new life, and my eyes shot open.

"It's happening!" I gasped, my heart pounding.

"What is?" asked Percy, looking up from a chicken carcass he was butchering.

"Bonded t-treasure," I stammered, struggling to speak as I felt the sparking power run through me like fire, my chest tightening.

"You're feeling my power at last!" Tera purred into my mind as she looked up at me, with her green reptilian eyes glistening in the firelight."

"Oh, this is exciting," said Percy, downing his knife.

"I-I need to stand," I said, shuddering. I struggled to my feet, as energy coursed through me.

"Channel it into something," said Percy, taking my hand and squeezing it.

"What?" I asked, my eyes flicking around the room. Bonded treasures were usually swords or daggers or bows, we didn't keep any of those just lying about.

"Anything!" said Percy, just as my eyes landed on his wooden cooking spoon.

Don't do that, said a little voice in my head, but it was too late. I had to let the power out, and I did. I let it pour into the spoon, of all things. It began to grow and twist, with thorns and twigs erupting from it as the light cherry wood began to transform. Darkening and thickening as it went, the spoon began to take on the form of a spiralling staff of pure ebony, dotted with the occasional jutting thorn and small errant tree branch. The end that had once been the bowl of the spoon shifted and transformed into a globe of knotted wood.

"Did you just turn my spoon into a bonded treasure?" Percy asked, letting out a howl of laughter.

"Shut up," I whined, cringing at myself.

"Touch it!" Tera urged me through my mind. Before I knew it, I'd crossed the room, and my trembling fingers were inches from the ebony staff. It was warm to the touch, smooth like varnish, and it thrummed with power. It was as if a spark shot up my arm as I laid hands on it. Suddenly, there wasn't one green light within me, but two. My sparkling emerald starlight, and Tera's larger, wilder, roiling ball of deep forest green fire.

"I feel her," I whispered.

"Finally."

"So, when considering dissertation topics, I urge you to look outside the box. Don't confine yourselves to the untapped potential of pure hues. I can promise you this, every professor on this campus has read more than enough on the potential of the void hue to draw in or expel certain enchantments."

"What did you write your dissertation on, Professor?" asked Europa, a particularly ambitious navy-hued member of my senior class. She reminded me of Astrid in some ways, but without the self-assurance that comes with being born pure hued.

"I wrote my dissertation and subsequent thesis on the resonant properties shared between certain hues of light, and certain types of dragons. For instance, green and yellow-hued light shares a certain resonance with the powers exhibited by forest dragons. Speaking of which, if any of you would like to include research on the powers of dragon riders in your dissertation projects, my office hours are—"

"Aster, you should probably get out here, mate, there is an envoy from the free folk arriving," said Nick, poking his head through a silvery portal that had manifested itself in the doorway of my classroom.

"What's that got to do with me? Professor Ophi is the head of free folk relations. Sorry about this, class," I said, flicking my attention between Nick and my students.

"They're here for Sirius."

"Oh, I see. Right, class, you all know where my office is, my office hours are from three till five every weekday. Must dash," I said, crossing the classroom and leaping through Nick's portal. I found myself in the grand hall of Streya University, where we held formals and large events.

"Professor Shepard, so nice to make your acquaintance," said a rather grand female centaur, who was leading a quartet of free folk representatives. Her coat was the colour of honey, and shimmered in the flickering lights of the hall. The humanoid section of her body was dressed only lightly, in strands of green taffeta, silk and amber, leaving very little to the imagination. Her voice was low and soothing, lending an almost lullaby-like quality to everything she said .

"And I yours, but you've got me at a disadvantage, as I don't know your name," I said, working very hard to maintain eye contact, which required quite a lot of neck craning as she was about three feet taller than me.

"I am Brigit, niece of Cerunos, and these are my companions," she said, gesturing to the trio behind her.

"Silus, Gerty and Prince Consort Bren." Brigit gestured to each of her companions in turn.

First was Silas, a faun with pitch black fur up to his waist, and a dark-skinned, well-muscled torso from the waist up. Unlike his compatriots, he was not adorned with jewellery, but wore heavy duty leather wrist wraps and had a hammer strapped to his back. Figuratively and literally, he was the muscle of the group.

Gerty, to his left, was to all the world nothing but a sagging heap of glittering black fabric, bound up with glistening silvery chains. Just one extremely long fingered hand was visible, holding her shawls and wraps to her body. This the classic wardrobe of a hag. Beneath the bundle of robes would be a stooped creature, bearing at first an uncanny resemblance to an old woman. Closer inspection would unveil their extremely long limbs, supported by two sets of knees and elbows, and taloned feet akin to a vulture. Hags, although off putting to look at, are well regarded within the free folk community. Their long lives and impressive minds made them somewhat like living libraries. Some of them had even been known to display prophetic powers, similar to those of mountain dragon riders.

Finally, there was Prince Consort Bren, the husband of the fairy queen herself. He was bedecked in long, shimmering topaz robes, that hung past his feet as he hovered at head height, about a meter off the ground. His wings were just a blur of pastel pink behind him, matching the rosy shade of his hair and eyes. He kept his position at the back of the quartet, a smile playing at his lips, as his eyes flickered around the room. This was by far the most well-born retinue of free folk I'd ever seen outside their own territory.

"It is a pleasure to meet each and every one of you. Am I correct in understanding that you have set out to meet my apprentice, Sirius Greyfellow? I believe someone is out looking for him," I said, shooting Nick a look over my shoulder.

"Vega is on it," said Nick.

"Cora Olympia enjoyed a warm relationship with the free folk. We would like to extend the same friendship to your apprentice." Bridgit's manner of speaking was slow, measured, warm and rumbling.

"You do understand he's just now coming into his powers? He won't be like Cora was," I said softly. I hoped they were not expecting Sirius to wade into some international incident on their behalf.

"We understand," said a crisp voice, from somewhere within Gerty's bundle of robes.

"Found him," came Vega's voice from behind me. I turned just in time to catch Vega and Sirius stepping out of a portal.

As he approached, Sirius fiddled with the top button of a fairly formal robe that ran from his neck down to his waist. It was missing the front and back panels, creating a sort of folded wing off each of his hips. I'd never seen him in anything so extravagant. It was cool and teal in colour, and matched his complexion nicely.

"Thank you, Vega. Sirius, may I introduce you to our guests, Brigit, of the forest of Cerunos, and her companions, Silus, Gerty and Prince Consort Bren."

"The pleasure is all ours," said Bren, fluttering forward from the quartet to offer Sirius his hand, Which Sirius took rather awkwardly. Something in me just knew he was worried that if he shook the prince's hand, he might inadvertently shake the whole prince. Luckily, Bren took the lead, and rather surprisingly, kissed Sirius's hand. There was something rather comical about watching a three-foot-something fairy bend forward and kiss the hand of a broad chested six-foot-something man.

"Errm... I don't know what to say," said Sirius, his eyes flicking to me nervously.

"There is nothing for you to say, we merely came to offer congratulations and greetings."

"And gifts!" said Brigit.

"Gifts?" Sirius asked, his eyes lighting up.

"Of course, how could I forget? Gerty, if you would be so kind," said Bren, without turning away from Sirius.

"Of course," the crisp, whispering voice emerged from inside the silken bundle, followed by a set of extremely long, impossibly thin grey arms . At the first set of elbows, the arms bent inwards like human arms would, but at the second set, which were closer to the shoulder, they bent outwards, creating a very crooked image.

Sirius was obviously struggling not to stare. So was I.

It didn't help that Gerty didn't step forward, but instead elected to extend her arms out around Bren's waist. At the end of each of her arms, Gerty's hands were formed into fists that appeared as spheres, owing to her impossibly long, spindly fingers. When they reached Sirius, she upturned them theatrically, and opened her fingers, which outstretched must have been a foot long each. In the palm of each hand sat a small wooden box, one studded with emerald stones, the other decorated with carvings detailed with gold leaf.

Sirius took them in with wide eyes. Before he could move to open them, Gerty flicked each latch with an almost whiplike motion from her little fingers.

"Allow me," said Bren, as he simultaneously pulled back each lid to reveal the contents in such dramatic fashion that I began to wonder if they'd rehearsed this display. Inside the emerald chest, lay a daisy chain of the most perfect daisies I'd ever seen. Each petal was immaculate, unbent and lustrous white. The stems were long, juicy and green, and bound together in perfect tiny knots. The pollen was full, fluffy and almost golden. Fairy alchemy had created this, and I knew immediately what I was looking at. The golden chest contained a short, twisted piece of petrified quaking aspen, the white wood having turned almost crystalline in petrification. It vaguely resembled the shape of a shepherd's staff.

"Are these… lenses?" asked Sirius, his eyes flicking back and forth between the chests excitedly.

"Good eye. A golden and a green-hued lens, the two hues we free folk feel most connected to. We thought they might aid you in your studies. Not to mention, our sources tell us, your master, Shepherd here, is intimately familiar with both, being born green to a family of gold."

My heritage wasn't hard to dig up. A lot had been made of my being named Cora's apprentice, but it was still a little unsettling to hear how much strangers knew about me.

"Is that true, Professor?" asked Sirius.

"It is," I nodded, and forced a smile.

"I don't know how to thank you," said Sirius, eyeing his gifts gleefully.

"Just do your best with the gifts you've been given, and of course, be a friend," said Bren.

"And now, we don't want to take up too much of your valuable time. We only need a few short words with your professor," said Brigit, as Bren floated back, and Sirius took his gifts from Gerty.

"Should I, errm?" Sirius looked again to me, slightly at a loss.

"You get back to class," I said, turning to follow the free folk. By now they had put a bit of space between themselves and Sirius, and were now watching me expectedly. A portal was opened for Sirius, who quickly stepped through, but Nick and Vega lingered. I assumed they were trying to guess what the free folk were saying to me.

"That was an extremely generous gift, I must thank you again, Your Majesty. Now, what was it that you needed me for?" I asked, approaching the group.

"Think nothing of it. As to you, I only wanted to extend thanks. My family is indebted to you," said Bren.

"It is?" I had no idea what he was talking about.

"I hear that you risked your life to save my niece, Ailsa, a few weeks back."

"Ailsa is royal blooded?" I asked, surprised.

"She's from my side of the family, not my wife's. But all the same, the House of Gloria considers itself indebted to you, Aster Sheperd."

I didn't know what to say. Bren turned and began to float away, then paused and turned back.

"You're no relation to the Shepards Pastor Shepherds, are you, by chance?" asked Bren.

"I am, actually," I said, forcing a smile.

"Well, I never. A Shepard that actually left the pasture. I never thought I'd see the day."

"I am one on my own," I said, forcing a laugh, as a pang of guilt shot through me.

"You certainly are. Well, next time you visit home, feel free to drop into the forest. We are neighbours after all," said Bren, giving a final wink before floating away from me.

The rest of his party followed his lead. When they were almost out of sight, a crooked arm shot out of Gerty's bundle of silks, and with it, an ancient voice that clanged like steel against stone rang through my mind.

"Careful of those who know the past, for they shall make that which was, that which is. He shelters amongst that which he becomes. Infinity hides in ancient stories, bleeding the stars to make them bloom, out in the endless dark."

Without hesitation or another word, the arm was tucked away again out of sight, and Gerty, barely having broken stride, rejoined the quartet. I began rummaging around for a pen to write down what I had heard.

I was in my office, enjoying my so far uninterrupted peace. It looked like another year of nobody in the senior class being particularly interested in including draconic theory in their dissertations. I was gazing out of my window, thinking it could do with a good clean, when something large and winged flickered past. It was too small to be a dragon, but too big for a bird.

I got up, crossed the room, and squinted out the streaky windowpane, trying to catch another glimpse. There was Sirius, of all people. He had sprouted tawny brown wings, and was somersaulting through the air. There was no courtyard below my office building, which meant there was no crowd to watch him. He was shirtless for his own benefit, then; at least I hoped so. I did somewhat worry that he might have been trying to show off for me. He was much more athletic than your average light walker, probably because he spent his free time doing aerial somersaults.

When I was an apprentice, I lived in the library, studying everything there was on dragons and draconic history, which was surprisingly sparse all things considered. And when I wasn't doing that, I was sneaking out to meet Percy. I suppose that was my version of secret aerial somersaults. I recalled the night we were caught taking a moonlit flight over the city. Rather than reporting us, Cora gave us a spare key to the disused astronomy tower. I'd have been lost in those memories for hours, were it not for the flash of bronze which caught my eye. Sirius was no longer flying under his own power. He was drifting away from the school, and struggling to resist whatever force had him.

I made a fist, focusing my light into my ring, which flashed navy, releasing a wide jet of water. Jumping through the shattered window, I bathed myself in bronze light, with glass and water twinkling around me as I shot through the air towards Sirius. He was being dragged quickly clear of the campus.

"Sirius, I'm coming!" I called, closing in fast. In the distance, I could see two cloaked figures, one of them with their hand outstretched towards Sirius.

"Professor, what's happening?" called Sirius, his voice full of fear.

"I don't know, just wrap your wings around yourself, this is gonna be bumpy," I called, pushing bronze light out of my spectacles and over Sirius.

Now, I could feel their will pulling him through the air. Gritting my teeth, I scrunched up my light and yanked on him. There was a moment's resistance, and then he was ripped free. I directed him towards a particularly plush looking bush, which he hedged into quite nicely. I landed in front of the bush, with about one hundred feet between us and the two cloaked figures that were coming this way.

"Stay behind me," I said, starting to gently will green light out of myself, and connecting with every root and branch I could find.

"Don't worry, Professor, I got this," Sirius's cyclopean

voice boomed, as he thundered past me. Once he was within fifty feet of our assailants, he lifted off the ground and started drifting aimlessly through the air, once again captured in bronze light. I couldn't not roll my eyes.

"Well, this is going well," I muttered to myself. I forced a jet of roaring flames out of my coal studded cane, only for the bronze assailant's companion to release a flash of aquamarine light and a heavy gust of wind from an ornate fan. My jet of fire was extinguished instantaneously, as Sirius ineffectually tried to breaststroke towards the ground.

"Sirius, get bigger!" I shouted, recalling the other day when I'd tried the same trick on him. There was a moment's hesitation, I might have even heard a laugh escape from the fan-wielding foe, before Sirius flashed grey and the cyclops began to swell. There was an audible groan as the bronze fighter sank to one knee, and Sirius thudded to the ground with an earth-shaking boom. At the same time, the fan wielder started to push light into his lens again, levelling it at me.

"Oh, no you don't!" I said, using my vines to whip his feet out from under him. His face slammed into the earth, eliciting a satisfying groan and a toe-curling crunch, as his blast of wind exploded out in all directions. I shielded my eyes with my arms, whilst gravel and dust filled the air. Then I flinched, as a familiar, weightless feeling overtook me, lifting my feet off the ground.

"Night, night," snarled the bronze assailant.

I clenched, and focused my light into the plants that had just caught the fan wielder. I was just beginning to restrain them, when I was jerked violently through the air.

My neck jolted painfully, and my body, no longer my own, was once more wrapped in bronze light. It was all I could do to catch myself, landing in the explosively blooming bush I'd just conjured out of the roots. My body ached and stung, as I cut myself while struggling, in a not-so-dignified fashion, to extricate myself from the wreckage of foliage and thorns. Meanwhile, the bronze-light wielder was standing over me, panting. I watched him, waiting for the tell-tale sign. Sure enough, his eyes squinted, and I knew he was summoning more light. In that instant, I thrust my coal studded cane up into his throat, as something Percy had once told me echoed through my mind: *Light walkers always forget you can just hit someone.*

He clutched his throat, wheezing, and I took my chance. Getting to my feet, I delivered another sharp blow to his temple. His eyes snapped shut, and he thudded to the ground just as Sirius's voice caught my ear.

"Watch out!" he said, his voice still magically deepened by several octaves.

But it was too late. I was buffeted through the air, with all the breath knocked out of me by an explosion of wind to my right. I groaned, dull pain wracking my body as I slammed into something hard, and immediately felt thick arms wrap around me. I fought to stay conscious, forcing my eyes open as I took in the world around me, all blurry and watery.

"I've got you, Professor," came Sirius's cyclopean voice, the hard thing that I'd crashed into being him, catching me.

"Make a run for it!" I winced, struggling to see what was happening, as I wriggled up in Sirius's grasp.

"I can't really move," replied Sirius.

"What?" I said, but realised what was happening as I asked. The fan wielder was glowing green, and foliage was beginning to obstruct my view, as it wrapped itself around Sirius, pinning him down.

"Get bigger!" I commanded. My chest was tightening, and I realised I couldn't move either. I tried to focus, to access my light, but as I closed my eyes and looked within, I felt my grip slipping. My head slumped forward, and my head swam. I opened my eyes, fighting the headiness, and all I could see were vines and branches and Sirius's thick, grey arm.

"Can't risk crushing you, sir," Sirius replied, and he was right. I was squashed right up against him. If his body swelled, I'd be crushed.

"Give up. Come quietly, and I'll let your professor live, Sirius," came a somewhat winded, but still snide voice, from outside our briar prison.

"Ignore him. Have you still got your red lens?" I hissed.

"Yeah, Orion picked it up for me after the incident the other day," whispered Sirius, although it wasn't much of a whisper being as he was, a cyclops.

"Don't try anything stupid," warned our captor. If my ears did not deceive, he sounded rather nervous. Although not as nervous I was, struggling not to focus on the thorn I'd noticed was growing towards my eye.

"Well then, point your hand away from us and blast him!" I hissed, urgently.

"I've not really got the hang of controlling my light through a lens yet, sir."

"So don't control it! Just blast!" I commanded. My eyelashes now flicked across the thorn with every blink, and I was struggling to crane my neck away.

Sirius didn't respond, the thorn kept growing, I kept craning, and then I noticed a glowing red armband among the mess of our limbs. Suddenly, we were rocked backwards by a huge wall of flames that exploded out of Sirius's hand. Luckily, he'd managed to stretch his arm out and away from us, but the heat was still intense. For a split second I could hear a scream, and then it was just the rush of wind and roar of flames. All I could see in front of me was red and yellow and gold, twisting and surging forward. Even behind the torrent of flame, my skin was scorched. I struggled to back away, finding myself pressed into Sirius's stonelike, cyclopean body, with sweat instantly beading all over me. Sirius wrapped his free arm around me, shielding me from the blaze, as yet more fire poured out.

"You can stop now, that's enough!" I struggled to shout, as the hot air scorched my throat with each breath, but the fire didn't stop. The heat continued to rise, and my body now soaked with sweat, squirmed desperately, as panic overtook me. I felt my breathing become short and ragged.

"P-please stop," I begged, struggling to find the strength to speak, as the world fell out of focus. My eyes fluttered shut. All I knew was heat and a terrible roaring sound and then all at once, it stopped.

"Professor, are you okay?" Sirius's nervous voice pierced my darkening world.

I took a deep breath, a cooler breath, and let my eyes

open. He was above me, glowing silver, and shrinking. I watched as his single, cyclopean eye went through the somewhat gruesome process of splitting into two human ones, as he returned to himself. I realised I was lying down. Looking up, past Sirius's worried face, dragons were circling above us.

"You stopped," I said, cracking a smile. I struggled to sit up, as burning pain stabbed my throat when I coughed, and I realised as I did that my head was pounding. It felt as though someone had left a bag of marbles in my skull for safekeeping. So, I gave up on sitting up.

"Is he okay?" I heard Percy's voice, followed by the rush and thudding sound of Styx landing behind us.

"I don't know, he got thrown around a lot," said Sirius, as Percy's worried face appeared in my eyeline.

"What happened? Aster, are you okay?" Percy asked, kneeling down next to me. I winced as he took me into his arms, with stabbing pain shooting through my side.

"Some guys tried to… kidnap me? I'm not sure, but Professor Shepard came to my rescue," said Sirius.

"Where are they now?" asked Percy, his sharp blue eyes darting about, surveying the scene.

"They, erm, I don't think there's much left of them," said Sirius, nervously.

I twisted my neck painfully, following his eyeline. Before us sat a smouldering trench that looked about twenty feet wide, two feet deep, and over one hundred feet long, blackened with smoking earth.

"Remind me not to try to kidnap you," Percy joked, nervously. I winced as his chuckles rocked my body, radiating pain from my side. Percy flinched, noticing my pain, and his body quickly became still as a rock.

"When you say he got thrown around?" Percy asked, with a newfound focus.

"I mean literally thrown around. One guy was using an aquamarine lens, and the other was bronze. Professor Shepard got blasted around at least twice," said Sirius. Percy's face fell into a frown.

"Could you go find Headmistress Vega or Professor Copper please, Sirius?"

"On it," said Sirius. With a flash of grey, a fresh set of wings sprung from his back and he took to the air.

"Can I do anything?" came Wayne's voice, again from outside of my eyeline, as wing beats blasted refreshing cool air from behind me.

"Take the rest of the guard and see if you can see anyone who looks to be making some kind of quick getaway," said Percy.

"Yes, sir!" said Wayne's disembodied voice, before the sound of more wing beats growing distant signified him taking to the air.

"Aster, I'm just going check your ribs, is that okay?" asked Percy, finally focusing all his attention on me as he began to gently unbutton my scorched robes. I nodded and swallowed.

"Go for it," I croaked. Percy forced a smile, then slipped one hand gently to my side. I shuddered and squirmed away, as stabbing pain shot through me.

"Sorry, sorry, all done," said Percy, recoiling his hand with a pained look on his face.

"It's okay." I tried not to wince as my voice cracked.

"I think you've broken a rib," said Percy, with little tears beading in his eyes.

"I'm okay!" I croaked. I coughed as my voice cracked again, and then winced as pain shot through my side. The whole ordeal somewhat undermined my point.

"I've got reinforcements," came Sirius's voice, followed by a flash of silver.

"Bloody hell, that's an impressive scorch mark," said Nick, as he appeared from one of his portals, standing over me and admiring the trench Sirius had blasted.

"Nick, we need a healer," said Percy, in a strained voice.

"That's why I brought him," said Nick. Marlon followed Nick and Sirius out of the portal, jogging in the way ancient men did that somehow seemed slower than walking.

"What seems to be the problem?" asked Marlon, kneeling beside me. He'd been an apprentice of Cora's about fifty years ago, but he'd never become a professor, he guarded the lens vault. General opinion was that he had been a bit of a let-down, although a lesser-known rumour was that he had been one of the most dangerous light walkers of his generation, having mastered every hue except for white and opal, making him one of the very few to master a pure lens. He didn't look so dangerous now. He looked old all over, save for his dazzling aquamarine eyes. Eyes, which made him like me, a wild-hued apprentice.

"Broken or bruised ribs, and he seems to have scorched his skin and throat," said Percy, anxiously.

"Don't worry, Outrider Percy, we'll have your husband back in one piece in no time," said Marlon, shooting Percy a wink. He slipped a hand into his robe, and produced a small ornamental needle with a topaz suspended in the eye. Within a second, aquamarine light was peeling out of him, channelling down his arms to his fingertips, pulsing yellow out of the needle. Without a word, he slipped his hand into my robe, but unlike before, it didn't hurt. Instead, warmth washed over me, like a hot soothing bath. An embarrassing little moan escaped me, as the aches and pains started to leave my body.

"Thank you, thank you so much," said Percy, his voice quavering between a sob and elation.

"Always a pleasure to help out a fellow apprentice, but now I'd best be off. Can't leave the vault unguarded, we could have a rush on lenses." Marlon smiled, shook Percy's hand and eased himself back to standing with a small grunt. His wrist flashed grey, and in the blink of an eye he was an eagle, taking to the sky.

"Thank the stars for old Marlon," I said with a chuckle. Sitting up, I still expected to flinch, but the pain was gone. I knew it would be, but knowing something isn't always the same as believing it, and yellow light is hard to get your head around. In some ways, yellow magic always struck me as one of the strangest of all. The power to permanently alter the human body. It made for great healers, but also carried the potential for great insidiousness.

"Do you still hurt?" asked Percy, so anxious that you'd be forgiven for thinking we were conducting this conversation on the edge of a cliff.

"No, I'm fine, don't worry."

"Okay, well I'm still taking you home," said Percy, as

he hooked his arm under my shoulder and helped me to my feet.

"Not yet. Sirius, are you okay?" Understandably, given the state I was in, Percy had forgotten that Sirius was the one someone had actually tried to kidnap.

"Oh, don't worry about me, Teach, I'll be fine," said Sirius, with a wink and a bicep flex. He was doing his best impression of a brave face.

"I want a guard put on him, give him Wayne," I said, scanning the sky to see if I could spot Nova.

"Can't give him Wayne; he's meant to guard the dim sick centre."

"Who's Wayne?" asked Sirius.

"He's a nice young man who tried to kill me once, but now he's under Percy's command, which means he can tell him to guard whatever he wants," I said, giving Percy a stern look.

"I don't need a guard, Professor, honestly, I'll be fine."

"You nearly got kidnapped, and I nearly died. And you're the new infinite, which means a lot of people have a vested interest in you now. It was naïve of me not to realise it before; you definitely do need a guard."

"Aster is right, you probably should have a guard," said Percy.

"So, make it Wayne, go on, who's gonna say anything? Nobody would bat an eye, go on," I said playfully, nudging Percy's ribs.

"I don't know..." Percy was hesitant, but he was weakening. I saw my opening and stood on tiptoe, craning up to whisper in his ear.

"If you give him Wayne, you can take me home right

now," I whispered, and watched the goosebumps appear along his neck.

"Wayne! Get down here, I've got a new task for you!" Percy bellowed into the sky.

* * *

I had to replace my robes after the kidnapping incident; the old ones were ripped and scorched beyond repair. I'd taken a few decorative liberties with the new ones. Rather than black, I had these made in a deep forest, the sort of green that looked black in the dark but caught the eye in the sun. They still had the double buttoned frontage, but now the buttons and the chain that hung between them were golden. Best of all was the lining: a vibrant, silky emerald green, with a pattern of larger-than-life autumnal leaves in wonderful burnt oranges and auburns falling across it.

"Morning Astrid, morning Orion," I said, as I entered my office. Both of them had their heads in a book. Astrid looked up from hers, something about the multiple applications of white hues when combined with other light walkers. Orion did not look up from his, which to my pleasant surprise was a book on the ancient history of the Sovereign dynasty.

"Morning, Professor. Is it true that Sirius was given a golden and a green lens by a fairy prince?" asked Astrid.

"It is, yes, although it'll be a little while before he progresses past just using the red lens," I said, sensing a note of jealousy.

"When will we be provided with our next lenses to begin practicing with?"

"When you need them," I said with a smile, but an attempt at sternness in my voice. Astrid opened her mouth, presumably to argue, but hesitated and, to my pleasant surprise, no argument was made.

"Sorry I'm late!" said Sirius, bursting into the office a second later. He was followed shortly by Wayne, wearing a guards' uniform, which was a little lighter than the traditional rider armour.

"Don't worry, just take a seat. Wayne you're free to wait outside or take a seat at the back."

"Who is Wayne?" asked Astrid, watching him intently as he crossed to the back of the room, where he diligently stood at attention rather than taking the perfectly good seat.

"He's my guard, because apparently when you're the infinite, people try to kidnap you," said Sirius, plopping down in his seat.

"I heard about that, is it true that you single-handedly fought off three beacons at once? That's what they were saying in the breakfast hall this morning," said Astrid.

"It was two, and Professor Shepard did most of the fighting off," said Sirius, with a nod to me.

"We both played a part, and we were lucky as much as anything," I said.

"He's being humble, he was amazing," said Sirius, with stars in his eyes, directed at me.

"Alright, let's get to the lesson," I said, trying not to let Sirius' words go to my head. Just then, Wayne cleared his throat rather loudly from the back of the room.

"Need something, Wayne?"

"I think Sirius is forgetting something, sir."

"Oh, right, yeah. I got this, I showed it to Wayne, but he said I should show it to you," said Sirius. He produced a somewhat scrunched up roll of fine yellowed paper with gold inlay along the edge.

"What is it?"

"It's an invitation, it says that me and someone called Tera are the joint guests of honour at a celebration being held by the Golden Court," said Sirius, as he handed over the invite.

"I wonder who Tera is," said Astrid.

"She is a forest dragon," I said, as I scanned the invite. I must have missed mine when I left home early to pick up my new robes.

"Aren't forest dragons especially rare?" asked Astrid, inquisitively.

"They're rarer than fire and swamp dragons, less so than grave, mountain and of course golden ones."

"So why would a forest dragon be the guest of honour alongside the infinite? I know they prize dragons highly, but it still seems odd," Astrid mused, speaking to herself more than anything at this point.

"She is my dragon," I said, putting the invite down, and staring at my desk as I felt several pairs of eyes pin themselves to me.

"I knew it," I heard Wayne whisper from across the room.

"Did you adopt her after a rider died or something?" asked Sirius.

"Nope, she bonded with me when she hatched."

"I didn't think that was possible," said Astrid.

"Nobody did until it happened. It took me by surprise

too." Everything I said sounded a bit too casual. The trouble was that giving it its due significance was liable to trigger the panic I was trying to suppress.

"Why did you even have an egg though?" asked Astrid.

"It was petrified, and then somehow… I unpetrified it." I still didn't really understand how I did that myself.

"The baby forest dragon you took to The Clutch, during Sovereign Lance's hunt… it's her, isn't it?" asked Wayne, from across the room.

"Could you tell?" I asked.

"I had a feeling, but I didn't think it was possible," said Wayne.

"So that means you'll be coming too then?" asked Sirius.

"I think all four of us should go." I caught a twinkle of excitement in Astrid's eye, although Orion still hadn't looked up from his book.

"What about Wayne, can he come?" Sirius asked.

"I'm not sure that would be possible," I said, and was surprised at how much Sirius face dropped.

"He can have my spot," said Orion, still from within the confines of his book.

"It's not a case of invites, it's more that Wayne isn't officially meant to be guarding Sirius. It won't be a problem in Streya, but I'm sure it would raise a few eyebrows in court," I explained.

"Oh right, secret guard," said Sirius.

"Why don't you want to go, anyway?" asked Astrid, looking to Orion. All she got in response was a shoulder shrug.

"Astrid, Sirius, do you have ceremonial robes?" I asked, improvising a distraction out of thin air.

"Do we need those?" asked Sirius.

"Oh gosh, I don't think I do," said Astrid, more melodramatically than I was expecting.

"Tell you what, take this and go and see my tailor. You can't very well turn up to meet a king in your school uniforms," I said, handing them the card for the shop that had made my new robe.

"What about money?" Sirius asked, looking suddenly nervous.

"There is a budget set aside for diplomatic essentials. I think we can get away with putting this under that, just don't tell Headmistress Vega." I gave a conspiratorial wink, and watched nerves turn to excitement on both their faces.

"Come on, Wayne, we're going shopping," said Sirius, and within seconds the three of them had scurried out of the room.

"Should I go too, sir, since apparently we're cancelling today's lesson," Orion asked.

"What is that you're reading, Orion," I asked, ignoring his question as I got up from my desk. Of course, I knew what he was reading, it had been in the bibliography of my dissertation, but I had a sneaking suspicion about why he might be reading it.

"It's about the Sovereign family history," said Orion shortly.

"Anyone of particular interest?" I asked, circling around to get a peek over his shoulder. As I had suspected, he was reading about The Sable Sorcerer.

"Nope," Orion lied.

"Now I think about it, that book is from the thesis section of the library, how did you come by it?"

"Professor Ithaca wrote me a special permission note to take it out."

"And why would she do that?" I asked, my eyes narrowing.

"She said it might be a good idea for me to be more familiar with the legacy of void-hued light," said Orion, finally putting the book down, having realised I wasn't going to be put off.

"I'm sure you're already quite familiar, aren't you?" I asked, finding myself already becoming annoyed at Ithaca.

"I am," Orion agreed flatly.

"Well, what have you learned so far from that book?"

"That it's probably not a good idea for a void-hued light walker to go anywhere near the Sovereign family. And that I don't think Ithaca likes people with void eyes."

"Want me to have a word with her?" I asked, already a few choice words were springing to mind.

"I'm used to it, sir," said Orion, with a resigned tone to his voice as his shoulders sagged.

"Has someone else said something?" I asked. There were some light walkers who held prejudice against people born of void hue. Luckily, in Streya at least, most people were more accepting.

"Not from here, I just mean with how I..." Orion's voice trailed off. Although I felt like I could guess where the sentence was leading.

"When you were younger?" I asked, trying not to

reveal I knew things about him that he perhaps would rather tell me himself.

"I grew up in a home, sir," he said, speaking rather quickly, like he was forcing it out.

"I see, and the other kids weren't too kind?" I hazarded a guess.

"The other kids were scared of me, but that's not really what I meant." Orion looked down at his shoes.

"What did you mean?" I asked, softening my voice.

"They found me in a box on the home's doorstep." His voice was very small now. I couldn't see his face as he'd leant forward and was staring at the floor, but it looked as though he might have been crying.

"I'm sorry, Orion, could I give you a hug?" I asked. He nodded wordlessly, and I wrapped an arm around his side and held him for a little while. After some time, he sighed and sat up.

"So anyway, I don't think I should go to this party," said Orion, rubbing his eyes, which were now red.

"And why might that be?" I asked, offering a friendly smile.

"Because the one time a golden dragon egg was taken and not returned, it was by someone with eyes like mine." He seemed to have gathered himself now and was speaking in a more even tone.

"The Sable Sorcerer?" I asked I watched Orion sag at the mention of the name.

"Yes, the most famous void-hued light walker ever, not exactly a good ambassador, is he?" said Orion, almost sounding embarrassed.

"You're a very smart young man, Orion."

"Thank you, sir. I think it's probably for the—"

"But in this instance, I'm afraid you're making a huge mistake."

"Sir, why?" Orion asked, looking confused.

"It's exactly as you said, Orion. The Sable shithead isn't a very good ambassador, is he?" I watched a hint of a smile tug at the corner of Orion's mouth. Getting a rush out of hearing a teacher swear was something that some kids never grew out of. I suspected Orion was one of those.

"No, sir, he's not."

"But he was also alive over one thousand years ago. There have been plenty of good void-hued light walkers since then."

"I know, but he's the one people always remember."

"So, perhaps it's time someone changed that," I said, attempting an encouraging smile.

"And how likely is that to happen?" Orion asked, grumpily.

"Well, I'd say you had a good chance of making it happen, Orion, apprentices tend to go on to great things. Just look at Headmistress Vega, she was no different from you just over a decade ago. Not to mention, you are friends with the new infinite, and you're being invited to meet the Sovereign family. You've got a lot going for you in the good and memorable category," I said, with a smile.

"You don't think the Sovereigns would mind someone like me being there?" he asked, a glimmer of hope flickering into life.

"Orion, do you know who else, besides a void-hued light walker, has stolen a golden dragon egg?"

"Who?"

"A Sovereign. During The Clutch uprising. And that was a much more recent event, not to mention, there have been more than a couple of void-hued light walkers in that throne room since the Sable Sorcerer."

"So, you think I should go then?" Orion asked, a full smile breaking across his face.

"Of course I do, you'd best catch up with the others," I said, getting up to hold the door open for him.

"Okay, thanks, Professor."

"Oh, and one more thing before you go. I'd suggest giving Professor Ithaca a wide berth, I'll be keeping an eye on her from now on."

"Me too, sir," said Orion, as he headed out the door.

* * *

To Sirius's delight, Wayne did end up tagging along. To no one's surprise, me, Percy, three apprentices and Tera, who'd grown to about the size of a large dog, all pilling onto Styx's back was a bit awkward. Consequently, Sirius, and Orion were riding with Wayne on the back of Nova, whilst Astrid, Tera, Percy, and I were all on the back of Styx.

"I never realised how much faster dragons were than light walkers," Astrid shouted over the wind, as Styx caught a pleasant warm updraft and soared up above the cloud line.

"Styx is actually slowing himself down at the moment. If he flew at full speed, we'd probably fall off," I called back to her.

"Is it true that grave dragons are the fastest of all?" Astrid yelled back.

"Aside from gold, perhaps," I mused. It was difficult to establish the standard traits of the golden dragon race, being as rare as they are, as each specimen could be an outlier. Sol, for example, could outstrip even Styx, but Elaine on the back of Khydra would not have.

"Who are they, Professor?" asked Astrid as we dropped below the cloud line again. I craned my neck behind, struggling to get a good view.

"Wyverns," Tera hissed into my mind, as she climbed across Styx to get a better view.

"Styx says its wyvern riders," said Percy.

"I wouldn't have expected Lance to invite them," I said, giving up on trying to get a look for myself.

"He must be feeling especially generous," said Percy, with a shrug.

"What's a wyvern?" Astrid asked.

"They are a cousin to the dragon, physically similar but without the connection to their riders or any elemental magic."

"They're big flying lizards," Percy shouted.

"Basically yes, big flying lizards. The Black Crater clan started riding them after the meteor dragons went extinct," I explained, as we began our descent into the Golden Cradle.

* * *

"Presenting this evening's honoured guests, Sirius Greyfellow, Slate Eyed, the Infinite, Apprentice to Aster

Shepard, by personal invite of Lance Sovereign, and Tera, Forest Dragon of Streya, first of her kind, bonded to Light Walker Aster Shepard."

It was strange to realise that my name was somehow tied to the titles of both the honoured guests of the evening, which almost made me seem important. I watched as Tera and Sirius made their entrance into the hall. Tera's eyes were fixed on me, standing beside Percy, Orion, and Astrid, but Sirius's were everywhere, never settling in one place.

Luckily, most people were distracted by his outfit; my tailor and also, I suspect, Astrid, had got a bit carried away. He was wearing a long, shiny grey robe that trailed at least two feet behind him along the floor, with dramatically draped kimono sleeves. Most eye catching of all, though, was the chest, which sported several concentric circles of clear gemstones. Set against the grey material, they shone in a silvery fashion, but as he moved, the light bounced and refracted, creating a shimmering rainbow of reds, greens, blues and golds. I'd no doubt the words *Outfit fit for the infinite* had been thrown about quite haphazardly.

Orion and Astrid had shown a little more restraint. Orion wore a loosely fitting black silk shirt and skirt that touched exactly to the floor. The entire ensemble was rather understated, but the way it hung off his slight frame was not unflattering. Predictably, Astrid had gone for a rather simple sleeveless white satin gown, offset only by her black beaded lens. Still enraptured with the lining of my new uniform, I'd had a loose silk tunic, with an open chest tied with golden thread, and a matching pair of wide-legged silk trousers, made of the same fabric: forest green with dazzling autumnal coloured leaves. I was also carrying my ebony staff, which I had no intention of telling anyone was formerly a wooden spoon.

Besides Sirius, Percy was probably the most impressive of our number, in his official knight's regalia. Similar to what Bors had been wearing, although where Bors was all greens, browns and golds, Percy's armour was a symphony of black and slate grey, with a deep blue cloak pinned to his pauldrons, to match the membrane of Styx's wings. A single pop of red was provided by the brooch attached to his left pauldron. A small enamel inlay depicted a burning red crack in a blackened craggy landscape, signifying his affiliation with the Burning Mantle.

"They are all looking at me." Tera's voice was smaller than usual, as she cantered towards me, not taking her eye off me for a second.

"Don't worry, I'm sure Sirius will make a show of himself soon," I spoke into her mind, as she reached me and began circling my legs.

"What do we do now then?" asked Orion, who'd positioned himself behind Percy and me, making us into a sort of human dividing wall.

"Well, exactly what Sirius is doing, I suppose," I said, watching him stride right up to a perfect stranger and start shaking hands. A crowd quickly formed around him.

"What do we say?" asked Astrid.

"'Hello, my name is Astrid, I'm one of the apprentices from Streya, what's your name?' Probably wouldn't be a bad place to start," I said, catching sight of Lance. To my horror, he seemed to be making his way towards me.

"Sounds awkward," said Orion.

"Would you rather meet Lance Sovereign?" I asked, lowering my voice to a whisper.

"Not right this second, I need time to prepare," said Astrid.

"Then I suggest you both go mingle," I hissed, as Lance's large frame pushed through Sirius's gaggle, closing in on us. Spotting this, Orion and Astrid scuttled off, staying close to each other, like pack animals moving in a herd for protection.

"Shepard," said Lance, nodding as he approached. He was dressed in a mix of armour and party regalia. His hands, feet and shoulders were sporting weighty looking pieces of armour, while his torso and legs were draped in flowing golden silks that shined beautifully against his deep golden-brown skin. His thick ropes of black hair were tied into a large bun on top of his head, with gold ribbons running through each rope, like seams in a coal face.

"Your Majesty," I said, offering a bow. To my surprise, when I straightened back up, I found Lance had dropped to his knees before Tera.

"Her eyes are bright, and her scales akin to that of a mulberry bush. A beautiful example of the forest dragon," said Lance, not taking his eyes off Tera. It didn't surprise me that Lance might be better with dragons than people, it wasn't exactly a very high bar to clear. Although his familiarity with mulberry bushes did catch me off guard. He reached out his hand towards Tera, and after a moment's hesitation, she bowed her head and allowed him to delicately touch her twisted brown horns. I felt her shiver against my leg as he did.

"He's all strength and power," she whispered, as she backed away from his touch.

"What does she make of me then?" asked Lance. Drawing himself up to his full height again, he towered over me, but he spoke with more warmth and friendship in his voice that I was used to.

"She thinks you're very powerful, and strong."

"As a king should be. But you needn't fear, little one. Your rider and I are allies, my strength is at your side," said Lance, directing his attention back to Tera.

"I like him." Tera purred into my mind, and without thinking, I let loose a small chuckle.

"What did she say?" asked Lance.

"Oh, only that she, errm, she likes you," I said, a little nervously. To my pleasant surprise, an unfamiliar smile cracked Lance's usually stalwart face.

"Well, the feeling is mutual, and I must admit, Shepard, I was wrong about you."

"Oh, how so?" I asked, a little taken aback.

"I underestimated you when Cora introduced us."

"Oh, don't worry about that, Your Majesty, it happens a lot," I said, hoping I sounded light-hearted and breezy, not pitifully mournful.

"Well, myself and everyone else were wrong. You've proven yourself to be a capable beacon in your own right, and somehow, you've performed the miraculous. I wonder, did you have any theories as to how it came to be that you were able to bond with a dragon?" asked Lance, with genuine curiosity in his voice.

I blinked, and hoped he hadn't noticed that every kind word was bringing me closer and closer to bursting into tears. I had to swallow hard around the lump in my throat before I spoke.

"I have my theories. During the star bloom, I used Tera's petrified egg as a place to vent my excess light, rather than turning my house into a jungle. And well, you see, it's slightly complicated, but I theorised that certain light walker hues happen to be resonate with certain types of dragon. Our magic is not always so dissimilar, allowing of course for the fact that draconic magic is typically much more potent that any normal light walker. That said, I believe my hue, that is green, is resonant with forest dragons. I believe in charging her egg with so much light, which is in a way, life energy, I inadvertently revived it. And in being so charged with my unique light, she was bonded with me, perhaps before she even hatched."

"Fascinating. Is there any way to corroborate this theory?" asked Lance, looking surprisingly engaged.

"Not that I know of, and as I say, it is only my own theory. I'm sure wiser heads will produce a different one at some point," I said, anxious not to seem overly satisfied with myself.

"Very well, I had better greet your apprentice, the new infinite. I believe the last time I met him I threatened him with Lustre," said Lance, with an uncharacteristic chuckle. He patted the gladius dangling at his side, before striding off into the crowd.

"Well, that was unusual," I said softly.

"People are finally seeing in you what I've known all along," Percy whispered into my ear, sending a shiver up my back. I allowed myself a minute to lean against him.

"I hope the others are having as good a night as me," I

said, taking a glass of sparkling wine from a waiter as he bobbed through the crowd.

"I'm sure they are. You know, Aster, I think your theory is probably right about how you bonded with Tera," said Sirius, as he snatched two odd looking vol-au-vents, and handed me one.

"I doubt it, it's just my theory after all," I said, with a chuckle. I sniffed the mystery pastry, detecting something fishy.

"And why shouldn't your theory be right?" asked Percy, swallowing his in one mouthful.

"Because I'm just me, Aster Shepard. Not some many times published academic genius who's working out the mysteries of our world."

"I wish you wouldn't do that," said Percy, solemnly. As he met my gaze, his large, light blue eyes almost drowning me.

"Do what?"

"Talk yourself down like that. You're not just Aster Shepard. You're Aster Shepard, the expert on draconic magic. Professor at the greatest magical university in the world. Master of the new infinite, and first ever light walker to bond with a dragon. Why shouldn't you be the guy working out the mysteries of the world?" This time the tears did tumble down my cheek, as I swallowed around the lump in my throat.

"Percy, I don't know what to say," I whispered, struggling to make any bigger sounds.

"I'm not trying to upset you, Aster, it's just, when I look at you, I see someone brilliant, and smart and funny and kind and I think everyone else is starting to see that brilliant person too. I just wish you would." The lump in my throat was becoming painful. I gulped some wine in the vain hope of finding relief. Then I flinched, as a loud clattering sound rang through the throne room, putting pause to my thoughts.

Before I'd even turned my head to find the source, Percy was already in front of me. One arm out, shielding Tera and I, the other rested on the pommel of Obol. The source of the clattering was a guard, by the looks of his uniform, a dragonless squire of the Whispering Woods. He had fallen backwards down the stairs leading to the entry-way, from which a fifteen or twenty strong crowd of extremely tall, well-muscled men and women was emerging. Bedecked in furs and weathered leathers, each was outfitted with weapons of almost comical proportions: hulking great hammers, claymores that could dig a trench and monstrous axes protruded at every conceivable angle. My eyes skipped away from them, and darted through the crowd, searching for my apprentices. Sirius wasn't hard to find in the centre of the throng, and Wayne was already at his side. He'd been standing guard around the edge of the room, but had quickly placed himself between Sirius and the intruders. Astrid and Orion were harder to spot. They'd found a place to congregate in a far corner of the room, worryingly near the entrance. They were talking to Bors, of all people. His armour was easy to recognise even from across the room.

"What is the meaning of this?" Lance's voice was so charged with power I thought I might lose my vol-au-vent as it crackled around the room. Golden lightning sparked between his hand and the sheath of Lustre.

"Where is the dragon?" came the gnarled voice of their presumed leader, a bald, olive skinned individual, who was perhaps an inch or so shorter than Lance, but broader. He had shoulders like cannonballs, arms like tree trunks, and a belly protruding like a beer barrel. In each of his massive hands, he held a long-handled hammer. At the head of each sat a large, craggy boulder. I could say with confidence that I would definitely not be able to lift even one of them off the ground. He looked to be in his late forties or early fifties, but with more power than most men would ever achieve at any age.

"Is that brute referring to me?" Tera hissed into my head.

"You will take not one step further without explaining yourself," said Lance, drawing Lustre and levelling its blade toward the hammer wielder. He snarled, his eyes narrowing to slits as he stopped halfway down the stairs.

"Is it true? Is it true that the court gave a light walker a dragon?" barked a younger man, who I guessed was the son of the hammer wielder. He was just as tall, but of leaner construction. He wore only a collection of leather straps across his torso, which bound a claymore I judged to be two meters long, strapped to his back. His was the most perfectly muscled body I'd ever seen. I suspected, anyone properly educated in human anatomy could use him in place of a diagram to pinpoint each specific muscle. His legs were covered to the knee by a skirt of furs, which were met by chunky fur boots.

"No dragon was given. A petrified egg was the gift," said Igraine, who'd joined Lance's side. She was bound up in a golden corseted gown that looked appropriately like an armoured bodice.

"We needn't explain anything to intruders." Lance growled.

"And yet, a light walker stands amongst you decorated with a dragon." The younger man glowered, his eyes falling on Tera as she circled my legs, behind Percy. He reached back, placing a hand on the hilt of his giant claymore. In response, Percy drew Obol, white mist pouring from its crystalline ice-blue blade.

"I'm no decoration!" Tera's voice rolled into my mind. My grip on my ebony staff tightened, as it began to hum with power. The great roiling fire of forest energy inside me was kicking up into an inferno.

"That light walker brought a petrified egg back to life and bonded with it. Something no one from your clan has done with a dragon for a generation," Igraine bellowed. Golden lightning was sparking off of her now too, and dancing back and forth between her and her brother. The hammer wielder gave a guttural snort of derision.

"Impossible, a weakling light walker could never master a dragon." His voice was halfway between a growl and a mocking laugh. He lifted his leg, taking a step towards me, and a bolt of golden lightning struck the floor before him. For all his bravado, he froze rooted to the spot.

"Leave now, before I have to separate you from your spiteful tongue," Lance commanded, as smoke issued from the tip of Lustre.

"We'll go, but let it be known that on this day, the Sovereign family chose a light walker over a tribe of the Draconic Lands," the son bellowed, his father seemingly momentarily without words. As he spoke, his eyes locked with mine, and an icy shiver ran through me. I'd rarely felt such pure, red hot hate. The air filled with tension, as time seemed to stretch into infinity. Then, all at once, everything snapped back into motion as the hammer wielder turned on his heel and walked back through his muscle-bound crowd.

"Well, I did think things were going too smoothly," I said to myself, as much as anything.

"Are you okay?" asked Percy, as he pulled me into a tight embrace. Tera climbed up onto my shoulder, although she was getting altogether too big to do that comfortably now.

"I'm okay, a bit rattled, but okay," I said into his chest, with my nose squashed against his chain mail.

"Is Professor Shepard okay?" I heard Sirius ask, before Percy let me go.

"I'm fine," I said, offering my best reassuring smile, trying to ignore the fact I could feel almost every eye in the ballroom on me.

"Professor Shepard, were those the wyvern riders we saw earlier?" Astrid said as she scuttled over with Orion by her side.

"I believe they were."

"Guess that means they weren't invited after all," said Percy, with a weak chuckle.

"Why do they want Tera?" asked Sirius. Wayne was hovering a few feet behind him, having not returned to his position among the guards.

"Because their dragons went extinct," said Orion impressively quickly.

"Correct, Orion. Meteor dragons, the last of them, died out a while back. I'd be surprised if anyone who had actually ever ridden one still lives," I mused to myself.

"I still don't understand why they'd want Tera though. A dragon can't bond with more than one rider," said Orion

"I expect they don't believe we actually bonded. It has, after all, never happened before," I said, running my hand over Tera's elegant neck as I spoke, watching the faces of the other riders throughout the party as I did. Looking for any hint of disapproval or revulsion at the sight of a light walker being bonded with a dragon.

"They are brutes and fools, and I wouldn't bond with them, even if I weren't bonded to you," Tera fumed in my head.

"Regardless, I think it's time we took our leave, so everyone can stop looking at me," I said, just loud enough for the group to hear, or at least that's what I'd hoped.

"I'll escort you all out," came a familiar voice from behind me.

"Oh, Professor Shepard, this is Bors. He says he used to know your husband, have you met?" asked Astrid, starting towards the door.

"We have," I said, catching Bors's eye as he walked with us.

"I wanted to apologise, for the other day," said Bors.

"What do you have to apologise for, you old goat?" asked Percy jovially, as we climbed the stairs out of the ballroom. Bowing to the Sovereigns as we went, we received a head nod of understanding in return.

"I was rude to your husband needlessly. After today's display, I've realised I've got much more respect for you and yours than the people aligning themselves against you," said Bors, pushing the door open for us, whilst Percy looked on in quiet surprise. To be fair, it was a very wordy apology by Bors's standards.

"That's very gracious of you, Bors," I said, as we meandered down the bridge towards Styx and Nova.

"What do you expect? He is a forest rider after all." Tera purred into my head.

It was his height that caught my eye initially. When someone is almost seven feet tall, it's hard to miss, even if they are wearing a cloak that covers them from head to toe. My first thought was that Lance was visiting the University of Streya in secret for some reason. But the way he walked straight past me, and my office, disavowed me of that notion. The only people Lance really knew in Streya were Cora and me.

Before I knew it, I was following the strange, cloaked figure, ducking into doorways, and weaving in between conveniently tall senior students. I needn't have bothered; the mysterious cloaked giant didn't turn around even once. I suppose being seven feet tall granted a certain sense of security. They did keep glancing at doorways, pausing as they passed each classroom and office. That's when it clicked: they didn't know where they were going, all they had was a name. When they paused in her doorway, I quickly came to realise that name was Ithaca. I watched the cloaked figure go inside and then waited five, maybe ten minutes before making up a reason I needed to speak to her, a reminder about some obscure historical fact or other, and knocked on the door, but got no reply. I pushed my way inside, but there was nobody there, just desks and chairs and a lot of dusty bookshelves. Remarkably dusty, actually. Not a single one of them appeared to have been picked up in months. There was a door behind her desk that led to the apartment above, but I didn't quite have the nerve to go poking around up there.

"So, I've decided that whilst we continue to work on control of your red lenses, we're also going to be making a lens. To help you understand more intimately the nature of what a lens is, what it is you're funnelling light into. There are some things you've just got to feel. My telling you about them or your reading about them in a textbook won't make an adequate substitute." This was another lesson plan I'd stolen from Cora. I'd made my own lucky rabbit's foot into a golden hued lens about a decade ago because of it.

"Which hues do we get to make?" asked Astrid, excitedly.

"Well, you and Orion were both interested in silver lenses, so I thought that would be perfect for you two, to work as a pair. Help each other when you get stuck, be each other's sounding board and research partner."

"And what about me, sir, the free folk brought me the two lenses I had on my list, besides red," said Sirius.

"Well, Sirius, seeing as you're currently capable of making an infinite amount of fire, and not extremely adept at controlling it, I think it would be prudent for you to be able to make an infinite amount of water too. To that end, you'll be making your own navy-hued lens, like my ring," I said, flashing the sapphire ring I wore on my ring finger. The band was polished and varnished, but the source was actually driftwood.

"And who gets to be my research partner?"

"That would be me, I hope it's not too uncool working with your teacher," I said, with a smile.

"Oh, not at—"

Knock Knock

"Come in!" I called. It swung open, and to my surprise, five figures walked in, four of them were Streya University board members. They were recognisable from the uniform; each wore a long sweeping black robe with one large stylised white star in the centre. The board was authorised to make decisions about all sorts of Streya University matters. Only Vega had the authority to deny their requests, although they rarely did anything the teaching body would object to. Most of them were former teachers, and all were former alumni. The fifth figure following in their wake was Professor Ithaca. Again, I found my eyes lingering on her shawl. The beads were black and dark purple. It looked as though they were woven into a pattern, but they were so similar in colour it was hard to make it out.

"To what do we owe the pleasure, governors, Ithaca?" I asked, my body tensing instinctively. Something wasn't right.

"Professor Shepard, it's a pleasure, as always, and I'm happy to say we've come with good news," said Governor

Dusk. A thickset older gentleman, he used to teach pure hue studies, though he himself was a bronze-hued light walker. His nervous tone did make me question the truth of his statement,

"What might that be?" I asked.

"We've come to lighten your load," said Dusk, who apparently was the governor's elected speaker.

"How so?"

"We've taken the decision that, given all your responsibilities, between your teaching in draconic magic, your diplomatic relationship with the Sovereigns, your position as master of Streya's apprentices, we think you've got more than enough on your plate without the added responsibility of mentoring the next infinite." I had a feeling that, that might be where they were going.

"You needn't worry about that. Sirius's mentoring is coming along quite well," I said, doing my best not to lose my manners.

"Given how important to Streya's future the new infinite shall be, we think it's best if—"

"His name is Sirius. You should learn it if you're interested in teaching him," I bristled.

"We wouldn't be teaching him. Professor Ithaca will be taking over his personal mentoring and development."

"No, she will not be," I said, figuratively and literally taking a stand, coming out from behind my desk.

"Shepard, you should look at this as a good thing, a gift. We're taking an enormous responsibility off your plate. The new infinite—"

"Sirius, his name is Sirius, and I'm sure he has an opinion on the matter," I said, giving Sirius a nod.

"I want to stay with Professor Shepard," said Sirius, with as much certainty in his voice as he could muster, although he looked nervous.

"I'm afraid that's not up to you infi—Sirius. The board of governors has decided this is for the best."

"And how do you work that one out?" I asked, taking another step forward, leaving only a foot between myself and Dusk, looking up into his nervous, watery bronze eyes.

"Professor Olympia was the bedrock of this place. We need Sirius to be able to fill her shoes, which means he needs all the attention we can give him. Especially since the kidnapping attempt," said Dusk, doing his best to inject some grit into his tone.

"Oh, I know. I know exactly how important Cora was, and I know exactly how important Sirius is, and I know exactly how ridiculous it is to expect him to fill her shoes. As for the kidnapping attempt, after that I assigned him a guard, something your board of governors failed to consider."

"Shepard, please let's not make this—"

"Astrid, fetch Vega for me," I said, cutting Dusk off. Astrid nodded, making for the door, but Dusk grabbed her wrist.

"That won't be necessary, miss," said Dusk, taking on the tone of an old man speaking to a foolish granddaughter.

"Take your hand off me or lose it," said Astrid, with impressive venom as her white eyes flashed menacingly.

"Aster, are you going to let your apprentices speak to me like this?" asked Dusk, aghast. At which point, I gave a snort of laughter.

"If you'd pulled that trick on Vega at Astrid's age, you wouldn't have been given a warning before you lost your hand, and Cora would have laughed. Now let her go." Astrid snatched her hand loose and scurried out the door.

"This is ridiculous, Aster. You should have just cooperated, we'll have your job for this. Grab the infinite," said Dusk, as two more of the board members took a step towards Sirius, now standing behind his chair.

"Nobody touches Sirius," said Wayne, emerging from the corner of the room, flaming bow drawn. The governors froze then began backing up, as a smirk creased my face. Then a shiver ran up my spine, as charge of power pulsed through the room, followed almost instantly by a flash of violet. Wayne's eyes glossed over, and a second later he folded to the floor like a silk scarf.

"What did you do to him?" asked Sirius, with panic in his voice as he knelt before Wayne's body, shielding him.

"Put the boy to sleep. He's fine," said Ithaca, emerging from behind her wall of governors.

"Orion, turn the lights out," I said, giving him the nod.

"Yes, sir." What little white there was in Orion's irises swirled and expanded, becoming completely black, and the entire room was enveloped in shadow. I took a deep breath, trying not to shudder as the chill of my light shrinking washed through me. I could see it on the faces of all the governors. It's a little unnerving, the sudden inability to shine your light into the world. Ithaca had shrunk back behind the wall of governors, hiding within her shroud.

"Now that we've disavowed you of the notion that you can brute force your way through this situation, why don't you try to explain to me why you think Ithaca would make a better mentor for Sirius than me?" I said, levelling my best withering look at the governors.

"Aster, please, call off the darkness, this isn't necessary," Dusk pleaded.

"Apparently it is, now talk," I commanded.

"Well, you see, Ithaca has a lighter load than you, and she's an expert in antiquities. She understands the history of the infinite, whereas you are—"

"I am what? No, wait, I'm not asking, I'll tell you what I am. I am the master of Streya's apprentices. Handpicked by Cora Olympia for the job. I know exactly how important she was, that's why I know how ridiculous your expectations of Sirius are. I am one of Cora Olympia's apprentices, in fact, I am the last apprentice of Cora Olympia!"

"And he was her favourite," said Vega, appearing in the doorway. Apparently, I could be heard down the corridor.

"I wish you wouldn't say that," I grumbled.

"Orion, you can lower this darkness now," said Vega. Orion looked to me for approval, I gave another nod, and suddenly the darkness he was projecting dissipated like smoke.

"Vega, will you please talk to Aster. This is for the best." Dusk's tone had become rather pathetic.

"Oh, I plan to. I plan to apologise to him for the rash and frankly insulting behaviour of our board members," said Vega. Her eyes were flashing like Astrid's had only seconds earlier. Dusk took a shocked step back into the crowd of governors.

"Vega, we were only trying to do what we thought was best." He was almost whimpering.

"Well then, you display an alarming lack of judgement. Aster is the best positioned person to help Sirius. I will cast down any plans you have that would compromise Sirius's tutelage in any way. As you know, the wellbeing of our new infinite is of paramount importance."

I'd been on the receiving end of Vega's towering, menacing monologues a couple of times in the past. I didn't envy Dusk, but I was enjoying watching him squirm.

"Perhaps we should leave," croaked Ithaca from behind the crowd.

"I'll show you out," said Vega, holding the door open for them each to file out in turn. Again, I found my eyes lingering on the purple and black beading of Ithaca's robe.

"Vega," I nodded appreciatively, as she headed out herself.

"Aster," she winked back at me, closing the door behind her.

"Orion, I've got a research project for you," I said, once I judged our visitors would be out of earshot.

"What is it, sir?" asked Orion, producing a notebook.

"I want you to look up any record you can find of legendary lenses that take the form of a shroud, or a shawl or a wrap, particularly violet-hued ones. And look for pictures," I explained.

"What for, sir?" asked Orion, looking curious.

"I have a little hunch. Take this, it'll get you into the thesis section of the library, just in case," I said, handing him a slip with my mark stamped on it.

"Thank you, sir, do you mind me asking why at all?"

"It concerns our mutual friend, Ithaca," I said, giving him a wink.

"I'm awake!" shouted Wayne, suddenly sitting bolt upright. His armour clinked so loudly I physically jumped.

"Are you okay?" Sirius asked, dropping to his knees by Wayne's side. Their eyes locked, and for a second, I was sure it looked like Wayne's cheeks were pinking up. Although it was hard to say for certain, what with all the red he already wears.

"I'm fine," he said groggily, as he rubbed his eyes.

"Do you mind if I take the rest of the day off, Professor? It's just… I don't think I can really focus right now," said Sirius, helping Wayne to his feet.

"Of course, Sirius, take all the time you need," I said with a smile, Sirius nodded his thanks and made for the door, followed closely by Wayne.

"Oh, hey love, welcome home. There's a note addressed to you on the kitchen table," said Percy from the rocking chair. Tera was curled up in his lap, her tail dangling down to the floor. It wouldn't be long before she was too big for the cottage; the expression, growing like a weed, seemed apt.

"A large bird dropped it off," Tera's voice lazily rolled into my head.

"How strange, I wonder if it's from the free folk," I said, picking it up. The fact it appeared to be torn from a notebook suggested it probably wasn't.

"Why is that?" asked Percy.

"Apparently, a large bird dropped it off," I explained, as I opened the note.

Dear Professor Shepard

I'm sorry I'm doing this in a note. Wayne says I should talk to you about it, but I just can't face that right now. I can't face anything right now. I think the universe made a mistake making me the infinite. It should have been someone smart and wise, like you. I can feel everyone looking at me, expecting something from me. Expecting me to be the next Cora Olympia. I can't be her, they got the wrong guy. I need some time away. To clear my head and to give you a break. I feel like my becoming the infinite has been nothing but trouble for you. Like literally from the moment it happened, you've been saving me, saving me from crushing the school and getting kidnapped, and now the governors are picking fights with you. I don't want you to lose your job over me, I'm not worth all this trouble. Please don't try to find me, I'll be okay, I promise.

Love Sirius.

"Fuck me!" I yelled, screwing up the note and tossing it across the room, my hands shaking.

"What's wrong?" asked Percy, getting up from his chair. Tera leapt from him, and glided over to my side.

"Is it me? Do I have some sort of stamp on my forehead? Some sort of marking that says, *Aster Shepard, loves to be abandoned by infinites who leave cryptic notes on his kitchen counter!*" I yelled and kicked the cabinet. Pain radiated through my big toe as a flurry of expletives tumbled out of me.

"What d'you mean?" asked Percy, looking bewildered and more than a little concerned.

"Read the note, I've got to think," I said, as I took up pacing back and forth through the kitchen.

"You do not have a stamp across your forehead, if you did, I would notice," Tera reassured me, her dazzling green globes intently focused on my forehead.

"Thanks for checking," I chuckled, in spite of myself.

"What are you going to do?" asked Percy, dropping the crumpled note as he finished reading it, and looking across the room at me wide eyed.

"I'm going to find him before someone else does, or he gets himself killed."

"You think someone will?" asked Percy.

"As soon as he loses control and burns down half of Streya or turns into a giant the size of the university, he'll have given himself away, won't he?" I huffed.

"Do we tell Vega or Nick?"

"No, I'm not sure what's going on, but I'm beginning to think there are people inside the school who don't have the best of intentions for Sirius. The fewer people that know, the better."

"So how do you find him first, where would he hide?" asked Percy.

"Hide, where would he hide? Where does a boy that can turn into anything hide?" I was thinking aloud to myself as I paced up and down the room, and then it flashed into my mind. The long, double elbowed arm, shooting out of a bundle of silks, the voice like metal clashing against stone, rocking my thoughts.

"Where is my old robe?" I asked.

"In the winter clothes closet I think, why?" asked Percy, bewildered again as I sprinted for the cupboard, with my socks slipping on our wooden floors as I went.

"A hag gave me a prophecy about a week ago," I yelled back, as I tore open the closet.

"And?" Percy asked, slipping along behind me.

"And I wrote it down, and I was wearing this robe at the time," I said frantically, riffling through the pockets until I found the torn off piece of paper in my breast pocket.

Careful of those who know the past, for they shall make that which was, that which is. He shelters amongst that which he becomes. Infinity hides in ancient stories, bleeding the stars to make them bloom, out in the endless dark.

"What does it say?" asked Percy.

"Well, it's three prophecies really, the first is some cryptic history nonsense, but the second two might help:

'He shelters amongst that which he becomes,' and 'infinity hides in ancient stories,' both sort of fit."

"He's not infinity though is he, he's the infinite, just like Cora was the infinite. Infinity is whatever power they share. So, the last part doesn't fit," said Percy, taking the note. He'd always been better with word games than me.

"So, he shelters amongst that which he becomes," I repeated.

"You already said it, Aster, he turns into giants, don't you get it?" asked Percy, his eyes lighting up.

"He's in the Titanic Lands!" I breathed as goosebumps ran down my back, realising if one prophecy was right, the others might be too. If only I knew what they meant.

"Which means we've got a head start, should we get going now? Styx could have us out in the Titanic Lands in a couple of hours," said Percy, as he started grabbing boots and coats and food from the pantry.

"No, not yet, I need to pick up a few things first. And Orion and Astrid, I can't just leave them behind. Cora told me to look after all the apprentices, not just Sirius."

"Okay, you collect them, what should I do in the meantime?" asked Percy.

"Grab everything we need, and find Wayne. He might have some more ideas about what Sirius was up to. Also, we might need Nova," I said, as I rushed for the door, pulling my shoes back on.

"I'm coming with you," Tera hissed into my head, carrying the ebony staff in her jaws as she pranced up to me.

"It'll be dangerous," I thought, locking eyes with her.

"Precisely."

"Alright, Percy, you take Tera, get Styx and Wayne and Nova ready, and we'll meet at the dragon's aerie."

* * *

I found both Astrid and Orion with their heads in hardback books from the thesis section of the library. They'd tucked themselves away in a pair of wingback chairs by one of the senior common fires, and each had a second book lined up and ready to open.

"Astrid, Orion, gather your things, we're going on a field trip," I said, grinning as they both jumped in their seats.

"W-when?" asked Astrid, producing a bookmark from behind her ear and closing her book.

"Tonight, time is of the essence. Pack outdoorsy clothes, your materials for making silver lenses and any books you can't face tearing yourselves away from."

"Why the urgency, Professor?" asked Orion, inquisitively.

"I'll level with you," I said, leaning in, poking my head between their chairs as I lowered my voice to barely a whisper.

"Go on," whispered Astrid, as they both leaned in with me.

"Sirius has run off, and we're going after him."

"Where to?" Orion hissed.

"The Titanic lands," I hissed back.

"Isn't that dangerous?" Astrid asked, nervously.

"There is a yellow lens and a violet lens in it for you.

I'm going to collect them now; do we have a deal?" I asked, straightening up again.

"Done," said Orion without a moment's hesitation. Astrid's brow creased for a second, and then she nodded.

"Well, I can't very well let myself fall behind."

"Okay, gather your things and meet me in my office."

"Before you go, Professor, I think we've found something," said Orion, grasping my wrist before I swept off in a dramatic fashion. I was momentarily buoyed by the excitement of being conspiratorial, forgetting for a second that one of my apprentices had fled the city.

"Can it wait?" I asked.

"It's about the shroud," Orion whispered, his eyes as full of life and excitement as two black voids could be.

"We've been working together on the research project you gave Orion," Astrid added.

"Okay, quickly, give me the headlines," I replied, caught in a tug of war between urgency and curiosity.

"We think it's The Shroud of the Night Mother," Astrid explained, as Orion flipped through the pages of the book in his lap, stopping when he came to an illustration.

"Look familiar?" he asked, holding the picture up for me to inspect. Across two wrinkled and yellowing pages, entitled *The Shroud of the Night Mother,* was spread a rather beautiful watercolour impression. A black shawl, completely nondescript on the front, but on the back, a moon and cloud detailed in shiny black beads, with a border of deep purple, outlining them against the black fabric of the shawl.

"Interesting," I muttered half to myself, recalling the myths my mother had told me as a child. I grew up in territory bordering Free Folk lands, so I knew more of them than most light walkers. Especially ones that had spent their lives in Streya.

"Do you know anything about it, or her?" Orion asked.

"I do," I replied. I was only half in the room with them, letting my mind drift back to Ithaca hobbling out of my classroom, and matching the watercolour to the eye catching purple and black beads of her shawl.

"We haven't had much chance to read about her yet, is there anything you could tell us?" Astrid asked, in the way a student might ask a respected teacher. For a second her reverence caught me off guard.

"Okay, quickly, but then I must dash, and you two get yourselves ready, okay?" I asked, the clock at the back of my mind was still ticking away, reminding me that although we were not yet searching for Sirius, others may still be.

"Okay," they both nodded.

"So, the stories all agree that The Night Mother was an extraordinary hag. She was said to have powers beyond the foresight of regular hags. Her prophecies, when heard, were believed to worm their way into people's minds and force themselves to come true. For instance, say she prophesied that you might receive a big windfall in your near future, a typical, innocuous prophecy, so you might think. Upon hearing it from her, you may suddenly feel compelled to go out and kill a rich relative, and everyone else in between you and the inheritance. Self-fulfilling prophecy was her power, in essence."

"And the Shroud?" Orion asked, hanging on my every word.

"You've got the text in front of you, read up on it, but not before you're packed and ready!" I hissed, straightening up.

"Yes, sir." Both of them rose, bundling books under their arms.

"And look for mention of Sky Everbright. I believe he was the last known holder of the Shroud," I said, turning on my heel and sweeping out of the commons.

I descended into the lens vaults, taking the steps two at a time, energised by a feeling of hope that perhaps I finally had an edge over whoever was after Sirius. Finally, I knew something I wasn't supposed to. The vault was guarded against students, but luckily teachers were allowed relatively uninhibited access. Orion, Astrid, and Sirius were already at their withdrawal limit, as students could only have one lens out on loan at a time. I, on the other hand was free to withdraw up to three lenses at a time for my own personal growth. Vega had mastered nine hues already, through liberal use of this privilege. She was only shy of yellow, void and opal. Personally, I'd never seen the need, and recently had had neither the time nor energy to dedicate to my own studies.

"Been a while since I've seen you down here, Professor. Returning those red lenses, are we?" asked Marlon, His brown robes, frayed at the edges, dragged behind him as he slid from his stool to my side, his long white hair swishing as he went.

"No, actually, checking out for myself today," I said, trying to seem casual.

"No time like the present, Professor. What can I get for ya then?" he asked, cheerily.

"Do you mind if I fetch them myself, Marlon? I like to get a personal feel for my lenses." That wasn't a lie. Even though in this case I was picking for others, I'd still like to find ones that I thought suited Astrid and Orion.

"Be my guest, Professor," said Marlon, as he ran his thumb over a small pendant on his chest, which flashed bronze. There was a moment's pause, then a rumble and a clinking sound, before several latches sprung open on the heavy metal door he sat next to, which swung open with an aching creak.

The door led to a corridor lit with torches and populated with thirteen arches, each glowing gently in a different colour. The first on the left was the red room, tiled in various hues of scarlet, crimson and vermillion. It was the largest of the rooms, and filled with many empty glass cabinets. Red was the most common of all hues, and therefore the easiest to acquire a lens for. However, for this reason, it was also the lens most often taught, so this room was usually half empty. Unlike gold or green, for example, which were not only not very highly thoughts of but also complex enough that very few people bothered. Therefore, their rooms were not only large, but full. Silver and bronze, on the other hand, were always in hot demand. All beacons tend to try to master one or the other. So, it is said that there would always be work for bronze and silver light walkers skilled enough to create lenses.

Fourth on the right was the violet room, which until

recently was the most strictly controlled lens. It was a relatively small space, and almost filled with decorative glass cabinets, each one containing curious oddities, like a glass eye on a chain, or a letter in a bottle, or a fragment of a fun-house mirror set in a brooch. For Orion, I selected a small metal object designed to cover and encase the top arch of the ear. From which hung a bell, with its chime removed. Symbolic of the idea that violet light could pass a silent message directly into the mind.

The yellow room was the last room before the three pure hues: on the right, void, on the left, white, and at the end of the corridor opposite the doorway, the opal room. Unable to ignore my curiosity, I peeped my head inside. The opal room was scantily stocked at the best of times, but now it stood completely baron, filled only with empty cabinets. Cora had been true to her word when she said she'd got rid of all the opal lenses. Luckily, it hadn't caused much outcry when it was announced, since almost no one ever tried to master such lenses, anyway. The news of Cora's disappearance had somewhat dwarfed the loss of a couple of semi-useless lenses.

Like all the other rooms, the yellow one was tiled in various shades of its colour. Filled with glass cabinets containing, in this case, small wands made of bone or the occasional pouch of dried herbs. For Astrid, I selected a palm-sized leather-bound book of pressed flowers, each famed for their healing properties, sealed with a small golden clasp and set with a topaz stone on the cover. She did love a good book after all.

"Thanks, Marlon," I said breezily, as I headed out the door.

"Good luck with the new infinite, Professor Shepard," he said, as I climbed the stairs. I made it halfway before covering myself in bronze light, and allowing myself to drift up as my legs began to complain.

I slipped a quick note to Vega under her door, explaining that my apprentices and I were going on a field trip, to escape Streyan politics and study in the wild for a week or so; only partially a lie. Then I went to meet Astrid and Orion in my office. Both armed with lumpy sacks of clothes, with the obvious hard corners of books poking out at various odd angles.

"Where to now, sir?" asked Orion.

"The dragon aerie. And I think whilst we're on our little field trip, you can call me Aster," I said, with a smile.

I lead them out into the courtyard and bathed the three of us in bronze light, before taking to the sky.

5

<u>A Field Trip.</u>

Ironically, although it was named the City of Stars, they were rather hard to see in the Streyan sky at night, Star blooms notwithstanding. The same could not be said of the sky of the Titanic Lands. Day had passed into night, as the seven of us crossed Streya's border. Here, the stars shone like crystals of every colour, set into a vast black tapestry. They provided a welcome distraction from my growing anxieties.

"Are you sure it is safe for us to be here, Profes… I mean, Aster?" asked Astrid, as she fidgeted restlessly on a hastily grabbed sleeping mat.

We circled the fire, flanked by tents that none of us seemed to want to sleep in. They were a bit mildewy, but I suspected our unspoken reluctance had more to do with the fact that nobody particularly wanted to feel on their own. I couldn't help reminding myself that Sirius had no such group to keep him company.

"We've got three dragons, two riders and three powerful light walkers in this camp. I'm not sure it's safe for anyone else," I said, forcing a laugh. I hoped I sounded more convincing to her than I did to myself.

"Don't worry, Styx is a light sleeper, he'll be keeping an eye out," said Percy, who was sitting behind me, with me between his legs as I lay back against him. Tera was curled up beside us, and seemed to be the only one of us who was able to get some sleep. Styx and Nova had settled beneath their wings, bookending our camp and making us significantly less attractive as a target for any errant giants that might catch our scent on the breeze. Not that there was much of a breeze, our campsite took up a tiny patch of the arid top land of the titans. I'd decided to start our search above ground rather than in the tropical canyons and cave systems below for two reasons. The first was that I prefer dry heat to humidity.

"So how are we going to find Sirius? I know you said you think he's here, but the Titanic Lands are huge, he could be anywhere," said Orion. He'd already laid himself out across his sleeping mat and was tying knots in some dry grass.

"Well, he can only go as far as he can fly. Remember, when undertaking a grey transformation into something that can fly, the practitioner still has to physically do the flying. The fact he's infinite doesn't mean flapping his wings won't start to wear him out."

"Can't we use the violet lens we got for Orion to

pinpoint his mind?" asked Astrid, as she stretched and yawned and rolled over for the seventh time.

"None of us have mastered violet. We'd be just as likely to give him an aneurysm by mistake if we used too much light, or just miss him completely," I explained.

"You do have a plan to find him though, right?" asked Wayne, anxiously.

"Well, sort of. Sirius doesn't just turn into any old giant when he transforms, does he?" I asked Astrid and Orion.

"You know, now you mention it, he does seem to always become a cyclops. When he does it on purpose at least," said Orion.

"Exactly. So my guess is, he is hiding among the nearest clan of cyclops to the Streyan border."

This brought me to the second reason I chose to stay above ground, which was that cyclops rarely, if ever, descended into the tropical canyons below. Perhaps, like me, they preferred a dry heat.

"And how do we find those?" asked Astrid.

"In the morning, Tera, Wayne, Nova, Percy and Styx will take to the skies to look for them. Cyclops tend to shepherd oliphants. Herds of which are huge and loud. They shouldn't be too hard to spot from the sky, and once spotted, we'll picked up."

"And what will we be doing in the meantime?" asked Astrid.

"Well, studying of course, this is a school field trip after all," I said with a wink, as I extricated myself from Percy's legs. I lay back on my sleeping mat, closed my eyes, and lied to myself about being ready to sleep.

* * *

"Does this remind you of anything?" Percy hissed from the sleeping mat next to mine, as I lay there, not really sleeping. I rolled over onto my side and met his beautiful ice-blue eyes, flashing in the firelight.

"Back when I used to sneak out of school to meet you," I whispered, the sound masked by the crackle of the fire.

"And Styx and I would fly all the way to Streya in the dead of night." I could only see his face when the flames of the fire leapt up high, but I could hear Percy smiling.

"Seems like every time we run off and break the rules, we find ourselves lying under the stars together," I said softly, rolling onto my back again to take in the sky. Twinkling yellows and whites and faint blues, and blankets of purple and green and red smudged the sky. It made me wish I knew how to paint. I always wondered what made up the colours of the night, space dust or radiation or perhaps a psychic field of the collective dreams of everyone sleeping on the continent. Probably space dust though.

"Do you think I did the right thing, breaking the rules again," I asked, as a faint streak of golden white tumbled through the sky above.

"Of course I do, you barely ever do anything else," said Percy. A second later, his lips pressed against my cheek, and I released the breath I didn't know I'd been holding onto.

* * *

By daylight, we could make out more of our dusty surroundings. The trees, for the most part were thin, dark, and spiny. The ground was parched, and the patches of grass that grew sparsely were dry and yellow. From the top of the hill that shadowed our camp, you could make out various oases surrounded by patches of green. Throughout the morning, smaller creatures had gathered to drink there, but so far, we had been lucky enough not to encounter any titanic denizens. People say that the desserts of the continent are red, or vibrant orange, that's how they turn up in paintings, but they're not. When you're in them, you learn that they're a sort of noncommittal, ruddy brown. The air was dry and hot, and somehow, out here when the sun shone on you, it felt personal. I hated sweating.

Our cyclops search party had already been gone longer than I expected them to be, and Astrid and Orion were becoming restless. I suspected that not having dragons lying around ready to protect them at the drop of a hat had made them slightly anxious.

"So, to start with, should I just try sending a message into your mind, Professor?" asked Orion, tugging on the bell chime dangling by his ear.

"Absolutely not," I said, already wishing I hadn't given him the damn thing before a sufficiently long and boring preparatory period.

"Why not?" asked Orion, looking disappointed as he flopped back on his sleeping mat.

"For the same reason Astrid won't be testing out her yellow lens on people willy nilly."

"What did I do?" asked Astrid, her bracelet flashing as

she released a puff of flame into the smouldering embers of last night's fire. A fire, which we definitely did not need in this sun.

"Nothing yet, which is a good thing, trust me. Yellow and violet lenses aren't as easy to practise with as red ones, or silver or bronze ones, or in fact, most lenses. They require a human subject, which means they're risky. Imagine, for example, Orion, that you try to send a message into my head, but you overdo it. When you overdo it practicing with a red lens, you release a big, uncontrolled ball of fire, but you can do that into thin air, you can do it safely. A big uncontrolled ball of psychic energy released into someone's head, as I'm sure you can imagine, is not ideal."

"So, how do we practise?" asked Orion, already looking more engaged.

"Usually, it involves trying to whisper a very small message, at a group of people. That way if you overdo it, at least the energy is dispersed through a lot of minds, not just one," I explained, remembering the time Vega accidentally gave the entire population of the senior commons a migraine.

"And me?" asked Astrid.

"Well, Astrid, didn't you grow up in a family of yellow-hued light walkers? You must be familiar with the challenges presented in trying to practise when you need live subjects, typically wounded ones, to practise on.

"My father ran a clinic, so we had no shortage of those. Regardless, I believe it's possible to practise on scars with minimal risk," said Astrid, running her fingers over the small leather-bound book that she'd slept with under her pillow.

"You're right, we'll have to see if Wayne or Sirius have any you can try fixing," I said cheerily. Percy had scars, but I wasn't going to mention them as I liked them exactly where they were.

"Do you really think we'll find him, Aster?" asked Orion, who said my first name as if he was trying to swallow a nectarine whole.

"Well, I'm not going to be the first master in the history of Streya to lose an infinite. So yes, we'll find him," I said with a smile, and enough conviction in my voice that I even convinced myself a little bit.

"Shadows on the horizon," said Astrid, pointing over my shoulder. I swivelled on my rocky perch, and my eyes fell on three sets of outstretched wings getting larger by the second.

"Do you think this means they found him?" asked Orion.

I nodded, but didn't speak. I couldn't trust my voice not to crack with excitement. Percy wouldn't come back before sundown without good news. I shielded my eyes as they came into land, their wing beats kicking up something of a dust cloud around us, and killing the unwanted fire.

"We've located a herd with a particularly suspicious member," Tera's voice curled into my mind as she trotted to my side. By now she stood level with my waist on all fours, and if she stood on her hind legs, she dwarfed me. Soon she'd be strong enough to support my weight in flight.

"You've got to see this," said Percy, as he gracefully dismounted Styx. The cool breeze drifting off his wings was reason enough to go for a ride, even if they hadn't found anything. Part of me felt bad for taking a seat on Styx's back whilst my apprentices mounted Nova, aware as I was of the constant heat she issued. Luckily, the part of me yearning for the relief of rapidly cooling down quickly froze out any nagging voices.

We took to the sky, with Tera undulating alongside us. I watched, somewhat transfixed as her body billowed through the air. The way a current of air would roll her neck, down her body and twist out of her tail, It was like watching the flow of the wind.

"*You admire my flight,*" she said softly, one of her fiery green eyes catching me. I smiled and nodded.

"*I admire your grace.*"

"*I envy Styx's speed,*" she grumbled back. I chuckled, and felt Percy's arm pull me a little closer.

"What's she saying?"

"She is jealous of how fast Styx can fly," I said, patting the grave dragon's cool scales.

"Don't be, Styx says being the fastest just means you spend your life slowing down for people," said Percy, eliciting a rumbling growl of agreement from Styx as he curled his wings, and we began to descend towards the ground.

"I don't see any cyclops," I said, squinting at the scene steadily growing larger beneath us.

"Well, that's what took us so long, they're sheltering," said Percy, as we swept beneath a large overhanging cliff outcropping and into the mouth of a huge, cavernous cave. A shiver ran up my back as we were engulfed in the cool shadows of the cave. The roof must have been as high as the towers of Streya, with long and threatening black stalactites glistening above us. It put me in mind of huge, needle-like teeth, dangling from the gaping maw of creatures that lived at some godforsaken depth beneath the ocean. Far below us, only barely visible within the shadows, pale mounds shuffled around the cave floor. Pale mounds I quickly recognised as cyclopes.

"Cyclopes don't shelter," I muttered to myself. In fact, their proclivity not to shelter was legendary. The story goes that millennia ago, a great cyclopean king was trapped in his own giant cave by a trickster. I couldn't properly remember it, but I knew it ended with him losing his one precious eye. Henceforth, they vowed never to live walled in. Personally, I suspected the reason had more to do with their three to five story high frames, arms as wide as tree trunks and skin thicker than most walls. Sufficed to say, they had little call for shelter.

"Exactly," said Percy, his voice dropping, whilst Styx and Nova landed as quietly as possible. We were only a little way away from the makeshift camp of cyclops and oliphants ambling about their enormous cave home. The oliphants were rearing up onto their hind legs, ripping moss and vines from the glistening wet walls of the cave with their huge dual trunks. Our presence didn't seem to bother them at all.

"Did anything else suggest Sirius might be here?" I asked, squinting into the low light at each cyclops. There must have been thirty of them at least, trundling about, kicking over stalagmites to make toothpicks and back scratchers as they went.

"Ever seen a cyclops like that?" asked Percy, pointing to the far corner of the cave. Muscular as cyclopes were, they all, at maturity, developed something of a potbelly and a hunch, causing their powerful arms and fists to eventually drag across the ground. I couldn't help but smirk when I followed his finger to the specimen leaning against the far wall of the cave. I found myself squinting at a figure five stories tall, with almost perfect posture, and clearly defined abdominal muscles. Wearing something resembling a makeshift kilt as opposed to the thread bare loin clothes of his companions. He also happened to have a luscious head of blonde hair that flopped half over his one eye. Every other cyclops in the cave, without exception, was bald.

"Even when he's hiding in a cave at the end of the world, he has to show off his abs," said Orion, with a snigger.

"You guys stay here, I'm going to go have a word," I whispered.

"Don't get squished," Percy whispered, planting a kiss on my cheek, as I let bronze light wash down from my glasses over my whole body, and gently drifted up into the air. I kept rising until I judged myself to be at a height to go unnoticed, then silently floated across the cave. Before long, I found myself hovering directly above the suspiciously in-shape cyclops with the wonderful hair.

"That isn't a very convincing disguise, you know?" I hissed down past my feet, talking to the glossy crown of his head.

The cyclops flinched, abandoning his lazy reclining

position as his head darted around for the source of the whisper.

"Look up," I said, stifling a laugh. A second later, I was met with one dazzling grey eye about the size of a grapefruit, that peeled to the size of a watermelon when it caught sight of me.

"Professor, what are you doing here?" From what I could tell, Cyclopes don't have the required anatomy to whisper. Luckily, none of Sirius' newfound clan seemed to care, as his voice echoed through the cave.

"Looking for you, well, finding you actually."

"How did you find me? I've only been gone a day."

"You came up in a prophecy from a hag that I received recently," I explained, as casually as I could.

"What, really?"

"Yep. Now, are you coming back with me, or do I have to drag you? Please don't make me drag you, you look heavy."

"I can't come back with you, Professor. I think people are out to get me in Streya, and I'm causing you so much trouble, I can't sleep at night over it. I don't like being a burden." Sirius' enormous grey eye swam with about a bucket's worth of tears, before he blinked it away.

I opened my mouth to speak, to argue I suppose, but then closed it again. I took a slow breath, and tried to imagine what it must feel like to be the new infinite. To be expected to fill the shoes of Cora Olympia. To deal with that, whilst shadowy figures were trying to kidnap you, and pushy governors that have never met you tried to control your future.

"I'm not here to drag you back to Streya kicking and

screaming, Sirius. But I do want you to come back with me. So, I promise we won't go back until we've got a plan to sort out at least some of what's going on. First things first, we need to work out who sent those kidnappers to get you, and make sure you're protected."

Sirius nodded, a hint of a smile playing at the side of his lips. "Why are you so good to me, Professor?"

"I suppose I'm trying to live up to the person I'm replacing. You might have some idea of what that's like?"

"Maybe an inkling," Sirius said, loosing a little cyclopean chuckle.

"And please don't worry about causing me trouble. My life had been becoming worryingly straightforward until you three came along. I needed the shake up," I said, returning a little laugh of my own. I wished I could put a reassuring hand on his shoulder, but to do so I'd have to drift right out of his eyeline.

"Do you think I could stay here then? Just until you work out what's going on and Streya is safe again?"

"I don't think it's a good idea for you to stay out here on your own, Sirius. If we can find you in a day, it won't be too long before other, less friendly people do," I said, walking a tricky balance between being gentle and also scaring him into seeing things my way.

"What can they do to me here? I'm protected, I'm part of the herd," said Sirius, gesturing broadly to the cyclopes dotted across the cave floor.

"Sirius, these people are powerful. If they want you out of here, they will get you out of here. Dealing with a few cyclopes is a low price to pay for getting their hands on the infinite, trust me."

"I'd like to see them try," said Sirius, puffing out his enormous chest defiantly. I'd done too good a job of scaring away his fears.

"Fine, but if your cyclopes bodyguards run off, I expect you to come find me," I said, turning my back on him and beginning to drift away, a plan already formulating in my head.

"Wait, really? I can stay?" Sirius bellowed. I didn't respond, I was scheming.

"Why isn't he with you?" asked Wayne, aghast, as I touched down with the group again.

"Just trust me a second. Percy, I need Styx to give the cyclopes a fright," I said, trying my best to ignore the slight panic in Wayne's voice.

"Oh, he's going to love this. You guys, make sure to keep clear of the exits," said Percy, mischief flashing across his face as he turned his attention to Styx.

"Is he going to do what I think he is going to do?" Wayne asked, nervously.

I simply nodded, as we pressed ourselves against the cave wall. A faintly blue glistening mist was already beginning to pour from his wings, and pooling on the cave floor like ribbons of cake batter, before melting into a baking tin. A perimeter of frost inched away from him, picking up speed as it went. Before long it had blanketed the whole of the cave floor in icy, whitish blue. My skin prickled with unnatural cold, as the still air became cloudy with the cyclopes' breath. It was for this power that the grave dragons were given their name, and it was also one of the least understood in all the world.

Even in the excitement of it, something rattled in the

back of my mind. Something primal that told me to run and hide and cower and make peace with whatever gods I hoped were listening, but I didn't. I watched, as out of the misty air, vague shapes began to appear. At first, just little circles, and then crude faces, moaning into focus. A shiver ran up my back, and my body went stiff as one of the faces loomed past us, crashing into a cyclops, and immediately encasing him in a shell of frost. Within moments, the cave became an echoing chamber of deafening low screams and growling and yelping and hollering, as more and more explosions of frost erupted, like corn popping on the stove. Cyclopes all around were struggling to control the rearing, trumpeting oliphants, already trying to make for the exit.

Then it happened. The ground in the centre of the cave cracked, and a pallid, off-white hand emerged from the earth, grabbing at a nearby cyclops' ankle. A crude command in a language that had never been written down burst from the creatures' mouths, and a stampede of oliphants and cyclopes made for the exit. I stuck out my hand, pressing Astrid and Orion well into the wall, as both of them looked on, wide eyed and shivering.

"That's enough." Percy's voice echoed through the now empty cave, as he placed a hand on Styx's neck. At once, the mist ceased to pour from Styx's wings, and within seconds, the faces were just crude shapes again, and then mist, and then nothing. The only audible sound was our chattering teeth, bouncing off the cave walls. The unnatural chill faded, as a few bony hands receded back into the earth. I'd never seen them make it further out than that, and Percy assured me that I didn't want to.

"Sirius, they've run off, are you going to come find me

now?" I called to the one remaining cyclops, still standing dumbstruck in the corner.

Sirius didn't put up much more of a protest once the cyclopes had fled. He came with us on the condition that we didn't go back to Streya, which suited me just fine. It was hard to know who to trust in the school, and if mysterious kidnappers could turn up once, there was nothing to say they wouldn't do so again. So, the field trip was extended, and it was one of the first lessons I hadn't stolen from Cora.

"Until we have a better understanding of what is happening in Streya, we're not going back there. So, in the meantime, I thought we could get cracking on making your lenses," I said the next morning, over our breakfast of the unidentified scorched thing Wayne had found for us. Absentmindedly, I poked at the fire with my coal studded cane. The clouds were looming low, and it was unusually cool that morning, especially by the typically hot and dry standards of the Titanic Lands.

"How are we going to do that without materials?" asked Astrid, the only member of our jolly band who wasn't especially pleased not to be back at home. She wasn't getting on very well with her sleeping mat.

"What materials would those be?" I asked, looking for a teachable moment to pounce on.

"Well, like the lava stone in my beads, or the sapphire in your navy ring. We don't have any of that kind of thing here."

"Ah, I see. You think lenses require rare and valuable materials to match the nature or colour of the hue you're making?"

"Well, don't you?" asked Orion, who'd only given me half of his attention at most so far this morning. The other half was still buried in his book of rare and powerful lenses. I smiled and shook my head. Reaching up, I removed my glasses to show them.

"How do you think this lens relates to bronze light?" I asked them around the fire.

"Are the frames not made of bronze?" Sirius asked, licking his fingers. He was the only one of us who'd managed to chew through the meal.

"Nope, they're varnished wood."

Astrid and Orion stared at the frames, puzzled for some time. Finally, Orion delved back into his book, and Astrid pulled out one of her own.

"Shall I give you a clue?" I asked.

"I'll get it," said Astrid under her breath, rapidly scanning the page.

"Yes please," said Sirius, discreetly rolling his eyes in both their directions.

"Think about what bronze light actually does," I said.

"It lets you fly, doesn't it?" asked Wayne. He'd been watching the class from a few feet away, since he found himself at a bit of a loose end. I had half a mind to ask him to go and find us something a bit more edible.

"No, it lets you control the mass and force of an object. To fly with it, you simply decrease your mass until you're lighter than air, and then exert force in the direction of travel you're interested in," said Astrid, giving an almost perfect textbook answer.

"Remember, a lens doesn't have to literally represent the hue it's producing," I said sagely, watching them ponder my cryptic clue.

"They weren't your glasses originally!" Orion blurted out, closing his book abruptly. I resisted the urge to grin triumphantly at finally winning his attention.

"Correct! In fact, I don't need glasses at all. The lenses are just normal glass, it's all about the frames in this case," I explained.

"So, who did the frames belong to?" asked Sirius.

"Anyone care to guess?" I asked, directing my attention to Orion.

"Someone who represented, or relates to what bronze light can do, like—"

"A bronze light walker!" Sirius blurted out excitedly, cutting Orion off. I simply shook my head.

"A mathematician?" Orion asked, more than told.

"Yes, correct. One of Cor— I mean, Professor Olympia's old students was fascinated by the concept of using force with the maximum of efficiency. Designing large complex contraptions that relied on counterweights and levers and axis and things like that to chuck stuff a great distance. She gave me his frames when I wanted to make a bronze lens."

In the end, his contraptions had proved altogether too powerful. He tried to use them as a means of transport, with himself as a test subject. Hence, the glasses being up for grabs. It was a miracle they'd survived his landing.

"So, for silver, we just need something that might

represent travel," said Astrid, inspiration firing in her eyes, as her mind raced.

"What about something like—"

Orion stopped mid-sentence, as an unfathomably deep rumbling sound issued from the sky above us. Styx, Nova and Tera stirred from their slumber, all turning their sharp eyes to the low-hanging clouds.

"Thunder?" asked Sirius, getting to his feet as the ground beneath us began to tremble slightly.

"Earthquake maybe?" Orion guessed.

"*Bigger,*" came Tera's voice. Already her claws were plunging into the dirt, coaxing out roots and vines, and forming them into a cluster around the camp, like a sort of giant bird's nest.

"Percy, what's happening?" I asked, doing my best not to let fear into my voice, as my breath ran short. Small crackles of lightning were ripping through the darkening sky barely a mile from us.

"That cloud's getting very dark. I think it's a thunderstorm," said Astrid, pointing to a cloud that had been rapidly turning from white to grey, and was now almost completely black.

"It's not the cloud, get low and hold on to something," said Percy, as he darted to my side. With his hand on my back, he forced me to my knees, not taking his eyes off the blackening cloud. The rumble grew louder with every second.

"Is this what I think it—" All the air rushed out of my lungs, as an impossibly large shape emerged from the cloud line. A great copper-hued fin flashed, as lightning peeled off into the clouds, and then the eye, the great, milky white eye, bigger than a house. I think I'd have screamed, had I the breath. More of the leviathan was emerging by the second. It must have been a mile long, maybe even longer, from its tail to the tip of its great bronze horn. It resembled an impossibly large whale, with a purple underbelly, lined with copper ribs. Lightning sizzled from its back, as it ploughed towards the ground. My body braced instinctively. A giant cloud of dust and wind exploded out in all directions, barrelling towards us and flattening trees and flinging stones as it went, and causing the very ground beneath us to shake.

"BRACE YOURSELVES!" Percy yelled, thrusting out a hand, and conjuring a wall of ice into the path of the cloud. With my eyes streaming, I took hold of the roots Tera had conjured. My body lifted clean off the ground, and it was hard to breathe, fighting to take the rushing air into my lungs. Suddenly, Percy's hand was pressed into my shoulder, forcing me back down to the ground, while the other wrapped around my hand, holding me fast to Tera's nest. I flinched, as a loud shattering sound filled the air, and cold and wet sprayed across us. Something dark and unrecognisable had smashed into Percy's wall of ice, fracturing it. Perhaps a tree dislodged by the gale. I tried to force light into my glasses, to make us all heavier, only to find they'd been blown clean off my face.

"I can't hold on!" I turned towards Orion. his whole body was waving in the air like a flag, as his fingers slipped from the vine he was holding.

"Got him," Sirius called from behind me, followed by a huge flash of grey light.

"He's slipping!" I screamed, the wind stealing most of

my voice. I watched in helpless horror, as Orion's fingers peeled free from the vine and he launched into the air, only to be snatched by a giant hand surging out of my peripheral vision. I turned back to find Orion clutched to Cyclops Sirius's chest, as he huddled on the ground.

"Is Astrid alright?" I bellowed, my vision going blurry as wind-whipped tears streamed down my face.

"Wayne has her," Percy yelled from above me.

"Tera, are you okay?" I thought as loudly as I could in every direction, as I couldn't catch sight of her.

"Styx has sheltered me in a sphere of ice. I'm quite safe," her voice rolled calmly into my head, just as the windstorm came to an abrupt stop, and relief washed over me.

My ears felt empty, and I could fill my lungs again. My hands were stiff and my knuckles white, as I prised them off the vines. An arm wrapped around my waist and pulled me back, and I found myself resting against Percy, whose heart I could feel pounding through his chest into my back.

"Everyone alright?" I wheezed. I turned just in time to catch a flash of grey light, as Sirius returned to his human form, in his shorts and a sun-bleached t-shirt. His wardrobe gave the distinct impression he used to live by the sea.

"You saved me!" Orion said, as he pulled Sirius into a tight hug. Sirius had about half a foot on Orion, so he had to go onto his tiptoes to fling his arms around Sirius's shoulders.

"Hey, don't mention it," said Sirius, as he gently patted Orion on the back.

"Is that a leviathan?" asked Astrid, wiping a tear from

her cheek as she and Wayne made their way over. She was hobbling a little, and looked as though she'd grazed her knee. Amusingly, her usually immaculately neat blonde hair had been wind swept to quite an impressive effect. It was the sort of hair style you'd end up with by some happy accident, and then never be able to replicate on demand.

"It is," I said, hesitant to turn back and face the thing. Even from this far away, there was something about looking at a creature that large, knowing it was alive, that made my stomach churn and my skin crawl.

"I've never seen one land," said Wayne, who seemed to share none of my reservations as he looked over at the thing. His eyes were about as wide as they had been during our first meeting, when Cora had blasted Nova straight through a portal.

"They almost never do. They even give birth in the air," I said.

Rattling off leviathan trivia, somehow made the whole situation feel less death defying. I slowly turned on the spot, looking past the rapidly melting wall of ice, and took in the sight of the leviathan. Again, my stomach lurched, and I felt as though I might be sick. I was somehow drawn into its huge, milky white eye, half closed, with little flickers of lightning flashing inside it. Its underbelly was armoured with what looked like six bronze ribs of external carapace, each of which was hundreds of feet long and as wide as a back-alley street. The same strange, almost metallic material covered all of its back like a shell. Even beached, a small blanket of cloud surrounded it, crackling with electricity.

"I'm going to go take a closer look," said Percy, from

behind me. I heard him take one step towards the creature, then let out a groan. I sagged as his weight slumped against me.

"Percy, what's wrong?" I wheeled around, struggling slightly to support him, until Wayne darted in to take the strain. I scanned Percy, hot, frantic panic flushing through me. His face was pale, but his face was always pale.

"My side," he groaned, slumping down onto the rock I'd formerly been perched on, hissing defensively as he gingerly raised a finger to the right side of his chest. He wore black leather, so it wasn't immediately apparent, but there was a shiny slickness to the place his fingers brushed against.

"You're bleeding!" My voice cracked as I lurched forward, only barely restraining myself from pawing at his side.

"I'm fine," he moaned, unconvincingly.

"You're not!" I almost sobbed, tears stinging my eyes.

"Let me look," said Astrid, crouching by Percy's side.

"Be careful," I begged, my voice shrinking.

"This might sting," Astrid said, apologetically, as she delicately ran her fingers along Percy's side. He flinched, and his jaw clenched, but he didn't make a sound. My eyes met with his, and he forced a smile.

"I'm okay," he whispered. I couldn't reply. A painful lump had filled my throat, leaving me to shake my head.

"Broken ribs, and a nasty cut. Must have been hit by some heavy debris. It'll need treating," Astrid explained, her voice suddenly calm and unemotional. Doing an impression of her father, perhaps.

"We've got to go back." The words spilled out of me, as my mind went blank with panic.

"We can't, we don't know who else is after me," said Sirius, panicking himself.

"I could treat it with my lens," said Astrid, reaching for the flower pressed book.

"No!" I darted forward, grabbing her wrist, more tightly than I meant to.

"Why not? I've seen my father do it a thousand times." She yanked herself away, glaring at me.

"Because yellow light isn't about healing, it's about manipulating the body. It's not just a case of willing him better. It's about making the bones and the flesh knit themselves back together. And what if you go too far? What if you fuse his skin and veins? Or turn a lung to bone, trying to fix a rib? Your first time using that lens will not be on my husband!" I'd been yelling. I hadn't meant to, but in the silence that followed, it became painfully apparent that I'd been yelling.

"Perhaps I could help." Tera's voice broke the silence, but only for me.

"Yes, please, Tera, go quickly." My heart pounded in my ears as I locked eyes with Tera. She slipped past Wayne and Astrid, coming to stop at Percy's side, her fiery green eyes glowed emerald, as she focused on his wound.

"What's she doing?" Sirius asked, taking a step forward.

"I can't believe I didn't think of it. I'm stupid," I muttered, watching as a small mound of moss started to grow out of the slick, shiny wound dripping red from Percy's side.

"You were scared," Percy said gently, reaching up with his left arm to squeeze my shoulder.

"Think of what?" Sirius asked.

"Dragon magic. It can share a resonance with our light walker hues, fire dragons and red hues for example. Forest dragons share with green and yellow," I explained, not taking my eyes from Percy's side for a moment, as the moss grew and flowers bloomed out of the wound.

"How could you be expected to know that?" asked Sirius, in a misguided attempt at consolation.

"I wrote my thesis about it," I replied, glumly, watching as the moss and flowers rapidly withered and dropped.

"Is that supposed to happen?" Astrid asked, leaning in. Her interest was hopefully a sign that she didn't intend to hold my outburst against me.

"It means it's done," I whispered, drawing in as close as I could. Percy's side was still sticky with a dark reddish brown, barely distinguishable from the leather. But it was no longer shiny, no longer dripping.

"I think it worked," I beamed. "How do you feel?"

"Fine." Percy flashed a smile, stood, and flinched. A moment later, a grinding, clunking sound filled the air, and my breakfast hit the back of my throat.

"What was that?" Wayne asked.

"His ribs grinding together," said Astrid, deflating, whilst the rest of us flinched.

"Percy," I whispered, my eyes swimming as they fixed on his pained face.

"I'm fine," he muttered, forcing another smile.

"It can't be," I heard Orion mutter from behind me, sounding almost as heartbroken as I felt.

"Tera's still young, her powers mustn't be developed enough," I said, turning to offer him an explanation, only to find Orion frantically scrambling around in the dirt and debris of the crash.

"Orion? What are you doing?" Astrid asked.

"It's gone!" he cried, looking up at us, his swirling void like eyes wide and desperate.

"What is?" Sirius asked, sounding utterly bewildered.

"My book! The book on the lenses! It's gone, blown off in the crash!" Orion wailed, still crawling around in the wreckage of broken roots and torn tents.

"I think we've got bigger problems than a missing bookmark," said Sirius, more gently than I could have managed. The sound of my husband's broken bones grinding together still echoing in my head.

"You don't understand! We can't go back without it," Orion all but wailed.

"What?" Astrid and I asked in simultaneous horror.

"It's the shroud! I was reading about it. Its last known owner was an opal-hued light walker named Sky Everbright. He went missing not long after his apprenticeship under Olympia."

"I read about him. He was a prodigy, he was studying ancient civilisations, using Opal light to look into the past. Streya went into mourning when he went missing," said Astrid.

"I know this, but why does that mean we can't go home?" I asked.

"It's a violet lens that infers on its owner some of the power of The Night Mother, the self-fulfilling prophecy."

"So, whatever she says comes true?" Astrid asked.

"Not quite, but it'll play tricks on the minds of those that see it and hear her words. I bet that's how she got the governors on side," said Orion.

"I see," I said gravely, as the weight of the problem dawned on me.

"Sorry, what is all this about a Night Mother and a Shroud? Why does everyone seem to know about this but me?" asked Sirius, looking bewildered.

"It's that shawl she's always got on, it's a powerful lost artifact," explained Astrid.

"But what does all this mean?" Sirius asked.

"It means Ithaca is lying about who she is. When she first turned up, she told us she was violet hued, but she wields a violet lens. And not only that, it means she was likely the person that made Sky disappear all those years ago. Which means she must be incredibly powerful, it takes more than your average light walker to defeat an opal."

"Plus, if she's gone after an apprentice before, who's to say she wouldn't go after one again?" said Orion, casting his heavy gaze towards Sirius, who was quickly turning as pale as Percy.

"I still don't understand why this means we can't go home. If we know all this surely, we should go back and confront her," said Astrid.

"And how exactly do we go about confronting a woman who can control destiny with her shawl?" snapped Orion.

"Well, surely there must be a way around that," Astrid replied, recoiling defensively.

"There is, I was just about to read about it, in my missing book." Orion scowled, casting his eyes around wildly.

"Ah." Astrid deflated, as my stomach twisted itself into a heavy knot. The solution to several problems at once was becoming clear, and I didn't like it.

"You guys go without me, I'll stay here. She can't get me out here, and Percy needs healing. I'm not going back. Don't worry, I'll be fine. You just go I'll—"

"Stop it!" Wayne reached out, grabbing Sirius by the wrist, as his pacing began to take him further and further from the group.

"There is another solution," I said dryly, my throat throbbing.

"Perhaps I could try to cover her in darkness. You must have noticed, Professor, that day in your office when the governors tried to take Sirius. The way she cowered away from my light?" asked Orion, offering Sirius and Percy an encouraging smile.

"I did—"

"So that settles it then, we go back, and Orion takes care of her cloak," said Astrid.

"That sounds dangerous," said Sirius, nervously.

"I could try," said Orion, getting back to his feet.

"The very fact that she is afraid of you is why you should be especially wary, Orion," I warned.

"I'm not scared of her," he replied, in a defiant and slightly juvenile tone.

"Well, you should be. If Ithaca was capable of

defeating Sky whilst he was in possession of that shroud, we have to be especially careful."

"So, what then?" Orion snapped, exasperated.

"We fight fire with fire."

"I've got you covered there," said Wayne, forcing a laugh.

"Not quite, Wayne. I mean, free folk magic. That's what the shroud is, and that's where we'll find the solution. The free folk could heal Percy too."

"I'm—"

"Don't you dare say you're fine again. I can still hear your ribs in my head?" I snapped. Pangs of guilt cloyed at my throat the moment I turned and saw Percy's face fall.

"And where do we get free folk magic?" Orion said, sulkily.

"Luckily, I just so happened to save a fairy princess's life a few weeks back, so they owe me a favour," I said, trying to force a smile. Percy had been putting on a brave face with broken ribs, the least I could do was reciprocate.

"You did what?" asked Percy, trudging stiffly towards me.

"Turns out, that fairy that Wayne's delightful friend took hostage, the one that they wanted me to trade my life for, Ailsa, she's Prince Consort Bren's niece," I explained.

"Your friend did what?" asked Sirius, turning a rather stern look on Wayne.

"It's all water under the bridge, we'd just best not mention who Wayne is to them, that's not really the point. The point is, I have a favour to cash in, and this seems like the time to do it," I said. Wayne visibly gulped.

"So … how do we get to the free folk to cash the

favour in?" asked Astrid, obviously eager to take her leave of the Titanic Lands.

"You can't portal into free folk lands, and there is no way Percy is up to the flight," said Orion, who seemed to have now set his heart on having a face-to-face confrontation with Ithaca, preferably within the next few hours.

"There is a little village on the outskirts of the forest of Cerunos, we'll go there," I said, catching Percy's eyes softening, as my stomach twisted again. I met his gaze and shrugged, as if to say, *needs must.*

"So, we'll portal there then?" asked Astrid, hopefully.

"Well, Orion is right, Percy shouldn't be flying right now. Besides, it's best we don't fly in. I suspect Ithaca, or whoever is after Sirius, will have worked out by now that we've gone after him with dragons. If they've got any sense, they'll have eyes on the sky above this village."

"Why would she be spying on this particular village?" asked Astrid, sounding puzzled.

"It's where I'm from. It'd make sense for me to hide Sirius there," I said, trying to squash the image of Mum's stacks of letters out of my head.

"So, are Orion and I going to portal us there?" asked Astrid, with a frankly worrying level of confidence.

"Are you mad? Your first portal being a long-distance travel with live travellers? Absolutely not, that'd be saving Ithaca a job!" I couldn't seem to stop myself from snapping at them anymore.

"So, how then?" asked Astrid, now sounding a little bruised.

"Nicholas Copper is going to send us. We just need to get a message to him."

"And how are we going to do that, since I assume you're not going to let me try to speak into his mind?" asked Orion.

"Believe it or not, my grumpy apprentices, I do have a couple of tricks up my sleeve that you have not seen," I said, slipping my hand into my pocket to take hold of my lucky rabbit's foot.

"So, how then?" Sirius asked.

"Gold light. We just need to wait for nightfall," I explained, watching their faces shift from pouty to puzzled.

* * *

I spent the rest of the day trying to make Percy as comfortable as I could, which as it turned out was not very comfortable at all, and trying not to bite anyone's head off. I wasn't particularly successful at that either. By nightfall, we'd all but stopped speaking to each other.

"Here we go," I said, rising from my hard stone perch to take in the sky.

Closing my left eye, I tried to work out exactly where we were in relation to the stars. I was never the best at reading star maps, but to me it looked as though we were directly beneath Sharman, the brightest green star in the sky, that formed the eye of the constellation of the forest dragon, Eden, which felt apt.

"Would you say we were directly beneath Sharman?" I asked the group at large.

"I'd say we were between Sharman, Sharman Minor

and Eden's Claw," said Sirius, holding his hands up, and forming a box to look through.

"Sirius is right," said Wayne, which wasn't very helpful since I was fairly sure he'd have said that even if Sirius was wrong. He'd been sucking up ever since Sirius heard the rest of the story of our first encounter.

"Aster never was very good at reading maps," Percy chuckled, then groaned.

"Careful," I winced, turning to him. The urge to touch him and hold him was overwhelming, but I knew I'd just make things work.

"I'm okay. I'm about to see something beautiful after all," Percy smiled, and my cheeks burned, although hopefully the darkness of the night hid that from my apprentices.

"What's he talking about?" Sirius asked, curiously.

"Just watch," said Percy, in a hushed voice. I shook my head and tried to ignore the feeling of

Percy's eyes on me. I found the twinkling green light within me, took a deep breath out and pressed it into my father's lucky rabbit's foot. There was a pause, then a glittering golden ring shone out of me into the darkness, and deep inside me I let go a call.

Come to me on a wing, a pulse of golden light carried my thoughts out into the valleys and crevasses and caves of the Titanic Lands like a wave, followed by a peaceful stillness.

"What now?" Sirius hissed, breaking the silence.

"Just wait," Percy hissed back. And they waited, five seconds stretched into ten and then twenty and then I heard it. The flutter of a tiny wing, and then another and another, and then a swarm of them. A cloud of small birds and moths, all of them with glowing golden eyes. When I opened my mouth again, it wasn't words that left my lips, but a harmony, a beautiful lilting, rising, falling wall of sound, reverberating out of me, carrying a message.

"Find Nicholas Copper, at the top of his tower, and tell him, this is where I am." As I thought of him, I envisioned Nick, in his high glass domed tower, and then I envisioned us, beneath the stars, just where Sirius had said we were. I held tight to the rabbit's foot, breathed out and let loose a whistle I could never normally muster. One last burst of golden light flashed from me, and my winged friends scattered into the wind, headed for Streya.

"I'm sorry, did you just sing to the birds and have them deliver a message for you?" asked Sirius, his mouth agog.

"This is why Styx says you're a princess," Percy chuckled, groaned, and the grinding sound set my teeth on edge again.

"It's an advanced golden magic, trans-species communication. It's supposed to be very tricky to pull off," said Astrid, filling the silence that followed like a living textbook.

"Well, I was born to it, my name is Shepard after all," I said, forcing a smile as we settled in to wait.

* * *

Whatever miasma of angst that had descended between us all, seemed to fade after I sent my message. Astrid, under Percy's instruction, had set about making a stew, after complaining that she was sick of the scorched and, in her words, 'inedible rubbish' that Wayne had managed to scrounge up for us. I wouldn't have put it so bluntly myself, but I didn't necessarily disagree. Sirius had found his way to forgiving Wayne for his past transgression, and they were now entertaining themselves by renaming the stars. Only Orion remained sullen, almost preoccupied; the idea of defeating Ithaca himself seemed to have taken root.

"How's that stew coming along?" Wayne asked, the savoury scents steadily overwhelming his interest in the stars.

"Patience, we have to let the flavours develop," said Percy. He tasted the tip of the stick he was using as a spoon and frowned. He was missing his spice rack.

"It's not as though we've got anywhere to rush off to anyway," said Sirius, as he bedded down on his sleeping mat, absentmindedly spinning his ebony armband on one outstretched forefinger.

"You're going to lose that," said Astrid, as she stabbed irritably at the stew.

"Please let's not lose two lenses in one day," I groaned, rubbing my palms into my eyes as I tried not to dwell on the fact that I couldn't fly anymore. I couldn't step weightless into the air and soar through the sky, with the wind sending streaks of tears down my face. I couldn't use bronze magic anymore, the first hue I'd ever dreamed of learning, gone. Lost in a pile of shattered twigs somewhere in the land of titans. Probably lying next to a book about lenses.

* * *

"Aster Shepard, you'd better not have misread these damn stars, where are you?" Nick's voice snapped me from my not particularly restful slumber. I could just about make out his silhouette about fifty feet from our camp, as the flashes of the beached leviathan cast him against the darkness.

"Coming," I called, groaning as I rose from my sleeping mat. My voice was met with a chorus of groans from my disgruntled and half-asleep apprentices. I inched my way past their discarded belongings, dispersed amongst the rubble and detritus of the landing, and carefully stepped over their silhouettes, cast in the light of the embers. I couldn't help noticing Wayne's head resting on Sirius's chest, as I slinked past the perimeter of what remained of our camp. Tera followed, gliding over the mess. Her eyes were like roaring fires of green against the darkness.

"A large man is here to see you," she whispered into my mind, bounding ahead and leading me to Nick, who I found sitting with his legs dangling over the edge of a rocky outcropping not far from our camp, staring into the darkness. He was wearing one of those floppy hats you see people sleeping in, in illustrated children's books. I watched him gazing into the night, only for a small flash of lightning to burn the silhouette of the leviathan into the black for the briefest of moments.

"Is that what I think it is?" he asked, as I approached. I perched next to him, and let my legs swing over the craggy edge.

"Yep, it nearly blew us all away when it crash landed. Percy was hurt, badly."

"How bad?" he asked.

"Broken ribs, he's in a lot of pain, but he'll live. You know how he is, tough."

"Good. In that case, it serves you right running off and leaving me back at the university, managing Vega's moods alone." Nick huffed.

"Has it been bad since we left?" I asked, guiltily.

"Bad? The governors are up in arms, when Vega isn't raging against them, she's ranting to me about you and Cora up and leaving her. Oh, and you should hear the rumours the kids are coming up with about you."

"Any good ones?" I asked, offering a feeble smile.

"My personal favourites are that you assassinated Cora to get her out of the way so you could kidnap the new infinite and raise him as your own personal super weapon. There is also another good one about you two eloping, which seems to neglect the fact your husband went with you." Nick's signature deep chuckle rolled out of him, and my feeble smile got a bit stronger. Nick could never hold on to a bad mood for long.

"I need your help, Nick," I said, when his laugh had died down to a titter.

"Only if you come back and set everything straight."

"I want to, Nick, but I can't, not yet. There are dangerous people in Streya, and they're trying to take Sirius away. The last thing Cora asked of me was to hold on tight to my apprentices, she had to know something like this might happen." Nick's face fell, and his thick, bushy brows furrowed.

"You know you don't have to do something just because it's what Cora wanted, right?"

"Nick, I know it's dangerous, but this is Cora we're talking about, she knew—"

"Don't 'Cora knew best' me. I knew Cora just like you did, Aster, and that's why I know she wasn't infallible. She was capable of being wrong, and maybe what she asked of you was wrong. What she asked of me certainly feels wrong."

"You mean keeping the anomaly secret?" I asked, sensing this mood of his probably wasn't really about me.

"Yes, I mean keeping the anomaly secret. We found, no sorry, I found a source of power out in the deep, dark, frozen places of space that radiates more energy than a star, and she wants it kept from everyone forever. Why? You should have seen her when I showed it to her, Aster, it was like she'd seen a ghost. Have you ever seen Cora scared? Cause I hadn't, not until that moment. Her letter be damned, I kept studying it, and you know what I found?" Nick was heated now. Spit flew from his lips as he spoke, and his eyes flashed silver against the night. I hadn't seen him this animated in years.

"What, Nick?"

"Somebody made it. Somebody like us. All that darkness, it's void light, swirling around, sucking and absorbing. That means it's there on purpose; it's there for a reason. It could be doing something to our world or our stars. Something is anchoring it there, and I can't for the life of me think what could be powerful enough to do that. And when the star bloom happened, it was putting off enough energy to wipe worlds out of the night sky, Aster, and she doesn't want anyone to know about it. So, yeah, Cora asked you to do something, but that doesn't mean you've got to do it. You've got a mind of your own, a brilliant mind, and you're not using it." Nick let out an exasperated sigh, and his shoulders sagged.

"How long have you been holding on to all of that?" I asked, placing a consoling hand on his shoulder.

"Too long," said Nick, laying back against the cool stone and gazing up into the stars. I lay back with him, propping myself up on my elbows.

"I know she was just a person, Nick, and maybe what she's asking me is wrong, but it doesn't feel wrong. She's not asking me to hide some arcane vortex in the deep dark of space from people. She's asking me to keep my apprentices safe when people come for them. That can't be wrong, can it?"

"It's certainly a less morally dubious request than mine," said Nick, flatly. All the fire had gone from his voice now.

"I'm sorry you got stuck with the dark scary vortex, when I just got teenagers," I said, with a small laugh, patting Nick on the back.

"So, what is it you need?" asked Nick, stifling a small chuckle.

"I need to speak to Queen Gloria, which means we're going to Shepard's Pastor." My voice dropped to a whisper, even though no one else was around.

"You've not been back there in a while. Looking forward to it?" asked Nick, in a gentle tone that suggested he already knew the answer.

"Needs must. We can't go to Gloria empty handed, or dusty and stinking, and Shepard's Pastor is right on the border."

"And you think there is a gift in the Pastor that will win over Queen Gloria?" asked Nick, sceptically.

"She owes me a favour. Once we've got what we need from her, I'll come back to Streya, I promise."

"Just be careful, Aster," said Nick, heaving himself back to his feet and dusting himself off.

"You be careful too, and keep an eye on Ithaca. Don't be alone with her, and don't let her think you don't trust her," I said, trying to sound as serious as possible. Nick paused for a second then nodded his understanding.

"Gotcha. Oh, and one more thing, what do you know about wyverns?" Nick asked.

"Well, if you ask Percy, he'll say big flying lizards. They're like dragons without the elemental connection, magic or intelligence, why?"

"A big flock of them was sighted, on the Streyan border. Just wondered if we should be worried?" Nick asked.

I shrugged. "I shouldn't think so. They were probably on a hunt that took them out of their usual territory. Or hey, perhaps whatever grounded that thing flushed them out. Either way, like I said, they're not like dragons, not as bright, shouldn't be a problem. You could use the dim sickness centre guard to scare them off if needs be." I caught myself smiling at the feeling of being useful.

"Right, well that's something at least. Shall we get you on your way? I assume you're not here alone, where is the rest of the merry camping band?" asked Nick, his usual jovial character re-asserting itself.

I turned and pointed back to the camp, just as the last

dying embers of the fire licked up into new flame. Wayne's work, I guessed.

* * *

"This is not how I imagined the forest of Cerunos would look," said Wayne, as we stepped into the cold, grey country light that emerges before the sun. When it's technically morning, but nobody in their right mind would ever think of it that way unless they worked on a farm or a boat.

"Well, perhaps you imagined rightly, as this is not the forest of Cerunos," I said, as I set off for a particularly high roofed barn a few hundred yards away across a dewy field.

"So where are we then?" asked Sirius, who seemed quite at home bounding through the fields.

"Somewhere we can make ourselves presentable. We are visiting royalty after all, and we just so happen to be on Cerunos' border," I explained.

"Care to be more specific?" asked Astrid, reminding me of myself, getting frustrated every time Cora insisted on being knowing and mysterious, rather than straightforward and direct. I understood why she did it now. It was so much more fun to be in the know, and it served as a good distraction from the pressure of being the one expected to have a plan.

"Shepard's Pastor."

"Shepard as in, like Professor Shepard?" asked Sirius.

"The very same," I said, trying the door to the barn with a gentle push. It creaked open without resistance, and smelt pleasingly dry inside. The barn was floored with dark wooden boards, and was largely empty. Dust swirled in disturbed air and light shone through the cobwebs, making them appear like golden glass. The edges of the barn were bordered by a series of hay bales with blankets thrown over them, offering their services as makeshift tables and couches. At the very back of the barn there was a staircase, which led to a second-floor balcony. It was haunted by the ghosts of guests past, looking over the edge, holding their drinks, and smiling down at the dancers below. Just before the staircase was a stage, with various instruments strewn about it. Try as I might, I couldn't resist a smile at my mother's party barn, and all the memories that it conjured.

"Make yourselves comfortable. We'll and introduce ourselves in the morning," I said, reclining across one of the blanketed bales.

"We've not been here in a while," said Percy, as he gingerly slid off Styx's back. He took a seat next to me and pulled the edges of the blanket around us both.

"Had to break the streak some time, I guess," I said, smiling weakly, wishing for nothing more than to curl up against him and hide in his arms.

I decided to leave Wayne and my apprentices in the barn, whilst we made first introductions. Introducing everyone at once would be a nightmare. With Percy on the back of Styx, he, Tera and I set off together to walk the track up to my family home. it was a large farmhouse that had in its heyday, housed myself, my three sisters, my mum and dad and my grandparents, although they had since passed, and I'd moved away. It was painted a deep mustard yellow, although Dad always insisted on calling it gold. Smoke was pouring out of the chimney as we wandered up the cobbled path. The smell of apples, cinnamon and baking pastry wafted out of the open front door. Dad opened it in the morning when he went out, and closed it in the evening when he got back, and anyone who wanted to pop round in between was always welcome. That's what they said, I'd never tested the axiom against a forest dragon, although I thought it unlikely to pose a problem.

"This is your home?" Tera asked.

"It's where I grew up, my home is in Streya," I spoke aloud so Percy could join in.

"I think you could have two homes, you know," said Percy, offering a gentle smile.

"You are nervous." Tera, I'd noticed, was rather fond of definitive statements.

"I am a little nervous," I agreed.

"Are they bad people?" she asked, in an unusually gentle register.

"Not at all, but would you mind waiting out of sight for a moment? This could get… hectic," I said softly, forcing a smile as I furiously blinked away a tear that had snuck up on me.

"As you wish." Tera bowed, and then disappeared into the hedge of wildflowers that

wrapped itself around the walls of my parents' home like a colourful, if rather thorny, scarf.

I winced as I helped Percy down from Styx. The sound

of grinding bones was unmissable, although he barely even flinched.

"You okay?" I asked, pausing with my hand raised to knock on the open door.

"I'm fine." he flashed a smile, and I resisted the urge to throw myself into his arms, before finally knocking.

"Room for a little one?" I asked, cringing at myself as I popped my head around the door.

"Is that my little professor I hear?" Mum's voice burst out of the kitchen full of excitement, and a moment later her face followed. She was in an almost floor-length navy-blue skirt, with a red apron covered in flour over a white frilly blouse. Her hair, like mine, was dark, long, and wavy, although hers was thinning a little now, and grey at the crown. She had painted her nails bright pink, but they were chipped and covered in flaky dough. Her face wore all the creases and markings of a life spent smiling in the sun, and her eyes were bright and golden.

"No need to make any f—"

A short, sharp whistle and a flash of gold from her eyes cut me off, followed momentarily by a streak of black fur shooting out the door. It probably took the form of a cat when it was still. Doubtless named Tatters, they were always named Tatters.

"I've sent Tatters to collect the others, won't be long. Can I fetch you some pie? It's ever so nice to see you, Percy dear. I think you might even be taller and more handsome than the last time we saw each other. When was that exactly? Gosh, last year, at mine and your fathers' fortieth anniversary I think it was, does that sound right, Aster dear? Anyway, sit, sit, I'll get that pie." Plenty of people talk to themselves, but no one could have a full conversation with themselves quite like Mum could. Especially when she was with company.

She shuffled us into the large living room as if sweeping dust along with a broom, and all but pushed us into a double wide squashy armchair. Squashy, misshapen furniture covered in blankets and cat hair was very in vogue in Shepard's Pastor.

"Haha, I don't think I've grown, Mrs Shepard, unless Aster's been stretching me in my sleep." Percy gave an easy laugh, he was better at my parents than me. I don't think she even noticed him flinch as his chest rose.

"Oh, what a laugh, stretching in your sleep, ha, you are funny Percy, funny and handsome, didn't my son do well. Oh, I can't wait for the others to get here, won't that be nice? I know, I'll do a nice dinner, what would you like Percy? You're looking a little pale. A roast perhaps? Love a nice roast, that'll put some colour in your cheeks." Mum chortled, her eyes glistening with the excitement of dinner plans.

"We can't stay long, Mum, just a flying trip, in and out before dinnertime." I spoke quickly, avoiding her gaze. Part of me was desperate to get away, another was disgusted with myself.

"Oh… well, you'll have pie on the fly." Mum beamed her dauntless smile.

To the untrained eye nothing was amiss, but the signs were there. Just for a second, the drop in the cheeks, and the shine in her eye. I was being disappointing again. I wanted to say something, to placate or soothe or justify, but finding the right words to answer that flicker had been one of the great failings of my life. I was musing on that, when the sound of bones grinding together twisted me back into focus. Mum had placed a hand on Percy's shoulder, and his ribs had crunched. Her expression changed in a second; her eyes furrowed, and her lips thinned as she looked at Percy's grimacing face, searchingly.

"Everything's fine," Percy answered a question not yet asked.

"Don't lie to your mother-in-law, Percy dear, what's wrong?" Mum asked, sharply.

"Broken rib, there was an accident. Please don't make a fuss, Mum, I'm gonna sort it out." I stared at my feet as I spoke.

"Don't make a fuss? You turn up out of the blue, flying visit, all mysterious, won't stay for tea and you're trying to hide a broken rib from me. Aster Shepard, you don't know your mother at all if you thought you were getting out of this without a thorough explanation." Mum huffed, then turned on her heel and stormed out of the room.

"Where are you going?" I called after her, half panicked, springing from my seat.

"To get Percy a piece of pie, the poor boy looks dreadful!" Mum yelled back.

"Oh." I slumped back into my chair, deflated.

"It's okay, I could eat some pie." Percy forced a smile, and his ice-blue eyes shined. You'd think they'd be cold, but he had such warmth to him, he always had. I'd almost got lost in them, when the sound of something clattering on the kitchen floor brought me screaming back into the present.

"Oh, my stars, there's a dragon in the window!"

Mum's voice carried through the whole house, as I let my face fall defeated into my hands.

* * *

"It's such a shame we didn't know you were coming in advance. We could have got the whole clan back together," said Mum, shooting me an admonishing look, as she offered each of my apprentices and Wayne a slice of pie.

"Who is everyone?" asked Sirius, bright eyed and interested, as he finished his second slice in two swift bites.

"Well, hang on I have to do them in order or I lose count," said Mum, putting down her pie to count off her fingers.

"There's really no need to—"

"Well, first of course there is our oldest, Andrea, named after my grandfather Andrew, she runs the local school now. Aster, I must have mentioned it in one of my letters. Gosh, you'll have to pay them a visit sometime soon, I remember your first day there in short trousers. Anyway, she's married a lovely local boy, and has a beautiful little girl named Ava." I almost choked on my tea at the mention of her name, although Mum didn't falter. "She has her second on the way, another girl, I suspect. Then of course, Aster, I named him that because the moment I saw those green eyes of his, I knew he'd be bright. Then there is Alexis, just eleven months between her and Aster, she's popping round. She's pregnant with her second, married to John, the oldest boy from the family one farm over. Then there is my baby, Anna, little miracle worker. She had triplets just a month back, I sent you a letter about it, but maybe it didn't arrive. We never heard back. Anyway, you've not met them yet, Aster, before you go perhaps you can zip over to see her, use some of that clever bronze light of yours." Mum was being tooth achingly sweet.

"I didn't know Professor Shepard had such a big family," said Sirius, enraptured.

"He doesn't mention us?" Mum asked, the slightest hint of a wound in her voice.

"I try to keep things… professional," I said, searching for a salve.

"Well, of course you do. It's a shame really, we don't visit as much as we'd like, none of us ever got the hang of that tricky silver light, and it's a devil to travel with all the littluns otherwise."

"Yep, silver's a tricky one," I agreed. I'd never put a great deal of work into trying to master it, but that fact didn't feel pertinent.

"So, Aster was the only one to come to Streya?" asked Wayne. Unwittingly picking at a scar that had never quite healed.

"Oh yes, we Shepards are like part of the furniture round here. But I remember the day the letter came—"

"Not 'the day the letter came' story again," said Alexis, as she trotted into the living room and slumped down next to me on the sofa, with her first daughter, my niece Amy asleep in her arms. I'd only seen pictures Mum had sent of her. She had the family hair alright, and no doubt, the golden eyes, too. It sounded cliché, but Alexis really was like a girl version of me. We were even the same height, same hair, same pale skin, same bookishness. Of course, her eyes were golden, but otherwise we were the spit of each other. People mistook us for twins growing up all the time.

"Oh, Alexis, you know how Ma likes to boast about that letter," said Dad, hobbling in behind her. They must have met each other on the road. He was in threadbare shorts that, by some miracle, Mum had kept white, and padded around in sandals. On top he wore something that was more patchwork than shirt at this point, and a leather cap cured by forty years of Dad sweating in the sun. All his hair had long since faded, but I was assured that in his youth he'd had a nice head of mousey curls, which would have matched his beard before it turned whitish grey. His eyes though, had never dimmed, big and warm and sparkly and golden. I'd always suspected Dad had a lot of light in him. I'd never seen his eyes grow dim, but couldn't say for sure, he barely ever used them.

"Hey, Dad," I said, offering a half-hearted wave.

"Well, aren't you a sight for sore eyes, come-er," said Dad, crossing the room and almost lifting me clean off the couch. He smelled of cut grass and wildflowers. I hugged him back, or did the best I could at least. Dad tended to squeeze the life out of me when he got his arms around me, before plopping me back down on the sofa.

"I don't see that it's much of a boast, he didn't get the place for being the best in our class. Did ya bro?" asked Alexis, digging an elbow into my side.

"Nope, or it would have come to you, wouldn't it?" I parroted my well-rehearsed line without deviation. It was true enough, Alexis was top of our class, I was a measly second. The fact that the letter came for me and not for her had been the source of some resentment.

"Well, that's just double the reason to boast, my brilliant daughter was top of her class, and my son. Well, Cora Olympia herself sent a handwritten letter requesting his presence in Streya.

"I remember when my family got the letter, asking for me to come to Streya to study under Professor Shepard, Mum turned into a swan on the spot." Sirius sniggered, and then Mum sniggered, and then they both burst into laughter. Orion and Astrid looked less amused. They would never have received a letter. Astrid had been sent for when she was seven, only one year into youngling classes, and Orion had grown up in the city.

"Oh, my goodness, Pan, why don't you nip upstairs and fetch the portrait we had done, you know, the one. From Frost Stars Eve, when Aster was apprenticing." Dad's name was Fry, but Mum found it hilarious to call him Pan, and it had stuck for as long as anyone could remember.

"Will do," said Dad, already making for their stairs.

"No really, Dad, there's no need," I protested, lamely.

"Won't take a jiff," said Dad, already a disembodied voice on the landing.

"What's the portrait of?" asked Sirius.

"Oh, its lovely, it's of Aster with Cora Olympia. Would you believe, she spent the whole holiday with us that year? One of the few Aster's spent with us too, since leaving for Streya. Wasn't it, dear?" It was just a question, but it came with a gullet full of guilt. I simply nodded my assent.

"And now, look at me, another infinite in my living

room, and a white-hued girl and a void-hued boy, and two riders, and three dragons on my lawn. Goodness me, if I won't be dining out on this for years. Aster, aren't you the lucky one? Such special students you have to teach," Mum said, beaming at Sirius, who beamed back. Astrid smiled politely, and Orion seemed incapable of making eye contact. In fact, he'd barely said a word since being shepherded up to the house.

"Damn sight more special than you were, aye?" Alexis hissed, and I rolled my eyes. She wasn't really bitter about it anymore, at least, I didn't think she was, but she did like to push my buttons. I could have said something about being the first light walker ever to bond with a dragon, but it didn't seem worth the argument, and Mum would only start gushing again.

"Found it!" called Dad, bounding down the stairs with the picture, which was passed around the room. It was met with a mix of genuine fascination from some, and polite recognition from others. It portrayed a rough likeness of myself, with my dark hair, pale skin and green eyes, set in a barely recognisable face, next to a much more convincing image of Cora. Understandably, she had occupied the majority of the artist's concern. She was wearing a shimmery, ice-blue gown, and I was wearing a silky, white turtleneck shirt, which had been entirely too thin for the season. She'd insisted on attending one of Mum's famous barn parties, and predictably, stole the show.

"Oh, isn't it lovely to have a full house again, Pan?" Dad nodded his agreement, his mouth now full of Mum's pie.

"Are you sure you can't stay the night? There are beds

for everyone," Mum offered, with a big bright smile and big hopeful eyes, that sank in my stomach like hot coals.

"Can't, Mum, time's of the essence. All we've got time for is a quick spit and polish and to rustle up a gift that's fit for Gloria." Mum's face sank again, just for a second. Just a flicker, but it sank.

"Oh... well, maybe next time. How's about you all start getting washed up, and I'll dig out a prezzie for you." She was all smiles and positivity, except for that *Oh*. It's funny how such a little word, just a sound really, could hold such disappointment and longing and heartbreak within it, enough to make me want to cry.

Mum handed me Gloria's present in the doorway, her eyes already watery in preparation for my departure. The others were waiting for me at the bottom of the path, allowing me a private moment to say goodbye, which I very much didn't want.

"Thanks, Mum, this is perfect." I forced an even tone as I slipped the little package into my pocket. A thimble that had apparently been passed down through three generations of Shepard women. Free folk are much more interested in that sort of thing than anything resembling money.

"See you again soon, Aster, don't be a stranger. You're all welcome any time you like." Mum stood in the doorway with Dad beside her as we turned to leave. Her voice was threatening to break, forcing a lump into my throat, as her previously watery eyes now shed tears freely. They always did, Mum was terrible at goodbyes. Dad wouldn't cry, but he'd get through more than his fair share of wine tonight.

"See you soon!" I lied.

Just as I was turning to leave, the sounds of horses hooves reached my ear. My chest tightened as a tall, well-muscled Shire horse trotted up to meet us. Its eyes glowed gold, as did those of the woman safely ensconced on its back. It was impossible to tell from horseback, but she was tall, her hair was thick, mousy and bore a slight curl, and her features were strong. She was my older sister, Andrea, with a swaddled baby in her arms.

"I hope you weren't planning on leaving before I even had chance to clap eyes on you, brother," said Andrea, flashing an easy smile as the horse lowered itself to the ground and allowed her to slip off.

"Busy," I replied, with a feeble smile and a small voice. My palms were sweating, as I tried desperately not to let my eyes be drawn to the bundle of blankets in her arms.

"Too busy to say hello to your big sister, gosh, things must be serious."

"I'm sorry, it's just—"

"Oh, hush I'm only messing, I can see it must be serious. Three dragons and two pure hues and the infinite all at the bottom of the garden. Mum's not gonna shut up about it for months." Andrea chuckled, throwing an arm over my shoulder as she pulled me towards her and planted a kiss on my cheek. She was the easiest to get along with of all my sisters, she'd been my rock, and I'd left her. In that moment, I'd have been quite grateful if a hole had opened up at my feet and swallowed me.

"It's nice to see you," I said, in a small voice.

"Not just me, here's Ava." I almost choked as Andrea unhooked her arm from my shoulder and carefully passed me the delicately wrapped bundle of blankets. My eyes stung as the covers fell from baby Ava's face. She was almost two years old now and should have been walking, but you'd never have known. She looked like a baby half her age, with skin paler than mine, nothing like her mother's healthy complexion. She was too light in my arms, too fragile. My heart thundered in my ears as I imagined slipping, and her falling away to nothing, like a house of cards. Her eyes opened, and breath escaped me, golden, and ever so faintly glowing.

"Do you see it?" Andrea asked, excitedly.

"Uhum," I mumbled, unable to speak.

"She's been growing, five ounces since the stars went bright. Fastest she's grown since she was born and she's been babbling too." Andrea sounded proud, beaming, not heartbroken at all.

"That's wonderful." I breathed. If I could have cut open my chest and poured my light into her, I would have, but I couldn't. Instead, I turned, teary-eyed to Andrea, and passed Ava back.

"Aster, it's alright, we're okay," Andrea whispered. Her kindness burned in my throat like hot coals.

"It was lovely to see you, bye." I was shaking as I turned on the spot and stormed down the path, not slowing as I passed the other.

"Well, they are lovely," I heard Sirius say brightly, as the rest of them started walking a few paces behind me.

"Great pie," Wayne agreed, happily. I rolled my eyes, and a tear slipped out.

"Are you alright?" Percy asked, as Styx sidled along beside me.

"I'm fine," I said, unconvincingly. Of course, he knew I wasn't, but we didn't have time for me not being fine. I could be not fine later.

"What is wrong, Aster?" Tera's voice was softer than usual. I let go a shaky breath, and thought for a moment before I answered.

"It's like I broke something, and now I have to go visit it, and smile at the papered over cracks. Like sitting opposite someone with a gaping chest wound, who's offering you a cup of tea whilst you try not to stare." It was easier to think the words than to speak them.

"What did you do wrong?"

"Shepards don't leave folks behind. If you cut Mum and Dad open, you'd find those words printed across their heart and in their marrow."

"So?"

"I left."

* * *

The point at which the woods stop being light walker territory and become the forest of Cerunos isn't marked. There is no border, and there are no signs. There are vague squiggly lines on maps, where the artist decided to start painting the trees in a different colour, but that isn't real.

All the same, you'll know when you cross that border.

You might look up into your husband's freshly shaven face and find that his eyes seem bigger, wider than they ever should be. Or you'll glance at your hands, and notice that your fingers have grown an extra inch since you last inspected them. Or you might look up into the sky, and wonder when it shifted from cloudless blue to a gentle lilac, with shimmering green clouds passing by. You might even swear to yourself that, for a second, you thought you saw a bird fly backwards. The lands of the free folk play fast and loose with the rules. Whether they found these strange lands and called them home, or this strangeness is the influence of the free folk themselves, is the cause of some debate. What is known, is that it is not wise to wander where you're not welcome.

"Stay close, everyone, and don't touch anything, especially if it seems like it might be alive," I warned them, clutching my ebony staff like a hiker's pole as we padded through the forest. As a green-hued light walker, I usually felt at ease in the trees and the dirt. That easiness faltered somewhat when there was a chance that the trees might start talking to you. Feeling Tera's power coursing into me from the staff was the best substitute I could muster.

"Yes, sir," said Orion, who apparently defaulted to reverence when he was nervous.

"Are you okay?" I asked, looking back at him over my shoulder. He looked anxious, he had a sweat on, although the forest was quite temperate. His eyes were darting this way and that, as if trying to follow an erratic bumblebee. The rest of my class seemed to be all together more awestruck by the surroundings. Astrid in particular was enjoying her extremely long, spindly fingers, and was drumming them against each other.

"Fine."

"You barely said two words the whole time we were at Shepard's Pasture." I lowered my voice a little as I spoke, not wanting to draw any undue attention to Orion.

"I just didn't want to delay getting back to Streya. To stop Ithaca before she does something we can't undo," said Orion. I frowned, I believed he wanted to stop Ithaca, although I got the sense his objections to her were all together more personal. That made me nervous, people tend to get a bit irrational when things get personal. Especially teenagers.

"Aster, I think there are eyes… in the trees," said Wayne nervously.

"I wouldn't be surprised, Wayne," I replied. I followed his eye line up into the canopy, but whatever he had seen was already gone. Although I did catch his hand sliding into Sirius's and didn't fight the grin playing at my lips. This must have been what it was like for Cora, watching myself and Percy not so sneakily sneaking around.

"Aster Shepard brings the infinite, two riders, two apprentices and three dragons into the forest," a lullaby-soft voice issued from the dark green denseness ahead.

"Brigit?" I asked to the forest in general. There was a rustling, and a moment later the familiar centaur emerged from the greenery. Her coat had a warm honey shine, just as I remembered, but unlike the last time we met, she wore nothing across her human torso. Part of me wanted to turn around and tell my apprentices to avert their gaze, but the free folk didn't do well with prudishness. So, I bit my tongue.

"What brings your merry band into my uncle's land?"

asked Brigit, in her singsong voice. I found myself wondering if she'd made the rhyme on purpose.

"We wish to visit Queen Gloria, I bring a gift and intend to ask a favour," I said, bowing my head slightly. Brigit smiled, her mouth splitting unsettlingly wide as she did, granting her a slightly alien quality. Her eyes flickered from maple to almost black and then maple again with each blink.

"The queen's domain falls under my uncle's protection. I can take you there, or you can take the Green Way." Her smile grew yet wider, as she ran a long finger across her tongue, then dragged it through the air. There was a shimmer and then a green portal yawned open, the sound of wind moaning through the trees rushed out of it.

"We're happy to be led," I said quickly, averting my eyes from the endless spiral of ever darkening green that had manifested before me. Very little is understood about the Green Way. What we do know is that it is a kind of liminal space. That, for all intents and purposes, exists outside of normal time and space. You could step into it here, walk ten strides and step out of it, in any forest of the free folk anywhere in the world. In some ways it was similar to silver magic, only silver magic creates a direct doorway between two places, in effect creating a fold in space, instantly travelling from one place to another. The Green Way, on the other hand, allows you to travel through somewhere to reach somewhere else like a shortcut. Most light walkers who have been brave, or foolish enough to use it extensively, lost their minds. Their ravings and writings becoming largely useless. However, there are shreds of sense that crop up again and again. Firstly, although the travel seems almost instant to those of us outside, it isn't always so quick for those within the Green Way. The second, and altogether more disturbing observation, is that you're not alone in there. It's never been clear what else is in there, but what is clear is that there are creatures that call the Green Way home. I was not anxious to meet them.

"Shame, there has recently appeared a shimmering doorway, we think you'd find it... fascinating." She dragged her finger through the air as she spoke, her words stretching into long sibilant sounds, whilst the portal evaporated.

"I'm sure I would," I said, suppressing a shudder.

"I wouldn't mind taking a shortcut," squeaked Wayne.

"He is a fool." Tera's voice pierced my mind sternly.

"You would," I said, shooting Wayne a look over my shoulder, before following Brigit, who'd already set off deeper into the forest.

"The queen will be pleased to meet the new infinite in person. Bren's recounting of your meeting certainly sparked her interest," said Brigit, as we picked our way through the forest. Foliage and undergrowth cleared a path for her that remained parted in her wake as she walked.

"She's always welcome to come and visit herself if she would like," said Sirius, attempting to be helpful, I'm sure.

"She rarely leaves the forest," said Bridgit, pulling back a curtain of vines, revealing a path that stretched seemingly endlessly in both directions.

"I leave you here, in the queen's domain," said Brigit, beckoning for us to step through.

I took a deep breath, felt the green fire flowing through my ebony staff, and stepped forward. Beyond the curtain, the canopy grew denser. So dense in fact, that I'm sure I'd have been standing in pitch black, were it not for the luminescent plant life. Flowers, and fungi glowing pink and green and yellow and blue and purple were all around us. Plant life you would never see outside the free folk lands, plant life even I couldn't conjure.

"This is amazing!" Astrid breathed, as her eyes grew unnaturally wide; doubtless the work of the strange powers of the forest, and glowed white with excitement.

"Don't touch anything," I warned again, scanning the neon forest nervously. The free folk wouldn't hurt us intentionally, but they did like to play games, and had been known to get carried away. I was about to take a tentative step forward, when a strong wind picked up. All at once, my hair blew back out of my face, and my cloaks flapped behind me, as words found my ears carried on the breeze.

"Follow the purple path," came a breathy voice, and a moment later, a formally technicolour strip of moss shifted to a bright purple hue.

* * *

As we followed the path, the glow intensified, before long drowning out all the other colours of the forest. Just as the purple path reached an almost painful brightness, we came upon a clearing. There was a large boulder in the centre, the size of a small house, completely blanketed in phosphorescent moss. Our trail stopped at the base of the boulder in front of a small, perfectly circular entranceway that was about four feet in diameter.

"I think we're here," I said, softly. I turned to face my

troop of riders and apprentices, hoping I sounded convincing. I was mostly operating on guesswork.

"Was anyone else expecting a palace?" asked Sirius, doubtless recalling the grandeur of The Clutch.

"Is a whole magical glowing forest not fancy enough for you?" Astrid sniped.

"Let's not bicker on the doorstep of royalty," I said, in the most level voice I could muster, although I had to admit, Astrid did have a point.

"No time to waste," said Orion, rather pointedly.

"Right you are," I said, as I stooped and stepped inside the small hole, doing my best not to gasp at the view. Almost the entirety of the house-sized boulder was hollow. Above me, collected in the domed roof, was a cloud of iridescent steam, its colours shifting like an oil slick. Occasionally, a drop of strange liquid fell from the ceiling, presumably condensation from the steam above, creating an effect not dissimilar to a faint drizzle of rain. The source of the steam could be traced down to a large chimney, which was connected to an elaborate arrangement of glass vials, domes, and test tubes, all containing various colourful liquids. The laboratory sat above a large fire pit, which appeared to have been excavated from the ground beneath the stone. The whole arrangement was elaborate and peculiar; it was hard to see any logic in the twists and kinks of the pipes and test tubes.

Although, all this oddness paled into insignificance beside the creature hovering just above the odd alchemical laboratory. It floated a few feet from the ground, hunched over, and in some ways resembling a ball. Strips of damp fabric of every colour and material dangled from it, pooling on the ground, making it impossible to know its true size. Its wings were a rainbow blur, and it wafted a sickly-sweet smell around the boulder. Strangest of all though, were its arms, all thirteen of them. Each arm was impossibly thin and they were of varying lengths, some with one elbow joint, some with two, and some with three. I believe I counted six on the longest arm, which stretched out from the floating body in the centre of the boulder to a spinning wheel in the far corner. The wheel was spinning what appeared to be thin air into fine golden strands, which tumbled into a glistening mound on the floor below the spinner. More arms craned up, shaking glass vials, or flicking them, or dropping unidentifiable liquids into them, whilst yet more stirred the three cauldrons, set low in the fire pit. I don't know how long I stood there with my mouth agape, watching the creature work. Eventually, a long, thin neck, rather like a swan's, extended itself from the ball of multi-coloured rags. The wrinkly, bluish-white skin of the creature's neck stretched until it became taught, with the colours of the fire and the vials reflected in its almost ghostly pallor.

"Hello, Aster Shepard." The voice sent a shiver through me, at once soft and sibilant, yet matched with an echo that sounded like metal crashing against rock. As the voice spoke, it reverberated off the walls, and its neck extended and folded backwards, until I found myself face to face with the creature, now upside down. Its hair was thin, but what little of it there was dangled wet and grey from the creature's blue-white scalp. Its left eye was closed, the right was an off white, with a green iris and a just slightly milky pupil.

"Hello… Queen Gloria," I said, offering a small bow, as my students and Percy, supported by Wayne, clambered into the boulder behind me. Each of them in turn did a fairly bad job of not gasping at what they saw. Gloria smiled and then, with a sickening creaking sound, her neck corkscrewed around until her face was right side up.

"She is more than a fairy." Tera's voice issued into my head, with an unusual note of fear behind it.

"Correct, little one," the two-toned voice echoed around the cave, although for all the world I could have sworn her thin black lips never moved. Gloria's eye flitted, just for a second, to Tera, who was cowering slightly behind me. A moment later, a jagged smile of razor-sharp teeth broke across her face, as her old green eye moved to my breast pocket, where I'd stowed the thimble.

"A gift? For me?" the voices whispered and clanged together. I nodded and slipped my hand into my pocket, producing the thimble. A small silver object that wore the dents and scrapes of a life spent practically.

"It's a—"

"A thimble, passed down through generations of Shepard women, given to me, by the Shepard that went walkabout. A prize indeed." As she spoke the six elbowed arm extricated itself from the spinning wheel and rotated around at the shoulder almost ninety degrees, before extending towards me. The thimble was plucked from my hand by two pincer-like nails that sat at the end of impossibly long fingers.

"I'm glad you like it," I said, feebly. I was struggling to conjure the right words, or any thoughts at all, that didn't revolve around Gloria's strange form.

"You've come for a favour, little Shepard, ask it." The dual-toned voice echoed through the stone.

"We need a way to neutralise the powers of The Shroud of the Night Mother." I almost jumped, as Orion's voice, with about as much force as I'd ever known it to carry, issued from behind me. He stepped forward to stand by my side, as his proclamation echoed around the boulder.

"And Percy, my husband, he was hurt, I was hoping you could heal him," I added.

"The void-eyed one is bold indeed." Her voices crashed together as two laughs filled the air, one soft and bubbling, the other harsh and guttural.

"I—"

"No... not bold, not brave. Angry. The void eyes are angryyyy." She almost sang the words, as she cut Orion off.

"Streya is in danger, we thought free folk magic might be the best answer to free folk magic," I said, making a plea to reason. The long-twisted neck nodded, and for a second all that could be heard was the popping and cracking of vertebrae, before the drips and bubbles of cauldron and condensation drowned out the dying echoes.

"You miss your opal-eyed teacher, poor children of the stars have lost their mother. Cora Olympia." She sounded out each syllable of the name as if tasting it.

"We do, we... I mean, I hope to protect Streya, she built it, it's what's left of her."

"You are what's left of her, left of her, how funny, how tricky she is," said Gloria. Another of her many arms curled back, twisting at the shoulder and bending at the second elbow, extending a long nail to scratch her chin.

"Can you help us?" asked Orion, with more steel in his voice than felt prudent.

"Of course I can. The question is, will I? And I will, in exchange for two more gifts," said Gloria. A long, grey tongue slipped past her lips to run along her countless teeth.

"What would you like?" I asked, resisting the urge to start rummaging in my pockets.

"First, the new infinite, I want something of him. Come forward, boy." Her milky, green eye drifted from Orion to Sirius.

"I've, errm, I've not got much on me, Your… Your Majesty?" Sirius's voice pitched up higher than I'd ever heard it as he stepped forward. I wondered whether Cora would approve of me doing this. Was this what she had in mind, when she told me to hold fast to my apprentices?

"I don't want your things, just you, silly boy." Her tone softened as she addressed Sirius, like a grandmother speaking to a lost child. The metallic clanging voice diminished. One of her arms extended out as she held his gaze, reaching towards him until her terrible, long nails were but an inch from his head. Part of me wanted to step forward, to pull him away and deny her, but I didn't. Somehow, I knew she wouldn't hurt him. She wasn't interested in hurting people; she was more complicated than that. I could see Sirius's jaw set rigid, his body was tense, and his eyes screwed tightly shut, as a nail slipped into his hair, then another slid past it. There was a small slicing sound, and then a lock of hair tumbled into another of

Gloria's outstretched hands, which snapped shut like a mousetrap.

"I… is that all?" Sirius asked, peeking open one eye, and visibly trembling.

"That is all."

"And the second gift?" I asked nervously, hoping she wasn't about to ask for a tooth or a toe.

"I wish to see something I've never seen before. The power of a dragon, melded with a star child."

I should have been relieved, she just wanted a show, but somehow that only made things worse. My heart was pounding, and sweat was beginning to bead on my fore-head. I suppose you could have called it performance anxiety.

"I've not really… tapped into Tera's power before," I said, adjusting my grip on the ebony staff.

"You will." Her voice clanged metallically now, the softer tone barely audible at all.

"Let us be the first of something, Aster," Tera's voice rolled into my head excitedly.

"You'll be great," Percy whispered, barely audibly from just behind me. I felt the gentle pressure of his hand just lightly resting on my shoulder. I took a deep breath and closed my eyes. There was my twinkling green starlight, and just beside it, the roaring verdant forest flame of Tera. For the first time, I breathed in and drew from both at once. Immediately, my muscles tensed as the power coursed through me. My eyes snapped open, and a smile peeled wide across my face; this felt good. Instinc-tively, I dropped the ebony staff, and for a second, it stood perfectly still and upright on the cave floor. Then it began melt into the ground, with bulging, vein-like roots surging away from it as it sank. I flung my arms wide apart, and felt myself drag something, a force, from the earth. There was a rumble, and a perfect, full-grown, black bark tree burst from the ground. Feeling a connection, I raised my arms wide, my muscles flexing, pulling against some invisible force, as I brought my hands together above my head. My hands passed in front the tree, and in their wake, leaves and flowers of every colour and shade sprung forth, mirroring the arc of my hands, until they met above my head and the tree stood proud in full bloom. Finally, I exhaled a shaky breath, and all at once, a golden rain of pollen tumbled down, quickly blanketing the floor in fine, shimmering powder. My head swam, and I staggered backwards, panting lightly.

"Are you okay?" asked Percy. He winced as he reached out to steady me, that awful clunking, grinding sound of bone and pain, setting my teeth on edge. His eyes twinkled in Gloria's firelight. Even through the pain, he could be distractingly beautiful.

"How did you know to do that?" asked Astrid, who'd plucked a pink flower from one of the further flung branches, and was inspecting it with fascination.

"Instinct." I breathed, still panting slightly.

"This is only the beginning, Aster." Tera's voice issued excitedly in my head, as she leapt into the air, landing among the black branches of my tree.

"Will that do?" I asked Gloria, whose head had turned away to inspect the tree more thoroughly.

"Beautifully," came both voices again, as her neck twisted back around. Her milky, green right eye was closed, but the left was now open. It opened much wider than the other, and appeared perfectly white. Until she blinked, and it rolled back in its socket, revealing numerous pupils. Some were round like a human eye, some were slits like a snake, some oval like a cat, and some that resembled a goat's eye. All suspended in one, skin-crawlingly large, white ball. It was hard to hold her gaze now; there was something about that eye. Besides the toe-curling horror of it, there was more, it almost itched at your mind.

"Had to get a proper look," she said, as if by way of an explanation. The milky, green eye opened again, and the many pupiled one closed.

"We've given you your gifts, now please, how do we overcome The Shroud of the Night Mother?" asked Orion, sounding both desperate and frustrated.

"Clue's in the name. Alice was a powerful old hag, none would deny it, but she did all her best work at night. Perhaps try shining a little light on the situation," said Gloria. Most of the clang had gone from her voice now, it was more of a soft, hissing whisper. As she spoke, she reached up to a high shelf above her spinning wheel with one of her longest arms, and hooked a finger onto something in the shadows. Gently, she lowered a small black lantern with grubby little windows into view, dangling it on the end of her nail. She extended her arm and held it before Orion. "Just shine a light through that, and you'll find that old shroud of hers to be little more than a rag."

"Thank you," said Orion, taking the lantern and holding it tightly with both hands.

"And my husband?" I asked, panic already fluttering to life in my stomach, as I sensed her interest in us wavering.

"You do not need me for that, tis but a trifle to one such as yourself, attuned as you are with forest magic." Gloria's eye roamed from me to Tera as she spoke.

"But I've never—"

"Now you must leave me to my work," said Gloria, gesturing broadly towards the jars and fires and cauldrons, almost all the softness of her voice was drowned in clashing, clanging metal and rock. With all thirteen arms splayed out behind her, she looked almost like some sort of horrifying peacock.

"Thank you for your time," I said, quickly. I reached out to one of the outstretched branches of my tree. Immediately, it shrank away, returning to the form of my black staff. It seemed unwise to linger once Gloria's invitation had expired.

"You may take the Green Way, if you like," she said, the harsher harder sounding voice growing louder still as we backed towards the exit.

"No, no need, we'll walk, take in more of your beautiful domain," I said.

"Shame, you'd so love to see the shimmering doorway," she said, sounding almost disappointed. Her long neck untwisted itself and recoiled inwards, until she was facing her cauldrons and vials again. I bowed a final hasty goodbye, and started ushering everyone back out of the hole before she decided she fancied a fourth gift.

I was the first to enter and the last to leave Gloria's boulder laboratory. Outside, it now seemed so dark, my eyes having adjusted to the cauldron fires and the iridescence. The purple phosphorus of the forest did little to combat the gloom, lending an almost claustrophobic air to the forest that wasn't helped by the expectant eyes gathering around me.

"Aster, you don't have to if you're not sure, I'll be—"

"Don't tell me you'll be fine, your bones are grinding together, you're not fine," I said, re-adjusting my grip on my ebony staff. I was clutching it so tightly, I'm sure my knuckled had blanched white, although it was too dark to tell.

"Tera, by my side, please," I willed into her mind, as I tentatively approached Percy, my apprentices and Wayne, who took a step back to give us space.

"How do I do this?" I asked, flushing with panic as I found myself face to face with Percy's wound.

"Just breathe," said Percy, smiling at me. He pulled apart the slit in his leather armour using his good arm, revealing the bruised skin and broken ribs beneath.

"We'll do it together," Tera's voice curled through my mind, as she trotted up beside me.

"Okay, together." I shut my eyes on the exhale, focusing on my fingers, and the thrumming power of the staff between them. The magic of forest dragons, of growth, and life, and renewal. One more breath, and then with a jolt, my arm buzzed as though a current was flowing through it. I couldn't have dropped the staff even if I'd wanted to. My eyes snapped open, as wide as they would go, as if my eyelids were being forced apart. Percy's side was glowing green, no, reflecting, I was glowing. I stared at the outlines of his ribs, focused, willed them back together, waiting. Time melted, seconds were indistinguishable from hours, nothing happened. But I couldn't stop, couldn't close my eyes, couldn't drop the staff. I wasn't sure I could even look away. And then I saw it: little vines, as fine as hair at first, sprouting from his skin. They thickened, coiling around his side like bandages, wrapping and threading together until all at once there was a grinding, clunking sound, my breath caught, the current severed and I dropped the staff. I blinked, and stepped back in panic, my legs trembling. My eyes shot to Percy's face, searching for pain, but there was none, or if there was, he was hiding it.

"Are you—"

"I think I'm fine," said Percy, tentatively. He reached around, running his fingers across the fine thicket of vines that had bloomed from his skin.

"Interesting," Astrid muttered under her breath, as she appeared peering over my shoulder.

"Let's see," said Percy. Without warning he reached up, stretching out his back, and flaring his rib cage. My stomach flipped as I waited for the sound of bone grinding against bone, but it didn't come.

"You're okay?" I asked, catching his ice-blue eyes in mine, holding my breath for his reply.

"I'm great!" Percy beamed, as he threw his arms around me and lifted me clean off the ground, and began to pepper my face with kisses.

The trek back out of the forest was like walking on air. The glow of the plants was brighter, and the birdsong had never been more melodic. At several points, I almost burst into song myself, beaming like an idiot and babbling into Percy's ear about the interesting plant life. It wasn't until we finally passed out of Gloria's lands, that someone broke me out of my giddy flow.

"What was she?" asked Sirius, as we passed through the curtain. Presumably, he'd been holding onto that question until he felt we were safely out of earshot.

"Not just a fairy, that's for sure," I said with a smile. I didn't know the answer, but for once I didn't particularly care.

"You mean, you don't know?" asked Sirius, sounding genuinely shocked, which I took as a compliment.

"I have my theories," I said.

"Well, don't keep us in suspense," said Percy, squeezing my hand, safely ensconced in his.

"Her voice, the errm, metal part of it, it sounded a lot like Gerty's. You remember Gerty, right?" I asked Sirius, recalling the day the quartet of free folk diplomats had come to visit him.

"The bundle of clothes with the weird arms... oh wait a second, her arms were just like the queen's, except she only had two of them." A flash of recognition registered on his face as he spoke.

"Inside that bundle of clothes was a hag. I think Gloria is probably part fairy, part hag."

"Wouldn't explain that eye though, or why she has so many arms," said Astrid.

"Maybe she's part fairy, part a lot of hags. Sorry, that's stupid, isn't it? Ignore me," said Wayne, who'd managed to step boldly into the conversation and shrink timidly out of it in one sentence.

"Actually, Wayne, that could make sense," I said softly,

only partially humouring him. I couldn't say how she ended up like that, but it certainly would explain things.

"I wish I'd counted her pupils to see if she had thirteen to match her arms," said Astrid.

"That would certainly be interesting," I said.

Conversation rolled on in that way for some time, until finally we found ourselves stepping back into the normalcy of the forest outside Cerunos' territory; the section of the map which would be coloured in a more muted green.

"Right, class, anyone know what's next?" I asked, turning around on the spot to face them all once we were all well clear of free folk lands. A flash of nervousness shot across Sirius's face, as excitement coloured Orion's.

"We're going home, finally," said Astrid, her voice full of relief.

"Indeed, we are." I chuckled to myself. Sirius wanted to hide, Orion wanted to confront a powerful and manipulative beacon, but I think Astrid was just sick of camping. Maybe I was more like Astrid than I'd first thought.

6

<u>The Battle for Streya</u>

As Styx carried Percy and I, his eternally frosty wings slicing through the air, the sharp wind drew watery streaks from my eyes, that tickled my skin as they streamed down my face. Just behind us, Nova carried Wayne and my apprentices, whilst Tera undulated through the air beside them.

All our chatter stilled as Streya grew on the horizon, becoming more than a distant spine of towers. Sunrise brought the city into sharper focus, as the expanse of the Titanic Lands, a rapid blur of brown aridness, vanished beneath us. We were crossing over the border into light walker territory, where the grassy forest kissed the desert edge. We'd be home soon, and we were returning armed, it was exciting. I think that's why we were so easily caught off guard.

"Something's coming," Tera's voice hissed into my mind, giving only a moment's warning

before we were engulfed in a storm of black leathery wings and gnashing teeth, surging up and

around us, appearing as if from nowhere.

"Hold on!" Percy bellowed, his arm coiling tighter around my waist as Styx banked,

screaming icy breath into the swarm, and tumbling through the air. Behind us, a scream pierced the flurry of wing beats, before a great column of golden red flame engulfed the sky above us, vanishing high into the sky, as tall as one of Streya's great towers. It had to be Sirius; neither Astrid nor Orion could sustain such a massive expenditure of light for more than a few seconds, if at all.

"We've got to land!" I screamed, over the clattering of teeth and the roar of fire. I squinted desperately into the maelstrom of gold flame, black leather, and occasional fleck of red scale, peeking out of what I now realised were dozens of wyverns swarming through the air around us.

"What about them!" Percy called back, nodding to the source of the flames. Styx dove, narrowly avoiding a great coiling lick of fire that whipped through the air just above us, singeing the hairs along the back of my neck. I had no answer for him. There was nothing I could do. We couldn't get close enough, not without risking being caught in Sirius's flames.

All we could do was watch, as more and more of the wyverns flocked towards

them, all but ignoring us. The further from Nova and Sirius we got, the less interested in us the creatures seemed. I could make them out more clearly now. Long, spindly creatures with small, nasty heads; rows of sharp teeth attached to about six feet of neck. Their front legs were long and taloned with large dark grey membranes which served as wings, whilst their hind legs were smaller and stouter, but still taloned. Their tails whipped out behind them, twice as long as their necks and jaggedly pointed at the end. They looked as though they'd been designed by someone cruel and overly interested in sharp objects.

They screamed through the air towards the whirling swirl of flame, until all at once, it vanished. I held my breath, waiting for what would come next. Dread filled me up for one agonising moment, as I asked myself why he'd stopped. All the world was consumed with wyvern screams, then, with a roaring rush, a great ball of fire exploded outward in all directions. I flinched away, shielding my eyes, and barely catching sight of Nova streaking out of the eruption. Percy threw his arms wide before us, creating a wall of ice to shield us from the blast.

With a jerk, Styx's flight path changed. With coiled wings, he shot through the air towards Nova, as wyvern bodies fell out of the sky and landed with a dull crunching thud all around us.

"Is everybody alright?" I called, launching myself into a stumbling run as I dismounted Styx. As I grabbed my ebony staff from my back, the vines that sprouted from it to fix it in place retreated at my touch. Tera came into a galloping landing beside me as I sprinted forward, already channelling green light into the earth around me, reaching for vines and roots, preparing to make weapons of them.

"He caught my hair!" Astrid scowled, as she slid down Nova's scales, planting herself on the ground. She cast her gaze skyward, to the black cloud of wyvern circling above.

"Where did they come from?" Sirius asked, dismounting himself, blanched unusually pale but not hurt. By some miracle, they all seemed to have escaped dishevelled, but otherwise unharmed.

"There's someone hidden." Percy's tone was granite steady and cold, as he stepped before the rest of us. He glared at a seemingly innocuous patch of grass fifty feet away, with his ice-blue sword, Obol, in hand, already misting the ground. I knew better than to dismiss Percy's instincts, and reached out into the ground, feeling my way ahead. My chest seized when I felt them, thick, strong and vital. The roots of a great oak, which should have been there but weren't.

"Reveal yourself, or he'll turn his flames on you!" I snatched Sirius wrist, thrusting his arm as threateningly as I could towards the spot where the tree should have stood. My heart was hammering in my throat. We were being watched.

"Aster, what are you—"

A low chuckle cut Sirius off, as the image began to shimmer, almost like the air above a roaring flame.

"You're very impressive, Professor Shepard. Although I'd expect nothing less from one of

Olympia's favourites."

I knew that croaky voice even before the illusion dissolved. It was almost like watching the warp and weft of a bolt of fabric pulled apart. The world unknitting before our very eyes. There she was, stooped and cloaked and ancient: Ithaca. She stood before a great oak, and by her side, a giant of a man who I also recognised. The freakishly muscled son of the leader of the Black Crater clan, who'd crashed the party Lance had held for Sirius and Tera. He wielded a giant claymore, the flat almost half a foot in width, with its point buried in the earth, it was almost as tall as he was. I didn't take my eyes off them for a second, but behind me, I willed a bloom of flowers at Orion's feet. Spelling out the word 'lamp'.

"What do you want!" I called, hoping to buy time whilst keeping one eye on the wyverns swarming above us. Only now, I saw that some of them were mounted. More Black Crater riders, no doubt hidden within Ithaca's illusion.

"Come now, we both know the answer to that. Give me the infinite—"

"NO!" Wayne barked, stepping in line with Percy, almost making me jump. A flicker of annoyance or perhaps amusement shaded Ithaca's cracked lips, as she took a long deep breath. The space between us stilled, as if the world were holding its breath.

"Give me the infinite, or Streya will fall." The words hung between us. Percy's grip on Obol tightened, as he glanced towards me. Whatever path I chose, he'd follow. Cora's letter flashed in my memory. *Hold on tight to your apprentices.* Nick might have been ready to disobey our old teacher, but I wasn't, and Ithaca was standing right in front of a very big oak.

"No," I repeated Wayne's words, flexing light into the ancient boughs of the great tree, coaxing it into a sudden, crashing swing. Its ancient bark shattered, as I made a giant's cudgel out of it. I watched, my stomach twisting, waiting for the impact, the thud and crack. The chief's son twisted, the flat of his blade absorbing the worst of the blow, as the oak lifted him off his feet and sent him skidding. But not Ithaca. I didn't blink. I could have sworn I didn't blink, but she just wasn't there. Where she should have been, the oak found only air.

"And I thought we were negotiating."

My breath stuck in my throat like a stone, as all of us whirled on the spot to face the source of the sound. She was behind us now, but there'd been no portal, not even a flash of silver. She cackled as our eyes met, seeing my terror, as black coils began to spread from her hunched form. A stretching, weaving tunnel of darkness reaching out, connecting us to her. This wasn't light walker magic, that much was clear. Percy moved first, slashing the air and releasing a crescent blade of ice, only for it to peel harmlessly away from her, furrowing the ground a few feet to her left. Percy never missed.

"It's the cloak," I muttered, flexing my hands around my staff until my knuckles turned white. I felt a hand on my shoulder pulling me back, and then Orion stepped forward. He held the dirty old lamp in one hand, and was channelling his void into it from the other. It flickered, like a gaslight sputtering to life, and then glowed. Warm orange firelight poured out of it as if from a lighthouse, meeting Ithaca's questing threads and dissolving them, sending them retreating like cockroaches in the sun.

"Now!" I cried, watching her cruel mask slip, as

Wayne's flaming arrows and Styx's icicle breath flew. We had her! I thought we had her, but then, once again, nothing but an empty space where Ithaca ought to have been.

"Seize the infinite!" Her voice rang out from further away now. I turned, spying her a hundred feet off or more, calling into the sky. The wyverns and their riders were still swarming above us.

"Orion! Stay close to Sirius," I commanded, throwing my gaze skywards as the cloud of black and leather and teeth started barrelling down. Styx and Nova roared into the sky to meet them.

"*Be safe*," I thought watching Tera rippling into the fray behind them, just before it hit me. Some invisible force knocked me sideway, staggering, then rolling through the grass into a heap with the others. Only Percy kept his footing, planting himself between us and the black crater chief's son, who was back on his feet and charging our way.

"It came from his sword. Watch his swings!" Percy called over his shoulder, pulling an icicle spear from the air and hurling it at the hulk of a man. The spear interrupted the next heavy swing of his blade, as he sprinted forth to meet him.

"Ithaca has gone!" The urgency in Orion's voice pierced the cacophony coming from above. I wheeled around and saw that he was right, she was nowhere to be seen.

"Keep your eyes peeled," I instructed, uselessly. I spread my light across the grasslands, reaching for her, feeling for her.

"How's she doing it? Just vanishing?" Astrid asked. Her wide eyes flitted wildly, as pure white light sparked at her fingertips. I didn't reply, I didn't know.

"It's got to be the cloak, right?" Sirius asked, pressing his back to Orion's, as the two of them turned in a circle.

"I just need to catch her in the lamplight." Orion spoke through gritted teeth, his expression a frozen glare, scanning the horizon.

"There!" Astrid's hand flashed as she hurled a bolt of pure brilliance, dazzling me. I flinched away, shielding my eyes, and when I opened them again, my stomach lurched.

"Aster!" Astrid shrieked, her face a mask of terror, as our eyes met from across the torn grasslands. Her bolt of light was already careening towards me. I blinked thickly, too stunned to move, then I saw it. The flash of grey, the burst of feathers.

"No!" I cried, my body finally moving again, as Sirius, already growing, already winged, shot from Orion's side. With his arms outstretched, he sailed through the air towards me, ready to tackle me aside, but there wasn't time. The blast connected, and Sirius's face scrunched in pain as his wings folded in, and his body thudded to the ground, tumbling past me. I turned, watching him skid with a painful groan, into the space between Ithaca and me.

My eyes were locked on hers, and hers were locked on him, like a snake that had spotted a mouse. I threw out my fist, desperately channelling light into my sapphire ring, as a volley of flaming arrows sailed over my shoulder. I watched them with bated breath, my light fizzling. They flew true, I was sure they did, and I waited for the thud of impact, and the scream that accompanied their searing heat. But it didn't come. She was gone, again, without a trace, but Sirius at least was still there.

"Orion!" I called, taking off at a sprint, chucking my gaze skyward as I pulled up networks of roots to secure Sirius from being snatched by swooping wyvern riders. Orion, not a natural athlete, had stumbled into a clumsy run, when the yelp froze him. A shocked, cracked sound that drew my eye back past Orion to Wayne, blazing bow still drawn. A wizened hand pressed a dagger to the bobbling lump in his throat. Astrid was already backing away, hands sparking and trembling.

"Everybody freeze!" Ithaca snarled, all her earlier cool confidence erased. Her voice was ragged now, she was panting. Whatever it was she'd been doing, it had cost her.

"Orion get h—"

Ithaca's grip tightened, straining Wayne's voice, but he'd said enough. Orion was already charging back, channelling into the lamp, which flickered with orange warmth. My eyes flicked to Ithaca, dreading what was about to happen to Wayne, but I didn't see rage. I saw a flash of purple, as her eyes flicked skyward and then down, a grin curling her lips. Then it hit him, like a streak of night. Wyvern and rider, slammed into Orion's side. His body went limp as the lantern slipped from his fingers, tumbling to a stop in the grass. I focused on the grass.

"I said freeze!" she bellowed again, just as Sirius shifted at my feet.

"Fine!" I muttered, raising my hands. I willed Sirius to stay down, as I slowly started to drag the lantern towards me. Fixing my eyes on her.

"Give me the infinite, or the legacy of Aster Shepard shall be the fall of Streya." Her voice was deadly, and she spoke my name like each syllable was a barb. I didn't reply. I kept my eyes on her, not on the lantern, never the lantern. I needed time, I needed her not to see what I was doing.

"Let her take me!" I needed Sirius not to say that. Not to struggle, achingly to his feet.

"Sirius, no!" I hissed, grabbing for his shoulder.

"Sirius, do—"

She pressed the knife into Wayne's bobbing throat, stifling his plea, as Sirius pulled himself free of my grip, glancing back to me. His eyes full. Mouthing the words, 'I'm sorry.'

"*Tera, I need you! Cut him off.*"

"Don't do this, Sirius," I thought and spoke at once. My eyes were pinned to Ithaca, watching her smirk grow then falter, as Tera slammed into the ground between her and Sirius. Battered and bloodied, but there, baring her teeth, driving Sirius back.

"Aster, please, I—"

Sirius choked and Astrid screamed. My stomach twisted; I'd taken my eyes off of Ithaca.

"You've made your choice. I'll pick the boy out of the rubble when Rex is done with you."

"Oh, my stars…," I breathed. I felt my eyes fill with tears, as Wayne slipped from her bloody fingers, slumping to the ground, spluttering scarlet. Ithaca vanished.

"No!" Sirius choked out a sob, collapsing to his knees. Tera only barely managed to see off a mounted Wyvern swooping low over her head with a snap of her jaws. I stood, watching. My eyes flicked from Astrid, pale and frozen in shock, to Sirius, slumped in the grass, to Tera, curled protectively around him, to the vast expanse of grass and broken turf, and dead wyverns, and to Wayne. Then Percy, charging through, with Styx swooping down to meet him.

"Come on, Wayne, they're on the retreat, we can catch them!" he called out, full of confidence at first. His sprint stumbled to a halt, scanning the field when he received no reply. Our eyes met. I opened my mouth, but no sound came out.

"Where's Wayne and Orion?" Percy asked, face already falling, as overhead Nova howled like she'd been ripped in two, and filled sky with fire.

We watched Nova, a streak of red across the sky, belching fire after the cloud of wyverns, beating a retreat away from the city border. My eyes were watery, as I swallowed around the heavy lump that had lodged itself achingly in my throat.

"They'll eat her alive." Tera's voice was restless inside my mind as she stomped anxiously, her neck craning, and her eyes glued to Nova's path.

"We can't follow her; they'll eat us too." My voice was coarser than I meant it to be, rough with grief and exhaustion.

"There's more coming!" Astrid's voice was full of panic as she pointed with a shaking hand over my shoulder, towards the centre of the city. I groaned, as I turned, about ready to give in, and was relieved to find not another cloud of black, but three distinct sets of wings, rising from the city.

"They're my men," Percy said, placing a consoling hand on Astrid's shoulder, as the black silhouettes flew down out of the sun, gaining colour and texture as they came into land. Three mature red dragons, complete with riders.

"We saw Nova chasing the wyverns, what should we do?" the first of them asked as he landed. Percy blinked, mouth falling open wordlessly, then looked to me. I swallowed the urge to bolt.

"Percy, you're the fastest. Get to the university, tell Vega what's happened. Tell her we'll meet her on the roof of the central building. Go now." I spoke as firmly as I could, willing my voice not to wobble. Percy nodded, crossed to me in three strides, pressed a kiss to my brow, lingering a little too long and then mounted Styx.

"Do whatever he says," was the last command he gave his men, before taking to the sky, becoming a streak of darkness and mist.

"Sir?" The rider saluted as he turned to me. I'd rarely felt more like a fraud in my entire life, as I wondered whether I should salute back.

"You three will carry Astrid, Sirius and me to the roof of the university's central building. You'll fly in formation around Sirius; we can't risk him getting snatched."

"I'm not going." Sirius's choked voice broke me out of my rhythm. He'd found his way to Wayne's side, and was crouched in his blood, struggling, with shaking hands, to close his eyes. I'd tried not to look at Wayne, tried not to see how young he looked, laying there, too pale, too still.

"We have to go, Sirius, it's not safe," I said, in my softest voice.

"Is that… Wayne?" one of the riders asked from behind me. I couldn't seem to answer. It had been Wayne, it wasn't anymore.

"He's gone!" Sirius answered for me, his voice sharp, but punctuated with a wet gurgling sob.

"Sirius, come, we've got to go," said Astrid, placing a hand on his shoulder, gentler than I'd ever seen her. He tried to shrug her away, but she stayed by his side.

"You should have let her have me." Sirius eyes were so full of grief and rage and fear, I could barely bear to meet them.

"I couldn't," I muttered, struggling for more words, better words, something that would help, or soothe, or console. But my eye kept drawing back to Wayne. Bloodless and cold. I realised none of us were speaking. We'd all run out of words.

"He wouldn't have wanted you to stay here." Astrid broke the spell at last, taking Sirius by the arm, all but heaving him up. He let himself be dragged to the nearest dragon, glassy eyed and quiet.

"Central building roof," was all I could manage, when I turned back to the riders. I hauled myself to the nearest dragon, affixing my ebony staff to my back as I went.

Vega, Percy, Marlon and a handful of others were already assembling on the roof when we arrived. Their attention was gathered towards the swarm of wyverns buzzing at the far edge of the city.

"Where have you been?" Vega asked as we landed, clearly struggling to keep the edge out of her voice. Her face was like thunder.

"There isn't time for that, we've got to talk about Ithaca, she's—"

"He was rescuing me," Sirius said hopelessly, slumping down a little way off from the rest of us. It was like watching someone drown in grief and guilt and self-loathing.

"What is he talking ab— Hang on, where are your glasses?" Vega cut herself off, caught between too many questions.

"Lost 'em. Doesn't matter. None of that's important. What's important is that Ithaca is the one that's been trying to kidnap Sirius. She tried again today, when we crossed the city border. When I refused her demand, she said she was going to destroy the city."

Vega gave a bark of dismissive laughter. "I'd like to see her try," she said, shortly.

"You don't understand, Professor, she's got this shroud and powers—"

"We've all got powers, we're light walkers, Astrid, this is Streya, the City of Light. We shan't be falling to one woman, no matter how scary she is!" Vega snapped, a little more harshly than I think was necessary.

"Well, regardless, she's taken Orion, and she's vowed

to take Sirius, so we need to do…" My voice trailed away, as I watched the cloud of wyverns scatter.

"Is that cloud getting darker?" Astrid whispered, pointing to the rapidly darkening cloud that they'd scattered away from.

"Not again," Percy groaned. His hand shifted to the hilt of his sword, as he stepped in front of me. I shook my head, swallowing hard, with the silhouette of a beached leviathan, carved into the night by lightning, burning through my mind.

"It can't be," I muttered, my heart racing. I was aware that all around me, the entire population of the roof had turned to see, to hold their breath together, as something large emerged from the cloud. but it was not a leviathan; there was no gleaming crest, no crackling lightning. It was brown and scaley, with horns that must have been three stories long, jutting out of its massive head. Behind it stretched a long, metallic bronze neck. At its shoulder, huge wings burst forth, dispersing the cloud wall for hundreds of feet all around it, as two sets of powerful legs dragged through the air behind it. It took me back to the old illustrations in text and storybooks. The stylised water colours, they'd not done it justice, they hadn't captured its magnitude, or the terror it wrought.

"A meteor dragon." My voice shook as it dawned on me, exactly how she planned to reduce Streya to rubble.

"But they're extinct," Percy said, flatly.

"Careful of those who know the past, for they shall make that which was, that which is." Gerty's voice clanged inside my mind, as I watched in unblinking terror as the creature's mouth yawned open. I didn't know what to expect. Fire dragons breath fire, that's plausible enough. But meteor dragons? Their power had only ever been described as devastating.

I waited for the glow of flame or energy, and then it hit me. Excruciating, mind rending, bone aching sound. Everyone around me hunched forward at once, eyes wide, mouths open, they looked as though they were screaming. They probably were, I just couldn't hear them. I could barely breathe, couldn't think, couldn't move, the edges of my vision blurred and darkened, then with an aquamarine flash, it was over. The pain, the sound, it all stopped, and there was just ringing. Terrible ringing, and the memory of pain and a trickling sensation running out of my ears. I looked around, dazed. People's lips were moving, but I couldn't make out what they were saying, just ringing. Then a second flash of yellow, and the world came back to me.

"Thank you, Marlon," Vega said, staggering back to her feet with a nod of genuine gratitude to old Marlon, from whom the last of a yellow glow was fading. I struggled to my feet, turning on the spot, my eye snagging on the strangeness of it. An almost invisible swirl of wind and dust had encircled the rooftop.

"All is calm in the eye of the storm." Marlon winked at me, his aquamarine eyes glowing brightly.

"That's as may be, but what are we going to do about the dragon?" I turned to meet Dusk's ever unpleasant voice, and found him stepping out of a large silver portal. He was stood beside Nick and several other governors and faculty members.

"We need Cora!" a disembodied voice called from somewhere within the scrum.

"Cora isn't here!" Vega snapped, glowering in the direction of the voice, before turning to me. "Aster, what about the Golden Court, if we could get a message to Lance, perhaps?"

"Even if they agreed to come, it would take hours for them to fly this far, even for a golden or grave dragon," I said. I shuddered as the ground beneath us shook, drawing my attention back towards the meteor dragon. It was on the move. It broke into a heavy gallop before leaping into the air, its impossible wings unfurling.

"We can buy you time." Percy nodded to the three riders who'd carried us here, sent to guard the dim sick centre. I couldn't help noticing that each of them had blanched white, although none objected.

"Be careful," I said, bolting forwards, and snatching Percy's hand as he went to mount Styx.

"Promise." Percy nodded, planting a kiss on my cheek before climbing onto Styx and pulling away. I reluctantly let him slip through my fingers. My throat quivered painfully as watched them take to the air, flying straight towards it and the cloud of wyverns that swarmed around it.

"What if we opened a portal, they wouldn't have to fly here?" Nick asked.

"Can't open a portal into the Golden Court, the whole of The Clutch is protected. Won't work," I answered in snatched sentences, struggling to fill my lungs. I watched as bursts of ice and fire lit the swarm of wyverns peppering the great brown-bronze hide of the thing. That was my husband, my Percy.

"So, we're on our own," said Nick.

"'Fraid so," I replied, trying not to let my voice crack.

"No. We are not." Vega turned solemnly to face the beast, squared her shoulders and the purple bangle at her wrist flared.

"This is Vega, Headmistress of the University of Streya, apprentice to Cora Olympia. I am calling to every light walker and beacon that can fight. Every apprentice that knew Cora Olympia. We are under attack. Everything Cora built is under attack. She is not here to defend it, but we are." Goosebumps raised along my arms, as Vega's voice rippled through my mind.

"Very rousing, Vega, but should we not at least consider trying to negotiate with them?" Dusk asked.

"Not possible," I said shortly, without turning to look at him. I was unable to tear my eyes away from the battle taking place in the distant sky above Streya. I watched, as the meteor dragon peeled away from its chosen course, beating a retreat further up into the clouds, as icicles exploded across its snout.

"Do we even know what their demands are?" I could hear Dusk bristling behind me.

"Hand over Sirius, and let her have her way with him. Like I said, not possible."

"Well, perhaps we should consider giving them the boy, that thing could level half of Streya." My shoulders tensed, and my throat bobbed. I wanted to turn, to bite his head off, in fact, part of me wanted to shove him off the roof, but Vega turned first, rounding on him.

"We're not giving up the infinite, for three reasons, Dusk. First and foremost, he is a student under our care, how could we ever presume to teach or take in students again if we gave him up? Second, it is unfathomably stupid to give a powerful enemy access to the infinite, you utter moron. Finally, we would never have even considered it with Cora here, and I'm not about to let her down now. You can go." As she turned away from Dusk, she flicked her wrist, and a silvery portal opened up beneath him. He vanished with a yelp, and a smile bloomed across my face, the first since Ithaca's ambush. Nick even whooped.

"That was brilliant," I whispered, glancing up to Vega, watching the ghost of a smile flicker across my old classmate's face. Then it happened, a silver portal shuddered into being beside us, and our old classmate Roma stepped out. Pale, slim, dark-haired, he'd always been somewhat avian in appearance, with his beady eyes and hooked nose, but age had softened him a little.

"Vega, Aster, Nick." He turned, nodded to us, and took to the sky, catching the first of Wyverns to approach us in a net of bronze light, and sending it crashing into a second. A second later, another silvery portal opened up beside Astrid, and then another. Two men in matching fiery red cloaks landed on the roof, glowing bronze. Then another portal, and a winged woman swooped down. I turned in a circle watching as dozens of light walkers, some faces I knew and some I didn't, poured onto the rooftop. Taking to the air, they fired bolts of fire and wind into the faces of the oncoming wyvern hoard.

"Who are these people?" Astrid asked, her voice breathless, and her eyes swimming.

"We're the arch beacons of Streya, girl. Now, pull yourself together," said a white-haired woman, as a flash of grey materialised, and scaley, red wings unfurled from her back, as she sprung into the air.

"Looks like it worked," Vega muttered, smiling a little broader now. I was almost starting to hope.

Percy and his men were doing all they could, tumbling, weaving, diving through the air, each of them pursued by a dozen wyverns at least. Peppering the great beast with everything they had, they were distracting it for now, but more and more wyverns were heading our way. I watched on helplessly, as beacons, other professors, and even some senior students flew out to meet them. Losing my glasses had somehow managed to become even more painful.

I was so busy wrapping myself in guilt, I almost missed him. A wyvern rider, tumbling out of the aerial fray, with his eyes locked on Vega. Standing tall, she was orchestrating the beacons, firing bolts of pure white light with frightening accuracy. His mount's eyes followed his, and as its leathery black wings folded in, it was picking up speed fast. My hand moved automatically. I snatched my coal studded cane, warm to the touch from within my cloak, and darted forwards, dragging it through the air like a brush. I painted a wall of flames across the roof, catching the wyvern, scalding the rider, and forcing him to double back before reaching Vega.

"Thanks." Vega nodded curtly, her eyes creasing to a squint, as two bolts of white light shot past me, dazzling my peripheral vision. Their shots flew wide of their intended target, as rider and wyvern retreated further into the sky, the light fizzling harmlessly in the distance. I turned and found Astrid, hands outstretched, face frustrated, sweat beading.

"Don't waste your light," I said, doing my best to sound like a teacher again.

"I've got to do something," she hissed, shaking her hands off. Her voice was trembling, and her eyes flitted about like a hummingbird as she watched the sky.

"Astrid, don't forget what makes white light special. You can amplify us all, focus on that. Find the best shot on the roof and give them a boost," I said, forcing a smile and a wink. I tried not to let my face shift, as a little way off behind her, I saw a beacon bathed in bronze, wearing blazing red robes was hit in the chest with a club. His shroud of bronze light dissipated as his face creased in pain, and he dropped out of view, my stomach dropping with him.

"Is something wrong, Aster?" Astrid asked, looking over her shoulder, following my eye line. She wouldn't see anything, he was already gone.

"Fine. I'm fine," I lied, tasting bile as I turned away and froze. A flicker of green was floating in the air at head height, vanishing just as a man in blazing red robes landed at my feet with a thump.

"Impossible," I muttered, looking around. For what exactly, I wasn't sure, although the loamy scent of the forest was unmistakable, for just a moment. A mountain crumbling roar that could split the air stole my attention a moment later. All of us turned to face the beast, its neck extended, as it blasted its voice to the heavens.

"What's it doing?" Nick yelled, whilst covering his ears. I didn't answer, I didn't know. And then it stopped. Retracting its neck, it pulled itself tightly together, before taking off at a lumbering gallop back into the air, each wing beat kicking up dust clouds three stories high.

"I think I know what it was doing." Astrid's hand was on my shoulder, pulling me away from the spectacle of the thing, turning me to follow her outstretched arm. Her finger pointed into the sky, passed the wyverns, up into the clouds, where a black spot had punctured the fluffy white, then another, and another, streaking through the sky, towards Streya. Towards us.

"Not good," I muttered, gripping my coal studded cane, knowing it would do me no good.

"Are they...?" Nick's voice trailed away.

"Meteors... if I had to guess." I nodded, my mouth turning dry.

"Right..." Nick nodded, wringing his hands as more and more of the beacons on and around the roof started to notice. Some were still locked in aerial duels with the swarming wyverns.

"What do we do?" Astrid's voice wobbled, her eyes swimming. I opened my mouth and closed it again without making a sound.

"Don't worry, I've got this," Nick answered for me, stepping forward, He cracked his knuckles, the many gold rings adorning his fingers catching the light as he threw his arms wide. Silver light peeled away from him in a rippling glow, making him seem like a giant, standing between us and the sky raining down around us. A tinge of pride plucked at my chest as a little speck of silver appeared in the sky and the rapidly growing black spot with its streak of fire vanished. In spite of myself, a laugh escaped me as another speck of silver flashed in the distance, jettisoning a flaming boulder into the side of the meteor dragon, releasing from it a yawning groan as the creature tumbled through the air. It began to swerve and weave, as more silvery portals released more boulders all around it.

"You're amazing, Nick!" I grinned, slapping a hand to his shoulder.

"Thanks, bud, just not sure how long I can be amazing for." Nick croaked, sweat already beading along his brow.

"I can help." Astrid's voice was leveller now, she took her place by Nick's side, her hand floating at the small of his back as she began to channel pure white light into him.

"Great!" I beamed, turning on the spot. I scanned the horizon for the next disaster, keeping an eye out for the next wyvern that might take a shot at Vega, or Nick. It took me a moment to notice what was missing, although I knew something wasn't right almost immediately. I turned again, my chest tightening, and my palms suddenly slick with sweat as it dawned on me.

"Tera, where is Sirius?" I threw my gaze skyward towards Tera, circling the roof, goring exposed Wyverns from the sky with her twisted horns.

"I don't see him," her voice hissed back as she dove down, making a strafing pass. Her emerald eyes caught mine for a split second as she searched.

"Was he taken?" I spoke aloud, my voice climbing an octave.

"Who?" Astrid asked, turning back to me as Tera came into a trotting landing beside us.

"Sirius, I can't see Sirius." I spoke fast, only able to breathe in snatched gasps, visions of Ithaca appearing and disappearing without a trace flashing through my mind.

"He can't have been, we'd have seen someone snatch him, we'd have heard it, he'd have fought." Astrid rationalised, turning away from Nick to scan the roof.

"Hey, don't stop." Nick's voice was horse, his arms sagging.

"Sirius has gone," I barked, by way of an excuse.

"He must be hiding," said Astrid, doing a better job of keeping her voice level than I was.

"Well then, find him!" Vega commanded, drawing my attention as she flung out her arm. A chain of white light materialised over my shoulder, catching a wyvern, which appeared to have been heading straight for me, binding its wings and leaving it to fall out of the sky.

"You caught all that?" I asked, uselessly readjusting my grip on my coal studded cane, trying to convince myself I'd have noticed it time to save myself. Doubtless I wouldn't have.

"Yes! Now go, and take this, you might need it," Vega said, shaking the bronze bangle from her wrist into my hand.

"Are you sure?" I asked, cradling it like it was a newborn.

"Of course, I've still got my silver lens, and you'll search quicker this way." Vega's eyes flitted hawkish through the sky, firing bolts of blue and white light as she spoke, her focus unyielding.

"Right," I nodded, turning to leave. I slipped the slightly too large bangle over my knuckles, my mind racing. Where would Sirius hide? If it were Astrid or Orion I'd head straight for the library, but Sirius was less obvious. I was at the top of the stairs that led back into the tower, and already walking the halls in my mind, when the air shifted. I froze, my hand on the handle of my cane, my mouth turning dry, as I told myself that what I could see out of the corner of my eye couldn't really be there. It was a bad dream, it had to be.

"I can't make a portal that big." Nick gave a dry, humourless laugh that told me it really was there. I turned slowly. I was breathless, and my heart was thundering, as if moving too quickly would provoke it, but nothing I did would change its path. It was coming for us all, regardless. Looming large over the city of Streya was a huge ball of flames and space rock, hurtling towards us like a great blazing eye. Fifty feet across at least, if I were to hazard a guess. Ithaca's voice rang in my head.

'Give me the infinite, or the legacy of Aster Shepard shall be the fall of Streya.'

"It wasn't an empty threat," I muttered, blinking stinging tears out of my eyes as I turned to the arrow of black and blue, darting around the meteor dragon in the distance. My husband. If I set off, I could reach him before the meteor hit. I could be with him. My throat bobbed painfully.

"Aster, what are you waiting for, I said find Sirius," Vega snapped, her tone unchanged.

"He won't be able to deal with… that." I was struggling to put any volume in my voice as I consciously didn't look at the city killer hurtling towards us.

"Leave that to me, you just find him," she snapped.

"But I…" My voice trailed away as my eyes darted back to Percy.

"Go now!" Her command rang in my ears, but I still couldn't tear myself away.

"I'll keep an eye on things," Tera's voice curled kindly into my mind. I swallowed, blinked away more tears, nodded, and disappeared into the bowels of the tower.

I didn't know where to start. I hurtled aimlessly down the empty corridors, bronze light thrumming out of Vega's bracelet. The stone walls creaked around me. Dust was shaken loose and spiralling in the air, as windows cracked and shattered. I checked the senior commons first, and found it deserted, like the rest of the school. The students had been evacuated, save for the seniors who'd elected to stay behind and fight and die.

"Percy has landed on the meteor dragon. He's fighting the rider."

"Of course he is," I muttered, drifting to a stop, as my stomach flipping nauseatingly.

"Where are you Sirius?" I spoke aloud, and to no one in particular. I tried to focus. To remind myself of what I was searching for, to prevent my mind from being dragged back to that thing in the sky over Streya. Or to my husband, locked in a duel to the death on the back of an extinct dragon. I couldn't blame Sirius for wanting to hide. I wanted to hide. To curl up on the green velvet couch in my office, that I never got to use, close my eyes and pretend none of this was happening. Then it hit me, maybe that was exactly what he'd done.

When I dispelled my bronze light, I had to jog to a stop as the momentum carried me just past my dark wood office door, left open just a hair. I tried it, but it didn't budge, the cracked masonry above had pinned it in place.

"Sirius, are you in there?" I called, pressing my shoulder to the door, trying to force it. It still didn't budge, and no reply came.

"Sirius?" I called again, louder. Again, no reply, I waited, breath held, I needed him to be there, I didn't know where else to look.

"Sirius, the door's stuck. If you're in there, I need you to say something." My voice sounded desperate, half given up. I was about to turn away when a flash of grey emanated from behind the door.

"Stand back!" My heart leapt, it was Sirius's voice, deeper than usual, but definitely Sirius.

"I have," I called, stepping to the side of the door. A moment later there was a heavy thud, and the door shuddered, shaking dust loose from the crack in the masonry. Another thud, and the door popped out of the frame like a wine cork, smacking into the wall opposite with a bang. Sirius stood in the frame, taller than usual, and broader, like he had been the first day he arrived late to my classroom. He looked tired now, his eyes red and raw. He didn't say a word as the grey light faintly peeled off him and dissipated. He shrunk down to his regular size, retreating back into the office. I followed him, ducking under the doorway and the sound of grinding stone, the crack above yawning wider.

"You found me," he muttered dryly, sinking down onto the green velvet couch, now layered with a film of dust.

"Vega says she's going to destroy the meteor." I tried not to let my face shift, as Tera's voice hissed into my mind. I refused to let my thoughts run back to the rooftop.

"I was worried about you." I spoke softly, sinking onto the couch beside him. He didn't reply, but flinched as the building shook. The shards of glass that still remained of my window tinkled almost musically. Something must have hit us.

"Is it bad out there?" he whispered, as if he were afraid of the answer it might receive.

"How much did you see before you left?" I asked, as his eyes flitted around the room, watching the cracks grow, and following the sounds of battle.

"That thing bursting through the clouds." His voice cracked as he dropped his face into his hands, pressing his palms to his eyes.

"You've seen the worst of it then." He didn't need to know about the rest, not right away. He needed peace, or as close to peace as we could get, anyway. I started to breathe out light, letting a faint green glow bleed out of me. I coaxed moss and small crawling vines out of the stonework and the bookshelves, papering over the cracks as best I could. It wouldn't hold the building together, it wouldn't even make us safer, but it could make things a little less scary.

"What are you doing?" His voice was hoarse when he

eventually spoke again, lifting his head wearily from his hands.

"What's it look like? I'm redecorating, of course!" I forced a smile, as a bead of sweat ran down my forehead into my eye, stinging it shut. The stinging eye forced me into a strange kind of involuntary, grimacing wink, which actually earned a half-hearted snort of laughter. Just over Sirius's shoulder, through the shattered window, the world was getting lighter. Almost like when you're on a picnic and the clouds clear and the sun suddenly floods your world, but whiter. I tried not to let my eye linger on it and looked back to Sirius.

"What do you think the infinite actually is?" he asked, when our eyes met. His had the look of a drowning man's, reaching for a lifeline. A distraction from what was going on outside. From what had already happened.

"I don't know. Whatever it is, I think it probably is not really infinite, just so unfathomably massive that it may as well be. I have my own theories about that as well, but I think Professor Copper knows more about it than me." My mind pulled me back to the anomaly as I spoke just for a moment, and the sheer power radiating off it. I hoped the memory of it didn't show on my face, if it did, Sirius didn't seem to notice.

"He was an apprentice with you, wasn't he?" Sirius asked, brightening a little.

"Yep, he and Vega both were. People called them the little infinities, because they were the brightest lights of our generation. Always got on Vega's nerves that she got lumped in with him," I said with a laugh, her scowling face flashing through my mind. My eye was drawn back to the window, and the light bathing the courtyard, so bright and white now it was almost bleaching walls.

"Which one of us was he most like? If you had to compare our class to yours?" There was a note of desperation in the question, or fear of what might happen next, once the conversation ended.

"Oh, Nick was most like you. He was the fun one, easy going, relaxed, he was the only one that could get Vega to lighten up. She'd be Astrid, I suppose, although the match isn't as close." Everything I could see of the courtyard was white now, almost painful to look at. Whatever was happening out there had to be Vega's doing, but even for her this was a lot of light.

"Which makes you Orion?" Sirius asked, not noticing, or not wanting to.

"I suppose, but Orion is much more special than I was. I just liked dragons; a lot of people didn't understand why Cora picked me," I explained, trying to keep my voice even, and my eyes on Sirius.

"People wondered why you picked me too, you know?" said Sirius. The very beginnings of a smile curled his lips, then faltered as something pulsed. We both felt it; someone had just released a huge amount of light. The air was suddenly thick with the static of it, hairs stood on end, skin pimpled.

"What was th—" The building rocked with the sound of it, a great rending thunderous boom.

"She did it… but she—"

"I know." I cut Tera's unusually soft voice off.

"Aster… you're crying."

"Am I?" I asked, blinking furiously. One stunned

finger reached up to wipe my cheek in a gritty swipe. I inspected my finger slightly dazed. It looked foreign to me, grey with wet dust.

"Aster, what's going on?" Sirius leaned forward, softened by concern. I swallowed and dragged up a smile.

"Did you ever wonder? Why you were chosen?" I needed the distraction as much as he did now. Sirius frowned and scratched the back his head, he knew I was avoiding something, he must have been deciding whether to let me.

"I thought you must have picked me for my good looks," he said eventually, cracking a forced smile of his own.

"Not your talent?" I asked, too tired to chastise him for flirting.

"I'm not that talented," he replied, flatly, his fledgling smile dropping.

"That's not true. Think about it. Everyone in this city struggled with the power boost from the star bloom. You seem to have got the hang of a much bigger one." It was true, he had, for the most part, got it under control. I wasn't at all certain I'd be doing any better in the same circumstances.

"I suppose," he conceded, nudging a piece of smashed stonework with his foot.

"I spent much more time thinking I was a mistake than I ever did thinking you were one," I added, possibly too candidly.

"But Cora Olympia picked you, Aster, no offence to you of course. I'm honoured that you picked me, but getting the Cora Olympia stamp of approval must have felt pretty good, and in the end, you proved she was right, as usual." He sounded in awe as he talked about her, most people did, especially the ones that didn't know her.

"Would you like to know a secret?" I asked.

"Percy has dismounted the meteor dragon. He is back on Styx."

"Go on." Curiosity drew Sirius closer to me, miraculously he didn't notice the little sigh of relief that Tera's words coaxed out of me.

"Cora picked you as well," I said, my smile genuine now.

"You're just saying that." His answer was quick, reflexive, but his eyes were wide and searching. Looking for a sign that I was lying, hoping he wouldn't find one.

"Nope, when she handed over the position of master to me, she handed over a list of three names with it. She said that picking each generation's crop of apprentices was a leviathan of a task and that she'd decided to save me the bother." As I spoke, an idea flickered into life, right at the back of my mind.

"She picked me?" he asked, his face breaking into a broad, believing grin.

"So do you feel like proving her right?" I asked, getting to my feet, clapping my hands together to shake the dust off.

"What do you mean?" he asked, looking bewildered, but following me up all the same.

"Do you know what drove meteor dragons to extinction?" I asked, beckoning Sirius to follow me with a nod as I marched us out of my office.

"Nope." He shook his head, following me down the

cracking corridor, stopping beside a shattered hole in the wall. Ivy hung limply, flapping in the breeze, framing the image of the university entrance. It looked more like an abandoned battlefield now.

"The riders of the meteor dragons picked a fight with the leviathan shepherds, and lost, badly," I explained, half thrumming with excitement, half furious with myself for not thinking of it sooner.

"Like the one we saw in the Titanic Lands?" Sirius asked, wide eyed.

"Yes, like that one, I want you to become just like that one," I said, struggling not to grin as his eyes peeled wider still, the memory of the thing doubtless flashing through his mind. The way its bronze carapace gleamed in the sunlight, the great purple underbelly crackling with electricity. The maw, a giant cave lined with stalagmites and stalactites. The eyes, huge white boulders, each the size of a house. Its body floating through the sky, held aloft by crackling clouds. The way the winds it summoned flattened every tree within a mile of us when it landed. It would be impossible for any light walker to become that thing. Save one.

"But, Aster, I can't." he swallowed hard, shifting nervously from one foot to the other.

"Yes, you can. You're the infinite, and you're my apprentice. You can do it. Now, do you trust me?" I asked.

"Styx was hit, they went down somewhere over the new town." My breath caught in my throat, and my eyes stung. My smile was suddenly so heavy it threatened to drag the skin from my face.

"Do you really think so?" Sirius asked, turning out to face the wreckage of the school.

"Of course, I do." I swallowed. My throat was now a thick, aching thing, filling with bile.

"Then fly!" I croaked, releasing a shuddering breath, green light rippling out of me into the ivy clinging to the university walls, yanking him out into the open air. I staggered forward, bracing myself against the broken brickwork, watching his fall. A yelp of surprise echoed off the stone before an explosion of grey light engulfed us both. My mind was already in the rubble and the wreckage of New Town buildings, with Percy.

"Tera, I need you. Guide me to him." I stepped out onto nothing, forcing light through Vega's bracelet, becoming weightless. With my ebony staff in one hand, and coal studded cane clutched in the other, I flinched into the gale peeling off of Sirius, almost buffeting me back into the stonework.

"Is that—"

"Sirius." I couldn't muster the energy for more explanation than that. I didn't care. Percy was alone in the city, or worse, but I couldn't think about worse. If I thought about worse, I wouldn't be able to find him. I needed to find him. I ascended, letting the wind toss me through the air like a feather, until I reached Tera. Her wings battled frantically to stay by my side.

"He went down over there." She thought it, and I knew where her eyes had settled: a cluster of half-wrecked build-

ings in the shadow of the meteor dragon. Not special, no different from a dozen other clusters of brown brick and new town grey stone.

"You fly recklessly," Tera hissed into my mind, rippling through the sky beside me. The wind whipped tears from my squinting eyes as we screamed through the air.

"That's what he always says," I thought the words. The dragon's roars would have drowned my voice had a spoken them out loud. Its great shadow swallowed us, and I slowed, letting my eyes adjust.

"Where?" I called, twisting through the air as thunderclouds gathered about Sirius's leviathan form, looming high above. The city was lit up in fleeting moments, still frames of dust and rubble and blood, burned into the eye in a flash of lightning. Behind the thunder, I heard it, a cry. A nail screeching its way down a chalkboard, emanating from the alleyway up ahead. Wyverns. Wyverns on the ground. My chest seized, and my heart thrashed inside me like a caged dog. I jolted through the air, using more power than I needed to, forcing light out of me in punchy bronze flashes, before stopping dead at the entrance to the alley.

He was there, not one hundred feet away from me. No sign of Styx, but chunks of ice as big as barrels lay about the clearing. Styx had tried to break their fall. Percy lay pinned beneath the shattered remains of a gable end. Only visible from the hip up, Obol's frosted blade was out of his reach. Instead, a large chunk of bloodied rock was in his hand, raised menacingly above his head. Piercing blue eyes trained on the seven snaking coils of black leather, spikes and teeth stalking down the alley towards him. Then he saw me, his eyes flicked up, and met mine. He smiled at me, the stupid fool, and the leader of the wyvern pack broke rank, darting forward.

It had a tear in its wing, it couldn't fly, but scuttled like a scorpion towards him, tail poised overhead. I'd never hated the sight of anything more in my life. My teeth set like stone, and my arm moved automatically, hurling my ebony staff like a black dart. It punctured the vile streak of leather and teeth at the neck, just below its jaw, pinning it to the cobbles. Its life pulsed out of it in a pooling vermillion puddle, seeping into the channels between the cobbles, dying them red. There was a beat, filled with just the choking death of the noxious thing, before its pack turned. The six of them trained their sickly yellow snake-like eyes on me, and charged.

I reached out, fingers poised like talons, and felt the staff. With a pull of my arm, five sharpened black branches burst from it like spears. They jutted and twisted violently, catching three of the wyverns, and pinning them to walls of the alley. Without a thought, I clenched my hand into a fist, and thorns erupted, ripping the three of them from the inside out.

The first of the pack had avoided my ebony spears. It was almost upon me, pouncing with its neck craning towards me as I raised my coal-studded cane. As its jaw snapped shut around the tip, I channelled fire down its gullet, and watched the light in its eyes go out.

The last two tried to flee. Turning to the clouds, they started to flap their leathery wings, but the alley was too narrow. They couldn't find their speed, couldn't get the sky beneath them. They latched onto the walls, scrabbling up, pulling down tile and brick as they went. Beneath them, my ebony staff dug its roots into the ground. The vines of it bulged the street and upended cobbles until, with a flick of my wrist, a great black tree exploded upwards. With one last, sharp motion, I threw my arms wide and watched the great thick tree tear itself in half, bludgeoning the stunned creatures, and cracking the stone walls before withdrawing, letting their lifeless bodies drop with hollow thuds to the ground.

* * *

I was floating, landing, running, staggering, falling and crawling to his side, my breath ragged, chest tight, arms and legs heavy, eyes stinging, throat choked.

"Aster, go easy, your eyes are dim." Percy touched my face with such tenderness I almost melted.

"Shut up!" My voice broke as I grabbed for more light, forcing a flash of bronze, coating the rubble pinning him down, and throwing it aside with a violent swipe of my arm.

"Baby, you're shaking." His voice was so gentle, tears slipped treacherously down my cheeks.

"You're hurt." I sobbed, my eyes flicking to the tacky darkness slowly oozing through his trousers.

"It doesn't matter." He said it so easily, as his hands laced around my neck, pulling me towards him. He pressed a kiss to my forehead, as my tears dropped into his wounds. "My Aster Shepard, my husband and my hero, my cry baby, you saved me." Then, I finally did melt, collapsing into his arms.

"I was so scared when I heard you'd been hit," I confessed, clinging to him. My heart was hammering in my chest so hard, I was sure it'd shake loose a rib.

"I'm sorry I scared you." He rubbed soft circles into my back as he held me. I wanted to sink into him, to give in to his warmth and soft words and the illusion of safety.

"I can heal you, like in the forest, with Gloria." I pulled myself away, my voice shaking.

"Aster, you're exhausted," Percy said, with just the slightest hint of firmness.

"Let me." Tera's swan-like neck extended as she padded forward, her curled talons scratching against uprooted cobbles. Her eyes met mine, a deep forest green so dark that in Sirius' shadow they were almost black.

"Carefully," I said, backing away to make room for her beside Percy. My breath was frozen.

"Of course." She bowed as she approached. Then her claws curled into the ground, piercing the stone as moss grew, then mushrooms, and flowers, all propagating out of dust and stone. Then the pale green leaves of a willow sapling, its branches slick with an abundance of sap, coiled up to Percy's wound, knitting it together. I breathed out. not realising I'd been holding my breath.

"Chew this," I said, tearing a strip of bark from the plant, and pressing it to Percy's lips. Percy opened wide and bit down obediently. "For the pain." I added quickly.

"Of course." He grunted around the bark, somehow grinning.

"Does it hurt much?" I asked.

"I'm fine," Percy lied, wincing as he moved. He tentatively put his weight onto his knees as he pulled me back into his warmth. I could smell him. "Now, tell me, is that who I think it is?" Percy asked, after a beat. He pointed one hand up into the sky, towards the great purple underbelly of Sirius, now floating almost directly above the meteor dragon. The ground rumbled as it leapt once more into the air.

"Yep," I replied, sagging into Percy's warmth.

"How did you get him to—"

"I shoved him out a window," I replied, the corners of my mouth twitching towards a smile.

"You what?" Percy sounded half scandalised, half impressed.

"I had just heard my husband had crash landed. I can't be held responsible for my actions in such circumstances," I replied breathlessly, watching the black wool blanket of cloud above Sirius flash menacingly.

"Fair enough." Percy almost managed a laugh, squinting against the lightning as the meteor dragon lumbered upwards.

"It's up to him now." I breathed, wincing as the meteor dragon opened its terrible jaws and loosed a bone grinding roar.

Sirius's leviathan form shuddered. His steady drift paused, as lightning crackled menacingly across the bronze panelling of its back and the clouds above the dragon flashed so bright, the world was for a moment blank white. I squinted until I could open my eyes again, a streak of lightning blazed against the clouds. It had pierced the dragon like a needle through yarn. Its roar became a pained groan, as its wings unfurled to their fullest extent, like a preserved butterfly pinned on a display mount. A moment later, it was losing altitude, plummeting towards the ground. It fell out of sight with an ear-splitting crash, and a cloud of dust exploded through the city in all directions. I covered my eyes and nose, as the dry film plastered my lips.

As the air cleared, I watched Sirius ascend, his body crackling with more and more lightning. The clouds gathered above him were almost glowing, as the flashes became near enough constant. Endless thunder shook the foundation of our trembling city.

"It's not over," Percy said, nodding to the titanic head rearing up over the city rooves a few hundred feet from us. Its wings were unfurling, raining stone and shattered tiles over our heads. Tera extending her wide brown wings to shield us from the debris.

"Should we help?" Percy asked, reaching for Obol.

"I don't think he needs it," I replied. A calm washed over me, as the meteor dragon gathered itself, its ridiculous hindquarters extending to push itself up into the air.

I held my breath, watching the hundreds of feet between it and Sirius vanish in a fraction of a second, before the light dazzled me. I squinted through the gaps in my fingers, struggling to keep my eyes open as lightning forked downwards, hitting Sirius's bronze carapace. Cascading around his body like a waterfall, somehow getting brighter, thicker and more potent as it went. It wrapped around him and forked down. The meteor dragon convulsed on contact, curling inwards as the last of its momentum carried it up yet further. A terrible, shrieking, curdling sound filling the air, before it finally fell silent, tumbling back towards the ruined city.

"It's dead…" said Percy.

* * *

"Do you think he'll ever change back?" Astrid asked, standing beside the frame of my shattered office window. She was staring up at Sirius's leviathan form, suspended above our ruined city.

"I don't know," I said, barely registering the question as I stared at my desk. Or more accurately, the small, grubby black lamp on my desk. People had died. Wayne had died. Vega had sacrificed herself to save the city, using up every ounce of her light to do it. The giantess of Streya was no more. Ithaca was still out there, and she had Orion.

"Here you go, love, drink," said Percy, slipping my fingers through the handle of a teacup. He was walking again now.

"He has to change back, doesn't he?" Astrid asked Percy, as he handed her some tea.

"He'll change back, and we'll get Orion back too, don't worry." Percy was looking at Astrid, but somehow, I felt he was talking to me.

"It all went wrong," I thought aloud, as I rubbed at a dirty smudge on the lamp with my thumb.

"We'll put it right again," said Percy, gently lifting the lamp from my hands and setting it aside. He knelt before me, taking my hands into his, capturing me in his eyes; ice blue and yet warm.

I'd first seen them on my virgin excursion to The Clutch, when I was attending a banquet. He'd been one of the Sovereign's guests. As a boy born to the Burning

Mantle clan, he'd been expected to hatch and bond with a fire dragon. The fact that he'd not only discovered, but hatched and bonded with a lost grave dragon egg made him eligible for a special tourney. Elaine Sovereign had honoured him with a personal meeting. We'd met waiting in the announcement chamber together; from the moment I saw him, I'd not been able to take my eyes off him. He caught me looking at him, staring I suppose, from across the chamber. He looked at me, and as he smiled, he caught me in his ice-blue eyes. I'd never been free since. They were so beautiful that day, and on this one too. So beautiful that I didn't even notice the glaring flash of grey light as it framed my office floor, shining through the broken window.

"He's changed back!" Astrid yelled, dragging me back to the present.

"Is he okay?" I asked, heaving my exhausted body out of my chair.

"He's grown wings, you know how he does, I think he's heading for the rooftop."

"Tera, can you intercept him for us?" I thought, at the curled pile of wings, scales and horns, gently rumbling like a giant cat in the corner of my office. There was a pause, before a glowing green eye peeled open, and Tera unfurled herself.

"Of course, Aster." Her voice was warm and kind, and she moved so elegantly. Her body undulated like a green wave on the ocean. She crossed the length of the office in a couple of bounds and leapt through the window. Her wings unfurled as she took the air, and a breeze caught her, carrying her up into the sky.

"She's quite beautiful, isn't she," said Astrid, watching Tera drift up to meet Sirius.

"She might be big enough to ride now," said Percy, placing a hand on my shoulder.

"D'you think he'll be okay? What with what happened to Wayne?" Astrid asked.

"Were they together?" Percy asked.

"I think so," I replied, and Astrid gave a barely perceptible nod of affirmation. Her eyes were still on Sirius.

"Then no, he won't be alright," Percy replied gravely. All of us stepped aside as Sirius came into land. His broad grey wings folded inwards as he tucked his knees to his chest, shooting through the hole in the wall where a window used to be, and rolled to his feet. Tera followed him in and slid through the room, curling herself into a spiral before coming to rest behind me, almost like a giant snail shell.

"Did you see that?" Sirus asked, his broad electric smile catching me off guard.

"Why did you stay up in the air so long after everything was over?" Astrid asked, her tone sharpened by the anxiety of waiting.

"I don't know… I sort of… how long was I up there for?" Sirius asked, his excitement shrinking just a little.

"At least an hour," she replied, her own edges dulling.

"I guess I lost track of time. It just felt so good, like for the first time I wasn't bottling it all up. Like I was stretching my legs, stretching my everything. Using my power rather than strangling it felt good." Sirius's smile was turning sheepish, his confidence ebbing away with every word.

"That makes sense," I said, kindly. I stiffly crossed the room, racing against the drop of his smile. He'd forgotten up there in the sky, channelling light, feeling his power, winning. He'd forgotten, and now he was remembering. It reached his eyes as I reached for his hands.

"Wayne!" He half barked, half choked on the name, like he'd had to force it out. His hands pulled away from me, covering his face.

"Sirius, I'm so sorry." I took a step forward, and he took one back, his stare crashing into me, grey, glowing and steely.

"You should have let me give myself up!" He half sobbed, half snarled.

"Sirius, I couldn't, you must know that," I pleaded with him, taking another step closer. He didn't back away this time.

"Couldn't lose your precious infinite?" His voice lashed, but the sting of it didn't reach me. I was too busy watching the tears streaking unimpeded down his cheeks.

"Now, wait just a minute, Aster was protec—"

"It's fine, Percy." I cut him off. He wanted to defend me, and I loved him for that, but I didn't need defending right now.

"He's still fine, I see, your husband. We trekked across half the country to make sure he was alright, didn't we? All you had to do was let me!" Sirius had backed his way up to the wall now and was slipping down, the anger slipping away too. His voice was wavering, as his yells became cries.

"Wayne wouldn't have wanted that," I said, softly, kneeling before him.

"And what about what I want?" He broke down. His head dropped, and his chest fluttered as his breathing became a series of chocked sob.

"I'm so sorry," I repeated myself, a tentative hand reaching towards his shoulder.

"We should have done something," Sirius words bubbled out of him between wet sobs.

"None of us could have done anything at that point." Astrid spoke from behind me, her voice almost unrecognisably kind.

"I could have!" he exploded, his voice a cracked yell, snot bubbling from his nostrils like a distraught child.

"No, Sirius, you—"

"I could have though! I could have done something!" He pushed himself up, his eyes wild, clinging to anger, his body faintly glowing.

"Sirius, you did do something, you saved Streya," I said, reaching out, only to have my hand slapped away. His form was beginning to swell at the edges.

"I should have been better. Like Olympia. If I were like her, Wayne wouldn't have…" His voice trailed away with a shudder. Again, I reached out a hand, and again, he slapped it away, his breathing coming in rapid gasps.

"Sirius, this isn't—"

"You should have made me better!" He was yelling again. He half lunged, half staggered towards me, baring his teeth. A blur of black rushed past me and caught him. Percy had darted between us, catching Sirius. Wrapping his arms tightly around the boy's chest.

"It's over now." Percy's voice was loud, and hard and firm.

"He should have made me—"

"It's not your fault." Percy cut him off.

"If he'd let me give mys—"

"Wayne wouldn't have wanted that." Percy's voice was as calm and clear as the surface of a lake on a still night. Sirius sagged, slumping into him, the grey light around him receding.

"I forgot," he squeaked.

"That's okay," Percy replied.

"How could I forget?" asked Sirius.

"It happens. It doesn't mean anything." Percy stroked his hair, cradling him as if he were his son, easing him slowly down to the ground. I swallowed around the lump in my throat.

"It doesn't mean you loved him any less." I croaked, placing a gentle hand on Sirius's trembling shoulder.

"He died fighting for me," Sirius muttered softly into Percy's shoulder. His sobbing had stopped.

"Because he loved you," Percy replied. It was young love, quick and fleeting. I couldn't have guessed if he'd have felt it in a month, but he had felt it. Just as Percy and I had at his age.

"What you're feeling now, this ache," I whispered into his ear, "it's just the love you held for him, now that you've got no place to put it. It's a good thing. You'll be glad of it one day." I glanced at my husband, smiling in that sad way.

"Promise?" Sirius's voice was that of a child's, small and scared and a little hopeful.

"I promise," I replied, easing myself down beside him. Percy gentling lowered Sirius' head into his lap.

"Astrid, why don't you go get some rest?" I said, watching her sag with exhaustion, as Sirius finally calmed. She nodded, glanced up, and met my eyes, her own were dim and framed in red. Then she cast her piercing white gaze down to the floor, and shuffled out of my office. For the first time, possibly ever, Astrid was speechless.

Not long after she left, Sirius's body uncoiled, his breathing becoming rhythmic and calm. Gently, and with a lot of shushing, Percy managed to lift him, and carry him back to his dormitory. Finally, we found ourselves slouched in the squashy wingback armchairs of the senior commons, staring at the pile of rubble that was once a fireplace.

"Aster?" Percy's large, calloused hand had wrapped around my own.

"Uhum?" When called upon, I found my voice had shrunk to barely a sound at all.

"You're crying." His tone was gentle, and his touch light, as he thumbed a tear across my cheek. I swallowed.

"Again?" I joked, choking on a laugh.

"What is it?" Percy asked, pressing on.

"I hope he wasn't scared." I forced the words.

"He was brave." Percy's voice was a low rumble in my ear.

"I know it's just… I just can't stop thinking about how scared he was the first time we met. How Cora had scared him. I hope he didn't die scared." The echo of my sob bounced through the empty room.

"He was brave," Percy repeated, because there was nothing else to say.

"You're right," I said, drawing a deep shuddering breath, before forcing myself to my feet.

"You need to rest." Percy reached for my hand, but I let my fingers slip through his. I couldn't let him pull me into his lap. I couldn't heed the exhaustion wracking my body, nor the tiny flickering ember that remained of my light.

"Can't. More to do," I said, shooting him a look, the kind of telepathic look spouses share. The kind of look that can beg, and plead. That can say, 'please don't fight me on this, I don't have it in me.'

"What's next?" Percy asked.

"We find Orion," I replied, squaring my shoulders and drawing a deep breath, fighting not to tremble through it.

"How?"

"I don't know."

7

<u>A Shepard and his flock</u>

"Bronze-hued light walkers and plenty with bronze lenses have been working throughout the night, clearing rubble and excavating anybody who has been trapped within. All told, almost two hundred casualties have been pulled from the wreckage," explained Marlon. He'd taken the lead in the rescue efforts once the battle subsided. How he had remained upright this long was a mystery. Most of the collected faculty and governors of the school had assembled for his briefing, almost all of us looking exhausted, pale and dim eyed. The leadership of Streya, run ragged.

"How many fatalities?" asked a grey-haired, navy-eyed lady I'm sure I'd been introduced to at some point.

"So far, thanks to the fine efforts of our yellow hued colleagues and yellow lens users, the death toll has remained mercifully low. Numbering fifty so far, we don't expect to find many more." I got the impression we were supposed to be pleased with fifty deaths, but I was struggling to see it as a silver lining. More like a dirty great red streak.

"We need to decide a new headmaster or mistress," Nick grumbled, slumped back in his chair. His were eyes red, and his dark skin dry and greyed by rubble dust. I doubted he'd slept at all.

"The governors will vote on a new candidate," said Marlon. Everyone in the room already knew that, but there was no other response to give. Nick shrugged and slumped back further. He wasn't really interested in the next headteacher, he was just reminding us of what had happened to the last one.

"What, if anything, have the Sovereigns to say about all of this? It was their people that attacked us." Dusk bristled at me, as Lance was at my beck and call.

"Well—"

"His Majesty Lance Sovereign has generously pledged to provide soldiers and resources to aid in the rebuilding of Streya." Magda's great niece, Serenity, cut me off, standing abruptly and parroting the message she'd delivered to me an hour ago. Which we'd all already heard.

"May I raise a new item for the agenda?" I asked, unsure if I should raise my hand or stand or just barrel on. No one objected, so I barrelled on.

"We need to find Orion and Ithaca. She was responsible for the attack. I believe she was behind the attempted kidnapping of apprentice Sirius, and she has taken apprentice Orion." Dusk wilted under my glare, a low whisper spreading around the table.

"Didn't you say that Ithaca had The Shroud of The

Night Mother in her possession?" Nick asked, his tone prickly.

"I did," I confirmed, trying not to take it personally. I reminded myself of the bullish young man who covered his insecurity with loud clothes and exposed skin, asking me to talk him up in front of his crush. A young Aster Shepard, rambling about the virtues of his roommate Nick, wouldn't have held any weight at all with the Vega Truelight.

"Well then, how do you expect us to find them, she has a powerful violet lens. It would be child's play for her to hide their minds from us," Dusk added, with renewed vitriol, as if he hadn't tried to personally hand Sirius over to Ithaca.

"I was hoping that the collective brightest minds of Streya all being in one room together might be able to come up with something," I snapped. The absence of their reply was deafening.

"Have you contacted his family yet, Aster? Given you were his master, the news should probably come from you," said Marlon, filling the heavy silence.

"He doesn't have one. We're it, we're the best he's got. Poor soul." I wrestled with my voice, which seemed to want to yell.

"Aster please sit down; you're going to wear yourself out," said Percy, following me with his eyes as I paced the floor of our cottage. He was stirring something that smelt fantastic. I hadn't the heart to tell him that I had no appetite at all.

"They're useless. The most powerful and learned beacons on the continent, and not one sorry idea between them."

"They're exhausted, like you are," said Percy as he lifted whatever it was he was cooking off the stove and set it aside.

"Yes, and they were all excited to get home to their beds. You know who isn't in his bed right now? Orion! We don't even know if he's still alive." My chest was tight, and my hands were sweaty again. Every time I let myself think about it, my body reacted as if I was standing on the edge of a cliff staring down at jagged rocks.

"He's alive," Percy said in a firm voice, taking my hands in his as he led me to my rocking chair.

"How do you know?" I asked. He'd told me before, but every time he did it helped. It helped to hear him being rational, because I couldn't seem to manage it.

"Because she took him. If she'd wanted to kill him, she could have. She didn't, which means she has a use for him, therefore, he's alive."

"You're right," I said, my chest inflating a little. "So how do we find him?" I asked, returning to my impossible question.

"I'm not sure that we can, maybe we just have to wait for her to come to us, she didn't get what she wanted after all, and the city's still standing. So, she must have demands," Percy reasoned, returning to his stove.

"What if she returns with another meteor dragon?" I said, getting up to pace again.

"There's no way she—" Percy was cut off by a knock at the door.

"Hello, anybody home?" A familiar, if slightly muffled voice carried into the living room through our post box.

"Impossible." I breathed, turning to face the door, as Percy moved to open it. Part of me wanted to run or hide, or pretend I was sick, or quickly master the art of turning invisible. Instead, I stood rooted to the spot.

"Percy! Darling! Don't you look handsome, and tall too, aren't you tall? Did you get taller?" Mum stepped through the doorway and pulled my husband into a tight hug. She was a flurry of questions and compliments, dressed in a long pink summer dress with a coarse brown farmer's coat hanging off her shoulders. She looked like she was about to attend what she would call, *a do*. This was Helen Shepard, at the height of her power.

"Haha, I don't think I've grown, Mrs Shepard, unless Aster's been stretching me in my sleep." Percy chuckled, repeating his tried-and-true line. I wondered if Mum would ever notice, but she didn't seem to, or gave no indication if she did. Percy ushered her into the cottage, followed, to my surprise, by my dad. I half wondered if I'd nodded off and this was all a dream.

"Stretching you in your sleep, oh aren't you funny and handsome too isn't my boy lucky? Now, Aster, my little professor, how are you? You look tired, have you been sleeping? You must sleep, you know. And eat, you look thin, your eyes are terribly dim, what's that smell? Is that you, Percy? Something smells gorgeous, doesn't it smell gorgeous, Pan?"

"Smells gorgeous," Dad confirmed, giving Percy a firm handshake, which became a hug.

"I don't understand," I said, thickly. I went limp, as Mum grabbed me and pulled me into a tight hug, which Dad quickly joined in on, almost squeezing the breath from my lungs. "How are you here?" I wheezed disbelievingly.

"Well, we heard about all the nastiness that had happened, and we thought we'd come down and, you know, help out," said Mum guiding me to back to my chair and kneeling in front of me, like I was a child. Her golden eyes were shining warmly. Shepard's eyes, just like remembered.

"How?" I asked, struggling to find a complete sentence.

"Oh well, you know, cleaning, laundry, do you two have a laundry basket? Pan, go and see if they have a laundry basket. Gosh and these cupboard doors could do with a good wipe down. I could go around with a mop. Have you got a mop? We can get you a mop if you like. I'll bake a pie; you wouldn't mind my borrowing your kitchen, would you, Percy? There's pie in it for you, of course." My mouth was opening and closing wordlessly, whilst Mum had one of her patented solo participant conversations.

"No. I mean, how did you hear about it and get here so fast?"

It didn't make sense. Word of the attack on Streya was spreading, but it couldn't possibly have reached Shepard's Pasture before this morning, and no one in my family had mastered the silver lens. Nick, perhaps? But he wasn't in any shape to be doing favours.

"Well, it was the funniest thing, we were sitting down to supper, Pan and I, and we heard a knock at our door, didn't we, Pan?" Dad nodded.

"We thought maybe Mr Mills one farm over, needed a hand with something. You know that son of theirs has been giving them the run-around recently. Have you heard? He was born grey; he's been shape shifting all over the place. I think it's quite funny actually, but his mother, my goodness, you should see her—"

"Someone was at the door!" I blurted out, before we got sucked into gossiping about the Mills. Which would inevitably lead to gossiping about every other neighbour in a five-mile radius.

"Right, yes, so we go to the door, and lo-and-behold, it's not the Mills, but a charming little fairy fellow, what was his name, Pan?"

"Bren."

"Yes, that's right, Bren."

"Prince Bren came to your door?" I asked, my eyes widening. I shot a look at Percy, he shrugged, just as lost as me.

"He was a prince? My goodness, he didn't say, he should have said, we'd have invited him in. Although I don't know what I'd have given him. What do you serve up for a prince? I've never been very good at elegant little picky bits. Do you think that's what princes eat? Like salmon puffs, I bet princes love salmon puffs."

"Focus, Mum." I groaned exhaustedly.

"Right, so lovely Bren comes to the door, and he says he knows you and you did a good turn for him looking after his niece. I said, well that sounds like our Aster. He's always doing people good turns, and then he said you might be in a spot of bother. He said that Streya had fallen foul of some nasty characters and that our son might need a helping hand, just like his niece did. He said he wanted to return the favour, so he whizzed by to drop us a call. So, we said, what did we say Pan?"

"We said—"

"That's right, Pan, we said we'd best get over there as quick as we can because our Aster might need us, and I have to say, love, you do look overtired. Have you been sleeping? Has he been sleeping, Percy? I don't think you've been sleeping enough."

"But how did you get here, Mum?" I asked, on the brink of frustrated tears.

"Well, Bren very kindly opened up a little green portal for us. He said if we stuck to the path, we couldn't go far wrong, and we were here in two shakes of a lamb's tale weren't we, Pan?"

"Just two shakes," Dad confirmed after dipping a finger to taste whatever it was that Percy had been cooking. There was a lump forming in my throat.

"You took the Green Way?" Panic flooded through me. I'd have lost my lunch if I'd eaten any.

"I don't know, love, I suppose so." She said it like it was nothing, so casually, like it hadn't taken a second thought.

"Mum, the Green Way is dangerous, you could have…

anything could have happened." My mouth was dry, somehow my tongue didn't seem to fit in it anymore, and my hands felt buzzy.

"Oh, foo dangerous! It was a hop, skip and a jump and we were here. Was no more dangerous than the garden path, and our little boy was in trouble. We had to come." She was beaming now, the lump getting larger and more painful by the moment.

"Course we did, Aster, your mum wouldn't have slept a wink for worrying otherwise. And you know how she is when she doesn't sleep," Dad explained, without raising his head from his search for a spoon. Percy kindly handed him a ladle.

"Aster lovey, you're shaking, come here." Mum stood, took my head in her hands, and held me to her stomach.

"Thank you for coming." I croaked, swallowed and tried to speak again, but only mustered a broken cry and all of a sudden, I was sobbing. Clutching my mother's dress like I was seven, and I'd grazed my knee.

"Oh dear, now look, you're all upset. Whatever's the matter can't be all that bad. Leave it to me and Pan, we'll fix it, won't we, Pan?" Mum ran her fingers through my hair.

"'Course we will," Dad replied, ambling over to rub my back as I soaked the front of Mum's dress with tears. The lump in my throat was melting away, little by little.

"Why don't you go take a little nap, everything will be better with an hour of sleep under your belt," said Mum when I finally let go of her dress.

"I can't, Mum, I've got to find Orion," I said, wobbling dangerously as I stood. My head was light and swimmy.

"That shy, void-eyed lad? Why where has he run off to?" asked Mum.

"He was taken by a woman named Ithaca. She has some magical artifact, and she's been hiding him from anyone with a violet lens or violet light, and I don't know what to do." The explanation rushed out of me like water from a well.

"He's been driving himself mad worrying about it," said Percy, gravely.

"Well, of course he has, he's a Shepard. Shepards don't leave folks behind," said Mum, repeating the words that would be emblazoned on our family crest, if our family was the type of family that had a crest. I didn't hasten to add that I'd already done a pretty good job of leaving them behind, but the thought was there all the same.

"We can help find the lad," said Dad.

"You don't understand, she's hiding him," I repeated, desperately.

"I doubt she's hiding him from dogs," said Dad sagely, as if that was supposed to mean something.

"Good idea, Pan. Aster you just rest, we'll get cracking. The sooner we find him, the sooner you can relax properly," said Mum, marching towards the door like a woman on a mission.

"Where are you going?" I asked, half dazed.

"We need to find some of this boy's things, so wherever he lives is where we're going." She beamed, beckoning Dad towards the door. She was in organiser mode now. She was the woman who'd thrown forty years of Shepard barn parties and built a community out of invitations and cajoling. And somehow, in that moment, she seemed more capable than every useless, stuffy old beacon in that meeting combined.

* * *

Mum and Dad sent word via carrier pigeon, of all things. We were to meet them at the dragon aerie, a place of harsh stone pillars and several inverted brick domes for its denizens to shelter in. It was large, and grey, and austere. Although, with Tera's presence, all that was changing. Now, moss was appearing within the cracks, and tracks of ivy were sprouting up the walls. Dangling flowers framed the porthole that faced out over Streya's border and the world beyond, like a ragged green curtain. The sun was high and bright, so bright that the glare of the city's web of light was almost completely washed away.

Styx looked changed too. A jagged scar ran along his freshly-healed left wing. Chipped and cracked scales decorated the hind leg on the same side, in a vaguely mouth shaped pattern. After the crash, he'd run himself ragged defending Percy and collapsed from exhaustion and blood loss two streets over. Tera had been diligently tending to him since she'd found him, but the marks would remain.

"We found some stragglers!" Mum called, trekking up the hill the aerie was built upon, looking down over Streya, with her summer dressed hiked up at her waist. Dad followed in her wake, and behind him, Astrid and Sirius.

"What are you two doing here?" I asked, easing myself up off the picnic blanket Percy had laid on the ground, doing my best to make it look easy. With two hours of sleep under my belt, I felt a little less frayed, but I wasn't exactly refreshed.

"You've got a plan to save Orion, right? I want to help." Sirius spoke first, his eyes were flashing, and his chest puffed. He was almost convincing, but the bed hair gave him away.

"Sirius, it'll be dangerous, remember what…" I let my voice tail off, cringing at my own patronising tone.

"Who better to take into a dangerous situation than the man who just felled a meteor dragon?" Sirius said, flashing a cocky and wholly unconvincing grin.

"Sirius, she's smart, she's tricky, brute force won't be the answer." I tried to be as gentle as I could.

"Please, Aster, I'll be careful, I'll do whatever you say." He was almost begging now, and closing the distance between us fast.

"Oh, go on, Aster, let the boy come," Mum chipped in, unhelpfully.

"Sirius, if you just stay—"

"Please don't make me stay here, I'll be climbing the walls. Orion is my dorm mate, the whole place is a reminder that he's missing, and the commons. I can't be in the commons, one glance at a fireplace and suddenly I'm thinking of…" His voice tailed off.

"Okay fine, you can come, but you do exactly as I say. No heroics, no charging in, no tackling anybody out of the way of anything, under any circumstances, got it?" I asked, doing my very best stern teacher face.

"Of course, thank you." Sirius nodded his thanks, whilst I imagined what my life would have been like if I weren't such a soft touch.

"Well, if he can come, I'm definitely coming," Astrid chipped in, timing her argument perfectly. I wouldn't have expected any less.

"Naturally." I sighed.

"Well, now that that's all sorted out, I think we're ready to get cracking," said Mum. She'd been fervently rubbing what looked like one of Orion's old socks, against various other bits of rag, and things that Dad had passed to her.

"Ready for what?" Astrid asked, watching the whole performance with thinly veiled disgust.

"I errm… I'm not…"

"She told me to root out his dirtiest clothes. Which was a bit tricky, actually. Orion's very neat, but I'm pretty sure those are the spare pair of socks he wore on our errm… field trip. He only brought two pairs," Sirius explained. He seemed less disgusted that Astrid, but no less curious.

"It's for the dogs," said Dad, shooting us a quick wink as he rubbed a dirty sock against an old tea towel, and right at the back of my mind sound rang out, clear as a bell.

"The dogs?" Astrid asked.

"Just watch," I replied, remembering the time Mum and Dad had scoured a whole forest for one of the Mills girls in an hour flat. I was a little annoyed I'd not thought of the idea myself.

"Ready, Pan?" asked Mum.

"Ready, Ma," replied Dad, as they linked hands. They stood out facing Streya and each put two fingers to their lips, letting loose a sharp whistle. Ringing sounds pierced the air, and waves of soft golden light began to radiate off them. They held the note for five or so seconds and then withdrew their fingers, but the light kept growing and the sound kept ringing. Without being prompted, Astrid stepped forward, placed a hand on each of their backs and engulfed them, just for a moment, in a flash of white. Mum wiggled excitedly as the golden light pulsing off them doubled in brightness, spreading further and further. Then it happened all at once, howls started to break throughout the rubble city.

"That should do the trick," said Dad, rubbing his hands together expectantly, as he watched the city.

"And my goodness me wasn't that boost fun? Was that you, dear? With those bright white eyes of yours? Aren't you a treat? I've never felt anything like that before. Have you, Pan?"

"Never felt anything like it," Dad agreed, still watching the city, as Astrid shrank a little from the compliment.

"So, what happens now?" Sirius asked.

"The little helpers come of course. Don't you worry, my lad, we'll find your friend," said Mum, clasping a hand to Sirius face and giving him a big wink. She had something in her that was so steadying, like a great big stone pillar, only soft, and warm, and in a summer dress. It was something that was hard to come by in Streya, but plentiful in the Pasture.

"Here they come," said Dad. I looked back towards the city just in time to catch sight of the first of them arriving. Little patters of feet and panting sounds and swishing tails and a blur of fur, as dozens of golden eyed dogs streamed out of the city.

"Now, come on kids, take a good whiff, and the fastest

of you, pick up a piece and take it with you. Spread that smell around." Mum gave her commands whilst kneeling, passing out ear scratches and tummy rubs as the horde of dogs breathed Orion in. The largest and fastest of them picking up rags laden with his scent, before bolting in all directions.

"Oh, I get it now," said Astrid, her face lighting up in that way it did when she learned a new bit of magic. It wasn't the sort she'd find in a textbook; golden magic didn't feature much in those.

"Well, of course you do, you're a clever girl," said Mum, beaming as she surveyed the pack of dogs quickly dispersing.

"Is there anything I can do to help?" Sirius asked, fidgeting.

"All that's left to do is wait, soon enough they'll catch his scent, and we'll be off to the races," Mum explained, cheerily.

"But what if he's not in the city?" Sirius's anxiety was beginning to remind me of my own.

"They take the scent with them, passing it on like a chain, that's why Mum was making more clothes smell of him. Of course, if he's on the other side of the continent, we'll be in trouble, but I think Ithaca won't have gone too far. After all, you're here and you're the one who she's got her eye on," I explained, pleased to find my ability to think rationally had returned.

As we waited, Tera and I coaxed twisted lengths of pliant vine wood from the ground and formed chairs for us all to sit in. I situated myself in Percy's lap, watching the sun pass over the city as we chatted. Astrid wanted to plan some complex, many staged attack on Ithaca, but that proved rather difficult without knowing where she was, who was with her or what she was capable of. That, and even Astrid's defences didn't hold out long against Mum's relentless onslaught of chitchat and gossip. Tera had taken up a position beside us, and as the day slipped on, more and more wildflowers bloomed at our feet, forming a steady carpet of pink and yellow.

Streya, even in its damaged state, had a kind of beauty to it. From the aerie's high vantage point, we could make out almost everything. The little cottages and ancient cobbled streets that encircled the giant that was the university at its centre. The more modern sprawling city that poured outwards, peopled with its great stone towers and statues. Pocked with its various parks and gardens, where Percy and I had spent our forbidden youthful days, hiding within the greenery. Streya was a university, with an old town built around it, with a new city built around that and, in spite of everything, it was alive.

"Well, I think the wait is over," said Mum sitting up in her chair, as the sound of panting drew near. It had worked, they wouldn't be back so soon without an answer, which meant relief. Although a little part of me was sad our time in our chairs watching the sun sail across Streya was over.

"I'll get Styx ready to fly," said Percy. The first dog had reached us now, a little whippet of a thing. It looked like somewhere in its lineage you'd expect to find a squirrel. Mum and Dad knelt, giving it some attention, whilst reading its mind with their golden eyes.

"Will all of us fit on Styx?" asked, Astrid nervously.

Four was quite a large load for Styx, which I'd not really considered before now.

"I'm not sure," I said, trying to estimate how much we all weighed and add it up in my head.

"I could fly myself, maybe?" suggested Sirius, hastily. Likely worried I'd revoke his and Astrid's invitation.

"You will ride me, Aster," Tera's voice rumbled firmly into my head.

"Are you sure?" I asked aloud, turning to her. She did look big enough, I had to admit, and the prospect did bring with it a certain excitement. It was every little dragon-obsessed light walker's impossible dream to ride their own dragon. The sort of thing you grow out of. I suppose part of me, even once she'd hatched, hadn't expected this particular fantasy to come true.

"Of course." Her voice was all serenity and confidence, and I was a rush of butterflies and excitement.

"Don't worry about it," I said, turning back Astrid, who'd been watching our half audible conversation intently.

"Right, boys and girls, we've got your heading, so gather round. Aster, fetch out that rabbit's foot of yours," said Mum, coming to a stand, whilst Dad continued to pay most of his attention to the dogs. Percy padded over with Styx, and we were all ready.

"I'm ready," I said, softly. I rubbed the foot twice between my thumb and forefinger for luck, before easing my light into it, and watching gold hum out. Mum put her hand on my shoulder, locked her eyes with mine, and a path rushed into my mind. I was running down into the Titanic Lands, through a great crevasse in the earth, down and down into the tropical jungle cavern. A short stream of water was running down, to a moss-covered porthole, leading to a low-ceilinged cave, with an underground lake and a few shadowy figures clustered at its far edge. I shuddered, took a steadying breath and let the golden light fade.

"Now, you go get that apprentice of yours back," said Mum, giving me a wink. I looked back over my shoulder. Percy had already helped Astrid and Sirius up onto Styx and returned to wait by my side.

"Thank you for everything," I said, giving them each a quick kiss on the cheek before turning to leave. I don't know if I imagined it, or if it was real, the small drop in the smile, a little sigh, but the stabbing guilty feeling was there again. I turned back to face them and immediately felt as though I was going to burst into tears.

"I'm sorry for leaving!" I blurted it out before I could think better of it, and found Mum and Dad looking somewhat puzzled.

"You've got to leave, Aster, to rescue that lad," said Dad, confusedly.

"No, I mean, I'm sorry for leaving Shepard's Pasture. I know I hurt you when I left, and I'm just… I'm just sorry." There was that lump in my throat again. Mum and Dad turned to each other, sharing one of their telepathic little looks. Dad smiled, and Mum turned back to me.

"Aster, you don't need to apologise for leaving, we never expected you to stay, did we, Pan? We knew since you were very little, those big green eyes of yours, the way you'd light up hearing stories about Streya, the City of Lights, and of dragons." Mum's smile shone as she spoke.

"Loved your dragon stories," Dad confirmed.

"But you always said Shepards don't leave folks behind." The words ached.

"You didn't leave us behind. Oh, my lovely, silly boy. That was just see you later, not goodbye," said Mum clasping a hand to my cheek.

"Has this been on your mind, son?" Dad asked. I nodded. My voice had deserted me.

"Is this why you've not been coming round to visit much? You know you're always welcome, even just an afternoon would be nice." Mum's eyes were sparkling.

"But you always look so sad when I leave, I feel like I'm letting you down, like I should stay longer." The words spilled out like water from behind a broken dam. Memories of Mum's sad 'ohs' and wobbling bottom lip crashed into my mind.

"Ma cries when Alexis goes back home, and she's down for tea every other day and lives one farm over, ya daft sod!" Dad chuckled and grabbed me, slapping my back as he hugged me.

"It's true, Aster, you know I do. Terrible with good-byes, aren't I, Pan?"

"You are, Ma, that you are." I found myself laughing and crying into Dad's chest all at once. A little weight eased off me, as I bunched his shirt in my fists. I was suddenly aware of a desire to reach back through time, and tell myself not to wait so long to reconcile. Not to hide away and leave so much unsaid, but of course I couldn't. So, I swallowed the little bit of regret that came with the relief.

"Helen, do you think we could come down for Frost Stars Eve?" Percy asked, as Dad released me. All at once,

Mum's face crumpled into a creased red smile sprung with happy tears.

"My stars, Percy, you bring my Aster and you can come for Frost Stars Eve and stay till summer!" Mum beamed, and grabbed us both, pulling us into a tight hug.

"That'd be nice," said Dad.

"Oh, do come, please." Mum sounded halfway between excited and begging as she squeezed us both.

"We'll come," I said, doing my best to squeeze her back.

"Oh, Pan, our boys are coming home for the holidays!" said Mum, letting us go to grab Dad and squeeze him too.

"So I hear." Dad chuckled wetly.

"Right, enough of this mushy nonsense, you go save that little apprentice of yours, and bring him along too if you like, bring the whole bloody lot of 'em, let's make it a year to remember," Mum said, shooing me and Percy away, her face shining with tears.

"Your family is rather emotional, Aster," said Tera, as she lowered herself for me. I climbed onto her lithe back, my eyes still on them.

"Yes, we are," I agreed, waving to them as Tera kicked off into the air.

"It's not goodbye! Just see you later!" Mum yelled, as we climbed into the sky.

* * *

Riding Tera wasn't like riding Styx, or Nova, or like flying myself. Her wings spent almost all their time outstretched, like sails, tilting this way or that to catch the wind. When they did beat the air, they did so in one singular, powerful motion, grabbing us and pulling us further up into the sky. I bobbed as we soared, holding fast to her horns as her body rippled backwards. It was as though we were at one with the wind. Free and easy, like breathing. Cool currents coaxed streaks to run from my eyes, and whipped my hair up. A refreshing chill flew over my scalp and down to the nape of my neck, washing something away with it as it ran off my back. I looked out over the cracked, arid Titanic Lands vanishing behind and beneath us, and caught a glimpse of a seam I recognised. A seam that part of me remembered.

"There," I thought, and Tera folded her wings as she twisted through the sky, beginning our descent.

"I've never flown beneath the ground before," said Tera, as we dove into the crevasse. Her wings tucked in neatly, so as not to catch the sides. She stretched her legs and began to half glide, half canter down the steep and craggy rock face.

"It's not so far now," I thought, remembering how the crevasse would soon open, becoming the mouth of a cave looking out over a tropical subterranean canyon. The air was growing thick and humid, as Tera's wings unfolded once more. Our entrance way opened halfway up the chamber wall and sloped down, leaving us to leap out into the open. The cathedral-like space was vast, lit only by the light that pierced through the hundreds of cracks in the ceiling, bathing half of the cavernous chamber in nourishing shafts of light, while the rest remained in hollow darkness. The cave walls were pocked with holes, which supplied trickling rivers and waterfalls, feeding the damp

and swampy ground beneath. Tera glided in circles, gently climbing until our heads almost grazed the ceiling, whilst we surveyed the floor.

"Fly lower, we're looking for another cave, maybe with water flowing into it," I thought, as I scanned the ground. It was impossible to pick out a cave from this height, but I had started to notice movement. What I'd initially thought of as stones, owing to their large size and greenish grey exterior, were actually creatures. Creatures big enough to comfortably seat four on their backs. Quadrupeds with frilled faces and large horns. As we flew closer, I made out their beak-like mouths, cutting through tropical trees like rabbits munching celery.

"What are they?" Tera asked, now circling just a few stories above the ground. Styx and the others had entered by now, and were circling above us.

"I don't know, they look almost like a cross between a giant bird and a giant lizard," I thought, as much to myself as to Tera. I'd heard the stories of ancient creatures that dwelt beneath the Titanic Lands, but I'd never seen them. Whatever the case, they didn't seem aggressive. Tera was more nervous of them than me. As we came in to land near a trickling stream, she breathed out a cloud of a thick purple substance I couldn't quite identify. Each beat of her wings was spreading it out around us. The eyes of creature it reached became heavy lidded, and they began to move more slowly.

"What was that?"

"Concentrated valerian pollen. It dulls the waking to ensure our safety," Tera explained landing with soft footfalls.

"You can do that?" I asked, more than a little impressed.

"I expect you can too, with the help of that staff," Tera replied, as Styx landed beside us and his passengers quickly dismounted. Little blooms of frost expanded out across the soggy ground beneath his feet.

"Stay behind us," I said to Astrid and Sirius, as Percy and I took the lead, following our little watery guide. We had to be careful not to slip, as the path sloped gently downwards. I fanned myself as we walked, already feeling the sweat sticking me to my clothes.

"Here," whispered Percy, holding Obol's ice-cold blade to my side, as he caught me pushing my damp fringe back from my face. All of us were creeping almost silently across the softened ground. A relieved shiver ran over me, as the cold mist that poured from the sword, chilled my clammy skin.

"Thank you," I whispered, slipping my cloak off, and draping it across Tera's back before I could sweat all the way through it. Percy did the same, stripping down to only his trousers and his black undervest. Sweat that ran like rivulets down his muscular arms to his fingertips, turned to ice at Obol's passing. Sirius, who for his part was barely ever wearing more than a vest anyway, quickly stripped down to just his shorts, leaving Astrid the sole member of the party still fully clothed. She'd taken to sheltering at the back of the group, never straying more than a few inches from Styx's perpetually cool wings.

On our way, we passed one of the grey-green creatures. Its head was bowed, as it drank from the stream we were following. Its head frill was grey on the outer ring, with circles of red in the centre that bore a crude resemblance to eyes. I was so drawn into the false red eyes, that I almost didn't notice what looked like a discarded and somewhat chewed sock beside the stream.

"We're close," I whispered, looking around. I envisioned the route my mother had passed onto me, recalling the mossy porthole. I looked and looked, but there were no obvious cave mouths yawning out at us.

"Anyone see anything?" I hissed, a little panic rushing to my chest. Had I taken us into the wrong tropical subterranean chasm? It was only the memory of a dog I was following.

"Aster, it's beside your knee," Tera's voice issued calmly into my mind. I looked to my side, knowing already that there was no great hole in the cave wall here. *"Look down."*

I followed her instruction and found a small inlet, more like a rabbit's warren than a cave entrance. Perhaps and foot and a half across, it was sunk into the wall of the cave, and almost completely concealed by a mossy drape. It had looked bigger in my memory, but it was dawning on me now that what I'd been shown was from the perspective of a little whippet of a dog.

"I've been very stupid," I grumbled, sinking to my knees to look into the hole.

"Well, we're not fitting through there," hissed Astrid.

"Oh, I can actually do something," Sirius said, excitedly and too loudly.

"Shhh!" Astrid hissed, elbowing him sharply in the ribs.

"Sorry, sorry! Just, okay, hang on." Sirius dropped his

voice to a whisper and released a low, slow exhale, as a gentle grey glow started emanating from him, little by little engulfing us all. I squinted into the light, watching him, and gasped as the world began to rush away from me. The trees and rocks were stretching upwards, as the ceiling vanished into the distance. The whole world shifting, as I stumbled, disoriented into Percy. He grasped my forearm and held me steady.

"You okay, Aster?" Sirius asked, in an unusually high-pitched voice.

"Just disoriented," I whispered, looking around at the plants and trees that were now gigantic. I felt a sudden pang of anxiety at the thought of running into another of those grey horned creatures.

"He shrank you." Tera sounded indignant.

"Oh," I said to myself, as it dawned on me what had happened.

"Good idea, Sirius," Percy squeaked. He took my hand and made for the now reasonably sized porthole, just as I'd remembered it.

* * *

"Now, you two stay back," I whispered, barely making a sound at all.

Sirius had returned us to our normal size, and we were huddled on the other side of the porthole. The trickle of water was widening fast. We were now within spitting distance of the little clammy dark cavern, which opened up into a large underground lake, complete with shadowy figures.

"So, when do we do something?" Astrid asked, in a barely audible voice.

"If it looks like, we're definitely going to die," Percy whispered, giving the two of them a wink, before we started creeping towards the opening that led to the lake chamber.

It was cooler here, and dark, and quiet. We hid our footsteps behind dripping sounds, and the moaning wind currents shuddering through the caverns. The waterway we followed reached a natural arch, after which the cave opened up. There was an underground lake. What little light that did penetrate this deep, glistened across its surface like silver dancing on black glass, reflected in the mirror sheen of the cave roof.

A small, soft glow emanated from the far side of the cave, a warm light, that cast giant shadows, tripping across the walls. It looked like two figures. One was stooped over something, casting the silhouette of a reader, the other was larger, and reclined against the cave wall. One had to be Ithaca, the other, perhaps a guard. There was no sign of Orion, they must have had him hidden in some other chamber of the cave. Whatever the case, now was the time to act.

With one hand gripped tightly to my ebony staff, I unclipped the grubby black lamp from my belt. Once I had it in hand, Percy turned to me, blew me a kiss and then broke away. He skulked towards the shadows, quickly vanishing into the blackness. I took a slow, steadying breath, and ever so gently, balanced the tip of my staff on the ground. It began to sink and spread into a carpet of roots and vines and earth, clambering over the clammy stone ground. With my free hand, I withdrew my coal studded cane. Taking one last breath, I snapped into action, pushing light into the lamp and the cane simultaneously.

The lamp flickered, and then cast out a cone of warm, yellow-orange light, not unlike the cosy glow of a hearth. Simultaneously, a bout of flame bloomed from the coals, and exploded across the lake surface. I didn't want to fight Ithaca. I just wanted to win.

The flames moved quickly, piling high, and spilling across the walls at the far end of the cave. Enveloping all, gold and red flashed across the slick, black walls. Part of me hoped that perhaps that was it, perhaps we'd won.

"Well, that was rude." The voice echoed, not from the corner of the cave, which was now steaming, but from somewhere further along to the right. Near where Percy had disappeared.

I twisted around, shining the lamp's homely light into the darkness. The image that met my gaze was strange. A hunched older woman, with waist-length grey hair that hung like seaweed, melting away as the warm light touched her. Another figure was emerging in her place, almost like a shell peeling back. There stood a slight man, short of stature, with wavy, shoulder-length, dirty-blond hair. His features were delicate and fine, and his age was impossible to guess. The focal point of the face, his twinkling opal eyes. Immediately, I wanted to run and hide.

My breath caught in my chest, as fear threatened to swallow me up. Stood just behind him, was the meteor rider that had threatened me that day in The Clutch. Although now, his muscled body was riddled with gashes and scars, and his left arm was gone completely, severed at the shoulder. Percy's work; he'd told me about their fight. If fear wasn't stampeding through me, I might have felt pride at that moment.

"Sky?" No sooner had the word left my lips, than a smile curled his. The muscled figure behind him made a move towards me, but Sky raised a hand and halted him.

"He knows who you are," he grunted.

"And?" Sky asked, not taking his eyes off me.

"And his filthy, traitor, rider lover did this to me. And you said his student was the one that killed Calamity," the rider snarled.

"Well, you did attack their city, I don't know what you expected them to do, Rex."

Rex's nostrils flared, as his one fist clenched, and his pectoral muscles flexed. He had his blazing angry eyes fixed on me, but he didn't move.

"You ordered the attack," I said, wondering if I could sow a little discord.

"That would have happened with or without me, I simply said when. You see, Rex and his people were rather aggrieved over that dragon of yours. That, plus the confidence that came with having one of their own again, after such a long while without. It was only a matter of time." Sky shrugged, affecting a tone of mock regret.

"That was your doing, wasn't it?" It made sense now. For an opal it would have been child's play to unfossilise an ancient meteor egg.

"Oh yes, that was me. All that energy I spent during the star bloom maturing the thing, wasted." For a second, Sky turned, shooting a brief glance at Rex, who retreated back a pace. I took my moment and started willing flowers to grow from the ebony staff, which now blanketed the entire cave floor. I couldn't use my light; Sky would see me, and the moment he knew my plan, it would already have failed. The staff, Tera's powers, that was my best chance.

"But why?" I asked, trying to keep him talking.

"I gave them their dragons back; they give me protection. It's not just Rex, you know, there's more of his kin throughout these tropical chambers. Keeping an eye out." I couldn't tell if that was a warning or a threat.

"Why do you need protecting?"

"Well, I didn't expect the world would take too kindly to me stealing the new infinite. But enough about me, let's talk about you, Aster Shepard. I'm impressed you found me, then again Cora did have a knack for picking winners, didn't she?" Sky's smile was unsettling. My body felt stiff and tight, and I was sweating again, even in the cold, damp cave air. I'd only ever seen one opal fight, and I'd never seen her lose.

"I thought you were dead." I croaked, changing the subject. Somehow, when I was the topic of conversation, everything felt much more dangerous.

"That was by design," said Sky, shortly. His smile was shrinking, and his eyes threatened to wander.

"Why? You were Cora's apprentice, and the only other opal in Streya, you could have been anything." I resorted to flattery, sensing his interest fading. I had to keep him distracted to let my flowers grow.

"This is a waste of time!" Rex growled.

"Hush now, Rex. We share something special, Aster and I, both of us were apprentices to that woman. That's a bond, and there is no need to rush things." The way he said *that woman* carried some venom.

"I'm not sure I'm quite in your league, Sky. Hadn't you mastered red, aquamarine, silver, grey, yellow and violet lenses by the time you graduated? Not to mention your eyes." I already knew I was correct. The loss of Sky was felt keenly; they don't erect statues beside Cora's for just anyone.

"I was something of a prodigy, yes." The smile grew again.

"So why fake your death?" I asked again, the first of my flower's heads was beginning to open in the shadows by the lakeside.

"I needed to get away from Cora. You must have felt it, her stifling influence." Sky's fists clenched and his jaw set. He hated her, it was plain as day.

"She did like to get her own way," I said, sheepishly, which earned a snort of laughter.

"Her own way? The woman's been controlling our whole civilisation for millennia, there is no other way than hers. Never has been."

"And you wanted to do things differently?" I coaxed, letting him talk. Talk and talk, until every shadow was a flower bed.

"I wanted to know things, that's what she was scared of most. You know opal magic can do more than control time. She wouldn't have told you, of course; it didn't suit her for people to know. Opal eyes can look backwards, into the past. I was learning things she'd let all of Streya forget. You know, at first, I thought even she didn't know about what I was uncovering, and then one day she came to me in the night. She didn't want me carrying on my research, told me to bury it, tell no-one. She made it seem like a request, but you know as well as I do, Aster, people didn't say no to that woman. I wonder, did she ever make a request like that of you?"

"She never asked much of me at all," I said, attempting a modest joke. Although Nick's words rang in my head. How heated he'd been over Cora's note. Over being asked to cease his research into the anomaly. Sky's eyes narrowed; it must have shown on my face.

"There was something, wasn't there?"

"She never tried to stop me personally, but—"

"One of your fellow apprentices, let me guess. Nicholas Copper? He likes to gaze up into the outer darkness, doesn't he?" Sky was speaking quickly now, excitedly, like he'd stumbled onto some hidden treasure.

"You got it in one, how did you know?" I asked, not really caring how he knew.

"What did he call it? That thing he found out in the stars? I found it too, you know. She hated that I found it." Sky was half ignoring me now. It was as though he was having a rehearsed conversation. Like this thought had been going around and around in his head for twenty years.

"He called it the anomaly," I said.

"Not a bad name, vague though. Impersonal. I suppose he didn't have my eyes, couldn't see it for what it was, what it had been. I could. Tell me, Aster Shepard, did you ever see the anomaly?" His voice was dripping with rage and excitement and smugness all at once.

"I did." My body was rigid. Sky's face, his eyes. It was like staring into the salivating jaws of a lion.

"And what did you think of it? How did it make you feel?"

"I threw up." His cackle echoed through the cave. Even Rex gave a little grumbling chuckle, although I suspected he hadn't the foggiest what we were talking about.

"Would you like to know what I call the anomaly?" Sky's excitement was at a fever pitch, like a child about share some awe-inspiring discovery with their parents. Like a beetle or something.

"What do you call it, Sky?" I asked, ignoring the little idea I'd hidden right at the back of my mind. I had a horrible feeling I might have been right.

"What do I call that twisting, writhing, stomach-churning monstrosity in the outer blackness of our stars, that Cora kept secret for a thousand years? Why, I call it, infinity."

My stomach flipped. The thought I'd pushed down, when I'd been struggling to sleep on cave floors and in absentminded moments, came screaming to the surface. Then I flinched, as along with it came a loud, echoing gasp from the cave archway behind me. Sirius, no doubt.

"We're not alone. Rex, go invite our guests inside."

Sky's twinkling eyes had shifted past me; he was now looking over my shoulder to the source of the sound. Rex grunted, took one step forward and then his back arched, there was a sharp wet slipping sound, and he groaned out his last breath. Cold blood sprayed forth, as Obol's glowing blue tip emerged from his sternum. Percy's hand was wrapped around his neck, dragging him further down onto the blade. Sky's eyes widened, Obol flashed, and a spray of red icicles exploded from Rex's body. Smashing and clattering sounds echoed throughout the cave. I waved my coal studded cane through the air, creating a wall of heat, and covered my eyes as the ice scattered in all directions. When I uncovered them, I looked to the spot where Sky had been standing. I'd hoped to see him on the floor, decorated with countless needles of bloody ice, but the space was empty, and Percy was glowing faintly opal.

"Is this your rider? He just killed mine." Sky's voice rang through the cave, as he strode out from the shadows behind Percy. I raised my hands in surrender, took a deep breath and held it, as every flower I'd cultivated in the cave expelled its payload of purple pollen. The time for talking was over. He couldn't have my rider.

"How did you—"

Before he could finish another smug sentence, I thrust my fist forward, firing a jet of glowing navy water from my ring, leaving a sucking tunnel of clear air, as it ploughed through the pollen cloud. Just as it was about to slam into Sky, it froze, enveloped by a blanket of opal light.

I raised my other hand, dragging thorny vines out of my flower beds towards him, but the space in which he stood was already empty. It all made sense now, how he'd done it, vanishing without a portal. He'd been stopping time. I watched for a sign of him, and jumped, as a moment later a spluttering cough broke out by my side.

I gasped, falling back in shock, and twisted through the air. Sky had been a foot from me, one hand outstretched, the other covering his mouth as he wheezed. Then it hit me, the heaviness, the slow feeling. I'd breathed it too.

"What is this?" He snarled, as his now purple saliva covered hand plunged into his cloak. Withdrawing a feather quill that flashed aquamarine, he released an explosion of wind. I flinched, stumbling to my feet, as I backed into the hard cave wall, my purple smog dissipating. I raised a heavy hand and released another jet of navy, but again Sky had already vanished.

"Look out, Aster!" I turned sluggishly to the sound, just in time to catch sight of Astrid, standing in the archway, with flames erupting from her outstretched hand. I followed the line of fire, barely catching Sky vanishing from my periphery. Then, there was a thud and a groan. Percy was free, the glowing shell that held him transfixed in time had faded.

"Percy's free," I mumbled, groggily, as a smile spread across my face. Something was dawning on me. Sky's magic was like Cora's, but his power wasn't. Cora would have frozen every single thing in this room. From me to each individual spec of pollen. We'd have been stuck, and she'd have luxuriated in her power as she did it. Sky couldn't, he wasn't infinite. He had to make do with flashes of time, he was freezing us from moment to moment, but that was all he had, a moment.

"Where'd he go?" Astrid's yell echoed through the cave, holding a sparkling white mote in her palm.

"Sirius?" I called, rubbing my eyes as I forced myself to stand, worried Sky might try to sneak him out of the cave whilst was still hidden.

"Here, Professor!" Sirius yelled, running out into the

open. I sighed with relief and then flinched as a tiny something flashed grey from the floor before him. Sky burst forward, growing rapidly, with his arms outstretched towards Sirius. I groaned, forcing my heavy body into a lunge. I raised my arms, calling every root and vine and blade of grass and flower stem up from the floor, and wrapping them around Sirius, holding him fast.

A flash of opal light filled the cave, and then a growl of frustration. Sirius was still held fast in my roots and grass, and Sky was on his knees ripping at the vines with his fingers, his head lolling forward exhaustedly.

"Aster, I'm stuck," Sirius called, nervously. He reared back, leaning away from the feral image of Sky clawing at his bound feet.

"Fire, Astrid!" I commanded, fighting to keep my eyes open, as she released another bolt of white. The pollen had done its work, Sky was spent and drowsy, like me. He didn't react in time. A groan reverberated through the cave, as the charge of whiteness hit him, sending him skidding unconscious across the flower laden cave floor.

"Find Orion!" was the last thing I managed to say, before I let the valerian sleep take me.

* * *

"Aster, WAKE UP!" Tera's voice ripped through my mind, as I sat up with a start. My shirt was soaked through, and plastered to my skin. The air was thick and warm, and filled with roaring, screeching sounds.

"What's happening?" I mumbled.

"He's awake!" yelled a voice I recognised instantly. I

beamed, my eyes snapping open, as I threw my arms around a somewhat startled Orion.

"Oh, thank the stars you're okay!" I said, squeezing him with all my might. Which wasn't very mighty.

"The others found me in the caves not long ago, but that doesn't matter right now, look!" he said, pushing me off of him, as he pointed upwards. I squinted into the light, watching the black blur of Styx flying overhead, pursued by a screeching wyvern, then another and another. I reclined back on my elbows, my chest tightening, and took in the scene. Tera and Styx were both dancing through the chamber, harried by at least a dozen or so mounted wyverns.

"Where are Astrid and Sirius?" I asked, lurching forward. I got to my feet and grabbed my ebony staff, which had been laid down beside me.

"We're here," said Astrid. I turned and found her crouched on a large mound of grey that could have easily been mistaken for a rock. She held a charge of white light glistening in her hand. Her eyes were focused, tracking the paths of nearby wyverns. Then, the mound she was standing on moved, pitching a large clump of earth and stone through the air, just narrowly missing a wyvern mid-flight, one large squinting eye following its path.

"Damn!" Sirius' deep cyclops voice rumbled.

"Any ideas?" Orion asked, nervously.

"Yes, actually," I said, grabbing my lucky rabbit's foot between my thumb and forefinger, as I pulled it from my pocket.

"Tera, try to clump them up, and get as close to the ground as possible, and tell Styx too," I thought, while

pushing as much light as I could muster through my golden lens.

"Sirius, put me down," Astrid commanded over the cacophony of battle. In seconds she was by my side, sending a rush prickling across my skin. My hairs stood on end, as her power flowed into me, and golden light sang out. Images of the great, frilled, bird-lizard creatures that populated this subtropical cavern filled my mind, as I let my voice ring out, calling them nearby. Little by little, the gentle giants of the underground crowded around us, their eyes glowing golden. I looked upwards, watching as Tera and Styx darted around each other, guiding the wyverns into a sort of swarming cloud of grey wings and razor-sharp teeth.

"What now, Aster?" Tera asked, as Styx shot overhead. I felt the cool breeze he carried with him catch in my hair.

"Everyone behind me!" I yelled as loud as I could. Within a second, I felt the wind at my back, as Styx and Tera flew barely over our heads, landing behind us. The cloud of wyverns skimmed the ground as they gave chase, flying headlong towards me. Finally, I released the last pulse of gold, and roared into the face of the gnashing beasts. The ground trembled, and all around us, my allied beasts stampeded forth. They met the swarm of wyverns head on, trampling and ramming and goring as they went. Within seconds, the chamber was filled with the echoed screeching and roaring and the grunts and yells of wyvern riders, locked in the heat of battle.

"Time to go," I said, as a wave of fatigue knocked me back, and I fell into Orion.

"Aster's exhausted," Orion shouted, nervously, as he struggled to hold me up.

"Rest." Tera's voice was gentle, as a blur of green and brown snaked around me, and pushed me onto her back.

"I'll fly myself and Sky out, Percy you take Orion and Astrid." A flash of grey followed Percy's call, as Tera began to climb into the air. I craned my neck, looking back. Sirius was flapping two pairs of large grey feathered wings, and had taken to the air himself. A body lay in his arms, tightly wrapped in a woven mesh of vines.

"My doing," Tera's voice issued into my mind, as we left the larger canyon chamber, entering the tighter seam. She half glided, half cantered upwards, until we burst out into the cool night air, and undulated up further still into the purple black sky, with the stars twinkling above us.

Sirius joined, hovering level with us.

"Are you okay?" I called across to him, his wings beating steadily.

"Don't worry, Aster, I've got this," he said, drifting closer as Styx shot like a shadow from the seam in the arid rocky ground. Doubling back on himself to release a gout of ice breath, he sealed our escape route behind us.

* * *

I watched as Nick, Sirius, Percy and Vega's father, Harper, bore the coffin out of the west wing of the university into the newly christened Garden of Vega. Initially, I was meant to carry the coffin alongside Nick, however, we quickly realised my considerably reduced stature next to my fellow coffin bearers would have made things rather awkward. Lyra, Vega's mother, seemed to take some comfort in her daughter's coffin being borne by the infinite anyway.

There were many funerals in the days that followed what came to be known as The Black Crater attack. Vega's was one of the largest. In her typical fashion, her coffin was white and huge. The ceremony took place in her memorial garden, which she would have hated. Vega had been solid and tangible and reliable. We should have named a supporting pillar after her. Not a garden that could be ruined by a hot summer or a bad rain. Her father led the ceremony, and a few faculty members spoke, although Nick's address was the only one I seemed able to take in. The rest felt almost like white noise.

"Vega was more than just a talent, or a rare hue, she was more than headmistress of this place. She was more than the Giantess of Streya. She was a friend and a daughter and a person who got scared and had doubts and unrequited loves. Just like anyone else. I remember one of the first lenses Cora Olympia allowed Vega, myself and Aster to practise with, which was navy. It was a beautiful crystal glass goblet. We were in the senior baths, which Cora had drained especially for this occasion. Vega was always the first to volunteer to try her hand, do you remember Aster?" As he addressed me, his silver eyes were red and sore and wet with tears, and his voice wavered. I nodded, but didn't speak. Not because I couldn't, I could have reminisced for hours about school with Vega.

I didn't speak because I wasn't crying, I wasn't gallantly holding back tears. In fact, if I were the one recalling how Vega strode forward and grasped that navy lens and proceeded to flood the baths. If I'd been the one describing how the water had exploded out of her with such force and such volume, that Nick and I were swept clean off our feet. Recanting that it was so cold that shock of it had stunned me. That had Cora not drained the pool, I may actually have drowned. If it were me telling that story, I'm almost certain I'd have broken out into a fit of hysterical laughter. It was bad enough that my shoulders were shaking at the recollection of it now, sitting one row back from Lyra.

Luckily, judging from the comforting hand placed on my shoulder by a person in the row behind me, it was taken that I was crying. That Nick's stories of nights shared with Vega in the library where she confided in him, had touched me. The idea that she'd been haunted by that day. The thought that she'd been so riddled with guilt at almost drowning me, moved me to tears. Then quite by surprise, a sob escaped me.

"Are you okay?" Percy asked, taking my hand in his, as the ceremony ended, leading me on a walk around the garden. Lilies, snowbells, elderflower, lots of white and perfumed air; she really would have hated it. There was to be a wake at the pub, which was apparently Vega's favourite. Not that I'd ever seen her frequent any pub.

"I wish she'd told me," I said, looking up into the sky, as I blinked a few stray tears away.

"About what Nick said?" Percy asked, intuitively.

"Do you remember the night that happened? We snuck out and met each other, remember?" Percy and I hadn't been sneaking out in secret for long at that point, so we were being extra cautious. Hiding in shadowy corners of the university that had fallen into disuse.

"Of course, your hair was still damp, and you couldn't stop laughing about it," Percy smiled, and ran his thumb under my eye, wiping a tear.

"Because it was hilarious, the look on her face when they fished me out of the pool. How confidant she was, and how abruptly it had all gone wrong." Again, the memory of it drew out a laugh and then a pang of something else. Some wasted longing.

"I remember you saying," Percy nodded.

"I just wish I could have told her it was okay, that she didn't have to worry about it. I have this image of her lying awake at night, not being able to sleep and then remembering that day and feeling bad about it. Again, and again, remembering that day and feeling guilty for some stupid accident she had as a kid that didn't matter. I was never upset with her about it," I said, holding Percy's ice-blue gaze.

"I know you weren't, Aster."

"I just wish she knew."

* * *

The position of Master of Streya's main duty is to oversee the education of each crop of Streyan apprentices. However, that isn't its only duty. There is also a ceremonial undertaking. When the apprentices graduate, it is the Master's honour to conduct the ceremony. This also goes for any other accolades that the apprentices might earn during their time at the university. Naturally, this honour comes with a ceremonial robe. A robe, which seemingly everyone including myself, forgot, would need to be altered when Cora handed off the position to me. Which is why, at the eleventh hour, beneath the stage of university amphitheatre, a flock of tailors and seamstresses were buzzing around me making adjustments.

"Does that pinch?" asked a man with a very thin moustache, whose name I'd already forgotten three times.

"No, it's fine." I had no idea if it was fine. It was impossible to know what he'd adjusted, as he was one of four pairs of hands working on me.

"How's the collar?" asked a lady behind me, fiddling with the emerald green ruffle collar that had been affixed to my lapels, and the cape of the same colour that dragged behind me. The former arrangement had been opal.

"Snug," I said, presuming that the pressure on my throat was normal, and that these things were probably never comfortable.

"Did this thing look quite so big on Cora?" Percy asked, looking me over with an appraising eye from the stool opposite.

"I don't know, it looked natural on her, everything did." I huffed, hiking up the long white robe that had been dragging across the floor, catching under my feet. I needed to let some air in; it was stifling underneath all my skirts and drapes and capes.

"Here," said Percy, waving his arm across me, releasing a gust of ice-cold air. I sighed at the momentary relief, rolling my head back to expose as much of my neck as possible.

"Well, now we know why she always held the graduation ceremony around the time of the Frost Star," I said, as I did my best to ignore the droplets of sweat running down my arms and pooling at the damp cuffs of my white trumpet sleeves.

"The ceremony begins in one minute, places please!" called the overly stressed, red-faced co-ordinator of ceremonies, whose name I'd also forgotten. It had been a hectic day.

I shuffled with Percy holding my cape behind me, wafting cool air onto my neck, reminding me why I'd married him. I turned and blew him a kiss, before taking to the stairs, climbing them to the rhythm of the orchestral music filling the air. The sky was cloudless and blue, the sun shining, and the breeze too gentle to offer any relief. It would have been a wonderful day, were I not wearing an outfit that weighed about as much as I did.

"Thank you all for being here today," I said, into a complex system of light refraction used to generate aquamarine light, which cast my voice out over the audience. In all the hustle and bustle and stifling heat, I hadn't had time to build a good head of stage fright.

The audience of the amphitheatre seated roughly five hundred. Most of which was filled with students and respected alumni. The front row to the left was reserved for significant foreign dignitaries. Most notably, Crown Prince Bren had made an appearance, along with his quartet and Igraine Sovereign. Her thick hair was pleated and twisted into the shape of a crown. Wearing the colours of the Sovereign family, fine black silks in her case, with golden dragons emblazoned across the long drooping sleeves. On the right were friends and family of the honouree, Sirius. He was the oldest of four I'd learned. The line from parent to child was clear, both his mother and father were tall and blonde, broad, olive skinned, with flashing grey eyes. The father, rather endearingly, couldn't seem to stop crying, and had ruined the decorative silk pocket square he'd been wearing when I was introduced to him earlier.

"Today, I have the lofty task of presenting one of my apprentices with Streya's highest honour, the title Champion of the City of Streya. This accolade is awarded only to those who, through their actions, have played an inarguable role in the preservation of our city. The first recipient of this award was my own master, Cora Olympia. Who almost single-handedly, repelled the behemoth stampede of the black night, some nine hundred and fifty years ago. Today, we honour Sirius Greyfellow, for defeating the meteor dragon Calamity during the Black Crater Attack on Streya. Without his courageousness, the death toll would doubtless be innumerably higher, and Streya as we know it may not have survived. Please now, come forward, to accept this award."

Sirius, who'd been waiting in the wings, stepped out to an explosion of applause. He was wearing the rather garish grey robes he'd had made for his party at The Clutch, although, mercifully, he'd had the draped kimono sleeves taken in. He looked a little flushed, either from wearing heavy robes on a hot day, or the embarrassment of having an audience scream for him, it was hard to say, really. As he reached me, I leaned forward and set to work affixing the glistening prismatic star pin to his chest.

"Congratulations," I said, forcing a smiling as I pricked my finger.

"It should be you getting this award, I'd never have left your office if you hadn't come and found me and talked me into it." Sirius spoke in my ear as he leaned forward to help me attach the pin.

"That's what teachers are for, just enjoy it," I said, breathing a sigh of relief as the fiddly thing clicked into place and I leaned back, seeding my position at the podium to Sirius. The crowd fell not quite silent, but as quiet as you can expect five hundred people to be.

"Errm, hello everyone, thank you all for coming. That is all I've got to say really, thank yous. Thank you to my parents and my family. Thank you to the friends I've made at Streya and special thanks to Aster Shepard. I'd never have been able to do what I did without you. Oh, and sorry to go on a bit, but one last thing. I just wanted to say I wasn't the only one fighting for Streya on that day, lots of people did, lots of people here now did, and some of the people fighting didn't make it. Like my friend, Wayne, he wasn't even a light walker, but he fought for this place, and he died. So, thank you, and I miss you, Wayne." Sirius sniffed, turned away from the podium and pushed his palms into his eyes as stepped back. The orchestra burst back into life, with a somewhat inappropriately lively song, as he descended the steps to sit with his family. His mother had now joined his father, and was bawling her eyes out. I watched him go, and did my best to restrain the grin trying to rip across my face as an idea occurred to me.

"Thank you, Sirius, for those poignant words. Which brings me nicely onto the second honouree of today's ceremony." I took a breath, and let the ripple of whispers break through the crowd. They didn't know about the second honouree. Which differed slightly from the panic breaking through the wings and beneath the stage. Those people knew there wasn't supposed to be a second honouree.

"It is my sober duty to announce our first ever honouree to receive the title, Champion of Streya, posthumously. The late Headmistress Vega Truelight. Who gave her life in the protection of Streya, and without whom the university would certainly not have survived. Vega, my colleague, Vega, my friend, thank you for all you did. All is forgiven." I smiled as a happy tear rolled down my cheek. The end of my speech may not have made sense to them, but I hoped if she were out there somewhere, it did to her.

"Now, if you would all follow us over to the grand hall, you're welcome to enjoy some refreshments with family and friends. Some representatives of the faculty and student body will show you the way. Enjoy!" I said, as I turned to the panicked co-ordinator of ceremonies, who was glaring at me from the wings, and started shuffling off stage, accompanied by more orchestral music. His eyes were bulging so dramatically, I thought they might pop out of his head.

* * *

"No, but Aster, seriously, thank you, that was bloody brilliant," said Nick, as he draped himself drunkenly across my shoulders.

"Pleasure's all mine," I slurred back, sagging under his weight.

"Now, you better go, cause I think Dusk just spotted you." Nick chuckled lazily, flicking open a silvery portal beside us.

"Come on, Percy, let's make like a banana and leave, or whatever it is," I said, sliding out from beneath Nick, who almost flopped onto the floor without me there to lean on.

"You mean split." Percy chuckled, as I attached myself to his side, wrapping my arm around his waist as we staggered through the portal together. We waved goodbye to Nick before it snapped shut behind us, leaving us alone, in our little cottage. We'd spent the majority of the party with Nick. Making a game of avoiding any and all members of the city government or the university board, whilst seeing how much free wine we could lay hand to. As it turned out, we were all extremely good at this game.

"Well, that was fun," I said, resting my hands on Percy's chest as I gazed up, my stomach aflutter as our eyes met. I could feel his heartbeat increase, as his breath grew short.

"I still can't believe you did that," said Percy, his large hands clasping my upper thighs as his voice dropped to a husky whisper.

"I'm out of control!" A jolt ran through me as he lifted me, my legs wrapping around his waist, my hands sliding up his chest, over his clavicle, my fingers knitting together behind his neck.

"What am I going to do with you?" Percy's voice rumbled low, and a shiver ran over my skin as the space between us closed. I could feel the static passing from my skin to his.

"Whatever you want." I breathed back, as our lips met in a soft, warm embrace. Our bodies rolled together, running against each other, as he carried me into the bedroom. I could feel his barely restrained strength in what little force he did apply. A squeeze of the hip, the pressing of him against me.

Our bodies moved together, clothes discarded in favour of the electric warmth of my skin against his. His powerful frame and mine becoming one, moving in rough and passionate harmony. I traced his muscles and found new scars as I explored him, listening for his gentle sounds, enjoying every gasp and shudder as he held me and tasted me. My nails, his back, his lips, my neck, his hands, my hair. His musk, and sweat and voice rolling through me, melting me. My whole world becoming him, as we created a symphony of whimpers, growls, and moans.

Until with a final grunt he fell into me, bliss and warmth rocked us, our bodies becoming a tangle of limbs. At last, we lay together, panting and exhausted, my head and my hand rested on his heaving chest.

"I love you," I said, playing teasingly with curled hairs of his chest.

"I love you too," he whispered back, kissing my forehead, as his arm wrapped around my back, cleaving me to him.

"Aster, it's time to wake up," a familiar voice issued from the darkness, as I sat up in bed and blinked the sleep from my eyes.

I could see a vaguely Percy shaped lump lying beside me, breathing softly into his pillow. The room was in almost total darkness, except for the little seam of vaguely green light peaking around the edge of the bedroom door. I slid out of bed and threw on my green silk dressing gown, before I tiptoed to the door and pushed it ever so gently aside. Slipping out into the cottage proper, my heart rate kicked up at the sight of it. The source of the light was a swirling green portal hovering just before the fireplace. The Green Way.

I don't know how long I stood there, gazing into it, the endless streams of green, flowing almost hypnotically into one another. The loamy smell of the forest wafted gently out, drawing me in, until I was standing just inches away. My hand outstretched. The Green Way is dangerous. People get lost in it, go mad from it. I knew that, and yet I felt so safe as I stepped inside.

Darkness, almost blinding darkness, swallowed me, and I froze, blinking into it. It wasn't blackness, but deep verdant green. The green of pine on Frost Stars Eve, and a sound, far off in the distance. I turned towards it, a flute maybe, or a panpipe. I wanted to follow it, but the voice rung out in my head once more, firmer now.

"Stick to the path."

Again, my breath caught in my chest. I turned away from the sound and saw it, my eyes having adjusted just a little, to the verdant darkness. Cobbles before me, stretching out as far as my eyes could make out, laid out almost like stepping stones. I only took seven steps before the endless world of green vanished behind me, and I walked out into the night. The Streyan night, I knew by the web of twinkling lens lights above me. The rainbow skein of Streya, and I knew where in Streya too, I'd been here before, recognised it by the hair.

Too bouncy, too full. Designed to flatter, carved from white marble, run through with seams of black. Core Olympia, looking out over her gardens. I didn't notice at first, so distracted by where I was and how I'd got here, that I was not alone. Before the statue, on a bench, sat a lone figure. Just as my eyes fell upon her, she turned, smiled kindly, and tapped the spot on the bench beside her. My legs almost folded up beneath me.

"Is this a dream?" I squeaked, staggering forwards. I studied her ageless face, her flowing silvery grey hair, her eyes glowing faint opalescence.

"Why not pinch yourself and see?" she asked, flashing a wink as she scooted along the bench making room for me. Her long black robe with opalescent threads pooled onto the floor beneath her.

"You d-died," I stammered, standing stock still, my body rooted to the spot.

"Did I?" she asked, in her leading way.

"You left us!" I flared, finding her calmness suddenly enraging.

"I did," she agreed, her smile faltering.

"You left me." My voice broke.

"I'm sorry. I had to." Her voice softened. I'm not sure I'd ever heard Cora sincerely apologise to anyone before.

"Why?"

"Sit down, Aster," she said, tapping the bench again.

"I met Sky, you know. He's in a prison cell now, below the school," I said, ignoring her command.

"I know."

"He had a lot to say about you," I spat, trying to hold onto my anger, although I could already feel it slipping. It was an act, a convenient foothold, saving me from falling into something else.

"I'm sure he did." Her voice was so level and even, and I was drowning and flailing.

"Why are you here?" I asked, My eyes were beginning to sting.

"I wanted to see you, to speak to you. You've done so well, Aster, and I knew you'd have so many questions. You always did." There was her smile again, her warm smile. The smile I'd craved for years, the smile that meant approval and achievement, and that I wasn't a mistake. Despite what so had many said.

"Well? What have I done well? Everything's fallen apart." I gasped, swallowing a sob, my legs trembled, and I sank onto the bench.

"Nothing's fallen apart," said Cora, taking my hand in hers. The many coloured metal bars running along her fingers and the black gemstone set into the back of her hand flashed in the moonlight.

"Vega died!" I choked.

"I know, I saw what you did for her today, I thought it was wonderful."

"You were there?"

"No, but I was watching."

"Why didn't you come back when we needed you?" The anger had gone, leaving my voice high and strangled.

"You didn't need me, Aster, you proved that." She smiled again.

"But you could have helped!"

"I did what I could." She squeezed my hand, her voice almost pleading.

"You did what you could? What do you mean, what did you…" My voice trailed away as the smell of forest and damp soiled wafted over me, bringing with it a memory. A man in blazing red robes, falling out of sight during the battle, a flicker of green, the scent of the forest and him landing, inexplicably, at my feet. "You did what you could." I repeated myself.

"Anything more, and I'd have risked giving myself away," she explained, solemnly.

"Were you there this whole time? In the Green Way, I mean?"

"In a sense," she replied, frustratingly vaguely.

"Why?"

"I had to hide myself away."

"From what?"

"Infinity," she said, heavily.

"Is it true? What Sky said? That's what Nick found, the anomaly, that is infinity?" I asked.

"It is." She nodded.

"Why keep it a secret?" She was right, I did have questions.

"If people knew what it truly was, it would be chaos, disaster."

"What is it, where did it come from?" I spoke with

sudden urgency, flooded by the rush that comes with being on the cusp of something.

"You've actually taught a lesson on that yourself." Her smile returned.

"I have?" I asked, wracking my brain for what she could mean.

"The Sable Sorcerer." She spoke the words, and a shiver ran over me. I remembered the anomaly, the rollicking, roiling storm of black, with a tiny little fleck of gold at the centre.

"It's the egg?" I asked, knowing it couldn't just be the egg. A golden dragon egg didn't generate storms of void magic around it like that.

"Come on, Aster, you know this. How would a light walker use an egg?" Cora prompted me, momentarily transporting me back to my days as an apprentice. I furrowed my brows, and thought about what was obvious, the simplest answer.

"It was petrified." I breathed.

"Correct." Cora nodded.

"A petrified golden dragon egg. What kind of spell could they possibly be fuelling with that? It'd be the most powerful source of light in the history of... history." The enormity of the thing was mind-boggling.

"A spell that draws light out of every star in the sky, and funnels it down into one light walker."

"That's why the stars were going out," I thought aloud.

"And the dim sickness was getting worse, and it was only going to keep getting worse," said Cora.

"But won't it happen again? Now that Sirius is infinite, won't he cause the same problem?" I asked.

"You saw what happened when I disappeared. The star bloom, that's what happens when an infinite dies. The spell has a failsafe built in, it gives it all back, all the power it's taken that isn't spent, replenishes the stars."

"But you were immortal, so it never got given back, the failsafe never kicked in." Goosebumps prickled along my skin as the realisation dawned on me.

"Exactly."

"And why the Green Way?"

"The Green Way exists outside of normal time and space; the spell couldn't find me anymore. For all intents and purposes, I had died."

"You were the shimmering doorway, weren't you?" I asked, shuddering from the rush of it. The kind of excitement you feel when all the pieces of a puzzle finally slot together.

"Shimmering doorway?" she asked, curiosity tugging at the edges of her voice.

"Queen Gloria mentioned it. She tried to coax us into The Green Way, but I didn't dare risk it," I explained.

"Ah yes, I think my presence did rankle her a little. I made my own room, with its own time in there to hide out in."

"But why the secrecy?" I asked.

"Because light walkers still need the infinite. It was made for a reason. This world is so big and so full of power. And if everyone knew how it was made, what it was, would the Sovereigns stand for it? What about those who suffer from dim sickness? At the first sign of an increase in the sickness, there would be a public outcry. Demand for the execution of the current infinite, to bring on a new star bloom. What if people decide they like the rush that comes with a star bloom more than they like having an infinite?"

"It would become a curse." I loosed a shuddering breath, as my mind spun out a thousand ways this knowledge could hurt people. Could hurt Sirius. "And what if the Sovereigns found out?" My stomach flipped at the thought of Lance discovering that the power of the infinite came from a stolen and petrified golden egg.

"Exactly, the truth is too dangerous," Cora nodded.

"And that is why you outlawed opal lenses, because people could use them to learn the past, like Sky did," I said, following the thought through to its logical conclusion, as if we were back in one of her seminars.

"And as long as the lenses existed, there was a risk that an infinite could master one, and use it to become immortal, like I was."

"Was?" I asked, the word ringing sharply in my head.

"Was." She nodded.

"Was, as in past tense. As in, you're not anymore?" I asked, feeling an odd pang of guilt as she shook her head.

"I'm not the infinite anymore."

"What happens to you now then? Are you coming back?" I asked, allowing hope to drown out the rational part of me, which already knew.

"I can't, Aster. Streya needs to learn to be without me, Sirius and the next infinite and the next infinite after that, they need to be free of me." Her eyes shone, the eyes of a being, that had seen a millennium. That had built a civilisation on her back. For a second, all those years flashed across her face, and all I could feel was terrible sorrow.

"But what about you?" A sob slipped out of me, not for the legend, not for the god, but for the person beneath all those years.

"I'll be alright, I'm going to travel. See the world, as me, not as the infinite."

"But you'll die!" I cried. Somehow it wasn't right, people died, but not Cora Olympia, she wasn't people, she was more. She was meant to be there, always.

"Don't cry for me, Aster, I've lived so many lifetimes." She smiled without a hint of sadness, pulled me close and kissed my forehead.

"You've done so much for us... for me." I spoke through shaky, trembling breaths.

"Too much, some would say."

"They're wrong," I barked.

"Sweet boy." She pushed my fringe from my eyes.

"I don't know how to thank you. I don't want you to go," I cried, and she shushed me softly, lowering my head into her lap.

"Shhh, Aster, it's okay, shhh." She soothed, stroking my head until the sobbing stopped.

"Will I see you again?" I asked, looking into her impossibly bright opal eyes.

"Perhaps. I don't know." She smiled back at me, little tears forming in the corners of her eyes, somehow, they stung worst of all.

"Then why did you come back? Just to make me lose you again?" I spat bitterly, then ached, regretting it in an instant.

"I never got to say goodbye to you." She smiled, and I

knew my petulance was already forgiven. That made the guilt ache all the more.

"I don't like to say goodbye. I take after my mother." I swallowed hard around the lump in my throat, and choked on a laugh. She chuckled, a warm kind chuckle, and a tear spilled down her cheek.

"Then, let's say see you later." She stood, holding my hands in hers, and I got to my feet.

Standing face to face with her, my hands in hers, my heart was racing, and panic began setting it. She was going, and I had to let her. I didn't want to, but I had to. I felt stiff and cold and sweaty and scared, and my throat hurt and my cheeks were wet. I could barely catch a breath.

"I'll miss you," I said, my eyes begging for her to stay, eking out every last second, desperate for her to stop. She ran a line through the air, and a green doorway peeled back in its wake.

"I'll miss you too, darling boy." She let the tears fall freely, her voice lingering in my mind. I held onto it with all my might, determined to remember. Her voice, her face. My master, my teacher, my friend, Cora.

"See you later!" I choked, and almost shouted, it felt urgent. I had to get the words out. Like if I did, she'd be bound to them somehow. Like they'd become prophetic and have to come true.

"See you later, Aster Shepard." She blew me a kiss as she stepped into the swirling green.

"Promise!" I demanded, my voice echoing across the empty park grounds.

I stared at the empty space where a portal had been,

and sunk to my knees, whimpering as they slammed painfully against the cold stone. It had been so quick, and so much of it I'd spent asking questions, hanging onto anger and thinking, rather than just being with her. I stayed like that, knelt in the park, in the night, staring at her statue. Replaying our conversation in my mind, despairing at the edges of the memory as they began to fray and blur. I stayed until the cold set in, and my teeth began to chatter. Finally, I forced light through my dead friend's bracelet, and flew myself home.

The cottage door clicked shut behind me as I slinked inside, like a rebellious teenager sneaking home past curfew. I was halfway to the bedroom door before I was caught.

"Aster?" Percy stepped into the corridor in just his underwear, Obol in hand. His voice was urgent, his eyes searching.

"Hi." I squeaked, and swallowed around the lump in my throat, begging myself not to cry again.

"Aster, what's wrong?" Percy was all softness and warmth, and in a second, I was in his arms, being pulled to his chest, as his hand cradled the back of my head.

"She's gone," I said, wrapping my arms around him, and pulling myself closer, as if I could burrow inside.

"Vega?" he asked.

"Cora," I said, lifting my head to meet his worried gaze. I felt his concern and also confusion, but most of all, I just felt love pouring out of him.

"I know you miss her," he said, kissing me softly on the cheek as he led me to my rocking chair by the fire, although I didn't sit.

"You don't understand, she came back," I whispered, holding fast to him. He was real and solid and safe and warm and wouldn't leave me.

"I thought she'd… died?" Percy said, as delicately as a person can say something like that.

"It's too complicated to explain now." I sagged exhaustedly, my head beginning to ache.

"Okay, that's okay, you don't have to explain. Do you want to tell me what happened?" Percy asked, kissing my temple, trying again to lower me into the chair. This time I let him, but pulled him down with me, climbing into his lap.

"We talked. I asked so many stupid questions. I wasted all of my time on stupid questions, and now I'm worried she doesn't know I—" I hiccupped.

"She knows you love her, Aster," Percy said, like he'd read my mind. I nodded, breathing slowly, trying not to let my breath run away from me.

"She said she wanted to say goodbye," I explained, when I'd finally collected myself.

"At least you got to do it properly, rather than in a note."

"We said see you later instead." I tried a weak smile, which Percy met with a kiss, beginning to gently rock us back and forth. Seconds stretched into minutes, as I listened to the rhythm of the chair and felt his heartbeat beneath me, breathing him in.

"Do you want to go back to bed?" he asked, as the first shafts of blue light that beat the dawn appeared in the window.

"Can we watch the sunrise?" I asked.

"Of course we can," he said, as we climbed off the chair and turned it to face the window.

"Tea? I fancy tea," I said, padding into the kitchen, conjuring water with my ring and boiling it with my cane that rested by the door.

"Tea would be nice." Percy nodded. I found my cheeks burning as I made the tea under his gaze. My Percy, reliable and steadfast and always here. I smiled to myself as I brought him his tea, and together, we climbed back into our chairs to watch the sunrise.

"I don't know what to do now," I said, as I sipped my tea, watching an arch of white light peak over the horizon.

"You can do whatever you want, Aster," said Percy, as the first shaft of morning spilled into the room.

The End.

AUTHOR'S NOTE

You may have noticed, in the acknowledgements, that I credit my brother as a co-writer. I thought now would be the perfect time to tell you a little more about that.

This world, of dragons and light walkers, free folk started life, not as a story, but a make-believe game that my brother and I would play together. The Golden Shot and Arms of Cerunos was all Henry as was the concept of a grave dragon. Whereas Aster Shepard and Cora Olympia were some of my creations.

We called this game Riders, which also happens to be the name of the folder in my computer, where you could find all the files that concern this book saved.

For years after, on sleepless nights, of which I had many, I would retreat back into this world, and these characters and tell myself stories. It was during these midnight imaginings that that the city of Streya and the many hues of light walkers were born. Eventually the stories became complex enough that holding them all in my head, whilst coming up with new ones became almost impossible.

Which is how it came to pass that I began to write them down. I hope to write stories about Streya, and the wider world and it's inhabitants for many years to come. I hope you'll read along with me.

ABOUT THE AUTHOR

Hey there! It's me again, the author. I just wanted to let you know that I have a website! If you liked this book and think you might enjoy reading some more, you should check it out.

In fact, I have a whole other trilogy totally complete. Now it's not set in Streya, or the world of Streya. The series is called: Adrian and Michael: A Song Of The Fay. It's a young adult gay romantasy, that straddles two worlds, ours, the human world, and the magical fay forest. Which you can think of kind of like a re-imagining of loads of Arthurian myths, all rolled into one.

So, if you got to the end of this story and found that the relationship between Aster and Percy had got you in the mood for a queer romance, I've got just the thing.

I also have a mailing list and everything (very high tech I know) but don't worry I won't spam you. I occasionally run giveaways through there though, free signed copies anyone?

Also, I have all sorts of social media, so you can see little clips of me being silly/having an existential crisis/with bad hair. Best of all, they're also all on my website, with handy dandy clickable links that someone else set up for me because I'm useless with everything of that nature.

If that sounds like something you're interested in, you can find me here:

albertjauthor.com

instagram.com/albert.j.writes
facebook.com/apjoynson
tiktok.com/@a.p.joynson

ALSO BY A.P. JOYNSON

Adrian and Michael: A Song of the Fay

A young adult gay romantasy, that straddles two worlds, ours, the human world, and the magical fay forest. Which you can think of kind of like a re-imagining of loads of Arthurian myths, all rolled into one.

These books are available in Waterstones and Amazon, and are a trilogy which should be read in order:

Son Of The Lake

Mothers, Witches, and Queens

The Stone And The Water

www.ingramcontent.com/pod-product-compliance
Lightning Source LLC
Chambersburg PA
CBHW031741180726
48283CB00005B/1619